THE SECRETS OF HARTWOOD HALL

A NOVEL

KATIE LUMSDEN

DUTTON

DUTTON

An imprint of Penguin Random House LLC
penguinrandomhouse.com

Previously published as a Dutton hardcover in February 2023
First Dutton trade paperback printing: February 2024

The Library of Congress has cataloged the hardcover edition of this book as follows:

Names: Lumsden, Katie, author.
Title: The secrets of Hartwood Hall: a novel / Katie Lumsden.
Description: New York: Dutton, [2023]
Identifiers: LCCN 2022019021 (print) | LCCN 2022019022 (ebook) |
ISBN 9780593186923 (hardcover) | ISBN 9780593186930 (ebook)
Subjects: LCGFT: Gothic fiction. | Detective and mystery fiction. | Novels.
Classification: LCC PR6112.U47 S43 2023 (print) | LCC PR6112.U47 (ebook) |
DDC 823/.92—dc23/eng/20220727
LC record available at https://lccn.loc.gov/2022019021
LC ebook record available at https://lccn.loc.gov/2022019022

Dutton trade paperback ISBN: 9780593186947

Printed in the United States of America
1st Printing

Book design by Nancy Resnick

Praise for *The Secrets of Hartwood Hall*

A SheReads Favorite Historical Gothic Mystery

"[A] captivating debut . . . Assured prose propels this well-crafted tale of family, friendship, and the cost of personal freedom. Fans of the great Victorian novels, in particular *Jane Eyre*, will have fun."

—*Publishers Weekly*

"Debut author Lumsden masterfully creates a believable atmosphere of the age, where science and logic are served side by side with the supernatural in everyday life." —*Booklist*

"In her atmospheric debut, *The Secrets of Hartwood Hall*, Katie Lumsden enthralls us with a quintessential manor-home mystery. Fans of gothic literature will savor the peculiar characters, the abandoned corridors, the deceptions and twists behind every door. . . . Ultimately a story about women and the haunting secrets they keep, Lumsden's debut reminds us never to trust first appearances. A mesmerizing debut!"

—Sarah Penner, *New York Times* bestselling author of *The Lost Apothecary*

"*The Secrets of Hartwood Hall* is exactly the book you want on a cold, stormy night when the wind is sneaking in the cracks. A thoroughly impressive debut with fantastically timed surprises throughout."

—Lyndsay Faye, author of *The King of Infinite Space* and *Jane Steele*

"I loved this fresh take on the gothic genre. Vivid, haunting, surprising." —Stacey Halls, author of *The Familiars*

"A full-blooded gothic mystery with bite, great characterization, and heaps of atmosphere. What a debut."

—Emma Stonex, author of *The Lamplighters*

FOR NICK

THE
SECRETS
OF
HARTWOOD HALL

When I think of Hartwood Hall, there are moments that come back to me again and again, moments that stain me, that cling like ink to my skin.

My first view of the house: a glimpse of stone, of turrets and gables, tall windows and long grass.

The sound of Louis's laugh. Bright and golden, eager and young.

Paul's hands in my hair, his body pressed against mine.

The silver locket, the dim portrait of the lost girl faded and worn within.

Lying cold in my bed at night, covers pulled tight around me, listening with my good ear to murmurs and taps in the darkness.

A figure in the distance, a shimmer beyond the lake. There, in the corner of my eye one moment. The next, vanished, leaving an empty impression behind.

The sound of a gunshot in the dark, running footsteps, burning flames, and black, black sky.

VOLUME ONE

CHAPTER I

FOUR WEEKS AFTER WE BURIED MY HUSBAND, I FOUND MYSELF IN the back of a carriage, trundling slowly uphill. The road was rough, the carriage ill-built, my black dress heavy, my eyes heavier. I had that kind of tiredness running through me that comes not from lack of sleep but from lack of rest, lack of calm. My body ached for something new.

Beyond the windows, I could see sweeping hills, tall grass swaying in hedged fields, rows of trees in distant apple orchards. We rattled by farmhouses and far-off villages, passed great houses set back from the road. Then green-brown wilderness for miles, not another carriage or even a laborer in sight. The sun streamed down on rivers and pathways, on dairy fields and scattered trees. This was a quiet part of the world, all mud and sun and sky.

I had caught the Great Western Railway from London to Bath the day before, emerged into a busy station in a cloud of steam. I'd stayed overnight in a quiet inn, then taken the post-chaise to a town I had never heard of. From there, a carriage was sent to meet me. I had thought at first it must be from the house, but when I inquired after Mrs. Eversham, the driver only scrunched up his nose and said, "I don't know, ma'am. Never heard of Hartwood Hall before now."

He had been instructed from afar, I supposed. He knew no more about Hartwood Hall than I did, and that was precious little. That the mistress was called Mrs. Eversham. That she, like me, was a widow.

That she, unlike me, had a child. Louis Eversham. My new charge. A boy of ten years old.

And that was all.

———>—<———

I had met only with an agent in London—a stout woman of around fifty with iron-gray hair. The study in her house in Cheapside was gray, too, with dull-colored furniture and cushionless chairs, a huge ledger adorning the pedestal desk.

"And you have been at several places, I see?" she'd asked, surveying my references.

"Yes."

"You are nine-and-twenty?"

"Yes."

"This last character is from three years ago."

I swallowed. Another mark against me. "I have been married, ma'am."

She glanced up, taking in my black dress, my widow's cap, with a quick nod. "A recent loss?"

I hesitated. If I told her how recent, she would think ill of me at once. "A little while ago," I said slowly.

That seemed to satisfy her. "You play the pianoforte, of course?"

"Yes."

"French? German? Latin?"

"Proficient in all, ma'am."

"You can teach mathematics and the sciences as well as reading and writing?"

"Certainly."

She glanced back down at her desk. "I see you have some trouble hearing."

"None that has ever caused me difficulty, ma'am," I said at once. "I cannot hear in my left ear, but my right is very good. You will see, I think, that my former mistress mentions it only to note how little it affected my abilities."

Once more she nodded, and I shifted uneasily in my chair. I needed work. I needed something. I had lost positions before because of my bad ear. Some mistresses caught word my hearing wasn't perfect and decided another woman would be more suitable for their child.

"That won't be a problem," she said. "I believe I may have something for you, Mrs. Lennox."

I breathed out. Here was salvation. A life to build. A fresh start.

———>·<———

That was a week ago. Characters from my previous employers had been sent, letters had been exchanged, and finally I was engaged. And now I was sitting in this carriage, heading toward my new life. It felt as though I had never been anything but a governess, as though it had been only a few weeks since I left my last place. Three years of my life, vanished into thin air. Three years of my life, and nothing but widow's weeds to show for it. I thought of Richard, his dark eyes, his freckled face, his gaunt figure those last few weeks.

I shut my eyes tight.

Beyond the carriage windows, the weather was turning. The sky had darkened from blue to mottled gray. I reached into my skirt pocket for my watch—well, Richard's watch, though it was mine now—and saw that it was not yet seven o'clock. I heard a rumble of thunder, and the coachman outside uttered a curse.

I had meant to think over future lessons in the carriage, to remind myself what a boy of ten might need to learn. But every time I tried to concentrate, I thought of Richard's face and my mind balked.

It was not my fault I was returning to work so soon. Everything else aside, I needed the money. I had spent the last four weeks in cramped lodgings, living off the sale of a necklace Richard had given me when we were first married. Even my mourning was reused: I had been forced to make the best of the black dresses I had worn when my mother died, darning here and there, turning out a seam, unplucking tighter threads at the waist.

A bad start, perhaps, for a widow—but it was not as though I had ever been a good wife.

———⟶⋅⟵———

Two hours later, the rain was furious and the darkness immense. The road seemed all turned to mud, and the horses were whinnying. I was about to call out and ask the driver how long it might be until we arrived when the horses began to slow.

Beyond the window, to one side, I could make out nothing but tangled hedges. When I looked to the other side, I could see the hazy glow of lamplight, just visible in the distance. Then the coachman's face appeared at the window, making me start.

"Sorry, ma'am," he said. He was wet through, tufts of gray hair matted to his forehead below his hat. "I don't know the way from here, 'specially in weather like this. See yonder—that's the village. Hartbridge, I believe. Bound to be a public house there. Someone'll know the way." He hesitated. "The track'll be rougher into the village. I could walk, or—"

"No," I said, not out of compassion for him as much as because I did not relish the thought of sitting alone in a storm. "You will only catch a chill on an evening like this."

He nodded. "Thank you, ma'am."

The road that led to Hartbridge village was indeed in a bad state of disrepair, and the carriage jolted over every stone, caught on each bramble. Gazing out the window, I saw shadowy shapes in the dimness— scattered farmhouses and cottages, I supposed, the occasional patch of what must be yet another orchard—and then the dark black of water, a river snaking its way through the landscape. We rattled over an old stone bridge, and back onto the rough road.

By the time we reached the public house, the rain was falling harder still. The building stood out, its lamps aglow in the darkness. It was an old, quaint sort of place, the walls made of sandy gray stone, the roof thatched.

As the coachman dropped from his perch and walked up to the inn, I pulled the window down. I could smell the cider from here, a tang of apples that filled the air. We were only a few yards away from the open door. A man stood on the threshold, looking out into the gloom, dressed in dark trousers and a worn shirt, with an apron over his clothes that told me he must be the landlord.

I turned myself around so that my good ear was nearer to the conversation. The rain was thunderous, but still I could make out the landlord's voice.

"You'll have to wipe your boots bloody hard before you come in here," he was saying.

"I don't want to come in," the coachman replied. "And you'd best not swear—there's a lady in the carriage."

The landlord gave an incredulous smile. "We don't get many ladies here."

"I'm taking her up to Hartwood Hall. Can you direct me?"

The man hesitated, and his expression changed from one of amused surprise to one of distaste. "Hartwood Hall?" he repeated. "Don't get folks going there much."

"Do you know where it is?"

He hesitated. "You certain it's Hartwood Hall?"

This was absurd. I opened the door and stepped down, feeling my boots sink into the mud. I was two yards from the carriage before I realized I had forgotten my bonnet. If the landlord had doubted I was a lady before, he would certainly do so now.

"Is there any reason," I asked, "why I should not go to Hartwood Hall?"

The coachman started when he heard me speak close at hand. "Ma'am, you might have waited in the carriage."

"Nobody ever goes to Hartwood Hall," said the landlord slowly.

"There is a family called the Evershams living there, I believe. I am engaged to be governess to the little boy."

He raised his eyebrows. Then, addressing the coachman, not me, he said, "It's north of here. Go back to the main road and on about a mile—there's a path up through the woods to the house. Once you come out of the trees, you'll find it. Big, grand place."

Beside me, the coachman was nodding, seemingly satisfied. He murmured his thanks and was about to turn back to the carriage when I said, again, "But is there any reason I should not go there?"

I spoke in the voice I used with young charges who would not confess to mischief.

"No reason, miss," the landlord said. "Folks say it's cursed, but I dare say a lady like yourself wouldn't believe such talk."

"Of course not."

The coachman took a step toward the carriage.

"What are the family like?" I asked. "Mrs. Eversham and her son?"

"Couldn't tell you. Never seen them since they came, and that was seven years ago now."

"And the servants?"

He shrugged. "They keep themselves to themselves. No one from hereabouts works up there, save Paul Carter."

My coachman was with the horses now, and my dress was becoming heavy with rain. I thanked the landlord, perhaps not very graciously, and struggled back through the mud to the carriage, thinking over his words.

Cursed.

How ridiculous. How thoroughly foolish.

I heard the horses neigh and sat back, wet through, as we began to move.

After a mile or two, I could make out the woods, a dense black shape in the distance. It was nearing ten, and I was late. The little boy would already be in bed.

The trees were mere shadows, twisting forms of curling branches and scattered leaves. Rogue brambles and undergrowth tapped and scratched at the carriage, and I heard the coachman swear and whip the horses to go faster.

Out in the darkness, amid the driving rain, I saw something stir in the woods, a shuffling, a shifting, a figure moving through the trees.

No, not a figure. An animal, no doubt. A deer in the moonlight, a bird preparing for flight.

Of course I did not believe the house was cursed—but when people feared a place, there was usually a reason. I must expect to find these Evershams strange.

At last we were out of the trees. As the horses pulled on, I saw rain falling on water, and a shadowy little building standing apart on the other side of the lake. I leaned out of the window to look up at the main house, and found my head soaked at once.

Hartwood Hall was very grand. I could tell it must be the shape of a horseshoe, with the middle part of the house set back from its two wings, a courtyard in the center—but in the darkness I could see only two towering shapes of gray stone, a dark void between them. I saw a dim light in a sash window in the east wing, and that was all. The rest of the house was dead.

This, then, was my new home.

We pulled up to the house, the horses complaining all the way. When we finally stopped, there was a splash of boots in mud and the carriage door opened.

"Here we are, ma'am," said the coachman.

While he took my trunk and carpet bag from the carriage, I crossed the cobbled courtyard. The gray walls of the house, surrounding us on three sides, blocked any moonlight the clouds had not smothered, and I had to wait for my eyes to adjust before I could make out the faint outline of a fountain in the center of the courtyard, a tree grown close to one side of the house, and an ornate brass knocker on the huge oak doors.

I pulled it forward, let it drop and bang.

We waited for some minutes in the driving rain. The coachman looked half drowned by the time I heard the heavy sound of bolts moving, and one of the double doors finally creaked open.

A woman stood before me. She was small, wearing a neat gray dress, her hair tucked beneath a mobcap. The housekeeper, to be sure. She looked somewhere between fifty and sixty, with little wrinkles about the eyes and a grave, set mouth. She held a candle in one hand.

"You are Mrs. Lennox, I suppose?" Her voice was clipped and low, the accent not local. She sounded as though she might, like me, have come from Hampshire or Surrey.

"Yes. I am sorry I am late. The weather—"

She nodded, and held the door open a little wider. As I stepped inside, she handed me the candle without a word, then took my trunk and carpet bag from the coachman and hauled them into the house. If he expected to be asked inside to dry himself by the fire, he was disappointed. He glanced between me and the housekeeper, then trudged slowly back to his horses. The housekeeper closed the door with a crash, and we were left alone in the dark.

She turned back to lock the doors, and I saw to my surprise that there were nearly a dozen bolts on the inside. She turned the key, pushed each bolt across, and then headed toward the stairs.

I eased off my muddy boots, lifted them in one hand, and followed her. The hall was all shadows. I was dimly aware that we had come to a wide staircase, which I walked up after her in silence. I opened my mouth once or twice to speak, only to find myself unsure of what to say.

At the top of the stairs, we turned left, heading down a carpeted hallway until the housekeeper stopped in the dark before one particular door. Setting my trunk on the floor, she pushed into the room.

I breathed out. It was cheerful enough: a glowing fire in the grate, a candelabra set on a chest of drawers. It was a good-sized room, with a curtained four-poster bed, a tall wardrobe to one side and a bookcase to the other. Across from that stood a dressing table that might double as a desk. The furniture was deep, rich mahogany, old but sturdy.

The housekeeper heaved my trunk in, and I tentatively placed my boots near the fire, embarrassed by my stockinged feet.

"This is your room, Mrs. Lennox."

I smiled at her.

She did not smile back.

"Thank you, Mrs.—?"

"Pulley," she replied. "I am the housekeeper here. You won't have had supper?"

I was too tired for food. "I am not hungry."

She nodded. "Mistress and Master are in bed. You shall meet them in the morning."

"Thank you, ma'am."

She nodded briskly, glanced once around the room to check that everything was in order, then took the candle from my hand and stepped out into the corridor.

The door closed behind her with a firm click.

I peeled off my wet gown and rooted through my trunk for my nightdress. Then I sat down alone on the bed in my new room. With my right ear toward the door, I could hear Mrs. Pulley on the stairs, the distant clatter of the kitchens. Then another noise, much closer at hand, and for a moment I expected her to reappear. But nothing followed. I wondered how close my room was to my charge's, if he was awake a door or two down, playing on his own in the dark.

I climbed into bed, my eyelids heavy. I turned my head, put my good ear to the bedsheets, and lay there, wet and weary, in the silence of myself.

CHAPTER II

I SLEPT LATE THE NEXT MORNING. THE THICK BED CURTAINS KEPT out the sun, and the mattress was comfortable—better than the one I'd had in lodgings these last few weeks, better than the bed in the spare room where I'd slept while Richard was ill.

A loud knock on the door finally roused me. I stirred slowly, rubbing my eyes. I'd half forgotten where I was, and when I opened the bed curtains, I stared blankly at the unfamiliar surroundings.

The flickering embers of my dream caught in my mind as I stumbled out of bed. I could still see Richard's face, hear the sound of hymns. He had been standing at my side by the altar where we were married, and when I turned toward him, his eyes were white and he was dead.

Another tap came and I hurriedly opened the door. Before me stood a maid—a young woman, not much beyond twenty, with a thin face and proud eyes and messy brown curls beneath her cap.

She was speaking as I opened the door, but in my weary state I caught only the word "dead" and in the seconds before I said, "Pardon?" I felt my heart constrict, and my first selfish thought was how hard it would be to have to find another position if the little boy had died suddenly in the night.

"I said you must be dead tired. I tried to wake you an hour ago."

"Oh." I swallowed. "It was a long journey. I am a little deaf, so please knock as loudly as you like."

She nodded, unfazed. "What's your name?"

"Margaret," I said, and then, with a sudden recollection of my position and hers, added, "Mrs. Lennox. And you are?"

"Susan. Housemaid. Well, maid-of-all-work, more like. There's no nurserymaid so I do for Louis, too."

"Have you been here long?"

"Eight months, nearly. Mary in the kitchen says the last girl got spooked."

"I beg your pardon?"

She glanced down at my nightgown and smirked. "You'd best get dressed and come to breakfast. Missus is always up late and Louis breakfasts with her, so they're still at table. I'll show you down."

—>—<—

Ten minutes later, wearing the neatest of my old black dresses, my hair scraped into a tight bun, I followed Susan down to the breakfast room. The house seemed friendlier in the daylight. The sun streamed over dust motes, making the marble staircase golden. It must have been a very grand house when it was first built, but the tiles were chipped now, the steps uneven, the red walls faded and solemn with some patches of brighter paint, as though vast portraits had once hung there.

We emerged into the entrance hall, and I kept myself to Susan's left so that I could better hear anything she might say. All of yesterday's shadows became clear—the chandelier, the console tables, the grandfather clock. Carved faces leered above the doors. They, too, were in some state of disrepair—the first was missing its nose, the second its ear, the third half its face.

To one side ran a long corridor, down which Susan pointed. "That way's the west wing—breakfast room and parlor and morning room and everything else. Missus'll tell you what you can and can't use. Stairs down to the kitchens and servants' quarters are behind the main staircase. The schoolroom's upstairs, next to your bedchamber."

Then, turning toward a door to the east of the main entrance, she said, "That's the library, there. Only room on this side of the house you'll ever need. Beyond that's the east wing." She nodded down a short stretch of corridor that ended in a closed door. "Did Mrs. Pulley tell you about the east wing last night?"

I shook my head.

"We're not allowed there," said Susan. "It's all closed up. Dangerous, like—rotten floorboards and such. Makes you wonder what the point of such a large house is if you can't use it all. Still, there's no understanding rich folk."

She looked me up and down as she spoke, taking in my patched mourning dress, as though to confirm that her assessment of me was right. It had been a long time since a servant had spoken to me so freely, and I was not sure I liked it.

"Anyway, stick west," she said. "Understand?"

We headed down the corridor, passing various closed doors before Susan stopped. I had barely a moment to feel nervous, to remember that the next few years of my life would depend on the people I was about to meet—and then the door was open and I was following Susan into a sunlit breakfast room, where two people sat at a vast rosewood table.

The first was a woman of perhaps five-and-thirty. She had dark hair—so very dark I might have thought the color false had her son's not been the exact same shade. Her eyes were a greenish blue, her skin pale, her frame tall. She gave the impression of someone who had once been very beautiful but had lost a little of her shine, not through age so much as care and trouble. She was in half mourning, wearing a mauve dress with white lace trimmings.

Across from her sat the little boy. He had his mother's dark hair, but beyond that the resemblance stopped. His eyes were bright blue, his features delicate. Had I not been told he was ten years old, I should have thought him younger, for he was very small. Yet he seemed to have a healthy appetite: his plate was piled with bread and bacon and eggs. He had a smear of grease on his cheek and a napkin tucked into his collar. His shorts were the same blue-gray as his waistcoat and his shirtsleeves were rolled up.

"You must be Mrs. Lennox," he said, and a shy smile spread across his face. After a glance at his mother, he crossed the room and held out his hand. It trembled before I took it, but it was somehow a strong handshake for a boy so small. "Mother says you're going to teach me everything."

"I will certainly teach you as much as I can," I replied. "I hope you are eager to learn."

"I hope so, too," said Louis. "And you are really my governess? I have never had one before."

Ten years old and never yet had a governess! I was about to ask if he had been away to school when my new mistress spoke for the first time.

"Come, Louis, let Mrs. Lennox sit down."

The boy, somewhat abashed, reclaimed his chair and tucked into a mouthful of bacon.

I hesitated. I ought, of course, to sit down next to my charge, but the place set beside him was to his right—it would be harder to hear clearly. The seat beside Mrs. Eversham was to her left, but I was not used to eating with the mistress of the house; it had never been the custom in my previous positions.

Perhaps seeing my difficulty, Mrs. Eversham inclined her head to signal the seat beside her, and I moved to take it. As I sat down, I saw Susan quit the room.

Mrs. Eversham, without standing, held out her hand to me. "I am glad to see you, Mrs. Lennox. Thank you very much for coming." I had never had a mistress thank me before, and I must have shown my surprise, for she gave a slight, cool laugh. "We are very out of the way here, I know. It will not be a grand position, but Louis's a good boy and keen to learn."

"He has never had a governess before?" I asked.

"Mama has been teaching me," he said, and his mother gave him a warning look for talking with his mouth full.

"It is time Louis had proper instruction," Mrs. Eversham said. "I am a poor teacher, I fear, and I am often away on business matters. I am going to London tomorrow, as it happens, so you will have a quiet first week here. You have met Mrs. Pulley and Susan, I think? I will introduce you to the others after breakfast. Do help yourself."

I had eaten nothing since a light luncheon the day before. I took bread and kippers and cold meats, and when my plate was full—though not quite as full as Louis's—I began to eat, thinking over all I had heard. I wondered what sort of business would take Mrs. Eversham regularly from home, and why she chose to live so far from London if she had cause to make frequent visits there.

As Mrs. Eversham poured my tea, she asked after my journey.

"A little wet," I replied, with a smile.

"I ran out in the storm," said Louis, "and Mother was dreadful cross."

"Of course I was cross!" The sudden urgency of Mrs. Eversham's tone surprised me. "Running out by yourself in the dark, on such a night as that! You know it is not safe, dear. You must never, ever wander off by yourself. You *know* this."

"Yes, Mother," he said, and looked solemnly down at his plate.

As I ate, Mrs. Eversham told me about the house. There was only a small staff here, she explained: a housekeeper and one housemaid, a butler, a cook, a kitchen girl, and one gardener. It was a surprisingly short list—at the Russels', where I had worked before my marriage, there had been twenty-five servants for a house not much larger. She told me that the building itself was three hundred years old, that the grounds ran down to the woods in the south, and up to the hills in the north. We were two miles from the village of Hartbridge.

"I came through it on my way here," I said. I half wanted to see what she would say about the village; it had been clear from the landlord's words that the Evershams were not favorites there.

"Oh, did you?" She paused. "I own I am not fond of the place. They are . . . small-minded, the people of Hartbridge, and don't take easily to outsiders. We never go into the village."

———>—<———

After breakfast, Susan took Louis upstairs to wash his face before lessons began, and Mrs. Eversham introduced me to the other servants. On the stairs, we encountered Mrs. Pulley, and I found her as impassive as last night. She inclined her head to Mrs. Eversham and merely blinked at me.

"You've met our new governess, haven't you?"

She nodded.

"Mrs. Lennox, if you need anything, ask Mrs. Pulley. She is the best housekeeper anybody ever had."

Mrs. Pulley's face remained expressionless. She said quietly, "Thank you, ma'am," and walked on.

Mrs. Eversham had no qualms about going into the kitchen itself. It was a large room, with bare wooden floors, a big range, and a mismatched array of plates lining the dresser shelves. It smelled of bread and apples, and I saw a pitcher of cider standing on one of the tables.

Here, Mrs. Eversham introduced me to the cook, Miss Lacey—"Just Lacey's fine by me, ma'am"—a tall, loud woman in her early forties, and to Mary, the kitchen girl, not more than eighteen, with dark blond hair and a pinched face.

"We're right glad to have you here, Mrs. Lennox," Lacey was saying. "If you can keep Master Louis out of the kitchen, everyone'll be happy. What an appetite that boy has! The food that goes out the larder while I'm asleep, I swear—enough to feed a man—and yet he's such a little boy, for all that he's trying to make himself big and strong."

Behind her, Mary muttered something under her breath.

"Oh, do be quiet, Mary. You'll be saying next that all that food vanishes into thin air!"

After we had left the kitchen, Mrs. Eversham showed me to the offices and introduced "John Stevens, our butler," who rose from filling out the household accounts. He was a man of about fifty, with dark hair, graying at the temples, and a gentlemanly face. He had a kind voice, with a faint northern lilt, and he greeted me with a cheer-ful "How do you do, Mrs. Lennox?"

"Very well, thank you. It is a pleasure to meet you."

"We are all glad to have you at Hartwood. I hope you will be happy here."

There was something so terribly earnest about those last words that I could not help smiling. "But of course," I said.

And that was all—five indoor servants, and no more. I wondered if anyone would dare ask me to help on laundry day. It seemed very singular, but Mrs. Eversham made no comment on it, as though it were quite normal to run a grand country house with such a small staff.

"The east wing is entirely shut up," Mrs. Eversham went on. "Please don't venture there—we never use it. That is the only part of the house that is out of bounds; otherwise, you must treat Hartwood quite as your home."

This, at least, seemed a warmer welcome than I ever had at the Russels'. There I had been confined to my own bedchamber and the schoolroom, banned from much of the rest of the house. Whatever the irregularities of Hartwood Hall were, I might find they worked in my favor.

On the way up to the schoolroom, Mrs. Eversham outlined my duties. I was to teach Louis from eight in the morning until four in the afternoon each day, and be his companion in the early evening until Susan came at eight o'clock to get him ready for bed. I was to teach him mathematics and the sciences, as well as reading and writ-ing, and modern and classical languages, and to walk with him in the grounds, to ensure he got enough exercise. In the evenings, my time was my own.

"There is one other thing I must mention." Mrs. Eversham paused, and a flush of color passed over her cheeks. "Whenever you and Louis are outside in the grounds together, you must never let him out of your sight. Of course it is different within the house, but please do shut and lock the doors whenever you come in." She tried to smile, though I saw she was very much in earnest. "You will think me an anxious mother, I know, but this is very, very important. You are always to know where Louis is. You are to watch over him constantly. Do you understand?"

I looked at her in surprise. Her face was pale, her brow furrowed in concern. I said, "Of course."

———>—<———

Louis and I commenced our lessons that morning. It seemed even stranger that he had never had a governess before when I saw the schoolroom, for it had been furnished perfectly: a fine wide desk for Louis and a larger one for me, a huge globe resting on mine, and a low bookshelf running along one wall, packed full of fairy tales and story-books. I spotted *Jane Eyre*, and Miss Edgeworth's *Moral Tales for Young People*, Pinnock's abridged histories, a leather-bound Bible, and several volumes in Latin and French. One shelf was piled up with paper and ink and pens. The inkpots were half full, and the black-board had evidently been used before.

Louis sat behind his desk, his legs folded beneath him. I pulled my chair forward before I sat down.

"Today, Louis, we shall start by becoming better acquainted." I smiled. "Can you tell me what your mother has taught you?"

He frowned in concentration, his forehead puckering. "We learned lots of things."

"And what is your favorite thing to learn?"

"I like learning about history," he said. "And I like reading—Mother is good at telling stories, and she always says that books are very, very important. I like French, too—but Latin is hard. I don't like arithmetic much, and nor does Mama, but I do like learning about the globes, and—and scientific things, when it's outside, insects and birds and everything. I like that. Not that we go outside much, but—" He broke off, seemingly confused, and finished by drawing circles on the paper with his pen.

"I'm glad to find you can read. Would you like to show me?"

He nodded eagerly.

"Pick your favorite book off the shelves and read me the first chapter. Then I'll read the next and ask you to write it down."

He chose Mary Shelley's *Frankenstein* and began to read aloud. He read well, not just with accuracy but with feeling—and though he struggled over some of the longer words, we had got smoothly through several pages before I had time to think that it was a strange favorite for a ten-year-old.

He stopped at the end of the first section and offered the book to me.

I read slowly to give him time to write, watching the movement of his hand as it traveled across the page. His handwriting was neat, though his press was too heavy, making the ink bleed into the page.

"Why do you like *Frankenstein*?" I asked, when I had finished.

He shrugged, suddenly shy. Then he said softly, "I like monsters."

CHAPTER III

We had luncheon in the breakfast room, just Louis and me. The table was spread with bread and hard local cheeses, and we both ate heartily. Afterward, I suggested we take a walk in the grounds. Louis was a thin, weak-looking child, and I was sure he ought to take more exercise than he did. He looked hesitant at the idea of a walk, but then his face brightened and he asked, "Can we see Paul?"

"Paul?"

"The gardener. He's my friend."

I smiled. "Do you have many friends your own age, Louis?"

Louis was busy putting on his boots and did not answer. When he finally looked up, he shook his head. "I don't know any other children," he said simply.

I studied his face for any traces of sorrow but found none; he seemed to take the isolation of his life for granted. I thought of my own childhood, playing in the river with the village girls, drawing hopscotch on cobblestones, racing marbles. My father had been a struggling surgeon; our home was small, our means always stretched— but I felt sorry for Louis, with his large, grand house and no friends to run and play with.

Out in the courtyard, the house towered above us. The roof was gabled, huge chimney turrets rising above graying sandstone. Gargoyles and statuettes were tucked in corners and above windows. I glanced around us, at the cobbles, the dried-up fountain, a worn statue of a woman's frame rising out of the stone. I took in the tall apple tree to one side of the courtyard, its bright leaves and ripening fruit—and beyond it, the east wing, where every curtain was drawn.

I followed Louis into the grounds. It was a warm, bright day, and the smell of fresh grass filled the air. To the south was the dark strip of woodland that enclosed half the grounds, a tight muddle of oak, ash, and beech trees. To the east of the house was the lake, its dark water shimmering in the sunlight. On the other side of the lake was a little summer house, and beyond that the countryside spread up into open hills. These were large grounds for only one gardener to manage, but everything seemed well ordered. The rose garden was elegant, the vegetable garden neat, the topiary impressive—even the unruly parts of the garden were carefully, purposefully wild.

"These are beautiful grounds, Louis," I said. "Do you often play outside?"

He hesitated. "Sometimes," he replied, "when Mother or Paul or Susan can watch me. I have to be careful, though. Mother says never to go into the woods or I might get lost."

"Are there deer here?"

He blinked at me, surprised by the question, until I explained that *hart* was an old word for deer.

"Oh. I didn't know that." He smiled, as though the idea pleased him. "No, I've never seen a deer. I should like to, though."

"The village is down through the trees, I suppose?"

"Yes," said Louis slowly. "We don't go there much. Mother is the only one who can take me and she is often away. On business," he added, in a very grown-up way, as though he knew all about it.

"Well, I can take you into the village, now that I am here."

Louis's eyes lit up. "Oh, would you? I should like that."

I looked across at him, this odd, lonely child. What a strange life his seemed to be.

For all today's warmth and sunshine, the grass was thick with last night's mud, and we tramped through it together. As we neared the east wing, I thought I saw something move in the summer house across the lake, a twitch of the curtains, and I stopped.

"Is there someone in the summer house?"

Louis shook his head. "Only Mama and I use it."

"Would you like to show it to me?"

Louis turned around. "But—but I want to show you my garden."

I smiled. "Your garden?"

"Yes, my garden. You'll like it. Paul let me choose everything in it. There's a big oak that has been there forever and ever and then Paul and I planted a little horse chestnut tree and lavender and Lent-lilies and primroses and magnolias and dahlias."

I glanced back at the summer house, but all was still. "Very well, then. Lead the way."

This he did, heading round the east wing, past curtained windows, across muddy grass, and up gravel pathways. The house's age, its shabby grandness, made it an impressive sight. Ivy and other creepers climbed between the windows, stretching up toward the roof. The east wing was nearly as much green as it was stone.

Beyond the house there was a small outbuilding that I assumed to be the stables; it was newer, with red brick and a tiled roof, with one ordinary door and one wide enough for horses.

As we came around the back of the house, I saw at once what must be Louis's garden: a swing strung up from an ancient oak, surrounded by an odd assortment of plants—a mess of flowers, thistles, and shrubs, with lavender and wildflowers carpeting the ground. It was beautiful, in its way, Louis's little arcadia.

And then I saw a figure move out from behind the tree—the gardener Louis had mentioned, no doubt. I stopped, colored, and stepped back.

The young man was leaning over, cutting the grass with a pair of shears. His hair was a light auburn brown, unruly about his ears. He wore dark trousers rolled up to the knee, thick worn boots—and nothing else. His shirt and waistcoat lay discarded on Louis's swing a little way behind him, and his back shone with sweat in the sunshine. Without meaning to, I watched him for a moment, his strong arms, his broad shoulders—and I thought of the last man I had seen in such a state of undress, of Richard's thin frame, months ago, in the days when he still summoned me to his room.

And then the gardener looked round.

He stood up, startled, and turned quickly to gather up his shirt and pull it over his head. I looked away, embarrassed, but at my side Louis was laughing.

"It is only us, Paul. You must meet Mrs. Lennox, my new governess. Mrs. Lennox, this is Paul. He made my garden for me."

The young man, now fully dressed, was scarlet. He approached us quickly, with a slight bow of his head.

"You'll forgive me, Mrs. Lennox, ma'am. I'm not much used to anyone being in the grounds at this hour. I'll remember in future."

Close up, I saw that he was even younger than I had supposed—five years my junior at least. There was something about his face, the line of his jaw, the color of his lips, that struck me. His hands were large, red raw, and hard-worked.

"Of course," I said. "There is nothing to forgive, Mr.—?"

"Carter, ma'am. I'm the gardener."

"Except here," cried Louis, "where *I'm* the gardener."

"Quite right, Master Louis." Carter smiled, and slight dimples formed in his cheeks.

"Paul is teaching me how to grow things," Louis said, turning to me. "The primroses I put in the ground myself."

I smiled as Louis showed me around his garden, pointing out each plant in turn, trying to remember the names for every flower and shrub. Carter had to prompt him only once, when the word *chrysanthemum* was a struggle. Louis's keen mind and eager explanations pleased me. He seemed an intelligent child—and more, too, a child who liked knowledge, who had stored up all that the gardener had told him.

We moved to a patch of dahlias, and with them came a rush of memory. Richard had brought me a bunch of these once, a few weeks after we were married, in the days when he had been shy, full of little gestures. He'd bring flowers for the dining table, buy volumes of sermons for me to read, order me clothes from London. Nothing showy, never too fine—good quality and plain, as all Richard's tastes were.

I turned back to Louis, shook the thought of Richard away.

Only when we had been through every inch of his garden did Louis seem satisfied. We were there so long that I half expected Carter to have resumed his work, but instead he stood back, surveying us, and I began to wonder if we were in his way.

"Come, Louis, we had better finish our walk and resume our lessons. Mr. Carter, good day."

The gardener's eyes met mine. "A pleasure to meet you, Mrs. Lennox."

"Paul's my favorite," said Louis, as we rounded the corner of the house.

"Has he worked here long?"

"Oh, ever so long. I don't remember when he didn't, though he did not always live up here."

"It is a large park for him to manage alone."

"There used to be another man, once, but I don't remember him much. Mother says he was a bad man and . . . prejudiced." He struggled over the last word, and spoke it slowly, as though unsure of its meaning. "But that was all long ago. Mrs. Pulley and Stevens have been here forever and ever, too, but Lacey and Mary are newer and Susan's only been here since Christmas." Louis stopped walking, his boots deep in mud, and grinned. "And now there's you. And you shall be my favorite, too, and more, for everybody else is everybody's and you're all mine."

———>×<———

We spent much of the rest of the day in the schoolroom, puzzling over languages. Louis's Latin was very bad, but his French showed promise. When the clock struck four, we went downstairs to the music room—a neat square room with pale green walls, an old grand pianoforte at one end, a harp at the other.

"Can you play the harp, Louis?"

He shook his head. "Mama can. She's very good." And then he frowned, as though he'd said something he shouldn't, and I wondered if Mrs. Eversham was shy of her talents. "I play the pianoforte, though. Shall I play for you, Mrs. Lennox?"

"Please do."

He was not perfect by any means. His fingering was jumbled and he missed one or two notes. His small hands could not stretch the octave and his timing was poor—and yet there was something almost mesmeric about the feeling with which he played, the rush of notes fueled by enjoyment. Yes, there was talent here.

When Louis had finished, he turned to me, smiling. "Will you play for me, Mrs. Lennox? I should like it very much."

→⟡←

We dined at half past six. I had been expecting Mrs. Eversham to join us, but Mr. Stevens came in and quietly explained that she would dine in her own room, as she was leaving early tomorrow morning for her journey. Louis seemed so unsurprised that I supposed this to be a regular occurrence. He tucked into his stew with great fervor.

My spirits were high over dinner; my first day seemed to have been a success. Yes, the house itself was a little unusual, and I did not quite know what to make of Mrs. Eversham—but I liked Louis. He was keen, clever, and I thought I could do well with him. And then he was lonely, too, and though my childhood had been a happy one, I had been lonely often enough in the years since I left home to feel for him. If he was a little alone, a little friendless—well, so was I.

Mary brought in the dessert. She moved slowly, shoulders hunched, head down, as though she feared meeting our eyes.

"Where are you from, Mrs. Lennox?" Louis asked, after she had gone. "Is it far?"

"Hampshire. It must be a hundred miles off."

"And you were married? Mother said so."

"Yes." I kept my voice steady. "My husband died."

Louis took another forkful of apple cake. He didn't seem to think this was especially sad, or that he needed to comment. He just accepted it as the way things were. "I'm glad you're here," he said. And then, more quietly, "Will you tell me the truth?"

"About what, child?"

"Everything." His eyes were suddenly bright. "I hate lies," he said. "I hate secrets."

I was momentarily taken aback, but I tried to smile it away. "It's good to like the truth, Louis."

"Is it?" he asked, and he seemed genuinely to want to know.

"Yes," I said, "and that is the truth."

I looked down at my plate to hide my face. Yes, better to teach Louis to always speak the truth, even if I knew *I* could not.

CHAPTER IV

THE NEXT MORNING, MRS. EVERSHAM WAS GONE. SHE HAD LEFT early, Susan told me, as I took my place at the table.

Louis was already digging into his breakfast, seemingly unaffected by his mother's absence. Susan, meanwhile, was less constrained without her mistress. She stayed longer today, asking Louis about his lessons, keeping her eyes on me. Before she left the room, she stole a rasher of bacon from the table when she thought I wasn't looking.

With Mrs. Eversham away, Louis and I settled down to our new life together. Over the next few days, I began to grow more accustomed to Hartwood Hall.

Louis's eager smile, his puckered forehead when he was struggling with a lesson, were soon familiar to me. There were a few gaps in his knowledge, little aspects of common sense he seemed to lack, and that odd pendulum between shyness and bright, urgent chatter. Still, I liked the boy—more, I think, than I usually liked my pupils at first.

I spent my days with him in the schoolroom, going over the books on the shelves or discussing history, helping him with his Latin or conversing in French, doing long sums on the blackboard. We ate together, walked together, played chess together. He took every lesson in stride.

I was coming to know the servants, too. Paul Carter greeted us in the gardens whenever we were outside, always ready with a smile for Louis. Mrs. Pulley was ever silent, but she nodded at me when we passed in the corridors, and though she did not smile at Louis—for she never smiled at anyone—I sometimes saw a flicker of affection for him in her face. Mr. Stevens was cheerful and polite, always eager to ask me how I was settling in.

I saw Lacey and Mary more than I expected to. For a cook and a kitchen maid, they were often upstairs, Mary serving at the table and helping Susan with certain duties, Lacey eager to gossip. She asked me more questions about my previous positions and my marriage than Mrs. Eversham had. I told her a little, but I did not tell her everything.

I sometimes wondered if I would ever tell anybody everything.

Susan talked to me sometimes as though Louis were not in the room, complaining about Lacey and Mrs. Pulley, moving around me so that I had to turn to catch her words. Her manner unsettled me. It bordered on familiarity, on insolence. There was something I did not like about the way she looked at me—indeed the way she looked at everything in the room, in the house—as though she was working something out, deep in the back of her mind.

———>·<·———

Toward the end of my first week at Hartwood Hall, I woke abruptly in the middle of the night, breathing hard. I had been dreaming of Richard again, and the scent of him, the tone of his voice, lingered in my mind. It took me a few moments to realize what had woken me. A noise, somewhere beyond my room, loud enough to pull me from sleep.

I opened my bed curtains gingerly and fumbled on the bedside table for a match. I lit a candle and got out of bed.

As I eased the door open, I saw the candle shake and sputter in my hand. I stood in the corridor, breathing in and out, looking up and down. But it was entirely empty.

A smile came to my lips. Of course I had heard nothing. Of course it had been nothing more than a remnant of my dream.

I took one final glance down the corridor—

And stopped.

There was someone there.

I whispered, "Louis?"

No reply. I stepped forward, my skin cold.

Whoever it was held no candle, but I saw movement in the darkness on the stairs, and I hurried after it. Was it one of the servants, wandering the corridors when they shouldn't be? Did Louis sleepwalk?

I was four steps down the stairs and my candle was casting twisted shadows on the wall. My footsteps creaked loudly on each step.

I caught a glimpse of a white nightshirt in the darkness below.

There was definitely someone there.

I moved quickly down the staircase, nearer and nearer to where the figure had been. I felt almost that I were still dreaming, as though the figure in the dark before me was Richard, walking away from me. I was losing him. Surely I could catch him, I could save him, if only I moved faster, if only I tried.

I shook it off. I was not dreaming. I was in my new home in the dark, following a blur of light.

As I reached the foot of the stairs I said, louder than before, "Louis?"

A moment's silence.

Then, "Mrs. Lennox?"

Louis's voice. I breathed out in relief.

"Are you all right, child? Were you sleepwalking?"

"No," came his voice in the darkness. "I heard you on the stairs and came to see what the matter was."

That was when I realized. The voice was not coming from in front of me but from behind. I had always struggled to tell.

I turned sharply round—and there was Louis, standing at the top of the stairs in a gray nightshirt, a candle in his hand.

I swallowed hard. I looked around the empty entrance hall, raised my candle, but I could see no one. Not a shadow. Not a movement.

"I thought . . ."

Louis was halfway down the stairs now. "What is it, Mrs. Lennox?"

"I thought I saw someone out of bed. I was following them, to check if they were all right. I thought it was you." I tried to smile. "It was probably one of the servants."

"They always use the back stairs," said Louis. "It must have been Mama."

"But she's away."

He blinked at me, and then his face cracked into a smile. "I am so sleepy I forgot," he said. "But I suppose you were only dreaming."

I was coming up the steps to meet him, but this gave me pause. I looked back over my shoulder, held the candle up high—but still there was nothing. What I had thought was a figure must have been a trick of the light, the white nightshirt nothing but the reflection of the moon. Only my imagination.

I reached Louis and put my hand in his. "I dare say you are right."

"Mother says I'm always right." He smiled. "You thought I was sleepwalking, but you were."

"I suppose I was. Come, we ought to go back to bed."

Louis squeezed my hand.

We parted outside my door. I watched him walk down the corridor toward his room, holding his candle aloft. When he reached his bedroom, he turned back. His face looked momentarily pained, and he said something. In the candlelight, I saw his mouth move, but the words did not reach me.

"What was that, Louis?"

He hesitated, and when he spoke again I was almost sure he did not repeat what he had said before. He said, "I'm glad you have come."

I smiled. "I am glad, too."

And then I blew out the candle and crept back to bed.

CHAPTER V

"What time does church start, Louis?" I asked.

It was Sunday, and I had come downstairs in my smartest black dress to find Louis waiting for me at the breakfast table. He was wearing his usual little gray suit, his sleeves rolled up, his forehead creased. "Church," he repeated. "But . . . we don't go to church." He looked down at his breakfast, suddenly solemn, as though he knew from books this was something to be ashamed of.

I could not hide my surprise. I had been in houses where church had been insisted on twice each Sunday, had been forced to trek through thick snow with several children to reach a service. But I had never been in a house where no service was attended.

A new thought struck me. "Are you Roman Catholics, Louis?"

"What does that mean?" he asked. "We went to the church in Hartbridge once, but that was years ago. I wanted to go again but Mama couldn't."

"Couldn't?" I repeated.

"Mother's too busy, and sometimes she's away, so there's no one to take me." He looked up at me. "I liked church, when we went. I like the music and I know all my prayers because Mother said I must learn them. I say the Lord's Prayer in bed and if I am ever in trouble. But there has never been anybody to take me to church."

"Well, I am here now," I said. "Should you like to go?"

"Oh yes, Mrs. Lennox, please."

I hesitated. I knew I ought to ask Mrs. Eversham, but she was away until tomorrow—and if the only reason Louis did not usually go was because she was too busy, that was easily remedied now that I was here.

"Some of the servants go, I suppose."

"Paul does."

"No one else?"

He shook his head. "Lacey and Mary have to do the cooking and Susan doesn't like church and Mr. Stevens is a dis . . . a dis . . ."

"A dissenter, Louis?"

He nodded. "That's it. And Mrs. Pulley, I don't know. Do you always go to church, Mrs. Lennox?"

I hesitated. Before my marriage, I had loved church. It had been a comfort to me. Not just because prayer was a release, a relief, but because church was *loud*. Because when I was a girl, after the accident, when my sudden deafness confused me and made my hands shake, my parents took me back to church and I heard bells and singing, all loud enough to penetrate the walls my body had created, and for the first time I felt real again.

But over the last three years, church had come to mean Richard. Church was hearing his sermons, seeing the congregation greet him after a service, all fondness and respect—and church, for me, was play-acting perfection, being the good reverend's wife, knowing that everyone kept half an eye on me.

The morning I found him dead, I prayed to God for forgiveness. I had not been to church since, and I both dreaded it and missed it with all my heart.

I smiled at Louis. "Nearly always, yes."

—————⟶⟵—————

An hour later, Louis and I were sat in the back of Paul Carter's trap, racing toward the village.

The gardener had seemed surprised when we found him. He had been pruning the rosebushes, wearing a dark suit and waistcoat—and, when I mentioned church, a frown.

"You're taking Master Louis to church, ma'am?"

"Yes, that's right."

He had stared at me, and I began to doubt myself. Then he swallowed and nodded.

"I was going to ride. You can both come in the trap."

So here we were, moving quickly through the woods until the trees grew thinner, down through the farmland and meadows and orderly orchards that had been mere shadows days before. It was beautiful here—the hedges tangled with honeysuckle and old man's beard, dark heather flooding the fields with purple. It was a warm but blustery day, and the wind was so strong I had to hold on to my bonnet.

Paul Carter said little. From the front of the cart, he barely seemed to register our presence, turning only once to smile at something Louis had said. He was sat directly in front of us, and it did not seem wrong for me to watch him, the quick precise movements of his arms to guide the reins, the ruffling of his hair in the breeze.

Louis was excited the whole way, peering at the cows and the orchards, the greens and reds of the ripening fruit blurring as we passed. When the village finally came into view, he squeezed my hand and grinned. It was not right, I thought, for this to be such a novelty to him.

There was the inn again, almost unrecognizable in the morning sun. We passed rows of little houses, built in yellow or red sandstone, all with low thatched roofs. We passed shops, too: a blacksmith's, a butcher's, a baker's, and a grocer's, lined up together along the main street.

Down one road I could see a mill at the edge of the village, the tall water wheel turning with the river's flow—and beyond it the arched stone bridge I had crossed on my way to Hartwood Hall.

We saw the people of the village, men and women, young and old, all heading in one direction. They looked mostly to be farm laborers—even in their Sunday best, I saw not one figure who might be taken for a lady or a gentleman.

We were clearly an object of interest. With every turn of the cart's wheels, another face looked up, another pair of eyes narrowed. Three

men out of the fifty we must have passed acknowledged Paul Carter
with some look of recognition. But none spoke to him, and none
spoke to us.

"Why is everyone looking?" Louis whispered to me as we neared
the church. His cheeks were pale, and when I reached for his hand, it
was clammy with sweat.

"Only because they do not know us," I said gently. It was certainly
not a very warm reception, but if Louis never came into the village,
they would not recognize him, and the sight of two well-dressed
strangers must have been a curiosity. Then I remembered the landlord's scowl when the coachman mentioned Hartwood Hall, and I
wondered if it was more than that.

"They look so hard," murmured Louis, "like they could see through
me and know everything."

"Hush, child. It's all right. It is merely because we are a novelty."

This seemed to satisfy Louis, but he kept his eyes on the floor of
the cart for the rest of the journey.

When we at last reached the church, Paul Carter alighted. He held
out his hand to help first Louis, then me. His skin felt rough, his
hands warm from the ride. He did not look at me as he released my
fingers and began to walk toward the church. It was an old building,
the reddish sandstone toned and weathered to gold, the windows thin
and arched, a few narrow cracks in the tall square tower.

Paul hesitated just inside the church door. Louis and I were behind
him, Louis's hand in mine. It was grand enough inside, for all that it
was small—ornate carvings lined the walls, and the altar and font
were made from marble. The pews were already half full, and I had
taken a step forward to find a seat when Paul Carter grabbed my arm
and held me back.

He released it at once, and flushed red. His grip had been strong.
"Sorry, ma'am. There's a box."

I blinked. "For Hartwood Hall?"

"Yes—where the old family used to sit. You'd best go there. Louis
oughtn't to sit anywhere else." He nodded toward the front of the

church, where two raised boxes stood on either side of the altar. In one of them sat a lady in a blue dress, with light brown hair. She looked about my age and seemed to be the only person in the church wearing gloves. "That one," Carter was saying. "The lady is the vicar's wife. She won't trouble you."

I hesitated. "Will you sit with us?" I asked Paul.

He stared at me. "No, ma'am, thank you. My . . . my family is here. Good day, Mrs. Lennox, Master Louis."

Louis was busy looking at everything and anything, so deep in contemplation of each person who passed that I had to tug his hand to make him move. His fear seemed to have evaporated, and I thought how strange children were, as I watched him run his hands along the ends of the pews. What a life he must have had, to be so enchanted by the everyday.

As we stepped up to the box, the church fell quiet, and dozens of eyes seemed to peer up at us. I saw mouths curved down into frowns, brows furrowed—and then each parishioner seemed to whisper to their neighbors.

Louis's hand began to shake in mine.

The lady in the box turned at our approach and looked as startled as the rest of the congregation. She smiled hesitantly, first at Louis, then at me, and said, "Mrs. Eversham, I am so sorry—had I known you were coming, of course I should not have sat here."

I flushed. So they did not even know in the village what Mrs. Eversham looked like. I kept Louis's fingers tight in mine, and something inside me shifted. I could have had a child like him, in another life.

"Oh, no, my name is Mrs. Lennox. This is Master Louis Eversham. I am his governess."

Her face relaxed. "Oh, I see. Do excuse me, Mrs. Lennox. Good morning, Master Eversham. My name is Mrs. Welling. I am the vicar's wife and I sometimes watch the sermons from here, but—" She rose to her feet. "Of course I will move. It is Hartwood Hall's box, after all."

"No, please, do stay." I spoke falteringly, aware of the congregation's eyes on us. "There is plenty of space for all of us, isn't there, Louis?"

Louis was not listening. He had already sat down at the front of the box and was busy staring out into the throng of people, meeting their steely gazes with his own curiosity. I smiled and took my place at his side, while Mrs. Welling sat back down.

As I glanced over the congregation, I saw Paul Carter. He was sitting at the back beside a family group: an elderly man, a married couple of about my age, and three whispering children. Carter's eyes met mine. He held my gaze, his expression unreadable. I swallowed hard. And then the man at his side said something and he looked away.

A moment later, the organ began, and a half-forgotten feeling washed over me. As I watched the front of the church, I almost expected Richard to appear, his mouth set, his eyes grave, ready for the service ahead. But instead I saw a different man, younger, smaller, milder. Mr. Welling was not much over thirty, with fair hair and spectacles, and a clear, distinct voice. He read well and spoke better, and even the little children stayed silent during the sermon.

Beside me, Mrs. Welling sat with her hands clasped together, watching her husband with a look of admiration, of pure love, in her eyes.

When Mr. Welling said, "Let us pray," Louis shifted beside me. Leaning close to my good ear, he whispered, "What should I pray for?"

"Anything you like, child. For your mother, perhaps."

"And for my father? Is it good to pray for the dead?"

I nodded, squeezed his hand.

"And for forgiveness?"

"It is a worthy thing to pray for," I murmured, "but I am sure you do not need it."

"I do," said Louis, and I saw his face pale. He muttered something I did not catch, and then someone glanced up from the pews below, frowning, and I signaled for Louis to be quiet.

I clasped my hands before me and saw him follow my example. I closed my eyes.

I prayed for forgiveness, too.

———— ⤙⤚ ————

When the service was over and the village began to file out, Mrs. Welling asked if she might introduce us to her husband. A minute later, we were in front of Mr. Welling, and Louis was putting out his little hand.

"Ever so glad to make your acquaintance, Master Eversham," said the vicar. "I hope we will see you again. Do bring your mama, won't you, my dear boy? How did you like the service?"

"Very much," said Louis, with a glance back at me. "Can we come every week, Mrs. Lennox?"

"I see no reason why not, child."

I looked around us. The church was nearly empty now, though I saw Paul Carter sitting at the back, waiting for us. The group around him had slowly trickled out, but his nearest neighbor, the younger man, lingered. He was dressed like a farm laborer, a messy cravat the only attempt at Sunday wear. As he rose from his seat, he looked back to Carter and said something. He seemed for a moment to be waiting for him.

Then Carter shook his head and the man left, frowning. As Carter turned away, our eyes met, and he saw that I was watching him. I turned back sharply to the Wellings.

"Will you dine with us one Sunday?" Mrs. Welling asked. "You might come after church."

The question surprised me, and I supposed she saw it, for she blushed.

"There is not much company, hereabouts. Dr. Rogers is a friend of my husband's, but he is not married, and—"

"What my wife means," said Mr. Welling, with a smile, "is that there is not one lady for miles around, and that you are the first she has met for half a year." He beamed. "Of course Louis is invited, too."

Louis tugged on my arm. "Oh, can we?"

"As long as your mother does not mind," I said gently. I looked up at the Wellings and smiled. "It is a kind offer. I shall need to speak to Mrs. Eversham, but I should be very glad to come if I am able."

Mrs. Welling was beaming. "Shall we say in a fortnight, perhaps?"

"Certainly."

———>·<———

Paul Carter barely spoke on the way home. He drove the horse as fast as he could, concentrating entirely on the road. As Louis and I talked, going over the sermon and what we would study tomorrow, I found my eyes drawn toward the gardener, his fixed expression, his defined movements. I thought of the young man who had approached him, how firmly Carter had shaken his head. We must have spoiled his plans by coming.

The sun was streaming through the trees as the cart emerged from the woods. Louis was telling me about his plans for his little garden, and I had just seen something like a smile from Carter when the house came into view.

There, on the doorstep, her shawl wrapped around her shoulders, stood Mrs. Eversham. Her face was ashen, her hands clenched into fists.

CHAPTER VI

"What on earth were you thinking?"

We were in Mrs. Eversham's study, me sitting as she had instructed, her standing, pacing, unable to keep still.

"I told you that we do not leave Hartwood, that you must be careful with Louis. This is not what I expected of you, Mrs. Lennox. I believed you were trustworthy. Your previous characters were very good. I thought—"

"I am used, ma'am," I said, as boldly as I dared, "to taking my charges to church. Louis wanted to go, and—"

"And you would take the wishes of a child over mine? Mrs. Lennox, you are in a position of trust in this house. It is your responsibility to carry out my wishes when it comes to Louis's education and life. I told you that we do not leave Hartwood. We never go to church. It is not— Louis is not—" She broke off. "Mrs. Lennox, how could you have so lost your senses as to take Louis beyond these grounds?"

"Mrs. Eversham—"

"I made it very clear that Louis must be watched carefully, that I wished him to be never out of your sight. We do not go to the village, Mrs. Lennox. The people there are suspicious—they are gossips of the very worst kind. Louis must, at all costs, be kept safe. I thought you understood this. Louis must never be taken from his home."

"But to church, ma'am! And Louis was never out of my sight, of course. I thought—"

"Well, you thought wrong!"

I breathed in sharply. Ten years ago, when I first became a governess, I might have borne my chastisement meekly. I knew it would be wiser to do so now, to apologize rather than defend myself. But I was not nineteen anymore. Mrs. Eversham had told me to be careful of Louis, yes, but she had not told me that we were never to leave the grounds of Hartwood Hall. She was being unreasonable, and from her strange mixture of agitation, anger, and embarrassment, I suspected she knew it herself.

"Mrs. Eversham," I began, speaking slowly and clearly, "Louis told me he had received religious instruction from you and that he was a Christian. He told me he wished to go to church, and that the reason he did not go was that there was no one to accompany him. It has been the custom in every place I have ever had to take the children to church on Sundays. Naturally I expected that this would be part of my duties here, that if it were otherwise I would have been informed. I am sorry if that was a presumption on my part, but I am sure you can understand it. If you do not wish Louis to attend church—and I wish you had told me so before—then Susan or somebody else will need to watch him on Sunday mornings, for I will not and cannot give up going myself."

Mrs. Eversham stared at me. She seemed too angry for words.

I had been here only a week, and already my position was in jeopardy.

This was madness. I could not afford to lose this place. If I was dismissed tomorrow, I would have nothing. I would have to sell Richard's gold watch, but even the proceeds of that would not last me long. I opened my mouth to apologize.

And then Mrs. Eversham sat down heavily in the chair across from me and raised her hands to her temples. "Forgive me," she said quietly. "I am very tired. It has been a long journey, and—and not what I had . . ." She swallowed, shook her head. Her face looked pained, but she did not meet my gaze. "I ought to have said something to you. Of course you would naturally think—" She broke off. "What was it like?"

The question surprised me. "I beg your pardon?"

"Was anyone—rude, or—did anybody act strangely? No one followed you?"

I frowned. That last question gave me a stab of unease. I wondered what she thought of the village that she should ask such a thing, what exactly she was afraid of. "No. To be sure, I am a stranger here and Louis nearly as much so—people looked at us, but that was all. We spoke to no one save the clergyman, Mr. Welling, and his wife—they seem very respectable people." I hesitated. "They invited me to dine with them in a fortnight and asked me to bring Louis. I said I would consult you before accepting such an invitation, of course."

She nodded slowly. Her eyes were dim, her mouth frowning, and it seemed as though some internal struggle were taking place. "You must go back to Louis now," she said, in a softer voice. "He will be wondering where you are."

All this she said without looking at me, her eyes fixed blankly on the fireplace. I watched her for a moment more, before rising and taking my leave.

—————>✂<—————

At dinner that evening, I could not help but feel embarrassed. Louis kept telling his mother about church, what the village had been like, what he had seen, and I was forced to sit there, inwardly wincing, torn between the gratification that I had caused this lonely child some pleasure and the distress of knowing that Mrs. Eversham disapproved. She glanced at me, once, when Louis told her about the sermon, but otherwise she kept her eyes on her son, as though I were not there at all.

After dinner, Mary came up to clear away the dishes. She seemed even more timid today—shuffling about, eyes downcast. She started violently when Louis dropped his fork, and I saw her glance at Mrs. Eversham warily—almost, I thought, as though she were afraid of her. Stevens came in with her, and lingered until she was gone. Once

Louis and I were half out of the room, I looked back to see Stevens leaning toward Mrs. Eversham, and caught the words on his lips: "No luck?"

"No."

I wondered what exactly Mrs. Eversham had gone to London for, what had left her so weary and dissatisfied on her return.

A few minutes later, Mrs. Eversham followed us, smiling. She told me that I was free for the evening, took her little boy by the hand, and quitted the room.

I was left alone and felt suddenly unsure of myself. What had I used to do with my evenings, in the days before my marriage? The Russels had sometimes made me help with the household sewing, and I had a distant image of myself sat alone at work in the darkened schoolroom. Beyond that, I could barely recall. I remembered my charges, the little boys and girls I had taught and cared for. I remembered hard and easy lessons, difficult and kind masters and mistresses—but my evenings? For the most part they had slipped from my mind, as though the time that had been solely mine meant nothing.

I left the drawing room and walked heavily toward the stairs.

When I passed Stevens in the corridor, he paused.

"Good evening, Mrs. Lennox. You are settling in well, I hope?"

"Very well, thank you. Louis is a good pupil."

"I'm sure he is." Stevens smiled. "I do hope you shall stay. Consistency will be beneficial for Louis."

I hesitated. Stevens seemed the friendliest face on the staff, so far—out of all of them, he was perhaps the most likely to tell me more about this family. "Has Louis's father been long dead?" I asked.

Stevens blinked. "He was gone before I came," he said. "I never met him."

"And how long have you worked here?"

"Seven years."

"Louis probably does not remember his father, then."

A pause. "I do not think he feels the lack," Stevens said at last. "The lack of friends his own age, perhaps, but . . . well, that cannot be helped."

This surprised me, for I rather thought it *could* be helped. "Surely there are some relations or friends or—?"

"No," said Stevens gently, before turning to continue down the corridor. "The Evershams are quite alone in the world."

CHAPTER VII

A SOUND WOKE ME. A FOOTSTEP, PERHAPS, A TREAD OUTSIDE MY door.

I drew back the bed curtains, fumbled for Richard's watch, and pressed the repeater. Four in the morning. I sat up straight, breathing hard. I thought of the other night, the trick of the light I had followed.

I climbed out of bed, lit a candle, walked once around my room to check everything was as it should be, then opened my door and peered out into the darkness.

The candle flickered and cast dark shadows on the walls—but the corridor was empty. Not a sound to be heard, not a soul to be seen. I shook my head at my own foolishness, but still I bolted the door as soon as I was back inside my room.

I could not sleep after that. I lay in bed, staring at the canopy, listening to the silent house, a headache pulling across my temples. When it was nearing six, the sun began to peek through the gap in the curtains. I rose, washed, and pulled on another black dress, then made my way downstairs to fetch a glass of water.

I was surprised to see a line of muddy footprints in the entrance hall beyond the stairs, and wondered who was up before me. The doors were still bolted across.

I walked slowly down to the kitchen, my head aching, my eyelids heavy. I half expected to find it empty at this early hour, but Mary was there.

I found her, to my surprise, not at work but standing on one of the sideboards, staring out a window. Here on the lower floor of the house, the windows were small, short, and set high up in the wall.

She turned abruptly when she heard me, nearly losing her balance. Her eyes were dark, her cheeks pale—though at the sight of me they flamed.

"Are you all right, Mary?"

"I was—I—I saw something." She glanced back out the window, then seemed to realize the strangeness of her position and reluctantly clambered down.

I could see little of the view out from where I was standing—just the blur of early-morning mist. "Something?" I repeated.

Mary hesitated. Then she stepped toward me. "I've been looking out for the ghost," she said. She spoke quietly, as though sharing a secret. There was a hint of fear in her voice, but a hint of glee, too, of triumph. "I *told* Lacey, I told her it's not Little Master, and it's not me—I told her it's not a person of flesh and blood, when anything's missing from the larder. I've heard about spirits like that, who can move things, take things. I tried to keep it off, like Mother used to say you could, if you tuck a shoe in a hole in the wall. But it keeps coming. And I saw it, just now, in the grounds—I know I did. It was far off but something was there, I *swear*."

I laughed. I could not help myself—partly because it was such a foolish, mad thing for her to say, but also because her very earnestness made me nervous.

She pulled back, stung. "Don't you believe in ghosts, Mrs. Lennox?"

"No, Mary, I do not think I do."

"Then what did I see?"

"A trick of the light, I suppose, or Mr. Carter, up early, tending to the garden."

Mary opened her mouth to speak once more, then stopped, suddenly abashed. I turned to see Lacey standing in the doorway.

"What's all this, Mary? Not scaring Mrs. Lennox with more fool-ish tales, are you?"

Mary said nothing. She refused to meet my eye, and instead went back to the sink and began clattering loudly about her work.

"Now, don't let that girl put you off, Mrs. Lennox," Lacey was say-ing, as though Mary were not in the room at all. "She has weak nerves, that's all. No such thing as ghosts, I dare say—only problem with this house is too many mouths to feed and not enough hands to feed them." She crossed the room, washed her hands at the sink, and I turned a little so that I could hear her better. "I ought to have a scullery maid as well as a kitchen maid by rights. When I worked in Taunton I had four girls under me, and here—well, I needn't bother you with my troubles, Mrs. Lennox, but it's always been a hard place, that's certain. And here in the middle of nowhere, too, not a patch of company for miles around." She pulled on her apron, wiped her hands on it. "Ah well, nowt to be done. Let it never be said that I am one to complain."

I hid my smile and told her I was sorry she had so much work to do. Then I filled my glass and went upstairs once more.

The footprints in the entrance hall were gone, and as I moved to-ward the library, the door of Mrs. Eversham's study opened and I saw her standing before me. Everybody seemed to have risen promptly today, and she had evidently heard me in the corridor.

"Good morning, Mrs. Lennox. You are up early. Will you come in for a moment?"

Within the study, her desk was a mess of papers, her pen lying as though just put down, her ink pot to one side. The window was open, the curtains blowing, and several sheets crammed with still-glistening words were fluttering in the breeze. I wondered what Mrs. Eversham had been writing at such length. The pages did not look much like letters, but I resisted the urge to look too closely.

"Do sit," she said.

I took the chair she indicated and waited as she sat down opposite.

"I have been meaning to speak to you. I—well, I have given it some thought, and I should like you to take Louis to church each week."

I could not conceal my surprise. I thought of her anger on Sunday, the hurried irrationality of it. Now she seemed entirely calm.

"It is quite right for you to take him," she went on, and though her voice was steady, I saw that this was hard for her, this admission that she had been wrong. "I had forgotten you were a clergyman's wife, and of course you take these things very seriously—as indeed ought I."

I could not help asking, "Are you sure?"

She stared down at the desk. "Yes, I am quite sure. Tell me, Mrs. Lennox—I have met Mr. Welling, once, and he seemed a kind man, but—well, his wife, what is she like? Are they . . . trustworthy people, do you think?"

"I should never have supposed them otherwise."

She nodded slowly. "And they asked Louis and you to dine with them? When was it—a week on Sunday?"

"Yes."

"Then you must go," she said. "Only—do be careful, please."

I stared at her, little knowing what to say. At last I managed, "Thank you."

She went on, in a low voice I had to strain to hear, "I am obliged to you, Mrs. Lennox. A mother always wishes to protect her children, but I do not wish to . . . to hold Louis back." She forced a smile. "That is all. I am sorry to have disrupted your morning."

I stood up to leave, took two steps toward the door, and then turned back. My head still ached. "Mrs. Eversham, is there something I ought to know about Louis? Has he been ill?"

"Ill?" she repeated, and I heard the panic in her voice. "What makes you ask such a thing?"

"Nothing—nothing to alarm you. I only meant, well, that you are very cautious and—"

"Oh." Relief filled her face. "No, there is nothing you need to know."

CHAPTER VIII

WHEN I TOLD LOUIS LATER THAT MORNING THAT WE WERE TO GO to church together each week—and to dine with the Wellings the Sunday after next—he could not keep the smile from his face. I had to work hard to hold his concentration on his sums; every time he settled down, pencil in hand, paper before him, brow furrowed, he would write four or five numbers before looking up again.

"And are we really to go to church?"

"Do you think Mr. and Mrs. Welling have ever been to Hartwood Hall?"

"Do you think the people at Hartbridge will look at us strangely again?"

At last I said gently, "Louis, I dare say we might discover all these things on Sunday—but arithmetic cannot wait."

Louis scowled. "But I don't *want* to do arithmetic," he said—louder, more petulantly than was his wont. A minute later, without a word from me, he looked shame-faced, anxious. He picked up his pencil and stared down at his work.

I could not quite make out these Evershams. Louis was a spirited, clever child, older than his years in intelligence, younger than his years in experience of the world. I could not quite tell which was the true Louis—my cheerful, eager pupil or that solemn, lonely child praying for forgiveness at church.

Mrs. Eversham was harder still to read. This morning's conversation in her study had left me bewildered. At first I had thought her merely an anxious, overprotective mother—but she was so earnest that she almost made me believe there was some real danger to Louis that she knew of and I did not.

No, I did not understand her at all.

Later, when we descended the stairs for luncheon, Mrs. Eversham put her head out of her study door and called for Louis.

"I shall send him on shortly," she said to me with a smile.

I walked to the dining room alone and found Susan there, dishing up cold meats, bread, cheese, and apples.

"Afternoon, Mrs. Lennox."

"Good afternoon, Susan."

She glanced round at me. "I hear Missus doesn't want you taking Master to church."

I pursed my lips. "You have heard incorrectly. Louis and I will go again this Sunday."

Susan raised her eyebrows. "I see. And Louis likes church, does he?"

"Yes," I said. I looked down at my plate, wishing I had not let her engage me in conversation. I did not think much of Susan, but if I was to remain here, to make Hartwood Hall my home, I did not want her to dislike me. It was not as though I could befriend any of the servants, not really—governesses both were and were not part of a household's staff; I had worked in enough houses to know that—but to be on good terms with them would be invaluable. I thought of my last place, with the Russel family—the maids who had muttered about me in the corridors, who always took the side of the children over me when they had seen them misbehave.

"So he likes book learning?" Susan asked.

I nodded. "He is a clever child. You would not know he had not had a governess before."

She threw back her head and laughed. "What do you think—that we killed the last one off and didn't tell you?"

I tried to laugh, but still, her words sent a chill through me.

Then she leaned over the table toward me. "You're new here, Mrs.

Lennox. You ever think there's something . . . *odd* about Hartwood Hall?"

I swallowed. "What do you mean?" I asked slowly.

Susan shrugged. "Oh, you know, lots of things. I reckon—"

The door opened, and in came Louis. Susan straightened, stepped back. She finished slicing the cold meat in silence and by the time Louis had finished piling bread and cheese onto his plate, Susan had left the room.

I hesitated. Then I said quietly, "Louis, do you like Susan?"

He screwed up his mouth and shrugged. "She says strange things sometimes," he said at last. "I liked Martha, who was here before Susan, but she left after Christmas, all in a hurry. Mother told me her father fell ill, but Mary says Martha saw a ghost." Louis laughed. "I shouldn't be afraid of a ghost," he said. "I'd like to ask it all sorts of questions."

———⋈———

That afternoon, we read together. Louis picked one of Miss Edgeworth's tales off the shelf and began to read aloud, slowly and carefully. I encouraged him to pause and ask if he did not know a word, and sometimes I, too, would stop and question him, making sure he understood what he had read.

During one longer passage, I found myself gazing out the window as Louis read, and I saw Paul Carter in the garden below us, trimming the grass. He looked up just as I glanced down, and for a second our eyes met. I looked quickly up at Louis once more.

"You must tell me about what kinds of books you like best to read," I said, when Louis had finished the story. "There might be others in the library that will suit you, and perhaps your mother will let us order some." I ran my fingers along the schoolroom bookshelves and came to one I had not heard of: *Miss Catherine*, by Emily Wilson. I lifted it, inspected the cover.

"That's one of Mother's," said Louis.

I looked up. "You mean it belongs in her study?"

"No, I mean, it's *hers*." A shy, proud smile came over Louis's face. "Mother's very good at stories," he said.

I thought of the papers in her study, of her trip to London. "Louis," I said, "do you mean that your mother wrote this—that she is a writer?"

He nodded. "A *novelist*," he declared, as though the word were sacred. "*And* she reviews books for newspapers. Only she calls herself Emily Wilson, like a—like a disguise. So that nobody will trouble us."

"I had no idea." I smiled. I liked Mrs. Eversham rather more for this knowledge—and I also wondered if it might explain some of her behavior. Perhaps someone who wrote and lived in stories could imagine all kinds of dangers for themselves, for their child.

I put *Miss Catherine* down on my desk. It would not be right, I felt, to read it with Louis, but there was no reason why I could not read it myself.

CHAPTER IX

I WAS TIRED AFTER A LONG DAY OF LATIN AND ARITHMETIC. WHEN Louis had gone to bed, I headed for the library, looking forward to a few hours of solitude with the novel I was reading. I had not yet started *Miss Catherine*, but it sat on my bedside table, waiting for me to pick it up next. I opened the door, candle in hand, and stepped inside. And there was Mrs. Eversham, sat in one of the armchairs.

She looked up from her book, and when her eyes met mine, I stepped back.

"I am sorry to disturb you, ma'am. I did not think there was anybody here."

"Do not go, Mrs. Lennox. You are more than welcome to use the library. Please sit down."

I hesitated. I would sooner have taken a book and gone upstairs than sat half an hour with her. It was not the done thing for a governess to sit alone with her mistress.

Still, I felt I could not now do otherwise. I crossed the room to another armchair, placing my candle on the side table. The library was an elegant room, and where the rest of the house was sparsely furnished, the library felt full. Every shelf was packed with leather-bound volumes, the mantelpiece lined with ornaments.

I took up the volume of Mrs. Radcliffe I had started earlier in the week, and glanced back at Mrs. Eversham, to see what she was reading. I spotted the title on the spine—*The Tenant of Wildfell Hall*—and smiled.

I tried to concentrate on my book, but Mrs. Eversham's presence distracted me. I was aware of her movements, every shift in position, every turn of her page. I kept wondering if she was watching me.

Perhaps half an hour later, Mrs. Eversham closed her volume and asked, "How is your book, Mrs. Lennox?"

I looked up, surprised. "Very diverting."

She smiled. "I have always liked novels."

I hesitated. Though it seemed almost a private matter to ask about, I could not help being curious. "Louis mentioned," I said slowly, "that you yourself are a writer."

I watched her expression closely, but I could not tell whether it was shyness or surprise that made her pause.

"I hope he was not wrong to tell me," I went on. "He is ever so proud of you."

A sudden smile. "No, no. I suppose it is right that you should know—after all, it is often what prevents me from devoting as much time to Louis as I should wish. But one must live somehow. And of course, it is a joy, too. I will not deny that." She spoke carefully, as though she were not much used to discussing this part of her life.

I felt I might press her, just a little more. "What sorts of novels do you write?"

"Oh, the sort that are rather looked down on, I suppose," she replied, and laughed—though not, I rather thought, at herself, but at those who might dare to disdain her. "Which is to say I write stories about adventurers and forbidden love and the occasional dastardly plot for revenge, and the critics bemoan my lack of moral virtue. But people read them, and I think I should find it rather dull writing long, moralizing works." She looked at me, as though to try to read in my face what I made of this, how it had changed my opinion of her. "I suppose you could say that I write the sorts of stories men do not like women to read."

I nodded. "My husband used to—" I stopped, frowned. I had not meant to speak of Richard.

Mrs. Eversham was looking at me steadily. "You have not been widowed long, I think, Mrs. Lennox?"

I shook my head. "Not long." Six weeks now—although of course I did not say that. I ought, perhaps, to be solemn and grave-faced at all times, to keep myself to the house and mutter Richard's name in my sleep, to cry when I was alone.

But I did none of these things. I dreamed of him, and that was all. I could not remember the last time I had cried.

Mrs. Eversham sat in thought. Then, "Did you love your husband, Mrs. Lennox?"

The question startled me. "Of course," I said mechanically, and I suppose she saw my frown, for she smiled, an odd, satisfied smile.

"You must think me very uncivil, Mrs. Lennox. I do not mean to insult you—it is only idle curiosity. I sometimes wonder how many wives love their husbands."

I said nothing. I thought of my parents, the easy way they had always had with each other when I was a girl, of the pure admiration with which Mrs. Welling had regarded her husband on Sunday. I had seen it, that kind of happiness, but somehow it had always passed me by.

I wondered if it had passed Mrs. Eversham by, too.

There was a pause. She glanced down at her book.

"Louis's father has been dead some time, I gather." It was almost a dangerous thing to say. She must know that I meant to ask about her own marriage, to judge if she had loved her husband any more than I had mine.

But if she was surprised or offended by the question, she did not show it. She only said, "Yes, a long time." Then she got to her feet, placing *The Tenant of Wildfell Hall* on the sideboard. "I had better retire to bed." She raised her candle, smiled that unreadable smile of hers, then turned and left the room.

I sat staring at the empty chair. What was I to make of her? I supposed that hers had not been a happy marriage either, that she, too, had found both guilt and relief in widowhood.

Well, we were both free now. A strange link to hold the two of us together.

I ought not to think like that. It was a sin to think myself free, just as it had been a sin to wish myself free all those years.

I shook my head as if to shake off such thoughts. I took my own candle and went up to bed.

CHAPTER X

"ONE . . . TWO . . . THREE . . . FOUR . . ."

I was in the library, my hands over my eyes. Today, we had decided to play hide-and-seek. When I had asked Louis what games he liked, he only said chess and solitaire, so over the last few days I had been trying to teach him new games, especially those that would give him the double benefit of exercise. We had played hopscotch in the garden, blindman's buff in the schoolroom, lookabout in the music room. And today—hide-and-seek.

I heard Louis laugh as I began to count, and then the sound of footsteps, followed by silence.

When I reached one hundred, I got to my feet and began my search. First, I checked the corridor, opening cupboard doors and peering behind curtains, making sure to look underneath the grand staircase. I found only cobwebs and dust—evidently Susan did not clean very thoroughly.

Next, I opened the door to the morning room opposite Mrs. Eversham's study. It was a pretty room carpeted with old Persian silk, the walls papered with faded flowers. Besides its two embroidered settees and an inlaid oak chest of drawers, the room was bare. There were not many places to hide, and once I had made certain that Louis was not lying beneath the settees, I moved on.

He was not under the coffee table in the parlor, nor behind the curtains of the dim card room. He was not behind the pianoforte in the music room, nor tucked beneath its settees. He was not under the

long oak table in the fine dining room; I had never been in there before, and it was at least three times the size of the little breakfast room
in which we usually dined.

He was not hidden among the piles of wood in the lumber room,
nor inside the empty oak chest in the green sitting room, nor behind
the long-case clock in the blue room. To one side of the west wing, I
found a long gallery, with bare walls and a chipped floor; the room
was entirely empty.

I could not think where Louis had gone. I paced back along the
corridor, and when I reached the entrance hall, my eyes fell on the
door to the east wing and I felt a prickle of unease. Perhaps I should
not have let Louis out of my sight, invited him to conceal himself. But
he surely knew better than to hide in the east wing?

I stared at the wooden door. I called out, very softly, "Louis?" and
when there was no response, I crept forward.

My hand was almost on the gold doorknob when I heard somebody scream.

I could not at first tell where it had come from, and my first thought
was *inside* the east wing—and then a shout and a hurry of indistinct
conversation made me realize my mistake, and I turned to see the
library door thrown open and a white-faced Mary stumbling
backward.

"You could've killed me," she was saying. "You could've scared the
life out of me. What are you doing sneaking about and hiding in
shadows like a little devil? It's enough to drive a person to distraction,
this place—never knowing who or what is round each corner. One
more fright like this and I swear, I'm finished."

As she leaned back against the wall, I saw Louis edging out of the
library, shame-faced and solemn.

"It was only a game, Mary," he said gently. "We were playing at
hide-and-seek, me and Mrs. Lennox."

"Did you plan it with Susan?" She rounded on him, her breath catching. "She sent me up here, told me Mrs. Pulley wanted paper and—and

she knew, didn't she? It would be just like her." She didn't wait for an answer. "Mrs. Lennox, he was hiding under an armchair, waiting, like a—like a cat or a rat or a ghost or I don't know what but—"

"It was only a game," Louis said again. "But Susan wasn't playing."

"Bloody stupid game." Mary was shaking her head, trying to breathe. I ought to have told her not to speak to her young master in such a manner, but she was so visibly shaken that I could not quite bear to berate her. Instead I laid a hand gently on her arm.

"It is simply a misunderstanding, Mary," I said. "You had a fright, that is all."

She stared at me, saying nothing, but my voice seemed to steady her.

"Why don't you go down to the kitchen?" I said, as softly as I could. "I am sure Lacey will make you a cup of tea."

She nodded and finally took a step forward, and I saw a spot of color return to her cheeks. She looked suddenly very young. "I—I didn't mean to be uncivil," she said, in a tremulous voice. "You won't tell Missus? Or Miss Lacey or Mrs. Pulley? Lacey thinks I'm mad but I'm not."

I said, "I won't tell," and she seemed to breathe easier.

With one last, unreadable glance at Louis, she hurried toward the servants' stairs.

Louis was standing very still. He looked a little uncertain, as though he, too, had had a fright. I reached out for him, put an arm around his shoulders.

"I didn't mean to scare her," he said.

"I know, child. It's all right. You didn't do anything wrong." I smiled down at him. "Were you under my chair all along?"

Louis nodded.

"That was clever," I said.

He glanced up at me, and I saw a faint smile light up his face. He looked rather proud of his own ingenuity. But a moment later his face was grave again. "I don't think I much like hiding," he said at last.

CHAPTER XI

As Louis, Mrs. Eversham, and I were eating breakfast the next day, Susan brought the letters in on a silver plate. Mrs. Eversham began to open hers—and then, to my surprise, passed one to me.

I stared at it, the neatly written address, the elegant hand. Who on earth would write to me? My parents were dead. My husband was gone. There was no one else; working as a governess was always a solitary occupation, and during my marriage—well, it had been a long time since I'd had anybody I could class as a friend. I had no one in all the world save the people in this house. I unfolded the inky pages and glanced down at the final signature.

The letter was from Cornelia Radwell.

Richard's sister.

> *My dear Margaret,*
>
> *I hope you will not mind my writing to you at your employer's house. I have had some difficulty in finding your address, so I hope you will forgive me for taking so long to write. You will believe me, I hope, when I assure you that I was entirely unaware of Mama's actions—Mama's accusations, perhaps it would be more correct to say—until very recently. My latest confinement prevented me from attending my dear brother's funeral, and since then I have been much occupied with Baby. I was made to understand only last week that you had been left no provision by my brother,*

*that it has all gone to Mama, and that you had gone to seek
out work, like—well, like a common person. I was much
distressed by it, of course, for I have always liked you, and I am
sure you were very good to Richard. I have no doubt that you
could never have done anything so very wicked as what
Mama says you did. I should hope I am above listening to
nonsense about poisons and plots.*

*In short, I should very much like to invite you to stay with
Radwell and me for a time. We have a quiet, comfortable life
here, which is really just the thing for a widow, and now that
the eldest children are growing into little men and women, you
are just the sort of person it would be good for them to have
about. If you will consider coming here for a time, I think the
arrangement would suit us all very well.*

*Dearest Margaret, I hope you will not bear against me the
actions of Mama and Richard—and I am sure, too, that you
will forgive Richard in your heart. He was so ill and confused
toward the end of his life. I am sure he never truly thought it
was your fault. They ought not to have let him make a new
will in such a state. When I think of what Mama has said,
really, I—*

"All right, Mrs. Lennox?"

I started, pulled abruptly out of my letter. It was Susan, still lingering in the corner of the breakfast room, watching me. When she
spoke, Louis and Mrs. Eversham looked at me, too.

"You're very pale," she said, and there was a flicker of something
more like amusement than compassion in her voice. "You're not
unwell?"

"No. No, indeed."

In truth, my head was pounding. I folded up the letter, pushed it
deep into my gown. I would read the rest later.

So Richard's sister, at least, did not believe all that their mother
had said of me. I wondered if she had really not known about the will,

if I ought to be grateful for Cornelia's sudden good opinion. Only, I had never liked Cornelia, and I did not think she much liked me either—she had married well, and I suppose she thought her brother might have done rather better. No, she had decided it was time for her children to have a governess and that, if she played her cards well, she might have me for free. That was all. And perhaps she wanted to anger her mother, who had always preferred Richard to her.

I tried to ignore Susan, and turned instead to Louis with a smile. "Come, have you finished breakfast? We have a morning of lessons ahead of us."

———————

It was evening before I read Cornelia's letter through. Mrs. Eversham took Louis herself immediately after dinner, and I was alone for the first time all day. I was all too aware of the letter in my pocket, the crinkle of paper as I moved—and yet I could not quite bring myself to look once more on Cornelia's words. Instead I sat alone in the music room, practicing the pianoforte. I had barely played in the three years Richard and I had been married, and the skill I'd once had, built upon by years of teaching, had slipped from me, as so many other things had. I was still a good governess—it had been the habit and purpose of my life too long for me to forget how to teach—but I had, I thought, been more than simply a good governess, and the person I had been three years ago might have done wonders with Louis's untapped mind.

I had been better then. Not happy, exactly. Not contented. But before Richard, I had been truer, cleverer. My conscience had been clean.

The first time I met Richard, I was playing music. I was working for the Russels then. The children—three girls, twelve, fourteen, and fifteen—were beyond challenging. They had no interest in their lessons, and no scheme of mine could change that. The more effort I made, the less they liked me. They pushed me and struck me and pulled my hair, mocked me and used my bad ear to their advantage, talking on the wrong side of me and shouting at me for not listening if I didn't catch everything they said. When I told Mrs. Russel their behavior was intolerable, that they were near impossible to teach, she told me I was insolent.

On one of my rare evenings off, I had tramped to the village church because I wished to pray in my own place of worship, rather than in the chapel I had to take the children to each week. When I found the church deserted, I sat down at the organ and played and played and played. I played until I forgot where I was, until I forgot my misery, the ache left behind by my mother's death some months before, the dreary monotony of my life, the cruelty of my pupils and their parents, the dull future that was all life had in store for me.

And then someone behind me coughed, and I turned and saw him. Of course I did not know his name then, did not know that his name would become mine. I saw only a clergyman, a man some ten years older than myself, with a strange expression on his face. At first I thought it was anger. It took me a moment to register that the look was something else, that he was intrigued to find a woman playing the organ without permission, that he was impressed by my skill. It took me a moment to see that he was looking at me with something like desire.

And I thought, here it is. A way out of my life.

———— >—<— ————

I reached into my gown and finally unfolded Cornelia's letter. I could put it off no longer. I stared at it, read it all the way through, and then walked steadily up to my bedroom. I held her letter over the fire, then pulled it back. I owed her something, I supposed. A reply, at least.

Dear Cornelia,
 Thank for your letter. I appreciate your kindness in offering to have me to stay. I have, however, found a situation in the west of England and am working as governess to a young boy.

*I am quite content here, and expect to remain in this position
for some time.*

Please give my love to the children.

Margaret Lennox

I looked down at my short letter. It was not uncivil, but it was
hardly an example of good sisterly kindness. Still, it would do. I folded
Cornelia's letter back up, slipped it inside the top drawer of my dressing table. Then I sealed my own letter and stood up to take it down to
the hall before I could change my mind.

Downstairs, I nearly knocked into Susan. I did not hear her coming, did not see her until a moment before we almost collided. She
stepped back, eyes wide, surprised.

"Dear me, Mrs. Lennox, I do beg your pardon."

There was something odd about her manner tonight. Her face was
flushed, her eyes bright, her smile wider than I had ever seen. I almost
thought she was intoxicated, but she seemed steady enough on her feet
as she walked away.

It was only when she had passed me by that I realized she must
have come from the east wing.

I wondered what had agitated and pleased her, if it was simply the
strange excitement some people take in doing what they ought not to
do, or if she had seen something. I thought of Mary outside the library
the day before, her raw panic, the fear she had of this house. I pushed
the thought away.

I placed my letter down on the silver tray in the hall, and hesitated,
my gaze lingering on the front doors. It was only nine o'clock, and I
had no wish to sleep. My mind was burning—Cornelia's letter had
unsettled me. I needed to distract myself; I needed fresh air.

CHAPTER XII

As I closed the doors behind me, I felt steadier. I passed through the dim courtyard, my boots loud on the cobbles, the fountain and the apple tree mere shadows in the dusk. I began to walk toward the woods, leaving footprints in the muddy grass. It was a warm, pleasant evening, and though the sun was nearly set in the sky, the moon was bright above me.

I had never liked the darkness. Ever since I was a girl, ever since I lost the hearing in my left ear, it had always been my sight I trusted the most. To be plunged into darkness, even for a moment, even the darkness of sleep, had always unnerved me. But there was a full moon tonight, and I needed this, the feel of the wind against my face, the sight of this grand open landscape. This was my life now. I was free.

I swallowed hard. It was wrong to think like that.

I had a sudden memory of Richard, standing at the top of the parsonage stairs, looking down at me as I came through the front door, his face a mask of panic and anger. I had gone for a walk by myself, strolled out into the fields. It was the first truly sunny day since we were wed a few months before, and I had not been able to resist. I had walked a little longer than planned, it was true, but I had told our maid where I was going, and it was not yet dark.

And there was Richard, staring at me, asking me, *Where on earth have you been?* as though I had been missing a week.

I only went for a walk in the fields, I said slowly. *It's such a beautiful day and*—

I was worried, he said, and his voice sounded so suddenly full of concern, of love, that it startled me. I could not imagine worrying about him like that. Guilt fluttered at the corners of my mind.

So I had said nothing when Richard gathered me up in his arms, kissed my forehead. I had said nothing when he said, *You mustn't do that again*, when he said, *I don't want you walking alone. It isn't safe.* But I learned to walk less often, confining myself to the garden, walking to and fro in the shrubbery, looking out into the hills beyond.

I was nearing the edge of the woods now. When I reached the trees, I stopped to catch my breath. I heard a sound, a crunch of twigs, and I could not tell which side of me it came from. I thought first of foxes or badgers, or one of the deer Louis said he'd never seen—and then, ridiculously, of highwaymen, of bandits, of Mrs. Eversham's earnest fear of everything beyond Hartwood Hall.

I spun around—and there stood Paul Carter, bathed in moonlight, looking at me.

"Mrs. Lennox?"

I tried to hide my surprise, my momentary fear. "Good evening, Mr. Carter."

"You are out late." His tone was not unfriendly, but it still sounded like a rebuke.

"So are you," I said.

He shrugged. "I've been clearing the path through the trees." He glanced back over his shoulder into the woods. "I've been at it five hours. It grew dark around me."

He was standing close enough for me to see the scratches on his hands. Close enough to see the thin stubble on his cheek, just visible in the moonlight. Close enough that I could have reached out and touched him.

I flushed, suddenly nervous. I did not know this man. I knew nothing of him, except that he was the gardener here, that he was younger than me, beneath me, that he was fond of Louis. That was all.

"Are you walking back up to the house?" he asked.

I nodded.

"Then we'll walk together." It seemed less of a request than a statement, but then he hesitated and added, "If you like."

He stepped forward just as I did, but he put himself on the wrong side of me and I had to step back and cross behind him to switch places. He looked confused for a moment, and then the explanation seemed to dawn on him and he nodded. I supposed somebody had told him about my hearing.

And so we began the long walk back to Hartwood Hall, and all the time I was oddly aware of him, the movements of his hands, his steady steps. I was more aware of myself, too. My hands suddenly seemed cumbersome, as though I did not know how I usually held them. Beyond the sound of our boots on the path, the whole world seemed silent, and I was painfully aware of the need to say something.

We both spoke at once.

"On Sunday—"

"How do you like—?"

We stopped, broke off, and he raised a hand, as though in supplication.

"I wanted to ask . . ." I began, and my voice seemed loud in the evening quiet. "Last Sunday, you were . . . you were displeased, I think, that Louis and I came with you to church. I hope we did not . . . disrupt your plans. I did not mean to inconvenience you, or . . ."

He was shaking his head. "No, I . . ." He looked pained. "It wasn't that. Only, I—I knew Mrs. Eversham wouldn't be pleased. That's all."

I frowned. "You might have warned me."

A slight smile. "What did Mrs. Eversham say?"

"She was angry, at first, but she has come around since."

"And you and Louis, you're to go to church tomorrow?"

"Well, yes."

He nodded, pushed a hand through his hair. "I knew she would never let Louis go to church unless she could see that it was safe. Mrs. Eversham can be stubborn, but she has sense, too. And it's good for

Louis, to see other people. He shouldn't be always at Hartwood. No child should."

"I quite agree," I replied. "Look here, Mr. Carter—you have been here a long time, I think, and I hope you will speak to me frankly. Do you think Louis lonely?"

"Of course," he said. "Everybody at Hartwood Hall is lonely." He looked sideways at me; I could not quite read his expression, but it seemed almost a question—and one I did not know how to answer. I wondered what kept him here.

I said only, "It would be good for Louis to spend more time in the village, Mr. Carter."

"Paul, please. Everyone calls me Paul."

I laughed. "As you are hardly likely to call me Margaret, I shall continue to call you Mr. Carter."

I almost expected him to be offended, but instead his lips curved into a smile. "Your name is Margaret?"

There was something about the way he said my name that made my skin prickle. It was almost insolent, and almost beautiful.

I opened my mouth to change the subject, and then stopped. As I looked up, I could have sworn I saw something flicker in the east wing.

"Can there be someone up there?"

Paul looked round. "What?"

"In the east wing? I thought I saw a candle."

His face darkened. "No. No one goes there."

"I saw Susan come from there today."

Paul shook his head. "You must have been mistaken."

I was not sure if he meant about the light or about Susan, but the east wing seemed all darkness now.

We walked on without speaking—and then, because the silence had stretched too long, I asked, "Why is it that people in Hartbridge don't like the Evershams?"

It was a long time before he answered. When he did, he spoke quietly. "It's a long story." He sighed. "There are all sorts of superstitions about Hartwood Hall. There always have been. When I was a boy, the house was empty and had been for decades. All the village children used to say it was haunted. There was always talk of ghosts and hobgoblins and phantoms, rumors that the trees here cast no shadows in the sun, that the rain when it fell made no sound. There used to be deer here, a long time ago—but they died out when my father was a boy. Poaching, I suppose—but folks round here have always said that the deer left, that they knew this place wasn't right. You see, in my great-grandfather's time, there was still a family at Hartwood Hall—proper squires, the sort who held harvest festivals and visited the poor. But the last squire had only daughters and they all married and moved away. Some distant cousin inherited, and he never once came here. It stood empty for decades and the stories grew up around it."

"You mean it is not Mrs. Eversham's family home?" I asked. "Or her husband's?"

"No. She purchased the property seven years ago." He paused. "When Mrs. Eversham arrived with her children, she was a young widow. No one knew where she came from."

I stared at him. "Paul, did you say *children*?"

I had not meant to call him by his Christian name. I did not say it like a superior speaking to a servant; I spoke his name as though we were equals, friends. I saw him smile at that, at me. Then the smile faded.

"Yes. That is the other reason why the village folks avoid Hartwood Hall. Mrs. Eversham's daughter died, five years ago."

I flinched. "What happened?"

Paul looked very solemn. "She was away from home with her mother when she was taken ill. One week she was playing with her little brother in the garden, and the next—well, Mrs. Eversham came back without her." He hesitated. "I didn't live at Hartwood then—I wasn't here when the news broke—but it was a great tragedy." I heard his voice catch. "She was not an infant, you understand—she was a grown girl of ten, as sweet and kind as any you might hope to meet. And afterward . . . Well, since Isabella's death, Hartbridge has feared Mrs. Eversham more and more. It must have made it so much harder to bear."

Isabella. Louis had had an elder sister—a sister he had lost when he was five years old. He must remember her, at least a little. And how much lonelier, I thought, to be an only child who had once been one of two. He ought to have learned hide-and-seek from her, not me. I thought of the old volumes in the schoolroom and wondered if she had read them as well, if Mrs. Eversham had taught her in that room as I did Louis.

I was surprised that Mrs. Eversham had not thought to tell me that Louis had such a grief, such a shadow hanging over him, that their family of two had not long been so diminished. Perhaps it seemed too private a matter to tell the governess; perhaps it was still too difficult for her to speak of. Mrs. Eversham's life seemed full of sorrow.

"But, Paul," I began, as I gathered my thoughts, "why should the people in the village fear Mrs. Eversham because her daughter died?"

He was frowning in concern, his eyes narrowed. "They think— some of them—that Mrs. Eversham was to blame. There were dreadful rumors, about her, about her husband, about the girl. My father thinks—" He broke off, as though irritated with himself that he had mentioned his own father. "Some of the village folks say that she is a witch, that she sold her soul, and her daughter's, to the devil. They say that she killed her own girl."

I shuddered. "Dear God. How dreadful."

"Hartbridge is a superstitious place. There have always been roads that folks won't pass on Midsummer or Christmas Eve, hills and lanes with tales about them spanning back generations." He frowned, screwed up his mouth. "But it's not only that. They don't much take to strangers here either."

"But you do?"

I had meant the Evershams, of course, but I supposed he thought I meant me, for his cheeks flushed, and I turned away to hide my smile.

Then he said, "Yes. I don't mind strangers," very softly, and when I looked round he was smiling, too, almost shyly, and I felt strangely young again. I wondered what would happen if I were to lean over and kiss him.

Of course I did not. I was the governess and he was the gardener and my husband had been buried for barely six weeks. But I thought about it, for a moment, about what it might feel like to have his arms around me, what it might feel like to belong to someone other than Richard, to know that his were no longer the last lips pressed to mine.

I must be careful of this man. Not just because he was beautiful but because something about him drew me in, because he had shifted something in me, opened a door within my mind I thought I had locked forever.

"I'm not really one of them," he said, his smile falling a little. "The villagers, I mean. They treat me like a stranger now."

"Because you work here?"

He nodded. "As I said, nobody likes this place. My father and my brother try to include me, but the other men, people who were my friends when I was a boy—they snub me now. Or they tell me to leave, to work elsewhere."

"And would you?" I asked. "I mean, is it worth it? To have your village take against you, for this?"

"It's my home." He stopped walking and turned to look at me in the moonlight. He grinned, a boyish grin. "Look around," he said, stretching his arms wide. "Tell me where else in the world I would find somewhere so beautiful to work."

I smiled. "It is lovely here."

When we reached the courtyard, I looked round at Paul.

"You don't sleep in the house, do you?" I said, and even as the words left my mouth, it seemed an odd question to ask.

"No," he said. "I live by the stables, to keep an eye on the horses."

"Of course," I said, as I turned to the doors.

"I'll see you in the morning."

"Until tomorrow, then."

"Good night."

I closed the doors behind me and stood in the empty hall, fighting the smile that came unbidden to my lips. And then I thought of Louis, Louis, who had lost a sister, whose life seemed so solitary, and whatever cure Paul had been tonight for my own loneliness, I felt a stab of guilt.

I bolted the doors and went quickly up to bed.

CHAPTER XIII

THAT SUNDAY, I WENT TO CHURCH WITH LOUIS AND PAUL, SAT NEXT to Mrs. Welling in the box, listened to the sermon, prayed and sang, tried to stop myself from looking round at Paul during the service. I thought, as I had the previous Sunday, of how different Mr. Welling was to Richard, whose flat voice had slowed readings to last hours, whose hands had fidgeted while he spoke. I watched the way Mrs. Welling looked at her husband and felt a guilty envy steal over me. How much easier it would have all been if I had been able to look at Richard like that, to love Richard like that.

I had been at Hartwood Hall for only two weeks, but already my old life felt an age away.

Some new feeling washed over me when Louis put his hand in mine during the sermon, and I realized with a start what it was. I was happy. Suddenly, abruptly happy. I could not remember the last time I had felt such a thing.

I glanced across at Louis and wondered, when I saw his lips move in silent prayer, if he prayed for his sister as well as for his father. I wondered how great a shadow her loss had cast on his short life.

I considered asking Mrs. Eversham about her daughter. I wished to know more—not for the sake of my own curiosity but because I did not know how much this sad event had affected Louis, and I knew I should not raise the subject with him without first consulting Mrs. Eversham. I did not know if Isabella was never spoken of by decree or by mutual reserve. And yet I knew I had no right to pry into sorrows so private. I did not want to ask her about her past, any more than I wished her to ask about mine.

It was the end of August now, and the weather was stifling. Alone in the schoolroom one evening, windows open, curtains fluttering in the breeze, I started reading *Miss Catherine*; I did not wish to read it in the library, where Mrs. Eversham might find me.

It was, as she had promised, an adventure story—the tale of a girl who, unhappy at home, oppressed by cruel parents, fled to find freedom, in search of a new life.

My first thought was that Richard would have hated it. We used to argue about books—or at least, I had argued at the beginning. The first time, I had not really realized what we were discussing, not immediately. I could hear his voice clearly still: *Margaret, you never read the books I buy you.*

And I had thought it was that, the thin sense of neglect he always felt. It tugged at the guilt within me, the feeling I could not shake that he was right, that I was falling short of the wife I ought to be.

So I had smiled, brushed it off. *There are days when I like to read sermons, Richard, and days when I like to read novels.*

He had frowned. *They are not good books, Margaret*, he had said, as though books could only be moral or immoral, a force for good or sin, not a force for enjoyment, a force for thought.

And it had seemed such a foolish thing to quarrel over, at first. So I learned to read the books he liked when he was in the house, to tuck my novels away on the lowest shelves, to read them when he was out, not to argue when they disappeared.

My second thought, as I read through Mrs. Eversham's novel, was that it was very good. I read a hundred pages almost without knowing, while the room grew dark around me. I thought of Mrs. Eversham, sat day after day in her study, ink pen in hand, surrounded by papers, pushing the loss and sorrows of her life into words, words, words. I liked her more for it.

I read until the sky was dark outside, my candle sputtering as it grew short. When I finally slipped next door to my chamber to sleep, my mind was so full of Mrs. Eversham's book that I barely heard the creaks and moans of the house in the dark.

→⟩⟨←

On Tuesday afternoon, the heat was so intense that Louis and I abandoned our lessons and walked down into the garden instead, heading for the shade of the oak tree by the lake. We read *The Children of the New Forest* together, Louis taking one chapter, me the next.

While I was reading, Louis leaned over and dipped his fingers into the lake, watching the algae on the surface split at his touch. He lifted them out, let the water drip from his skin, then did it again, as though he had never done so before. When he looked round at me, he was smiling.

I put the book down on the grass. "When I was your age," I told him, "I lived near a river, and the village girls and I used to go swimming. My father didn't approve, because I was supposed to be growing up a lady, but I used to love it."

"I have never swum," said Louis. "Is it hard?"

"Not when you know how."

He dipped his hand again. "The water's cold," he said, but he looked delighted.

I smiled. "Put your feet in."

Louis looked down into the lake's depths. "Oh, I daren't."

I laughed and pulled my own boots off. Then, raising my skirts a little, I dipped my bare feet into the water. The cold made me shudder, but it was welcome in the hot sun, and the look of impressed surprise on Louis's face gave me a rush of triumph.

"Try it."

Beside me, Louis unlaced his boots and gingerly put his feet into the lake. He giggled, took them out again, put them back in, smiling at the feel of the sun on his wet toes. He took such pleasure in small things, this child who never went beyond Hartwood, for whom new wonders were so easy to find.

I dipped my feet further in and Louis did the same, rolling up his trousers to his knees. He laughed again.

Beneath my toes I felt something cool and hard at the bottom of the lake. I was bending over to pick it up, feeling in the mud until my fingers closed on something small and metal, when I heard a voice say, "What on earth are you doing?"

We both turned sharply. It was Mrs. Eversham, standing behind us, her face anxious and alert. I had not heard her approach, and I supposed Louis had been too caught up in the lake to notice. Now his smile only brightened.

"Mother, the water's so cold."

She did not reply, but instead only looked at me. "Mrs. Lennox, the lake is not a safe place for Louis to play." Her voice was labored, and I saw that she was angry, that she was trying to control her anger because Louis was present. A knot formed in my stomach.

"There is no harm in it." It irked me, the implication that I would not have kept Louis safe, but I reminded myself what I knew of Mrs. Eversham—that she was changeable, anxious, that she had lost her daughter and was forever seeing dangers to her son. "We have only just put our feet in."

"Louis cannot swim," she said, and her voice caught.

"I know. He told me. I would not have let him go in further."

She nodded, but I could see from her face that she was still displeased. Louis had moved back onto the grass and said, "But the water is so cold, Mother, and it is so hot today."

"Look at your feet, Louis—they are covered in dirt." Although her voice was softer, it was still sharp. "You mustn't do it again." She addressed Louis, but she glanced at me as she spoke.

Louis said softly, "Yes, Mother."

I said nothing.

"Very well then." Mrs. Eversham looked down at the book on the grass. "I will leave you to your reading," she said, turning to me. "But please—don't go so near to the lake again."

And then she was gone, leaving Louis and me standing alone, our wet feet sinking into the grass.

All the time she was speaking, I had kept my fist closed around whatever it was I had pulled from the mud, but now I opened my hand and saw within it the tarnished gold of a wedding ring.

I closed my fist again and turned back to Louis with a smile.

———>·<———

That evening, I cleaned the ring at the washstand in my bedroom, then held it up above the candle, watching the light flicker off the gold. The ring was discolored and seemed to have been in the lake a long time. It looked to be a woman's and the initials engraved on the inside were *L* and *G*. I turned it over in my hand, wondering what past inhabitant of this place had dropped, or maybe thrown, it into the lake. I looked at my own wedding ring, the plain gold encircling my finger, and then slipped the one I had found into my dressing-table drawer.

It was only when I laid the ring on top of my papers that I noticed my letter from Cornelia was gone.

CHAPTER XIV

THE NEXT MORNING, MRS. EVERSHAM WAS QUITE EASY WITH ME, and the incident at the lake seemed forgotten. Still, the heat remained stifling, and I could not keep my mind from that letter. I had searched my room, opening drawer after drawer, but it was nowhere. If someone had taken it, had read it—well, what would they think? What would they do? I could not bear the thought of anyone here reading Cornelia's words, of the secrets of my old life tarnishing Hartwood Hall.

I ought to have burned it.

After dinner, Louis and I sat together in the music room. We had become quite good at duets now, me taking the lower part, Louis the melody, and we were just about to embark on another when the clock struck seven. Louis looked round, and I turned, too, to see Susan standing in the doorway.

"Master Louis, your mother wants you."

So it was to be one of those evenings. Every few days, Louis would be suddenly called away from me to spend the evening with Mrs. Eversham. I did not know where they went; I supposed she took him up to her own room, for they never seemed to be anywhere downstairs.

"Good night, Mrs. Lennox," said Louis, as he got down from the piano stool. I watched him leave, saw his eagerness to see his mother, the joy on his face as he walked away from me.

Susan watched him, too, though she did not follow him. I

turned back to the piano, heard the door close, and went on playing my part alone.

As I played, I began to feel a sting of unease, as though someone was watching me. I looked round sharply, and Susan was still there. She had closed the door, yes, but she had not left. She was sitting upright and very still on the settee, looking at me steadily.

And I knew at once who had taken my letter.

"Received any more letters lately, Mrs. Lennox?"

I opened my mouth to speak and my mind went blank.

I would lose my place. Of course I would lose my place. Mrs. Eversham was already uncertain of me, had twice found fault with my behavior. And if I could not find another position, if a poor character from Mrs. Eversham stood beside the fact I was a widow, that my hearing was imperfect—well, what would I do?

I swallowed hard, tried to compose myself.

Susan wasn't looking at me. Her eyes were fixed on a patch of fading sunlight on the floor, and when she spoke her voice was even, almost curious. "What do you think Mrs. Eversham would say, if I showed her that letter? From your sister-in-law, I think it is?"

"It says nothing," I said, and it surprised me how much my voice shook.

Susan wrapped a stray thread from her dress around her finger. Still she did not look at me. "I don't know about that."

"It says only that my husband left me no money. He was very ill."

"But that's not all it says," said Susan. "The letter mentions *accusations*. It mentions *poisons*."

Cold seemed to spread over me. I felt suddenly sick, and I wanted more than anything to stand up, to leave the room, to run. "It's not true," I said slowly, and even as I spoke the words I heard how they must sound. I could not keep a glimmer of guilt out of my voice.

"We'll see what Mrs. Eversham thinks about that."

I said nothing. My mouth was dry. I had a sudden image in my mind of Richard, his skeletal figure in what had been our marriage bed.

I shut my eyes, tried to think, tried to concentrate. There was always a solution to any difficulty, always some way to wipe out a problem.

"What do you want from me?" I asked. "If you want money, I have none."

Susan shrugged. She snapped the thread from her dress. "You have a fine watch, though. Must be worth a bit."

I swallowed hard. I felt for it in my pocket, ran my fingers over the carved initials. Richard's watch, real gold with silver inlay. It ought to have gone to his mother, just like everything else.

"It was my husband's," I said. "Would you like a dead man's watch?"

"Nothing wrong with a dead man's watch," said Susan. "Not like he's going to haunt me." She looked up now, and a grin spread across her face. "No such thing as ghosts anyway," she said, and held out her hand.

I kept my eyes on her face as I handed over the watch, took in her smile of satisfaction, of amusement. She slipped it into her pocket.

"Got any other jewelry?" she asked.

I shook my head.

"Don't lie. Got a wedding ring, haven't you?"

"And what would Mrs. Eversham think if she saw me without it?" She shrugged. "Nothing else?"

"I have nothing, Susan. You read the letter. He left me nothing."

She frowned, put her hand in her pocket as though to make sure the watch was really there. "All right," she said at last. "This'll do, I suppose." And then she smiled again, broad and terrible, and left the room.

I stared after her, my hands shaking, my mind whirring. I had thought Susan a simple country girl, fond of the sound of her own voice, perhaps, with an odd sense of humor. Now I saw something else in her: the thrill of it was clear in her face. She did not really want my watch; she wanted the strange pleasure of being able to take it from me.

And I realized, too, that she did not care about what the letter had said, other than that she could use it against me. She did not care what or who had killed my husband.

The weight of Richard's watch seemed missing from my pocket. I'd had it for weeks, since the morning I went into his room and found him dead.

It had been on his bedside table, ticking the rhythm his heart no longer beat. I looked down at his wide, staring eyes and reached out, as if to touch him, to close his eyelids, to stroke his cold face. But instead my hands fell on the watch at his side, and I slipped it into my pocket.

I hardly knew why I had taken it; the will had not been read then and I did not know that he had left me nothing. I knew only that I was tired and miserable and free, that I had failed the world in some grave way.

I did not want something to remember him by, because I did not want to remember him. But perhaps I thought I needed a reminder of what he had done. Of what *I* had done.

CHAPTER XV

I BARELY SLEPT THAT NIGHT. I LAY AWAKE IN THE HOT DARKNESS, staring up at the canopy of my bed, thinking over Cornelia's letter, Susan's threats. I could not let her ruin what I was building at Hartwood. I liked it here. I liked Louis. There was so much I might do for him, so much I had to teach him. And some part of me felt that if Mrs. Eversham were to read the letter and dismiss me it would mean, unequivocally, that I had done wrong.

I could not let that happen. I had given away Richard's watch, and now I would have to be careful.

But I did not know what to make of Susan. I could not tell if she had acted on impulse, seen an opportunity and decided to profit from it, or if it was something more deliberate, more thought out than that. I could not tell if it was all over, whether now that she had taken the watch she would be satisfied and quiet. And even if she did nothing more, there was one member of the household who thought worse of me, who knew a little too much.

I rolled over, blinked my tired eyes. I must not let Susan unnerve me. She was young; she would not be here forever.

I shut my eyes, put my good ear to the pillow, and willed sleep to come.

—→✕←—

For the rest of the week, Susan kept looking at me at breakfast. She would stare until I met her gaze, and then she would smile. She was enjoying herself—and it made my skin crawl. I did my best to try to pretend her away.

I would have to conquer this. She had my watch. I must not let her have my fear as well.

Mrs. Eversham seemed to notice her behavior, for I caught her frowning at Susan sometimes, saw her turn away when she entered the room, making almost as much effort as I was not to look at her. Louis was the only one who greeted her with a smile. I weighed up in my mind whether there was something I could say to Mrs. Eversham— not the truth, perhaps, but a tale bordering on the truth—but the thought gave me a cold, uneasy feeling I could not shake. I could not think of any half-truth, any lie, that might credibly be believed. And besides, I did not want to talk about Richard. I did not want to *think* about Richard.

I tried to avoid Susan. When my day of teaching was over and she had put Louis to bed, I would keep to the schoolroom or my own room with the door bolted, or walk through the grounds. I often saw Paul, still hard at work, rake or spade in hand. Sometimes I dodged him, turning in another direction. Other nights I told myself that it was mere foolishness, that I was not some schoolgirl unable to stamp out a vague feeling, and I made myself walk directly into his path. We did not talk as we had done the night he told me about Isabella, but we would quietly bid each other good night.

One evening, I had been in the library and was just closing the door behind me, candle in hand, on my way upstairs to bed, when I heard voices. As I turned, I saw Louis and Mrs. Eversham standing close by the east-wing door. They looked as though they had come from within it—indeed, there was nowhere else they could have been.

I hid my surprise, both at the late hour and at where they must have been, and only bade them good night—but the next morning, I asked Louis about the east wing, if he had been there with his mother.

He looked at me, then glanced down at his book, clearly embarrassed. "I told Mother I thought there were ghosts there," he said, "and she said she'd show me there weren't."

I smiled. "And were there any ghosts?"

Louis frowned, twisted the collar of his shirt. "I don't think so," he said slowly, and he sounded almost disappointed, "but you never can tell."

———>—<———

That afternoon, Louis could not settle to his studies. We struggled through Latin after luncheon, but he kept fidgeting, gazing out the window. He was excited about our dinner at the Wellings' house tomorrow; it was a strange novelty to him, and he could not focus on anything else. In the end I suggested we finish lessons early for the day, and we left the schoolroom together.

As we came down the stairs, I saw Stevens and Susan talking together in the hall. I had rarely seen them speak before, except in passing, but now they stood close together, engaged in what seemed like very earnest conversation. Susan's expression looked fierce.

One phrase escaped—Stevens's voice, suddenly raised: "That is enough!"—and then Louis stepped heavily on the next stair and Susan looked up with a start.

When she saw us above them, she gave an odd kind of smile, muttered something to Stevens, and then walked quickly past him down the corridor.

Stevens turned, and though he smiled at Louis, it was a thinner smile than usual, and I could see that his cheeks were pale.

"Are you all right, Mr. Stevens?" I asked, as we reached the foot of the stairs.

He looked at me, and I saw a flicker of something like fear pass across his face. "Of course," he said. "Just a household matter."

I wondered, for a fleeting moment, whether it was possible that Susan might have some information regarding him, too, if she had tried to disrupt more lives than mine. But Stevens seemed so composed, so ordinary, so thoroughly proper and good, this middle-aged butler who had worked here for many years. What secrets could a man like him possibly have?

His usual smile had returned now, and he was asking Louis about his lessons and the dinner tomorrow in a manner completely free from agitation. It was impossible, I thought, that Stevens could be like me, that he could have anything to hide.

"Come, Louis," I said, when he seemed in danger of regaling Stevens with every possible dish the Wellings might serve us. "I believe I promised you a game of chess."

CHAPTER XVI

As the church was emptying the next day, Paul approached Louis and me to say that he would take us back later that afternoon, after our dinner at the vicarage. We arranged a time to meet, and then he turned away. I watched him as he went, his walk, the turn of his shoulders. I waited for him to look back at us, and smiled when he did.

I led Louis through the crowd, his hand in mine, conscious of the villagers turning to look at us. There was nothing menacing, nothing dangerous, in their expressions, but each of them stared, long and hard, and I felt my chest tighten.

"I hate it when they stare," muttered Louis, as we emerged into the morning sun.

"It's all right, child."

"I *hate* it." He spoke with more vehemence than normal.

"Louis, it is not good to hate," I said, surprised.

He looked down at the ground. I wondered if Mrs. Eversham had been right all along, if we ought not to have come into the village.

"But it's all right to hate bad people," said Louis. "Like the devil or—" He said something else, but he turned away from me as he spoke, to gaze after a group of children playing in the street, and his voice was muffled.

"It's never good to hate," I said. "The Lord teaches us to turn the other cheek." I knelt down, reached out to hold his shoulders, turned him back toward me. "Louis, the people here, they do not understand us—that's all. We must be better than they are, and try to understand them."

"Paul understands me," said Louis, his face still dark, "and he's from the village."

"But Paul knows us, and these people do not," I said. "You shall see, Louis—we shall come here week after week, and this time next year no one will look at us strangely."

He shrugged, but I could see the clouds lifting from his face.

A moment later the vicar and his wife were out of the church, and Mrs. Welling's face lit up at the sight of us waiting for them.

—⟩-⟨—

Dinner was a handsome affair. We ate soup, followed by roast beef and potatoes, with carrots and Yorkshire puddings and two side dishes, one of broiled fowl and the other of curried mutton. Louis ate with his usual hearty appetite, but I measured mine, trying to make sure there would be leftovers. For all that the beef was a good cut and the gravy thick, it was easy to tell that the Wellings were not wealthy, and I doubted that this fare was what they usually ate on Sundays. From the light flush on her face when I complimented the food, it seemed that Mrs. Welling did the cooking herself. They had only one servant, a girl called Jenny, who could not have been much more than fourteen. They seemed to treat her more as a favorite niece than a maid.

The vicarage was not large. It was a cottage built of red sandstone, with a thatched roof and gables, and climbing plants running over the walls. The garden was neat but small, just a short lawn and nursery garden, with one tall beech tree at the end. Inside there was a sitting room, dining room, and kitchen, and space upstairs for surely no more than two bedrooms and a study. You would have known it to be a gentleman's house, though, for the steps were clean, the carpets brushed, and the furniture worn but sturdy. We ate off scratched but real silver.

Louis was to my left around the table, and I had to strain or turn to hear him clearly, but he was suddenly too shy to say much, and the Wellings and I carried the conversation. They were straightforward people; they said what they thought. Mr. Welling talked a lot about the church over dinner, about life in Hartbridge, about his days as a curate in Liverpool. Mrs. Welling talked about how beautiful Somersetshire was, about the charity work she did in Hartbridge and in the neighboring village of Medley, about how the people were not quite like them, and—said without a moment's awkwardness—how lonely they sometimes were, how glad they were to see us.

I noticed, again, how much they loved each other. Not as some husbands and wives love, with comfortable fondness, but with something more than that. I saw their fingers brush each time they passed a dish between them, saw Mr. Welling reach out to put his hand over his wife's, saw her touch his shoulder when she stood up to fetch something. They smiled at each other every time their eyes met, and while one spoke the other would watch in rapt attention.

There was something about the considerate kindness with which they regarded each other that half reminded me of my parents. My mother had been dead nearly four years, my father ten, but I remembered well their shared looks, their quiet affection, how they had so often seemed to communicate without words. I had known, before Richard, that not all marriages were like that—I saw Mr. and Mrs. Russel daily, their stony silence, their stormy tempers—but I had hoped, somewhere deep within me, that Richard and I could become such a pair as my parents had been, as the Wellings seemed to be. It had seemed the ideal, then—a house of my own, a person to share my life with.

When Mr. Welling praised the food, smiling brightly at his wife, I thought of the first time I had cooked for Richard, a few days into our marriage.

I had thought he would be pleased. I always had a degree of confidence as a governess, a certainty that I was good at my work, and I wanted to master this, too—the work of being a wife, whatever that might be. And if I could not love him, not really, not enough, then I could do this—all the rest of it, domesticity and comfort, building a life. So I cooked what I knew was his favorite dinner, smiled when he declared our servant had outdone herself this time.

But I made dinner tonight, I said, smiling.

He stared at me. His face fell. *We have a servant for that work.*

There is too much work for Betty to do alone. Of course some of the household duties will fall to me.

His mouth was set. *It is not appropriate for a lady of your position to be in the kitchen.*

But a clergyman's wife—

You are not merely a clergyman's wife, Mrs. Lennox. You are a gentleman's wife. You are my *wife.*

But I thought—

He had looked at me, his mouth set in that expression of his that almost counted for a smile. *You must always ask me, Margaret, if you are unsure,* he said, more gently. *I will guide you. Your behavior is within my care.*

———✦———

After dinner, Mr. Welling asked Louis if he'd like to see some of his books on plants and birds, and they sat at the dining table to go over them, as though Louis were one of the men at a dinner party—which he of course loved. Mrs. Welling and I drank tea together in what she called the drawing room, though I expected it was their parlor and morning room, too.

As Mrs. Welling poured the tea, my eyes found the clock on the mantelpiece. There was an hour left until we were due to meet Paul. I wondered what he was doing at this moment, if he was with his family, at the public house, walking the lanes to pass the time. I tried to push him from my mind.

"Hartbridge must feel very different from Liverpool."

"Oh, ever so different." She paused. "It is partly that we are so out of the way here. I am used to a bustling town, to docks and warehouses, and here it is all fields and orchards. Most of the village people are farm laborers or work in the mill, and everybody is busy in apple-picking season. It is a harder parish for Matthew, in many ways—in Liverpool the congregation wavered, and many within the parish went to chapel or to the Roman Catholic churches instead, but here we have other difficulties. They all come to church without fail each Sunday, but the superstitions run deep." She gave a wary smile. "Many of them are harmless. After the apple picking's done, the people here go 'pixy-wording,' as they call it, to collect the apples they think the fairies have held on the trees until the end. And on Old Midsummer Eve, Matthew caught several of village lasses in Farmer Bell's orchard, trying to cast spells to show them their future husbands."

And yet they called Mrs. Eversham a witch. "How long have you lived here?" I asked.

"Three years," she said.

"And how long have you been married?"

"Five years." She smiled. "It doesn't seem like it."

Five years. Five years and still so in love. And then I thought, too, of the way they both looked at Louis. Five years and no children. They must feel it. And if I knew nothing of love, I did know something of that. I longed to reach out to her, to place my hand on her arm, to tell her I understood. Hadn't we tried for the best part of three years? *We.* The only thing in all the world Richard and I had been united on.

I had always longed for children. I had married Richard for an escape, yes, and in the hope of affection, but also for children, for a future, for life beating within me.

Every night for months and months he moved on top of me, and then I would bleed again and know that it was over. A year passed, two, and no child came.

Of course I told Mrs. Welling nothing of this. I only smiled.

"I used to be a governess, before my marriage," she said.

I could imagine her as a governess—fond, quietly stern when she needed to be. "Did you like teaching?"

"Sometimes." She gave a small frown, and I wondered if she had worked for people like the Russels. "This life suits me better, though."

I paused, and then, because her manner had made me warm to her, because I had been lonely, too, I said, "We have swapped. I used to be a clergyman's wife."

Her smile slipped. I had meant to speak lightly, but of course she understood my loss as she would her own, imagined me as heartbroken as she would have been.

"Yours has been a recent loss, I think?" Her voice was solemn, soft.

"Yes."

I saw her eyes fill with tears, and I felt like a fool.

"I am so very sorry," said Mrs. Welling.

"Yes." My voice sounded all wrong, too cold, too harsh. I said, "I am glad to have found a home at Hartwood Hall."

This brought a slight smile. "How do you like it here?"

I thought of the creaks in the night, of Mrs. Eversham's temper and her anxiety about Louis, Mrs. Pulley's silent frowns, Susan's threat.

And then I thought of Louis's eager face, Paul Carter's broad smile.

"I like it very much."

"I am glad." She glanced, almost longingly, toward the dining room. "Louis seems a sweet boy."

"He is. Very clever, too."

"I am pleased he is coming to church now. Matthew and I have both often wondered why the Evershams did not come. There are all sorts of rumors in the village, but—" She broke off, and for the first time since I had met her, she looked a little embarrassed.

"Mrs. Eversham is very solitary," I said. "She is often away on business, and there is nobody to take Louis—but now that I am here, she has asked me to bring him every week. Some of the servants are dissenters, and they avoid the village because Hartwood is not thought of kindly here."

Mrs. Welling nodded solemnly. "I am afraid it is true."

I sipped my tea, wondered if Mrs. Welling knew more. I said, slowly, carefully, "I suppose it is all about the little girl."

She sighed, as though she were relieved I had heard the story. "It is a terrible thing, to lose a child. It was all before we came here, of course, but it must have been a very difficult time for Mrs. Eversham. And some of the village folk here are quick to judge. There have been stories . . ."

I looked at her. "Stories?"

"Foolish things, really. Mrs. Eversham's daughter died away from home—and was buried away from home, too, I gather. There was no funeral here, and there is no grave in the churchyard—and of course that gave rise to rumors. Some people said—well, Hartwood Hall has always had a reputation for being haunted, simply because it is the oldest house for miles around, and there are all sorts of tales about Mrs. Eversham dealing in the dark arts. Jenny told me that some say the daughter didn't die a natural death at all, that Mrs. Eversham sold her to the devil." Mrs. Welling sighed, shook her head. "I suppose it is no wonder Mrs. Eversham avoids the village." She sipped her tea. "Louis must miss his sister."

"I do fear that he is lonely. It is a solitary place."

She nodded. "I once walked up to Hartwood Hall. We had been here for only a few weeks and I kept expecting the Evershams to turn up at church. I thought I'd see the place where they lived. It was such a long walk, and when I finally got there, I was amazed. Such an imposing house, but so old and dingy and so—I can't think of the word for it, but it made my skin crawl. When I saw it, I think I half understood why the people of Hartbridge think it an evil spot." She gave a slight laugh. "Paul Carter told me I was trespassing and chased me off the property with as much gallantry as he could."

I smiled. I could imagine just how he might have done it, quietly, firmly. "Do you know Mr. Carter, then?"

"Oh, not well. He's the only one from Hartwood Hall who comes to church—except you and Louis now—so Matthew and I have come to know him a little. He seems a good sort of man."

"Yes," I replied. "I am sure he is."

CHAPTER XVII

WHEN WE LEFT THE VICARAGE, THE SKY HAD CLOUDED OVER AND grown darker. We found Paul waiting for us outside the inn at the edge of the village, just as he had promised. I wondered what his day had been like, if he had gone back home to his family.

He leaped down from the cart to help Louis up. He offered his hand to me, too, and I hesitated before taking it. His skin was rough, scarred, warm. He looked up at me before he let go.

I looked away.

"How was your afternoon?" I asked him.

"Pleasant enough," he said, and though he did not elaborate, he smiled. He turned to Louis. "And how was your first dinner party, Master Louis?"

Once we were settled in the cart, our hats pulled low to shield us from the rain, Louis began to tell Paul of our afternoon's adventures. He had talked through all Mr. Welling's scientific books and how marvelous dinner was by the time we reached the woods and were plunged from the dusky evening into near pitch black.

I blinked as my eyes adjusted, and for a few moments I could see nothing at all. Then the blurred outlines of trees began to form before me, and Paul's back, shoulders, and bowed head became a rough silhouette of gray against black. I looked around, willing my eyes to find clarity. There was Louis at my side, silent now, perhaps nervous, too, his skin almost luminescent in the darkness. He looked like a ghost. And there, on my other side, was the inky blackness of thick trees.

I could hear the clop of the horse's hooves, hear Louis's soft breathing. But beyond that, everything was muffled. I wished I had sat on Louis's right, so that I might have listened to the woods instead, the splitting of twigs and the snarls of animals, the rush of the wind and rain through the trees.

A kind of cold fear stole over me. It was foolish, ridiculous, childish, how much I hated the dark. I took Louis's hand in mine and tried to tell myself it was only for his sake. His palm was cold from the rain, and I thought abruptly, dreadfully, of Richard, how cold his hands had been in death.

Then I thought of Isabella, and a picture came into my mind of a child with paper-white skin walking through the woods, bare feet on mud, coming closer, closer.

I blinked in the darkness—and somewhere, among the trees, I thought I saw something. A flash of movement. A deer, I thought. Or a child.

Impossible.

There was nothing there.

I gripped Louis's hand. I was riding through the woods in the dark with my charge. I was a governess. I was a widow. I was not a girl stuck at the bottom of the well, my clothes damp, the blood pounding in my head, my eyes, my ear, my consciousness slipping, my body failing.

I was not a child anymore.

It was another aching few minutes before we emerged back into the light, onto the track up to the house. I breathed out, took in the dusky blue of the sky, the gray clouds scattered across it. I kept Louis's hand in mine, even as we drew up to the courtyard. Paul walked with us to the front doors and stood beside us, talking to Louis as I knocked.

It took a few minutes for Mrs. Pulley to answer, and when she did, she only gave a curt nod—but Mrs. Eversham was right behind, moving quickly forward to greet Louis. He wrapped his arms around her, and as he began to tell her about his afternoon, I felt a kind of pang, and I dare say I looked at them just as Mrs. Welling had looked at the dining-room door when Louis was behind it.

Mrs. Pulley followed them down the corridor, and I hesitated on the threshold, glanced back at Paul.

"Not scared, were you, Mrs. Lennox?" he asked, smiling.

I swallowed. "I don't much like the dark," I said. And then, because there was something in his open face that made me wish to speak more, I said, "When your hearing is as mine is, it is—well, I am even more reliant on sight. If I cannot trust my eyes, then . . ."

His smile was gone and he nodded earnestly. "I am sorry. I did not mean to—to make fun of you. I would never—" He broke off.

"It is quite all right. You have not offended me."

He said, very quietly, just loud enough for me to hear and low enough for me to know he meant more than he said, "I shouldn't like to offend you."

"No."

Then, in that same quiet voice, "Did you always . . . struggle to—?" He stopped himself. "Sorry. I've no right to ask."

"I don't mind, Mr. Carter." I hesitated. "I fell down a well, when I was thirteen years old. Cut the left side of my head open, damaged something in my ear beyond repair. I was there for hours before my parents found me."

He looked appalled. "Dear God, how did you not bleed to death?"

"I tore my dress and bound up my head with it."

"Most children would not have thought of that," he said.

"I was not most children." I glanced at him; it touched me that he looked impressed. "My father was a surgeon and I had seen him bind up wounds before. I suppose they brought me up to be practical—my mother taught me for the most part, but my father showed me bits and pieces of his trade." I paused. "Still, I thought I was going to die. It was midnight before I was found. I suppose that does not help with my fear of the dark either."

"And yet you walk out in the grounds in the evening."

I shrugged. "One has to conquer it somehow. Are you never afraid, Mr. Carter? We are very isolated here."

He grinned. "Nothing to be afraid of."

"And yet Mrs. Eversham has ten bolts on her front doors."

His smile slipped a little. "She's a cautious woman."

I nodded. "Well, good night, Mr. Carter."

"Good night, Mrs. Lennox," he said. And then, as he turned away, I heard him murmur, "Margaret."

I wished I had not told him my Christian name. I liked the way he said it, and I did not like that I liked it.

I shook my head as I stepped into the house. I ought to avoid Paul. I closed the doors behind me and began to lock each lock and bolt each bolt, just as Mrs. Eversham had taught me.

CHAPTER XVIII

WHEN I CAME DOWN TO BREAKFAST THE NEXT MORNING, I FOUND Mrs. Eversham just finishing her meal and Louis helping himself to bread and butter. Susan was standing in the corner, watching over them. Mrs. Eversham looked up when she heard me enter and rose to her feet.

"Mrs. Lennox, I am glad you are up, for I wished to say farewell. I am leaving this morning. I have just received a letter and—well, I must go at once. I am not sure how long I will be away. I will leave Louis in your care, of course."

"Of course."

"Thank you, Mrs. Lennox." She turned. "Susan, will you tell Carter to bring the cart round to the front?"

Susan tutted—quietly, but loudly enough.

Mrs. Eversham looked up in surprise, and their eyes met. "Yes, Susan?"

Susan pursed her lips, paused for far too long, and then finally nodded and left the room. I watched her go with an odd feeling of relief, not just because she was going but because she had behaved sulkily. It would be all the better for me if Susan made Mrs. Eversham dislike her by her own behavior—especially if she did decide that Richard's watch was not enough, that she wanted to tell the mistress about my letter.

Mrs. Eversham smiled at me. She rounded the table and kissed her little boy goodbye.

Within a few hours, she was gone.

The next morning I woke to a loud knock on my door, and opened it to find Susan standing there, face set, arms folded.

"Good morning, Susan," I said, as steadily as I could.

She did not greet me. She said, "I want paper."

"Pardon?"

"I want paper," she said, "and you'll give it to me. Paper and ink. I want to send a letter."

"I—"

"There's plenty in the schoolroom, isn't there? You'll get me some. Two sheets'll do. Half a bottle of ink. And a pen."

I stood there, my hands shaking. It was bad enough to have given up my watch. It was worse, much worse, to know that she could demand anything of me at any time, that any request she made I must comply with, or risk everything.

I would be stealing from Mrs. Eversham. It was only two sheets of paper, and it would not be noticed, but Susan might ask for far more in the future.

I hated that I was afraid.

She slipped her hand into her pocket, took out Richard's gold watch, and wound the chain around her fingers.

"Well, Mrs. Lennox?" said Susan.

"I shall get paper for you," I said mechanically.

Susan's lips flickered into a smile. "Good," she said, and turned to walk away.

I fetched the paper and ink for her before breakfast, slipping it into her hand when I passed her in the corridor. And then I went and ate with Louis, studied and worked and spent my day with him. In his presence, I felt calm. The schoolroom was a place of safety. His wide smile was all the balm I needed.

Without him, in the evening, fear crept toward me, the constant prickling of Susan's glances, Richard's face forever in my mind.

I must *do* something. There must be a way out of this situation.

—————⟩•⟨—————

The following evening, I found myself entirely alone. Louis went to bed at eight o'clock, and Lacey and Mary were busy downstairs baking the bread for the week. Mrs. Eversham was still away. Mrs. Pulley had retired early with a headache and it was Stevens's evening off—goodness knew where he went in this desolate spot, but he was not here. Susan was supposed to be minding the house, but she put her head into the library at a quarter past eight to tell me she was going out, that I was not to tell anyone, that if Mrs. Pulley asked tomorrow, she had been tidying the parlor the whole time.

I watched her go, then crept out into the corridor to see the front doors shut behind her. I itched to close the bolts, to lock her out. But I did not want to lock Stevens out, too, and I could not afford for Susan to have further reason to make trouble for me. The moment I was no longer useful to her, she would show Mrs. Eversham my letter.

Unless, of course, I could get it back.

I stared at the closed doors. Susan would not return for a little while, at least. She sometimes carried my watch about with her, and it might be that she carried the letter, too—but it was possible that it was secreted somewhere in her own room. It was possible—just—that I might be able to reclaim it.

I glanced around the empty hall, then walked cautiously downstairs. I reached the end of the staircase and walked down the first stretch of corridor without meeting anyone, though when I rounded the corner, I heard the clatter of pans in the kitchen. The hallway was dark, here in the cellar, and it took me a moment to adjust to the dimness.

I went quickly up to Susan's chamber door, trying to tread as lightly as I could. I hesitated, my hand on the doorknob. If Mary or Lacey came out into the corridor, what on earth would I say?

I thought of my letter and swallowed hard. I must risk it.

Slowly, I turned the handle—and found the door locked.

I ought to have known. Of course Susan would lock up her room when she was not within it. She might have guessed I would try to get my letter back—and besides, someone willing to pilfer from others in the household would hardly trust anyone else not to do the same to her.

A new thought struck me. I turned along the corridor and paused outside the housekeeper's office. Mrs. Pulley was asleep at the other end of the corridor, and there was a chance, perhaps, that if there was a spare key to Susan's room, I would find it here. My head pounded as I pushed the door open and stepped inside, pulling it closed behind me.

The room was dim, illuminated only by one window set high. I quickly scanned the desk and the shelves: there were a few labeled keys strung up on hooks beneath the servant bells—I spotted keys for the summer house, for the front doors, the back door, Mrs. Eversham's study, the library—but none for any of the servants' rooms. I stepped forward and began to search. Forcing myself to breathe more slowly, I worked methodically, easing open drawer after drawer—but there were no more keys to be found.

I froze at a sudden sound. It must have come from the corridor outside. I crept forward, pressed my right ear to the keyhole, waited. Footsteps first, then Lacey's voice came clear.

"Mary—what are you doing?"

A hiss came back. "I heard the ghost. In there."

"You heard no such thing, lass. No doubt Mrs. Pulley is up again, that's all. Come back to your kneading." Lacey's voice sharpened. "I mean it, Mary—I'll have none of this nonsense."

Another few footsteps, growing softer. I held my breath, waited, my heart thudding. At last, when there seemed to be silence outside, I rose unsteadily to my feet, then slipped out into the empty corridor. I hurried back up the stairs.

CHAPTER XIX

AT THE TOP OF THE STAIRS, I STOOD HESITATING IN THE HALL. THE keen sense of frustration was almost overwhelming. I could try Susan's door again, another time, but no doubt she would rarely be so careless as to leave her door unlocked or unattended. I was as trapped as I had ever been.

My mind was busy, my nerves frayed. I did not want to go into the library, as I often did. I did not want to plan my lessons in the schoolroom. I knew even *Miss Catherine* could not hold my attention tonight. I longed for distraction, for Louis, for anything to get Susan and Richard out of my head. I thought about walking in the grounds and found myself thinking not of grass and moonlight but of Paul's blue eyes, the soft way he had spoken my name. I dismissed the thought and turned.

And there, facing me, was the entrance to the east wing.

I crept forward, reached for the doorknob. It would be locked, too, of course. And yet—

And yet I turned the handle, and the door creaked open. I stood motionless, my heart pounding.

There was no one around. No one need ever know. After weeks of passing this forbidden part of Hartwood Hall and wondering what lay within, of course I was curious. And where was the harm? I would be disturbing only empty rooms and dust.

One door had been locked to me already tonight. Now that I found another open, it seemed impossible not to step through.

Some small voice inside me whispered that it would not be safe, that I had been told as much, that there would be loose floorboards, hanging beams, that I would get hurt. But Mrs. Eversham had brought Louis to the east wing to prove there were no ghosts, and I was half sure Susan had been sneaking around in here, too. There would surely be no danger I could not avoid. And besides, the voice was Richard's voice, telling me that I was too rash, that I ought to take better care of myself—and I did not want to listen to him, not tonight. I felt suddenly reckless.

The door creaked as I pushed it further, and I found myself at the edge of a wooden-floored corridor. I couldn't see very far, because the corridor turned abruptly a few feet away from me, just as it did in the west wing. It looked almost to be its mirror image. Gloomy light was trickling from somewhere around the corner, leaving stripes of gold on the floor. There must be a window out of sight, where the curtains had been poorly drawn, letting in the last of the evening sun. The walls were a faded cream, the floorboards bare and exposed. The corridor smelled faintly of dust and damp.

Before I knew what I was doing, I had stepped forward and pulled the door closed behind me.

I breathed out. I was in the east wing, and that thought alone brought a chill to my skin.

I was being foolish. It was nothing but an empty wing of an old house. No secrets, no mystery.

No ghosts here.

I tried the first door I came to, turned the handle, felt it give. I peered into a long, thin room lined with wooden benches. An old chapel: cobwebbed pews, raised altar, faded, whitewashed walls. The last of the evening light streamed in thin stripes through gaps between the curtains, but still the room was dim.

It felt cold here, and I tugged at my shawl. In one corner, a branch of ivy had worked its way between the stones and was crawling up inside the house, clinging to the ceiling. When I ran my finger along one of the benches, it came up thick with dust.

I walked through the chapel slowly, trying to steady my nerves, to observe everything, to remind myself that this was nothing more than a deserted chapel in a deserted part of a half-deserted house. There was no sense being afraid of shadows.

I turned to move back to the corridor, and stopped. There were footprints in the dust, clear marks standing out in the gray. I shivered, swallowed.

I was being foolish. They were my own, of course.

Emerging from the old chapel, I could see a little more of the corridor before me, though the far end was in shadow. I saw no sign of danger—no broken floorboards, no crumbling walls. But now that I thought of it, it was Susan, not Mrs. Eversham, who had told me the east wing was dangerous, and no doubt Susan said whatever she liked. Mrs. Eversham had only told me not to come here.

I stepped forward, tried the next door along, and found it locked. I tried the next. Again, locked. The next one, and the next. All locked.

And then I pushed another and felt it give.

It was so terribly silent in this part of the house. Not a creak from upstairs, not the distant sound of a clock, not the rattle of windows in the breeze. Even my own footsteps, my own heartbeat, seemed quietened.

I opened the door and looked at the room before me.

It was large, perhaps intended to be a sitting room, and white sheets were thrown over most of the furniture. The curtains were drawn untidily, but in the chink of dying light creeping through, I could make out the shapes of settees and tables, even of a piano. In the corner, a mirror was propped up against the wall.

Something moved.

In the mirror, something behind me.

I started back, cried out, reached instinctively for my penknife. Every governess in England is always equipped to mend and cut pens.

But there was nothing there. The room was still—no movement but my own. As I stared slowly around, searching, I saw my shadow move, flickering in the thin strips of light. That must have been all I had seen.

I put my hand over my mouth. Someone might have heard me cry out. And it was nothing, after all—the slight oddities of this house and Susan's threats had led me to expect some monster lurking in the east wing.

It was not like me. I was not usually one to start at my own shadow, to be given to fancies. Even when Richard, in his last few days, had told me he saw angels, I had told him that he was delirious, when I might have told him he was blessed.

There was another door within this room, and I stepped toward it, pushed it open.

The next room was similar, silhouettes of furniture beneath faded sheets, an old mirror in the corner, its face to the wall. One of the sheets was rucked up, revealing a red-cushioned armchair, faded with use. The curtains on the far window were pulled back, and the windows were caked in grime, but—

No, it was not a handprint. It was just the way the dirt had fallen. That was all.

It was a dead place, this part of the house.

The thought made me shiver.

In the corner of the room, a narrow stone staircase led both up and down. I made my way to the first step down, then hesitated, looking into the grim darkness of the cellars. In pitch black, I would be lost entirely.

Upstairs, then.

I climbed carefully, emerging into what must have once been a study. In this room, the furniture was uncovered but sparse: a small settee, a desk, a dresser in the corner, a stained marble fireplace.

I saw something glinting on the mantelpiece, illuminated in a narrow ray of light. I stepped forward. A silver chain, thin loop after thin loop, with a silver filigree locket at the end. I opened it, almost by instinct, and stared at the picture within.

It was a miniature of a girl of seven or eight years old, in a white linen dress, with a ribbon in her fair hair. Her face reminded me of

Louis's. I did not have to wonder who she was, this little girl, with her solemn eyes and her smiling mouth. The dead girl. Louis's sister. Isabella.

I wondered what the locket was doing here; perhaps Mrs. Eversham had been so pained by the memories it brought that she had felt the need to shut it away in the forgotten half of her house.

I laid it down gently, stepped away. It was no business of mine.

A moment later, I was out in the corridor, walking slowly on, trying door after door. The layout seemed to mirror the floor beneath. Here, too, there were no rotting floorboards; there was no decay—just dust and faded wallpaper.

Each door I came to was locked fast. I was nearly at the end, heading toward the main section of the house, when I tried another handle and felt the door ease open.

And it was then that I heard something.

Singing.

A woman's voice, or perhaps a child's.

Soft, barely audible.

I strained to listen, pivoted to better catch the sound—and lost it. Everything was suddenly silent—very silent. I wondered if it was possible I had imagined it, or even if it might have been Louis, unable to sleep, singing in the west wing of the house, if the sound might somehow have carried here. I pushed the door open as hard as I could and took in the empty room. It was entirely empty, without a single item of furniture. Nothing but faded walls and long floorboards with a faint stain in the center.

And then I heard footsteps. Clear, distinct steps. Loud creaks on floorboards. There was no doubting these, but I could not tell if they were right behind me or from the floor below, even from the attics above.

I breathed in, breathed out, waiting for them to cease.

But the sounds did not stop.

It must have been Mrs. Pulley, up and recovered from her headache.

Or Lacey, perhaps. Or even Susan, if she had come back early, if she had seen me slip through the forbidden door to the east wing and decided to torment me.

It might be an intruder. I thought of all the locks Mrs. Eversham kept on the doors.

Or—

I did not believe in ghosts.

But Richard had told me, once, that he would haunt me.

And I could not get the face of the girl in the locket out of my mind.

Another step. Someone was either right above me or right behind me.

Somewhere, a shadow moved.

I ran.

First to the end of the corridor, to the door I hoped might take me to the familiar upper landing. I shoved it hard, rattled the handle until my hands hurt. It was no use. It was locked.

I wheeled around, barely taking in the corridor ahead of me.

I was tearing down the corridor, heading for the stairs that would take me out, away, anywhere but here.

My skirts were flying, my hair coming loose.

I wanted to call for help.

But I was not supposed to be here. I had broken the rules.

I hurtled down the staircase, my feet slipping as I hurried to the lower floor.

I could have sworn I felt breath on my neck, that I heard someone else's heartbeat besides my own.

I pushed through the first door I found, cutting through another abandoned room, barely taking in the long table, the old chairs, focused only on the door at the other end. I fumbled with the key already in the lock and finally burst through the door.

Straight out into the open, sunlit evening.

Straight into the figure who awaited me.

CHAPTER XX

I HAD BEEN RUNNING SO HARD THAT I WAS KNOCKED BACKWARD, and I sat for a moment on the grass, staring up at Paul Carter.

Well, at least it had not been Mrs. Pulley. Of all the people who might have caught me where I should not be, I was glad it was him.

I had come out on the side of the east wing, not far from the stables. Though it was late, the sun was still faintly aglow, and the idea of ghosts and intruders lurking within Hartwood Hall now seemed preposterous. And yet still my hands were trembling, my heart hammering. I glanced over my shoulder and saw where I had come from: a narrow oak door, sunk back into the brickwork.

Paul Carter held out a hand to help me up, and I took it cautiously. His grip was strong. I let go quickly and pulled myself up. When I was on my feet and had brushed down my black skirts, I looked across at him.

He was observing me steadily, an unreadable expression in his eyes.

I opened my mouth, and did not know what to say.

"Margaret."

I managed, "Paul," and got no further.

"With all due respect"—he waved toward the door behind me—"what on earth were you doing?"

I swallowed. I had no excuses beyond curiosity, and my mind was swirling too much to think. I was his superior in the house, of course—but he had been there far longer than me, and his word would hold more weight. I could not afford for him to tell anybody.

"I was—exploring," I said at last. "I—I know I should not have been, but—well, I have been over the rest of the house and the door to the east wing was unlocked and I just started walking and . . ."

Paul was looking at me strangely; I supposed that I had been talking too fast, that my voice was shaky. "Margaret, are you quite well?"

"I—I thought I heard someone." It was almost a relief to say it. "In the east wing—I heard someone."

"And that's why you were running?"

I swallowed hard. "Yes."

Paul was still observing me. He hesitated, opened his mouth to speak. I half expected him to upbraid me, but instead he said, "Would you like a cup of tea?"

I looked at him. I was standing in the evening sunlight and my teeth were chattering and my skin felt cold. At my sides, my hands shook. I hardly thought before I said, "Yes."

—⋈—

The place where Paul Carter lived was not quite what I had expected. Half of the old stables was still in use; the other half, bricked off from the horses, seemed all his. The room he led me into was part workshop, part cottage sitting room. There was a dresser full of seeds and bulbs, each drawer neatly labeled with a pencil drawing of the plant within; a long rough dining table that he must have made himself; and a few upright chairs that had come from the house. In one corner, there was a low armchair. In the other, a fire, with a few pots and a kettle held over it. Against one wall hung the tools of his trade—rakes and trowels, buckets and saddles and knives. There was a workbench, and vases and pots of flowers dotted around the room, as though he could not bear to be away from the garden, even here. Above us, reached by a ladder to one side, was a hayloft. I supposed he must sleep up there.

While I sat down, he filled the kettle from a bucket by the fire. He had taken off his jacket and was standing with his back to me. I watched as he lifted two chipped teacups from a shelf above the fire, took out some tea leaves from a caddy, and filled a dented copper teapot. He did it all carefully, slowly, with measured exactness. He brought down milk, in a discolored china creamer, then moved a chair round to the other side of the table, so that he could sit on the right side of me and pour the tea.

He handed one cup to me. I took it and gulped.

"Better?"

I nodded. "Better."

I looked down into my teacup and wrapped my hands around it. The shaking seemed to have finally stopped. But I was in his home. The place where he slept. I ought not to have come.

"Do you think—? I was so sure I heard someone in the east wing. My hearing isn't always good, but—"

"It was probably Mrs. Pulley. She goes there sometimes, I think, to check on things."

"But she is not well tonight—she's in bed with a headache."

"Perhaps she felt better," said Paul, raising his own cup to his lips. "Or it might have been Stevens."

"He's not here. It's his evening off."

"It might have been any of the servants. It won't have been an intruder." He smiled at me, and I tried to smile back. His smile seemed so young, as though the five or six years between us made a vast difference.

"You will think me mad, but for a minute I thought it might be a ghost."

His smile slipped. "There are no ghosts here, Margaret."

He spoke my name very softly, and the hammering in my heart was back.

"Nor anywhere," I said. "I know that. I am no fool. Spirits and ghosts and curses—it's all bunkum and nonsense. I know that. But . . ." I sipped my tea. "I just keep thinking of the girl who died. Isabella." I swallowed. "I saw something, in the east wing. A picture of her. I suppose it made me nervous."

I thought of Richard, too, his voice clear in my mind in the east wing. I tried to push the thought from my mind.

Paul looked at me steadily. I wondered what he made of me. He was not looking at me like he thought me a fool.

"Nothing about Hartwood Hall need ever make you nervous."

He spoke so earnestly that I found myself smiling. "Why do you love this place so much?"

I had not meant it to sound like such an intimate question, but Paul looked up, smiled. It lit his entire face.

"I used to sneak up here when I was a boy," he said, "when the place was deserted. The woods here are very thick, much denser than other patches of trees hereabouts, especially for people used to cultivated orchards, and I suppose that gave rise to the rumors about it being haunted. One day my brother brought me up to Hartwood, just to scare me. I suppose he thought it would be a lark. But I wasn't scared." He paused. "James and I, we used to swim in the lake, run round the park, get lost in the woods. We even snuck inside the house. We found a bunch of old keys in the stables and we explored every inch of the place. James used to put his hand on the windows to leave marks in the dust and tell me it was the ghost." I could hear the smile in his voice. "By the time Mrs. Eversham came, we were older, and my brother had stopped coming, but . . . well, I still loved the place. The grounds were unkempt and chaotic—but there was beauty, underneath it. I knew that. I wanted that. I used to pinch seeds from the farm and plant them in the grounds—I started the rose garden long before I worked here. All my childhood, my mother was ill and the work on the farm was hard and—well, Hartwood was my escape. I thought it was paradise."

"Paradise," I repeated, smiling. Hartwood Hall was beautiful, grand, impressive, charged with atmosphere—but I had never thought it a paradise. "How did you come to work here?" I asked.

"Stevens offered me a job. He found me . . . loitering in the gardens, I suppose, just after my mother died." Paul shrugged. "My family were very much against it. They have their own farm, you see. It's only small, just cornfields and a few sheep, truth be told, but my father has always been proud of it, especially when so many smaller home-steads hereabouts have been bought up, made into bigger farms. But all my life I had wanted something more, something . . . different, I suppose. Different from what my father had, different from what my brother wanted. It's never seemed enough to me, to plant and grow food, to make ends meet, to shear sheep and create nothing but . . . *useful* things. The gardens at Hartwood, they're not useful, but they're more—more real, somehow, for that. Corn is just corn. Gardens can be anything." He sipped his tea. "Father didn't want me to work at Hartwood Hall. But the wages were good and the harvests were bad and we needed it. That's all. They still don't like it, but I send home half my pay and they don't complain."

"It must be hard for you to work here," I said, "when so many people distrust the place. If I were in your position, I might not stay."

"Are you not in my position?"

I smiled. The first few times we had met, he talked to me as though I were a lady. Now he spoke as though I were a servant. In a way, of course, I was both. "Not quite," I said. "I have nowhere else to go."

"Nowhere?" he repeated. "No family?"

"None."

"But you could find another position."

"Not easily." I tapped my left ear. "The hearing—it doesn't help. And then I haven't worked for a few years, and my characters are out of date. And it's harder, if you've been married—some families don't want widows. Too solemn, too somber."

He was looking at me, his gaze piercing. "You don't strike me as somber."

I smiled. "Just mad?"

"No, not mad. You don't have to be mad to see ghosts in the dark."

"What then? What do I strike you as?"

Paul hesitated. I had been in jest, but he seemed to take the question seriously. He was examining me, his eyes moving over my face, my hair, the neckline of my black dress.

"Clever," he said, and something in my stomach twisted. "Strong. Not somber, but—well, a bit regretful, perhaps. And good. Definitely good."

I could not smile at that. "I am not sure I am a good person, Paul. I don't think good people see ghosts."

"And did you really see a ghost?"

"No," I said softly. "Perhaps the shadow of one. I don't know."

"And you're all right now?"

I nodded. Then, quietly, I said, "Thank you, Paul. I am glad it was you I knocked into."

He was looking at me again. His eyes so blue. Too blue. He said, "I don't believe you're not good."

I thought of Richard, his sallow skin, his pleading eyes.

Margaret, I will haunt you.

He had not thought I was good.

I looked away, and I felt tears in my eyes. Ridiculous. Foolish.

And then Paul put his hand very softly over mine and my skin came alive with something that was not fear. He was running his fingers over my knuckles, his thumb over my palm, as though to comfort me—and then he lifted my hand to his lips and kissed it.

Not like a gentleman kisses a lady's hand. Not like that. No, he kissed each knuckle in turn, and I sat, motionless, my heart aching, knowing I was on the precipice of something, knowing that if I moved now I could never go back.

I was here for a new start after the ruin that had been my marriage. I could not afford to fall in love.

I did not mean to kiss him. I knew only that I wanted him, that his hands were rough and his eyes were bright and that if I kissed this man then the last lips on mine would no longer be my husband's. So I pushed myself forward, out of my chair, and pressed my lips against Paul's.

He was startled. Then I felt his mouth hard and hot against mine, and he was standing up, his arm around my waist, his hand in my hair, his body against mine.

He tasted like tea, like grass, like fresh air on a hot summer's morning.

This was impossible. I had been at Hartwood Hall less than a month. I had been a widow for two.

I will haunt you.

I pulled back sharply, disentangling myself from him, my face scarlet.

"I am so sorry," I said, stumbling over my words. "Really, I—I do not know what came over me. I should not have—"

He was half smiling, a kind of confusion spreading across his face, and I was not sure whether it was the last few moments he could not believe had happened or this, now. His eyes were brighter than ever. He was too beautiful. He opened his mouth as though to speak.

I did not wait. I did not stay. I hurried as fast as I could from the stables, out into the evening air.

VOLUME TWO

CHAPTER I

FOR THE NEXT FEW DAYS, I AVOIDED PAUL. I STAYED INSIDE, KEPT out of sight of the gardens, tucked away in the schoolroom or the library. I taught Louis, struggling through Latin and French and arithmetic. I watched him writing, his pen making indents on the desk beneath. We tackled the planets, and he listed for me all the kings and queens of England, and all the wildflowers that grew by the lake. I focused on my work. In the evenings, I planned my lessons, or read books in the library, trying to lose myself in words. I finished *Miss Catherine*, astounded by its power. I could not quite reconcile the novel with the woman I knew. I tried to imagine anxious Mrs. Eversham sitting in her study, pulling words from her mind. I started half a dozen other books but could not concentrate on them.

If anyone had seen me kiss Paul, I would lose my place. Whatever it was about him that drew me in, I had to conquer it, forget it, hide it somewhere deep in my troubled mind.

Susan shadowed me. With Mrs. Eversham away, she lingered longer in the breakfast room every day, talking to Louis, looking at me. One day, she even sat down at the table and began to help herself to cold cuts and bread. She said nothing as she ate, but Louis looked at her in surprise. When I opened my mouth to speak, I saw Susan pull the watch chain from her skirt pocket and wind it slowly round her fingers.

She seemed impressed by her own daring, and perhaps a little fearful of it, for she ate fast and kept glancing at the door, as if expecting Stevens or Mrs. Pulley to come in and spoil her fun.

———✦———

One evening, I went out into the grounds. It was Paul's evening off and I had heard Mrs. Pulley say he was down in the village, so I thought I might be safe from an encounter with him. It was a warm night, and I had just completed one circuit of the house and was rounding the corner of the east wing when I saw a shadow mingling with my own on the grass. I turned, startled, half expecting to see Paul after all—but there stood Susan.

I did not know how long she had been following me. She might have been a few steps behind me since I left the house.

"Evening, Mrs. Lennox."

"Susan."

She grinned. I had never hated someone's smile so much. "Pleasant weather," she said.

I said nothing. I looked down at my boots, at the grass, anywhere but at her. I wanted to turn and run, but somehow I could not move.

"I was thinking," said Susan, "that it's not enough. That fancy watch, I mean. It's pretty, to be sure, maybe worth a pound or two, but it's not *a lot*, is it, for a secret like that? It's not . . . *adequate*, that's the word." She grinned. "I want something else, Mrs. Lennox."

Nausea rushed through me. "I have nothing."

"You have money."

"Susan, I don't."

She waved her hand dismissively. The gesture did not seem hers, and I wondered if she had caught it from some previous mistress, if she had stored it up, stolen it like she had stolen my letter. "You'll have your wages next quarter day," she said. She glanced up, gazing into the windows of the east wing with a smirk. "When they come in, you shall give me half."

My surprise overtook my panic. "Half? What am I supposed to dress myself on?"

"The other half," said Susan. "There's food enough here. You shan't starve. I'll hold you to it, Mrs. Lennox. And the next quarter. And the next."

I stared at her. This was madness. I could not let one letter and a housemaid's schemes ruin what I had already built at Hartwood Hall, the life I could have here. This was too much.

I said, "No," and with the word I felt my courage rise.

Susan stared at me. "Oh?" She took one step closer to me. "Then who shall I tell first, do you think—Mrs. Eversham, or little Louis?"

Her words stung. I had thought of being sent away, of being parted from Louis, but I had not thought of Susan telling him whatever she thought she knew about me. Mrs. Eversham would be shown the letter, to be sure, but Louis would just be told a story, a tale to make him hate me. My hands began to shake and I steeled myself. "You will not tell anyone," I said, endeavoring to keep my voice steady.

"Oh, and how will you stop me?" Susan grinned. "Kill me, like you did your husband?"

I flinched. I stood motionless, caught. The fight drained out of me as the gardens seemed to spin. I tried to say "It's not true," but I could barely hear myself pronounce the words. They sounded faint. They sounded like a lie.

"Listen to me, Mrs. Lennox," said Susan, her voice fierce, the smirk gone. "I set the rules now, not you—I am done with following other people's rules. There's a few weeks before next quarter day. You have until then to make up your mind to be wise. Understand?"

I said nothing. I stared at her. I could not get Richard's face out of my head—the flicker of his frown when I had done something wrong, the frank disappointment in his face that I had let him down, again, his familiar voice telling me that I must try harder, that I must listen to him, that I must be a better wife.

I kept telling myself that I was free, but I knew I was not.

I looked at Susan's fierce expression and felt myself crumple. I said nothing, only nodded. I was not that steely, determined girl anymore, the one who had bound up her head with her own dress in the dark. Now I was just afraid.

CHAPTER II

THE NEXT MORNING, I SAT DEEP IN THOUGHT AS LOUIS BENT OVER his handwriting exercises. It did not seem right that Susan had charge of him in the mornings and evenings—she only helped him wash and dress and ready himself for bed, but I could not shake that stab of worry that she spent so much time alone with him.

"Louis," I said gently, "is Susan kind to you?"

He looked up from the paper before him. He did not seem surprised by the question, but he frowned as though he was trying to consider it fully. "I—I think so," he said at last. "Not kind like you are, Mrs. Lennox, but she is never *un*kind. Sometimes she asks questions."

"Questions?"

"About Mother, like where she is when she's away and if I remember where I lived before. But I don't remember anything before Hartwood Hall. I have been here forever and ever." Louis shrugged. "Once she bought me a bag of bonbons," he said. "That was kind, wasn't it?"

I tried to nod. I wondered where Susan's questions had been leading. I wondered, too, if she had questioned him about me, but dared not ask. Instead I said, "You would tell me, wouldn't you, Louis, if she was unkind to you—if anyone was unkind to you?"

"Of course," he said, but he looked puzzled and solemn as he began to write once more.

I longed for and dreaded Sunday. A few hours away from Hartwood Hall would do me good, I knew—to get away from Susan, to see Mrs. Welling, to pray. But after what had happened, I was anxious about encountering Paul. I did not want to see him—and yet, somehow, I desperately did.

I did not know what Paul might have made of my behavior—what he might have made, even, of his own. He must know, as I did, that it had been a foolish, impossible moment, that neither of us could afford to put our positions in the household in jeopardy, as such a connection, whatever it was, would surely do. I did not think he would tell anyone—I believed I could trust him that far—but I did not know how it would change his behavior toward me.

He would say nothing, surely—not in front of Louis—but he would look at me, and that would be enough.

I was hesitant as Louis and I walked out toward Paul's cart. It was a hot day, the air thick, and my black gown felt warm and heavy. Paul was already sitting up at the front of the cart, reins in hands, shushing the horse. Usually he waited beside it.

And then he turned and smiled. It was a beaming, innocent smile, like nothing and everything had happened.

I swallowed hard, fought the smile that crept to my lips. The day felt suddenly even warmer.

It was mid-September now, but the summer had by no means left us. The sun was hot, and the orchards beyond the hedgerows shone in the light, dappled green, amber, gold, and red, the ground ruddy with fallen apples. I spent the journey to church trying not to look at Paul, talking only to Louis. If Paul noticed, he gave no sign; he was as easy with us as always.

Louis and I sat next to Mrs. Welling in the box, and the stares from the congregation seemed less troubling this week. Fewer people muttered as we passed. This time next year, perhaps, no one would look at us twice. The thought made me smile. I should like to still be here, in a year's time.

Away from Hartwood Hall, I could look at the situation more rationally. Susan's behavior could not last forever. The footsteps in the east wing must have been one of the servants. The noises in the night were merely my imagination, the signs I was still not used to this big, old house. In time, the troubles I had at Hartwood Hall would slip away.

As we left the church, Paul's brother approached him. They exchanged a few words I could not catch, and then the man frowned, shook his head. Paul glanced round at Louis and me, and his eyes met mine. My heart jumped, and I made myself look away. Paul turned back to the man, bowed his head, and walked out into the sunshine.

He was quiet on the way home. Louis sat at my side, cheerful and talkative as always, while ahead of us Paul kept his eyes on the road, speaking only when Louis directly asked him a question. When we finally reached Hartwood Hall and alighted from the cart, Paul lingered, as if half expecting me to send Louis on and find an excuse to speak to him. But I did not. I turned away, took Louis's hand in mine, and walked through the courtyard.

I did not look back.

CHAPTER III

THE HEAT GREW MORE INTENSE THAT WEEK, AND ONE MORNING I suggested to Louis that we go down and work in the summer house. We went to the housekeeper's room to collect the key; Mrs. Pulley was at work upstairs, but Lacey was soon able to find what we needed.

Ten minutes later, we were tramping down through yellowing grass, the hot sun high above us. Louis had seemed happy enough at first to take our lessons somewhere other than the stifling schoolroom, but as we neared the summer house, he grew sullen, wondering aloud if we ought to go back, saying that it might be even hotter in there, that it was a long walk from the house.

"Louis, whatever is the matter with you?"

That quietened him. He muttered, "Nothing," and changed the conversation, talking loudly about yesterday's lessons as we approached the summer house.

I saw Paul in the distance, chopping firewood just outside the stables, his jacket off, his shirtsleeves rolled up. He looked round, raised a hand in salutation. I made myself look away.

As I turned the key in the summer house door, Louis kept glancing over his shoulder, and as soon as it was open, he cut across me to step inside first. Once over the threshold, I saw his tight shoulders drop a little. I supposed it was not as hot as he had expected. He looked round at me with a sudden smile and stepped forward to let me in.

It was a small building, the inner walls plain wood like the outside, with pictures hung up here and there, sketches of the Italian lakes, framed poetry with illustrations. The floor was covered in an old Persian rug, and on it sat two large armchairs, a little coffee table squashed between them. At the back stood a bookshelf and a large oak blanket chest.

I drew back the curtains from the front windows and pulled the door shut behind us. Then I took the left-hand armchair and Louis sat down beside me, papers and pen folded in his lap. It was cooler in here, and I found myself smiling.

"That's better now, isn't it?"

Louis nodded. "I like it here."

On the coffee table sat an open book, an empty porcelain teacup, and a silver teapot. I reached out to move them to the floor until the lesson was over and I could take them away.

The moment my fingers touched the handle, I drew back. The teapot was *warm*.

"Louis," I said slowly, "who uses the summer house?"

"Only Mama and me."

"None of the servants?"

"They oughtn't," said Louis hesitantly. He was looking at the teapot now, looking at my hands. "I suppose they might."

Unease crept over me.

Mrs. Eversham was away.

One of the servants, then. Susan would have no scruples about being where she ought not to be.

Or Paul, perhaps. I thought of the chipped cups in his rooms, the easy familiarity with which he wandered the grounds. It was possible, but it seemed unlikely.

I reached out to touch the cup. It was cooler, and my disquiet began to slip away. The teapot was metal, in direct view of the glass in the door. It had probably been warmed by today's bright sun.

I was imagining things. I tucked the teapot and cup under the table, and closed the book. It was *The Old Curiosity Shop*.

"We ought to read this after *The Children of the New Forest*," I said, holding up the book.

"No."

I looked up, thinking I must have misheard. Louis was staring down at the ream of paper on his knees, frowning hard.

"It's a good book, Louis. You'll like Dickens."

He was shaking his head, his face pale. There was an odd kind of panic in his eyes. "I said no!" His voice was louder now, and with one violent motion, he shoved the book from my hand. It dropped hard to the floor, falling open on its back, pages fluttering.

I flinched back from him, startled. I was as surprised as if he had struck me.

Louis looked down at his hands, bewildered. It was almost as though he did not know what he'd done, as though he had, for a moment, completely lost control.

Then his face crumpled, and he sank down into the armchair. He curled back into it, pulled his arms around himself. I heard him mutter under his breath.

At first, I could not hear the words. They were too soft—gentle enough, I thought, for an apology. And then I heard something else, caught the lilting sound of something my mind made into "Isabella."

Ah.

I leaned forward, put my hand softly on his arm.

"I don't want to read it," he muttered. "They used to read it together, Mama and—" He broke off. He had clearly not meant to let the name slip before and seemed not quite aware of having done so. I wondered if Mrs. Eversham had come here to read the book she used to read with her daughter, if she kept it in the summer house to keep it out of Louis's way.

"I don't want to," Louis said again.

"It's all right," I said, and though he was not crying, though he was ten years old and I had known him only a month, I knelt down beside him, pulled him into my arms, and hugged him tight.

I did not know how long we sat like that. At last, Louis disentangled himself from me, his cheeks still pale, his expression penitent.

"I'm sorry I was bad," he said quietly.

"It's all right. It does not matter."

"Mother will be angry."

"She doesn't need to know," I said. "It can be our secret."

Louis's eyes widened at that, and he shook his head. "Not a secret," he said, his voice strained. "I hate secrets."

I smiled. "Not a secret, then." I leaned down to pick up the book, dusting it off. "See? No harm done. And you are sorry, so we needn't tell your mother."

Louis sat frowning in his chair. "But badness is still badness even if you're sorry."

I swallowed hard. "It depends on how bad you were, and on how sorry you are," I replied, but even as I spoke, I wondered if that was true. I ought to have a better answer for him. "Come, child," I said. "See, I have forgiven you, and now you must forgive yourself. It is only a small matter, and we shall forget it."

Louis nodded slowly. Then, "I like it when you call me 'child.'"

I frowned. I had not realized I was doing it. "Do you?"

"Yes. Sometimes my name does not seem like it's me. Have you ever felt like that, Mrs. Lennox?"

I swallowed. *Mrs. Lennox* never sounded like me. *Mrs. Lennox* sounded like Richard's mother. "Yes, Louis," I said, "I have."

He looked down and bit his lip. I was about to go on when he asked, "Can we do sums now, please?"

I smiled. "Of course."

We did his sums together, papers on our laps, pencils in hand. I watched Louis's mood shift, saw his frown change to one of concentration, saw him push whatever feelings had come over him away. I looked across at him as he worked, this clever, sweet, lonely boy—this boy who could not bear to read a book his sister had loved, and who could not tell me this, because his mother must have told him not to.

No wonder he hated secrets.

CHAPTER IV

I COULDN'T SHAKE ISABELLA FROM MY MIND ALL THAT DAY. I HAD resisted the urge to ask Mrs. Eversham about her daughter, for fear of the pain it might bring her. Paul had told me all he knew—but there might be somebody else who could tell me more about her, about how Louis had taken her death. I did not quite dare to question Mrs. Pulley, and Lacey was too much of a gossip; she would only tell Mary, and it would fuel her strange mutterings about ghosts. Stevens, then. I would ask Stevens.

I purposefully came across him that night in the corridor, leaving the library just when he was passing, and he smiled at me, turned to bid me good evening.

"Wait a moment, Mr. Stevens, I—I want to ask you something." I swallowed. I had already made it seem too much, too pressing, and I feared he would think my questions presumptuous.

Still, he walked a few paces down the corridor with me, his expression all attention. "What is it, Mrs. Lennox?"

"Mrs. Welling, the vicar's wife, she—she mentioned to me that Louis had once had a sister. Forgive me for asking about it, but you have been here a long time and must have known the girl. I worry about the effect that her death has had on Louis."

Stevens hesitated, and I studied his expression. He looked torn, as though he could not decide how much to tell me, how much to keep back. When he spoke, his manner was constrained. "Mrs. Lennox, what you have heard is true. Isabella Eversham, she—" He broke off, and I saw a flash of grief in his face. "It was many years ago now, Mrs. Lennox, and Louis, I believe, has recovered. His sister is much missed, of course, but he was very young, and I do not think he remembers her clearly. You have nothing to fear, I think. The wound has healed, for him."

"It seems such a tragedy," I said.

"Yes." He hesitated, ran his hand over his chin. "Listen, Mrs. Lennox, you had better not ask Mrs. Eversham about Isabella. It will only distress her. We are not—that is, nobody in this house speaks of her."

We had reached the stairs now, and Stevens seemed keen to be rid of me, as though he thought he had already told me too much. He said quickly, "Good evening, Mrs. Lennox," and walked away.

I stood motionless in the corridor, looking after him. I thought of the book thrown to the floor in the summer house, of Louis's pained face. His wounds did not seem healed to me.

———>·<———

The next morning, I was roused by several knocks on my door. I scrambled out of bed and found Susan standing before me. I wondered if I had overslept—and then I saw her expression, hard, cold, amused.

"What time is it?" I muttered at last, for one of us must say something.

"Just after six."

"What do you want?"

"A *favor*." She smiled, shrugged. "There's something I want you to do for me."

I swallowed, waited, wishing I could slam the door on her and walk away.

"A letter came yesterday," she said, "for Mrs. Eversham." She looked at me steadily. "I want it."

I blinked. I felt suddenly sick.

"I saw Stevens put it in her study. I want to know what it says."

I steeled myself enough to ask, "Why?"

Susan scowled. "That's none of your concern, Mrs. Lennox. What *is* your concern is that you are going to get it for me. You are going to go into her study, and you are going to find it and bring it to me. The room will be locked, so you'll need to take the key from the house-keeper's office—but Mrs. Pulley sleeps until seven, so there is time, if you move fast."

I stared at Susan. I must say no—I could not possibly do as she asked. I could not betray Mrs. Eversham like that; I knew all too well, after all, what Susan liked to do with other people's letters.

And if I was caught, there would be no excuse—I would be dismissed at once, the very thing I had given her Richard's watch to prevent.

Enough. This would have to end now. I must say no—and face the consequences. I would tell Mrs. Eversham, when she came home. I would go to her, explain as much of the truth as I dared.

After all, there was one thing I must remember, one factor in my favor that might be enough to save me: Louis liked me. He would not want me to go.

Mrs. Eversham might come to a different conclusion to Susan, even if she was presented with the letter.

"I can't, Susan," I said, but I heard the weakness in my voice, how little it would take to topple my defenses.

She folded her arms. "And I say you can, and I say you must."

I opened my mouth but the words would not come.

"Hurry up," said Susan sharply, her eyes bright. "You'd better dress yourself—you have work to do."

———>·<———

My heart was pounding, my mouth dry as I dressed quickly and stepped out of the room. At the top of the stairs, I told myself I would not do it. In the entrance hall, I told myself I had too many scruples, that I was not so far gone as this. And then somehow I was descending the servants' stairs, slipping unseen into Mrs. Pulley's office. When I lifted the key to Mrs. Eversham's study from its labeled hook on the wall, I looked around once more for a key to Susan's room, thinking of my letter locked behind its sturdy frame, of all the power bound up in that one sheet of paper. But none of the keys on the wall were for the rooms in the basement, and there was still no sign of any others.

At this early hour, the corridors were empty. I trod softly as I climbed the stairs once more, as I crossed the hall to Mrs. Eversham's study.

I had been in Mrs. Eversham's study before, but it was unsettling to stand in her room when she was not there. I closed the door quietly behind me and glanced around, breathing hard.

The whole room was mahogany—dark wooden desk and chair, dark wooden paneling beneath red paint, dark wooden shelves lined with books. I saw familiar titles—*Jane Eyre, Deerbrook, The Half Sisters, Olive, The Haunted Man*. I looked down at her desk, the orderly piles of paper. The majority were covered in her own writing—pages and pages of literary reviews for newspapers, a few sheets of what seemed to be a new novel, closely written lines and crossings-out as she revised her work. My eyes fell upon one letter in another hand. It could not be the letter that Susan meant—after all, if that had arrived yesterday, it must still be unopened—but I read the last few lines poking out from beneath a stack of paper, almost without meaning to:

You must come at once. I believe I may have found—

Some part of me dearly wished to pull it from its place, to read and read, to see what I could learn about Mrs. Eversham. I thought of her words about husbands and wives, and the miniature of her dead daughter hidden in the east wing. There were so many things about this family that I did not know.

But I was not Susan. I did not wish to profit from other people's secrets.

I took in the room once more, the bookshelves, the blotting paper, the pen and ink, the stacks of Mrs. Eversham's work—and there, finally, I saw what I—what Susan—was looking for. A small cream envelope, placed neatly on the mantelpiece. I stepped forward, lifted it between my fingers.

And stopped.

I could not do it. Mrs. Eversham—changeable though she might be, unreadable though she sometimes was—had been kind to me. And if Susan truly thought something in this letter might harm Mrs. Eversham, surely it would harm Louis, too. I could not let that happen. I could not bear it.

My heart was beating fast. I stood still with the letter in my hand, thinking, listening. I turned my good ear toward the door, but I could hear no sign of anyone coming to disturb me. Still, it would not be long before the household woke. I must think quickly, act quickly.

I would lie. Yes, that was it. I would tell Susan that I had not managed to find the letter, that she must have been mistaken.

I weighed the options up in my mind. I could hide the letter somewhere else within the study—but if it was out of sight for Susan, Mrs. Eversham, too, would not find it. Or I could take it myself, keep it hidden, give it to Mrs. Eversham with some convenient lie when she returned. Whatever Susan thought it might contain, it would be safer, surely, with me.

Light was streaming into the room, and the carriage clock on the desk read seven.

I pushed the letter into the pocket of my skirts. I would have to be careful. If Susan knew I had taken it, she would get me dismissed.

I crossed the room slowly, put my ear to the keyhole before I dared open the door. I glanced in both directions, but the hall was deserted. I stepped out, closed and locked the door behind me, slipped the key back into my pocket, and breathed.

It would be all right, I told myself. Susan would not find out, and Mrs. Eversham would be safe. It was too late to save myself, but I could try my best to save her.

All I had to do now was return the key and face Susan, lie well enough for her to believe me, and keep that letter hidden.

I moved toward the servants' stairs and made my way down. At the bottom of the staircase, I glanced around the dim corridor before stepping into the housekeeper's room and replacing the key on the wall.

Next I went to the kitchen, in part to settle my nerves, in part to give myself a reason to be downstairs at all. When I asked Lacey for a cup of tea, she pursed her lips. Still, she filled the kettle and struck up a conversation—asking how I'd slept, how I was liking Hartwood, what I thought of the village when I'd been down to the church.

"It's a strange place, Mrs. Lennox, I tell you. Most of the folks down in Hartbridge are like Mary—all superstitions and rumors and goodness knows what. They can't abide the thought of this place. The way they look at me when I go down to market, and never a kind word spoken—I swear, it's enough to drive a body out of their mind."

I answered her mechanically, keeping my voice as steady as I could. I pressed the letter between my fingers in my pocket and pretended all was well.

—————>✦<—————

By eight o'clock I was frantic. I knew how to lie—I had told white lies to Richard often enough—but I was afraid of Susan. She might suspect, might search me. There was no knowing what she might do.

I waited alone at the breakfast table. As I watched the clock on the mantelpiece, time seemed to slow. One minute past eight. Two minutes past. Three.

And then the door was opening, and in came Louis, followed immediately by Susan. She looked at me and held my gaze. Then she turned suddenly to Louis as he stepped toward the breakfast table, a bright smile on her face. "Louis, I just saw a kestrel at the window—go and see."

I am not sure Louis knew what a kestrel was, but Susan's tone made him curious. He hurried toward the window on the far side of the room, his eyes wide and eager.

Susan crouched down at my right.

"Well?"

"It was not there." I kept my voice low and steady. "There was no letter."

"What?" I heard the frustration in her voice.

"It was not there, Susan. I tried, but there was nothing."

She was silent. I dared to turn a little, and saw that her brow was furrowed. "Stevens must've taken it himself," she muttered at last. "Wonder what his game is." She scowled. "You took the key back?"

I nodded. I had got this far, and I hardly dared speak again. I watched Louis at the windowsill. He had opened the window and was leaning out, trying to catch a glimpse of a bird that was not there.

Susan stood up quickly. Then she crossed the room, a wide smile on her face as she approached Louis. "No sign of it? It was there before. I'm sorry you missed it." She put her hand on Louis's shoulder, then looked back at me and smirked.

CHAPTER V

ALL THAT DAY AND THE NEXT, A LINGERING FEAR DISTRACTED ME from my lessons. I still had Mrs. Eversham's letter in my pocket; I dared not leave it in my room—after all, I knew Susan was not above searching through my things. She did not seem to suspect that I had lied to her—certainly she had not challenged me yet—but she watched me carefully. After Louis had gone to bed, I sat alone in the library, trying to read, but I could not concentrate.

I shut my book and stood up. Enough. I needed air, outdoors, something to distract me.

I tried to tell myself that I was not looking for Paul, that I was not hoping to catch sight of him in the gardens.

I walked through the courtyard, the walls of the house towering above me, and I breathed a little easier when I emerged into open air. The sky was dim and dusky, the sun a red glow behind the house. It had rained earlier, and the ground was muddy underfoot.

When I reached the woods, I took my bonnet off, held it in my hand to feel the wind in my hair, and spread my arms wide to the sky and the world. I made myself look at the trees, take in the quiet, the stillness, reminded myself that there was nothing here to be afraid of, that Susan would grow tired of tormenting me, that I would get over this feeling for Paul. I stared into the darkness and tried to steady my thoughts.

Then I glanced back to the house, a jagged silhouette in the distance, the sky darkening beyond its turrets and gables. Both the east and west wings were dim tonight, and the middle of the house, sunk back behind the courtyard, seemed only a gap, as though the house were not one but two.

I turned myself around and around, taking in the grounds, the rose garden, the topiary, the summer house, the lake, the—

I stopped. I had spun myself too fast, and when I looked back to the lake, it was gone.

And yet I'd seen something.

I was sure I had.

There, a moment ago, as the last rays of sunlight caught on the water, bright and blinding, I had seen someone. A figure standing by the lake, illuminated in the evening sun.

I squinted, blinked, but it was gone.

I stepped cautiously forward. If there had been someone there, had they had time to move? Could they have slipped into the summer house or hidden in the long grass? Surely they must still be nearby.

Otherwise—

I hurried forward, my skirts thick with mud, my boots struggling in the wet ground, up toward the summer house. I circled the lake, my eyes darting around. I kept looking over my shoulder, half sure I had heard something—a breath, a suppressed laugh, a footstep some-where behind me. But I found only empty grass and a sky growing ever darker.

When I reached the summer house, the windows were dim. I tried the door and found it locked. I lit a match, held it up, squinting to see in as the flame danced before me. But all I could see was furniture and empty patches of floor.

No one was here.

I turned back, my heart still hammering. I retraced the path back to the spot where I thought I had seen the figure. The grass was long here, and whoever it was might have lain down in it, crept away while I was searching the summer house.

I squatted down in the grass, squinting through the long blades of green.

No one was here now.

If there had been someone here, they must have hidden themself and then slipped away. *If.* But there must have been, surely—for otherwise there were only two possibilities: one, that spirits walked the earth; or two, that I was going mad.

Richard had told me once that I was too rational, that he did not think it proper for women to be like that, that God had not ordained that everything had an explanation.

I rose slowly to my feet. I would remain calm. I would steady my breathing. I would go back to the house and bolt the doors and go quietly up to bed. I would read my book and fall asleep. I would wake up tomorrow and the day would be new.

Or—

I looked north, up the hill, beyond the house, to Paul's stables, illuminated in the gloaming.

I had kept away from him this last week. I had tried my best. But tonight I wanted to be outside myself, to blot out the sight of that shadowy figure by the lake.

I wanted to feel something.

I lifted my skirts out of the mud and walked up the hill.

I stood in the doorway for half a minute before Paul noticed me. He was working on some kind of trellis, leaning over it at his workbench, his back to the door. He wore only his shirt, sleeves rolled up, trousers, and braces. His feet were bare. I watched him work, trying to tell myself that this would be enough, that it was a comfort just to look at another person, to know there was someone real, here, solid and alive, that any moment I would walk back to the house.

And then Paul turned and stared. He dropped the piece of wood in his hand.

"Margaret?"

I bit my lip. I had nothing to say, no reason for being here, aside from that I had wanted to come, that I had been afraid and now I was no longer afraid.

"What is it?" he asked.

"Nothing," I said. "Just—" I broke off, swallowed, looked down at my muddy boots. I shouldn't have come.

And then Paul said, "Oh," like he had realized something, and when I looked up, he was grinning at me, a frank, boyish smile. I felt a pang of guilt—and something else, too, a rush of something more than desire. I thought, *I could fall in love with this man*, and somehow the thought did not trouble me as much as it had before.

His smile slipped a little. "Margaret, are you all right?"

I swallowed. "I—I thought I saw someone. By the lake. I don't know, but—I could have sworn I saw . . ." I hated how shaky my voice sounded. "Someone was there one moment and gone the next."

He crossed the room toward me and put his hands gently on my shoulders. They were so warm. I hadn't noticed I was cold.

"Margaret—"

"Do you ever think that there's—I don't know—something wrong with this place?"

He was frowning. His face was close to mine. "What do you mean?"

"I have only been here a month, and sometimes I feel like I'm going mad. I keep hearing things, seeing things—things that don't make sense. All Mary's talk of ghosts and all the mystery around Isabella, the fact no one speaks of her. Everything is . . . strange here."

Paul looked at me steadily. "Am I strange?"

I gave a slight smile. "No. Not you."

"It is only a house, Margaret," he said softly. "That's all."

So I breathed in and out, told myself that it was true, that he was right, that of course I knew he was right.

Just a house.

Just people.

Just a man, in front of me, his warm hands on my skin.

I didn't want this conversation anymore. I didn't want to be myself.

So I leaned forward and kissed him.

I had my arms around him before I knew what I had done, and his hands were in my hair, my eyes shut tight. He smelled of the gardens—that familiar scent of mud and grass and summer air. His arms were warm, his hold tight. He didn't hold me like Richard had, like I was some fragile ornament, like he might break me if he tried; Paul held me like he wanted to, like the only thing in the world that mattered was his arms around me, his lips on mine.

"This is wrong," I said. I didn't pull back; I didn't even try. I stood, a breath away from him, my arms still locked around him.

"It doesn't feel it," breathed Paul. I could feel his words. Not just hear, not just see, but feel.

I said nothing. Too many reasons, too many sins.

But he was right. It did not feel wrong. It felt less wrong than anything had in a long time.

"Because you're a lady and I'm a gardener?" he whispered. "Is that it?"

"No," I murmured. "Not that."

"What then? Because you're older than me?"

That brought a smile to my lips despite myself. "Not that much older."

"What then, Margaret?"

"I'm a widow," I said, and it made me wince. I had always hated the word.

Paul pressed his lips very gently to mine. "How long?" he asked.

"Not long," I said. "Not long enough."

"Did you love him?"

I hesitated. I said, "No," and looked Paul full in the face, to see if he judged me, to see if he dared.

But he only smiled, a faint smile, and held me tighter still. His expression did not falter.

I thought of the figure by the lake, the nightmares that haunted me—and somehow that "no" seemed to give me permission. I kissed Paul again, harder this time, pressing myself against him. I felt his lips smile, felt him wind his arms around me, his hands on my back, on my arms, in my hair.

And I thought of Richard—that night, a few months into my marriage, the first time I had been too tired to hide the flinch that came automatically when he kissed me. He had pretended not to notice, had kissed me a little harder, lifted my nightdress like he always did. And afterward, lying side by side, he had asked me if I loved him.

And I said, *Of course.*

We lay in the dark and I felt Richard shift as he heard the tone of a lie in my voice. I held my breath, waiting for his sorrow, waiting for him to ask again. But when he spoke, he sounded angry, not hurt.

Because you know, Margaret, he said, *I am your husband. It would be a grave sin indeed if you did not love me.*

Now I felt Paul's body warm underneath mine, his breath hot against my neck, and I knew the mud from my skirts would be on his trousers, on the floor, on his skin. His skin. I barely knew what I was doing, only that I wanted to touch him, to be near him—that if I were with this man I would no longer belong to Richard. I would be someone else's, and perhaps if I were someone else's, I would be my own again. It was not quite enough to wash every stain off me, the stain of Richard's touch and Richard's death, of Susan's words in the music room, of the endless voice in my head telling me that this was wrong, that this was a sin, that my husband had been in the ground only two months and that it was my fault he was there, that I should never have come back here, that I should never have sought Paul out, that this was madness, insanity, entirely impossible—

But somehow I was pulling Paul closer to me, and I was unlacing my corset, tearing at my chemise, fumbling with buttons and ribbons until all our clothes lay discarded around us, and we were on the floor, my skin on his skin, his body warm beneath me.

And after that I thought no more.

CHAPTER VI

I WOKE EARLY IN MY OWN BED, MY MOUTH DRY, MY HEAD ACHING. I had forgotten to close either the window curtains or the bed curtains, and my room was filled with light.

The previous night came back to me in flashes. The smell of Paul's skin, his breath warm against my neck, the feel of the scars on his hands, his hair beneath my fingers, the cool of the floor against my legs.

Had I really done that? Had I really been so foolish?

It would not have happened, I told myself, had it not been for Susan. Her threats, the danger she posed—it was too much. And it would not have happened, either, had I not seen that figure by the lake, had I not *thought* I had seen that figure by the lake. It would not have happened if I was in my right mind.

And yet.

And yet here I was, lying in bed with a foolish grin spreading across my face.

My body ached for Paul, even now. It was new to have someone want to touch me and think well of me at once. I was used to Richard, Richard, who, even when he raged and railed against me, had still reached for me in the dark.

At least I did not have to fear getting with child—that was one consequence I knew was impossible. I thought of Richard's blank eyes, his face filled with pain, telling me that if I really loved him, God would have given us a child—as though my empty belly were simply another reminder of all the other ways I had failed him as a wife.

I rolled over in bed, pressed my face into the pillow. If anyone had seen us, if anyone were to find out—

I had been wary leaving Paul's rooms, had looked around me, walked fast. I was back in the house before Mrs. Pulley had bolted the doors. I had been as late on many other nights, walking in the grounds, and no one would know I had been doing otherwise.

I would be more careful next time.

I shook my head, made myself get out of bed. That was a foolish, dangerous thought. There must be no next time. There must never be a next time.

———→·←———

After I had washed and dressed, I went downstairs for breakfast. I was strangely composed, as though last night had cleared my mind. I would avoid Paul, conquer whatever feelings were simmering inside me. The figure at the lake was nothing—just the trick of a tired mind. I knew that, in the light of the morning, with the sun casting shadows on the floor.

And then I opened the door of the breakfast room, and stopped.

Mrs. Eversham was sitting in her usual chair, helping herself to bread and potted meat as though she had never been away.

"Good morning," I said, taking a seat across from her. "I am glad to see you back. I hope you are well?"

"Quite well."

"And your business completed?"

A flicker of sadness crossed her face. "Not as successfully as I hoped."

I thought of the letter I had seen in her study. *You must come at once. I believe I may have found—* What, or who, was she looking for? I colored at the memory and put my hand instinctively into my pocket, to where her other letter was hidden. It was none of my concern.

"Still, I am glad to be home," she said. "What have you been doing while I have been away?"

I thought of Paul's hands on my thighs, his lips on my neck. I looked down at my tea. "Louis's lessons are progressing well," I said slowly. "We have finished *The Children of the New Forest* and his French is much improved."

Mrs. Eversham nodded. "I am glad to hear it."

My fingers closed again on the contents of my pocket. I glanced toward the door—there was no sign of Susan yet, and it was still a quarter of an hour before she usually appeared with Louis. I would get it over with, rid myself of the letter and the guilt that came with it. "A letter of yours got in with mine a day or two ago," I said, handing her the envelope across the table. "I meant to give it to one of the servants this morning, but I may as well hand it to you."

She hesitated as she took it. She seemed to think my explanation, or perhaps my manner, a little strange, but the letter distracted her. I saw her inspect the postmark, then open it at once, her eyes eagerly scanning the lines. I looked away as she read, poured myself a cup of tea, tried not to watch her solemn expression.

By the time Louis arrived at the breakfast table, she had folded up the letter and was able to greet him with a bright, cheerful smile.

That morning, Louis and I worked on our French, going over tenses again and again. He was making good progress, and he seemed to like the language—certainly more than Latin.

"Would you like to go to France, Louis?" I asked, as we packed up our papers.

Louis frowned a little. "Well, yes, I should like that, but . . ." He trailed off.

"But what?"

"But we never go anywhere," said Louis.

"To be sure, you may not travel much now, but when you are no longer a little boy, when you are a man—"

"I shall always stay here," he said, and he sounded so certain, so determined in his childish way, that it pained me. His world was so very small, and it saddened me that he could not reach beyond it.

————>·<————

I did not walk in the garden that evening. Instead, after Louis had gone to bed, I went up to my own room, bolted the door, and tried to read. I had not seen Paul that day. When Louis and I took our daily walk, he had been absent, whether on purpose or by accident I could not tell. Somehow, this comforted me; if I could avoid him, if we only met once a week at church or in passing, I could stop all this before I fell too hard.

But I dreamed of Paul that night. I dreamed of his arms around me, our bodies pressed together, his lips against mine. We were not in the stables, in the dream. We were locked together in a bed, sheets tangled around our bare bodies, my face in his hair, his breath hot and quick against my neck—and then I looked up, and I realized it was not my room in Hartwood Hall but my room in the parsonage, and Richard was standing in the doorway.

CHAPTER VII

I POURED MYSELF INTO MY WORK. LOUIS AND I STARTED A NEW BOOK together—*Jane Eyre*—and puzzled over arithmetic. On the way to church that Sunday, I tried to address only Louis, not Paul, and during the service I endeavored not to glance out into the congregation. But every time I accidentally met Paul's eyes, he'd smile. It was a slight, simple smile, wrinkles around his mouth, dimples in his cheeks. It shot a mixture of guilt and pleasure through me. I made myself look away.

—⊰⊱—

One afternoon that week, I gave Louis a painting lesson. We shut ourselves up in the schoolroom with reams of paper and pots of water and a dozen brushes and paints. When the desks proved too small for Louis's ambitions, we laid out paper on the floor and lay on our fronts to work. We were painting a picture of Hartwood Hall itself, tall and imposing, gray and towering on the top of the hill, the lake in the foreground, the woods a border at the bottom of the page. It had been Louis's idea to depict Hartwood, and his idea, too, that we would do it together.

We made a game of it. I used my penknife to mend his pencils while he worked. Then he took the house and I focused on the gardens—or else we picked a color each, and everything gray and brown was my responsibility and everything green and blue was his. It was no great work, for neither of us were true artists, but it was pleasant to attempt it together, to see Louis's small hand working away at one corner of the painting while I drew long strokes across the top.

Louis had seemed happier these last few days, more content. The stormy boy from the summer house was gone, and the shadows over him seemed to have lifted. He was less painfully thin than when I had first arrived.

Sitting back as he finished the painting, watching him spread blue over the sky, I felt a surge of pride wash over me. I had been here five weeks and already I had helped him. Already he had helped me. To think what I could do here in a year, two, three.

"Look," said Louis at last. "It's finished."

I took it all in: the wide painting, the splashes of blues and greens, the twisting stone of the house. He had given the gargoyles distinctive faces and added in three figures on the lawn: himself, Mrs. Eversham, and me. I stared at it, moved beyond words—and it was then that I noticed a fourth figure, standing by the woods.

"Who is that, child?"

Louis hesitated. Then he said, "The ghost, of course. All old houses must have a ghost."

I looked down at the little pale figure, its fair hair and white dress, and I realized with a start that he had painted his dead sister into the picture, as though the house could not be complete without her. My eyes filled with tears.

"It is very beautiful," I said. "We should be proud of our work today."

Louis grinned. "Can we ask Mother if I can put it up in my bedroom?"

I glanced down at the ghostly figure, wondering what Mrs. Eversham would make of it. "I think it belongs in the schoolroom, don't you?" I said. "We can hang it above the books."

"Perfect," said Louis, and beamed at me.

CHAPTER VIII

LOUIS AND I WERE IN THE MUSIC ROOM, JUST BEGINNING A NEW duet, when I heard something—a shout, I thought, the rising cadence of an argument. We turned to each other in surprise, and then before I could stop him Louis was racing toward the door. I followed him into the corridor—I could not have judged at first where the sound had come from, but as we descended the servants' stairs, the commotion became clearer: Mary shouting, Susan's yelled replies, and the muffled lower voices of Stevens and Lacey.

When we rounded the corner, Mary was in the doorway of her own room, the others standing close around her. Mary's face was pale with anger or fear—I hardly knew which. Susan looked half annoyed, half amused. Lacey looked flustered. Her attention was all on Mary, but I saw that Stevens was watching Susan with a thoughtful expression on his face. Mary and Susan were both talking at once, their words interrupting each other so often I could hardly make out what was being said, though I did catch an "unacceptable" and "cruel" from Mary, and a "liar" from Susan.

At the sight of us, Stevens laid a hand on Mary's arm. She stopped talking, flushed redder still, and glared at Susan.

Susan glared back.

"Mrs. Lennox, Master Louis, apologies for the disruption," said Stevens. "I am sure it is only a misunderstanding—do not let this interrupt your lessons."

At my side, Louis turned, having heard another step behind us, and moved aside to let Mrs. Pulley through. Her face was set with stark disapproval.

Nearly everybody in the house was here now. I wondered that Mrs. Eversham had not heard, too.

"What is the meaning of all this noise?" asked Mrs. Pulley sternly.

Susan and Mary started speaking at once, and Mrs. Pulley raised a hand to silence them.

"One at a time—yes, Mary?"

"Look—look what she did." She spoke emphatically, moving out of the doorway. I could not help myself; I peered in along with the others.

Mary's room had been . . . upset—that was perhaps the best word. The wardrobe was open, and a few items of clothing lay discarded beneath it. The little shelf of trinkets below the high window seemed to have been knocked about; some glass beads were scattered on the floor, the window wide open above it. The bedclothes were pulled back and the mattress raised a little on the iron bedstead, as though someone had been searching underneath.

Mrs. Pulley was frowning hard.

"It was fine an hour ago," Mary was saying now, her voice fast and breathless. "I was going down to the vegetable garden for Miss Lacey and then I realized I'd forgotten my cap and it's a hot day so I came back here for it, and first my door's stuck and then I hear something like . . . like someone crashing around in there, and when the door gives, it was—like *this*. The window was shut when I left it, so whoever did it must have got out that way." She caught her breath, then rounded on Susan. "And then *she* comes in the back door and starts asking me whatever is the matter, as though it weren't *her* who had been in here, trying to—I don't know—"

"You're a liar," said Susan. Her tone was fierce, but I saw a flicker of amusement in her eyes. She was enjoying this.

There was something unnerving about the room, the scattered belongings, the open window, the pages fluttering in the wind. The window was small, set high in the wall. I would not have been able to climb through it, but Susan was scrawny, tall enough to reach it, perhaps, if she stood on the shelf. It must, surely, have been her—there was no other explanation. I wondered what she had been looking for. Something to threaten Mary with, perhaps.

"It wasn't me," said Susan, all innocence now. "I've been cleaning the flags in the courtyard all afternoon and I've only just come in." She glanced at Mrs. Pulley, then turned toward me. "Mrs. Lennox can tell you," she said, and her voice was very steady. "She saw me through the window just a few minutes ago—didn't you, Mrs. Lennox?"

I stared at her. She had no doubt that I would lie for her, that I would save her to save myself.

"Yes," I said, and felt shame run through me. "Yes, I saw you."

"Well then," said Susan, turning triumphantly back to Mary. "Can't have been me. Must have been the ghost."

Mary flinched.

"You saw her?" Mrs. Pulley repeated, turning to me.

I swallowed. "Yes."

Stevens was staring at me. He, I thought, did not believe me. The corridor suddenly felt very crowded. I tried to breathe, to calm myself. I looked down at Louis and made myself squeeze his shoulder. He looked a little afraid, gazing past the others into Mary's disordered room.

"Told you," said Susan. "It was—"

"Quiet, Susan. We shall have no more nonsense about ghosts." Mrs. Pulley's expression was unreadable, her eyes hard. "There will be a perfectly rational explanation. Mary, you must have left your window open. Perhaps an animal or—"

"But—"

One look from Mrs. Pulley silenced Mary. She stood still, scowling at Susan.

"I am sure you all have work to do," Mrs. Pulley went on. "Master Louis, Mrs. Lennox, you will have lessons to attend to." She turned back to Mary and said, with an almost imperceptible change in tone, "You may take the rest of the afternoon off, Mary, to put your room back to rights." Mrs. Pulley nodded, as though to dismiss us, and marched back to the housekeeper's room.

Lacey went back to the kitchen, muttering to herself, and Stevens headed down the corridor. I led Louis back upstairs, but glancing over my shoulder, I saw Mary and Susan still standing in the corridor. Mary's face was flushed with anger—and, behind it, perhaps, fear. She stared at Susan, lost for words, and then she retreated into her bedroom and slammed the door in Susan's face.

—————————⟶⟵—————————

That evening, after Louis had gone to bed, I ran into Mr. Stevens in the corridor. I was coming from the music room, he from the drawing room, and we walked together for a few paces.

"I hope you are settling in well, Mrs. Lennox," he said. "You have been with us—what, nearly six weeks now?"

"That's right."

He smiled, but his smile was a little hesitant. "This afternoon was out of the ordinary," he said, after a moment. "I shouldn't like you to imagine the household is often in such chaos." He paused, and panic rippled through me. "Mary is a little nervous, at times. She and Susan have never taken to each other. If you had not seen Susan outside, I should have almost thought that . . ."

He left the sentence unfinished, waiting for me to end it, to correct him, to tell him that I had not seen Susan. I thought of the day I had seen the two of them talking at the foot of the stairs, the fear in Stevens's expression.

Was it really possible that he knew exactly what Susan was like?

Stevens was looking at me sideways, as though he saw everything I meant to hide.

I met his gaze and kept my voice steady. "Yes, it is most strange."

We were at the foot of the stairs now. He turned toward me, a half-agitated smile on his pale, lined face. "You must tell me, Mrs. Lennox," he said, "if there is ever anything troubling you at Hartwood Hall. You might find I am able to help."

He looked very earnest, but anxious, too, I thought; he meant every word but was afraid I might confide in him. Instead I stepped back, forced a smile. "Thank you, Stevens. I am not easily frightened, I assure you. It would take a lot to unsettle me."

He looked half disappointed, half relieved. "I am glad to hear it," he said, as he turned away.

Climbing the stairs, I thought over my words. I *was* easily frightened these days—but what, after all, was another lie after one far worse? And it had been true once, a long time ago, before everything, before Richard. I had once been hard to discompose, hard to scare. The person I was three years ago would not have started at shadows by the lake or thought she heard ghosts in the east wing. She would have turned to Susan and fought back.

I went into my room and sat down heavily on the bed. It seemed like a lifetime ago that I had been that other person. I had lost her somewhere along the way, and I did not know how to find her. She was dead and buried, like my husband, and I could not get her back.

CHAPTER IX

I SLEPT ILL THAT NIGHT, AND WOKE LONG BEFORE THE DAWN. WHEN the sun finally broke through, I rose from my bed and crossed the room. The grounds beneath my window were half in darkness, half in sun. I watched the line between shadow and light move for a few minutes, looking out at the miles of woodland beyond the gardens, stretching on into the distance.

I looked back to the grounds, the neat path around the house, the rose garden beneath my window. And there was Paul.

It could scarcely have been much after seven, but he was leaning over the rosebushes, pruning them, a look of steady concentration on his face. I watched him, his careful movements. Each wilting flower he plucked he put in a sack beside him, collecting them like they ought to be savored. I wondered if other gardeners worked with such reverence.

And then he looked up, and his eyes met mine.

I ought to have moved from the window. I ought to have stepped back, shut the curtains, returned to bed. I knew that. But somehow I stayed where I was, in my nightgown, watching him look up at me.

He smiled.

And even though I had been avoiding him, even though I had told myself that I must put distance between us, even though I knew that I must end this before it truly began—all I wanted was to see him.

I had not been drawn to someone in this way since I was Paul's age, perhaps younger. In my first position as a governess, there had been a dancing master who had filled my head for months. But it had never been quite like this. I had never been so irresistibly caught.

I dressed quickly, tying my stays and chemise with shaking fingers, pulling on the first black dress I found. I opened my door quietly, stepped out into the corridor, and moved down the stairs as softly as I could. The hall was still dark, the occasional streak of sunlight making the dust glow gold. I paused on the stairs, listening, but heard nothing. The house seemed quiet, as though everyone else was still asleep.

I eased back each bolt on the front doors. I turned the key in the lock. I stepped out into the cool morning air.

Paul was not in the rose garden. I had to walk once around the whole house before I found him, standing in the doorway of his rooms in the stables. He watched me approach.

"Good morning." He grinned at me. "I wasn't sure if you'd come."

I swallowed. "Nor was I."

He stepped back into the room, held the door open for me. I followed him inside.

I do not know what I had expected. The hurry and flurry of last time, perhaps, him reaching for me, our hands and bodies meeting. Instead I felt suddenly awkward, standing in the corner as he lit the stove beneath the kettle.

"What's the matter?" he asked, as he set two teacups down on the table. "You look pale. Couldn't you sleep?"

He was looking at me very steadily, and I swallowed. He signaled for me to sit down, but I leaned against the table instead, feeling my cheeks flush.

"It's this house, I think," I said. "I like Hartwood Hall, I do—Louis is the perfect pupil and in some ways it is an ideal situation but—" I broke off, frowned. "Hartwood Hall is a strange place. To have such a grand house, half shut up and in such a state of disrepair—for there to be so few servants—the way the people down in the village view

Hartwood—and then for Louis to have never had a governess before, for him to so rarely leave the grounds. It is all . . . irregular." And Susan, of course, although I could not tell Paul about that.

He was standing right in front of me now, and somehow his hands found their way to my waist. It sent a kind of thrill through me, almost made me lose my train of thought.

"Margaret, Mrs. Eversham has had a hard life. It is not so very strange that a wealthy widow should choose to live a retired, secluded life, especially after the death of a child. You must see that."

"Of course, but—"

"But nothing, Margaret. She is a good woman. That is all."

His hands on my waist were warm, soft, and his eyes were fixed on mine. "You have a lot of respect for her," I said.

"Of course I do. So should you."

"I do, but—"

He kissed me. Not hungrily like the last time. Softly. Tenderly. He pulled me into him, wrapped his arms around me, and his warmth seemed to spread through my body. It would be so easy to slip into this, to fall headfirst.

"We shouldn't, Paul," I murmured.

"Perhaps not," he said, and his voice shook. "But here you are."

His lips were warm, his hold steady. I put my arms around his neck. I kissed him harder. I closed my eyes, felt his hands in my hair, his lips on my throat. I pulled him to me, as though I could not get close enough. All my resolutions of the last week were vanishing fast. I knew only that I wanted this, his hands on me, his lips on my skin. I wanted to live in this moment and forget all the rest.

I opened my eyes, wanting to look at him in all his beauty.

And I saw something else.

A figure framed in the window. A face looking in at us.

"Paul."

He looked up at me, hearing the panic in my voice. "What?"

"There's someone out there."

He turned, followed my eyes to the window. The windows were grimy, and I was less certain now, but surely, surely, there was someone out there.

Someone had seen us.

We would both lose our places.

I would lose Hartwood Hall, would lose Louis.

Unless it was Susan. Susan cared for money more than morals. If she had seen us, she would not tell. She would only ask for more.

I was not sure which I feared most.

Paul moved toward the window, squinting out into the morning light. "I can't see anyone," he said. He hesitated, then marched toward the door, thrust it open before I could say anything, before I could hide, and stepped outside. He closed the door behind him.

Alone, I drank the tea we had forgotten about, tried to tidy my hair. I felt sick. I did not know how I had been so very, very foolish.

Paul was gone for several minutes. I saw him pass by the window once, but that was all. The grounds seemed empty now. I tried to listen for his footsteps outside but heard nothing. At last the door clicked and he appeared once more.

"There's no one there," he said. "I promise."

"But I saw someone."

He shook his head. "If anyone was there, they are gone now." He moved toward me, reached for my hand. I flinched away.

"Paul, don't you understand? If we've been seen—dear God, we must both be mad! We could both lose our positions."

"Margaret—"

"What would you do?" I asked him sharply. "You have been here longer than me. What would you do if you lost your place?"

He said nothing. He looked down at his boots. "I don't think I would," he said slowly.

I wondered why he seemed so certain—whether it was because he had been here longer or because he was a man. A sudden surge of anger ran through me. "But I would! Paul, this is ridiculous. I should never have come. The risk is too great. We can't—I can't—"

His face fell. I saw something like confusion, like pain in his expression, and it made my heart ache. He reached out for me, and I pulled back.

"But—"

"I have to go, Paul."

I pushed past him toward the door.

"Margaret, wait—" His voice sounded choked, but I did not let him finish. I closed the door hard behind me.

I walked slowly back to the house. I went the long way around, so that it would seem to anyone who came across me that I had just been out walking, taking the morning air. I made myself not look back. I told myself it was over, that whatever glimpse of love this had been, it was too risky, too dangerous.

I let myself in through the front doors and closed the bolts behind me. I stepped softly up to my own room and washed my face to hide the tears.

CHAPTER X

I WAS IN THE LIBRARY, GOING OVER *JANE EYRE*, REFRESHING MYSELF with the chapters Louis and I were to cover in our next lesson, when Susan came in. I did not hear the door open, but a sound made me look up. She stood in the doorway, watching me read. I shivered. I had been trying to avoid her, but she had a habit of always being there when least expected. I wondered if this was it, if she had seen Paul and me, if she was about to ask for more.

"Susan?"

A smile rose to her lips. She stepped inside, closed the door behind her, and sat down next to me. She said nothing. She did nothing. She merely sat there, watching.

"Susan, what do you want?"

Again, she said nothing. She sat quite still, her gaze not leaving my face. She looked at me as she always did, fierce and steady, eyes like a challenge.

Then she reached into her pocket and pulled out something small and round and gold. She held it up between her fingers, shutting one eye as though to look through it. An old, worn wedding ring. The ring I had found in the lake. "Came across this in your room," said Susan, with something like a smile. "Not yours, is it?"

"I found it," I said.

"Well, I found it, too. Thought I might keep it."

I said nothing, though my face burned. I supposed I had no more right to it than her, but I hated the thought of Susan rifling through my drawers when she was supposed to be cleaning my room.

"What do you want from me, Susan?"

She looked at me steadily for a moment, then shrugged. "I want . . . information, I suppose," she said at last.

I stared at her. "What—?"

"Listen, tell me—and you had better tell me; I shall know if you're lying—does Louis ever speak about his sister?"

That threw me. "What has that to do with anything?"

"So you *have* heard then, about the girl?" Her voice sounded different now, curious, less fierce.

I thought of how I had asked Stevens about Isabella a few days ago, and felt a moment's shame—true, I had asked for Louis, because I wanted to help him, but that did not change the fact that I, too, wanted to *know*.

"Does Louis talk about her," Susan went on, "about how she died?"

"No." I kept my voice as steady as I could. "He has never spoken of her." It was, after all, almost the truth.

She narrowed her eyes. "But you know?"

"I—I have heard about it, yes."

Susan frowned. She looked disappointed, but not as though she did not believe me. "Have you never thought," she said, "that there's something *strange* about this family?"

I blinked. I wondered what she knew about Isabella's death that I did not. I wondered if she had gone back to Mrs. Eversham's study after I had failed her, if she had searched the papers there, discovered some grave secret. I wondered what on earth she would do with it, and I felt a prickle of fear run through me.

"You think *you've* a lot to hide, Mrs. Lennox, but you're not the only one. What if I told you I have it all lined up? What if I told you that this family, this house, is going to come crashing down?"

"Susan, I don't know what you—"

She stood up abruptly, hurriedly took a cloth from her apron, and began to dust the bookshelves. I stared at her in amazement for a moment until the door opened and Mrs. Pulley appeared.

"Susan, you're wanted downstairs," she said, in the same cool voice she always used. She did not look at me, but Susan did; as she followed Mrs. Pulley to the door, she glanced back, held a finger up to her lips, and left.

I did not want to stay in the library after that. I looked for Louis and Mrs. Eversham, hoping the sight of them together would push Susan's speculations from my mind and remind me why I was here, that I was valued, that I had a future at Hartwood Hall. I moved from the music room to the drawing room, the morning room to the parlor, but I could not find them anywhere. They would be upstairs, no doubt, in Mrs. Eversham's room, where I could not follow.

I went to my own room and bolted the door behind me. I lay back on my bed, shut my eyes, and let images of Susan and Richard haunt my dreams.

On the way to church that Sunday, I avoided Paul's eyes. I tried not to speak to him directly. I kept my eyes and my thoughts on Louis, forcing a stream of conversation between us all the way, asking him how he was enjoying *Jane Eyre* and quizzing him on Bible verses, turning the conversation again when he tried to ask Paul about flowers and birds.

I was all too aware of Paul. I could not move without noticing him; I could not keep him out of view. He was listening to our conversation. I could tell from every movement of his arm or slight inclination of his head. He did not turn, did not look at me, but he listened. My cheeks were flushed all the way to the village.

When Paul pulled up outside the church, he said nothing, but he jumped down from the front of the cart and held out a hand to help Louis and me down. Louis took it. I did not—but Paul waited for me, trying to catch my gaze. I would not let myself look at him. I would not let myself feel.

We sat quietly in church, Louis and I, Mrs. Welling at our side. We listened to the service, murmured familiar words, and I let the loudness of it, the sound and noise and glory, wash over me.

Forgive us our trespasses.

I thought of Richard, his gaunt frame lying motionless in our marital bed.

Lead us not into temptation.

Paul, his blue eyes, his warm hands and broad smile, the feel of his weight against me.

Deliver us from evil.

Susan, her watchful stare, her fingers twitching the chain of Richard's watch.

I turned, almost without meaning to, and looked out into the congregation. Paul was not looking at me. He was looking toward the front of the church, and he looked so sad, so solemn, that all I wanted was to step down from the box and put my hand in his.

I shut my eyes and prayed.

I would conquer this love, this infatuation—whatever it was I felt for Paul. I would get over my fear of Susan. I would stay here and make Hartwood Hall my home, keep watch over Louis, build myself a better life. I could do it, I was sure.

I prayed to God that I could do it.

———>·<———

And then, ten days later, everything changed.

CHAPTER XI

It was a quarter to eight in the morning, just as I was sleepily fastening my dress, when there came a soft knock on my door. I finished the buttons hurriedly and rushed to open it. There stood Louis in his nightshirt, bleary-eyed and red-faced, his mouth curled into a frown.

"Whatever is the matter, child?" I said gently, kneeling down to his height.

"Susan didn't come," said Louis. "I waited and waited but she didn't come. And I can't dress myself because I can't reach all the buttons. And Susan always combs my hair and Mama says I do not do it well myself. And now I shall be late for breakfast and lessons, but—"

"I will help you, Louis. You needn't worry." I stepped back to retrieve my shoes, pulled them quickly on, then held out my hand for his. "Susan must have overslept, that is all. Come."

He led me along the corridor to his bedroom. Just as we were about to enter, I saw Mrs. Pulley turn the corner, her footsteps silent as she moved toward us. I explained that Susan had not come for Louis this morning.

Mrs. Pulley always looked grave, but there was something more particular today in her expression. "Susan is unwell," she said shortly. She spoke in a soft voice—I suppose hoping that Louis might not hear, but it only made it harder for me to do so. "In truth, Mrs. Lennox, I am afraid she may be very ill. It would be wise for both you and Master Louis to avoid the kitchen and the servants' quarters today."

I stared at Mrs. Pulley. I rarely heard her speak so many words together, and it unsettled me. I thought of Susan, this girl who had caused me so much pain and fear, lying shaking and shuddering in bed. I could not help a guilty flicker of relief.

"Let me know if there is anything I can do. I'll help Louis to dress."

She nodded. "Thank you." She gave me what I supposed to be an attempt at a smile, tight and forced, then moved off down the corridor.

In Louis's bedroom, I saw that he had brought his clothes out of the wardrobe himself. He had got as far as unbuttoning his shorts and shirt and then stopped. Again, I thought what a strange child he was, sometimes so far beyond his years—at times like this, so far below.

I helped him to dress. It had been among my duties to do so in one or two places and I was no stranger to little cravats and shirts and jackets. As I was teaching him how to fasten his shirt himself, I was surprised to see a long scar running the length of his back. It looked deep, a thin red gouge in his skin.

"Where did you get that scar?" I asked him, as he pulled on his waistcoat and I tightened the back.

He was silent for a few moments and I wondered if I'd been wrong to ask. But he said, at last, "I don't remember," and then, "Mama won't tell me, but Bella said—" He broke off, confused.

"Your sister?" I said carefully. I ought to have left it alone, not pressed him further, but I had lived for nearly two months in this house of secrets and I wished to know. I thought of Susan, trying to find out if Louis ever spoke of his sister, and I felt ashamed that I had asked.

Louis was looking at me now, his eyes wide. "You know about Bella? But she's a secret."

I said nothing. I waited.

Then, "She's not here anymore, but I see her sometimes."

"You see her?"

"Sometimes. When I'm sleeping or—when it's dark, I can see her.

In the woods, that time, after we'd had dinner with Mr. and Mrs. Welling, I thought I saw her, in the trees. And she said, once, a long time ago, that the scar was because Father threw something at me, because Father was a devil."

I felt suddenly and terribly cold.

"Bella was my friend," said Louis.

And then he began to cry.

In all the time I had been there, I had never seen Louis cry. He was the sort of child to face his fears, to talk eagerly about a lesson he had struggled over a moment before, to put on a brave face if he fell down. Even in the darkness of the woods that night, he had held my hand lightly, though he saw the shade of his dead sister among the trees.

The thought of Louis seeing Isabella's ghost in the woods unsettled me, but not as much as the thought of his father, Mrs. Eversham's late husband, hurting him.

"Come, child," I said gently. I knelt down, put my arms around him. "It's all right now. It's all right."

He sniffed and coughed, and as I drew him toward me his forehead was sticky and hot against my cheek. He put his arms around me, sniffing and sobbing, his face crinkled and red, his eyes wet.

"Hush, Louis," I said, drawing back from him. "Tell me what the matter is. You must miss your sister."

He nodded. He was breathing hard, trying to calm himself, and I saw him blinking back his tears. The violent sobbing had begun to subside, but still the boy looked miserable. "Sometimes I don't remember her," he murmured.

"Do you remember your father?"

"No. I remember Bella telling me about him. That's all. Mama never speaks of him."

"Some marriages are unhappy, you know, Louis," I said gently.

"Mama's afraid of him."

"It does us no good, Louis, to be afraid of the dead."

He sniffed again, hard. He wiped his eyes on his shirt.

"Are you well again now?"

He nodded, but I could see he did not trust himself to speak.

"Shall we go down to breakfast?"

A pause. And then, muffled, "Mother mustn't know."

"That you've been upset? Well, not if you don't want her to. Come, we'll wash your face and no one will be any the wiser."

———>×<———

We were late to breakfast in the end, but nobody seemed to notice. By the time we got downstairs, the whole house was in disarray. Paul had ridden into the village for Dr. Rogers and brought him back, and Susan was pronounced to have the measles. Lacey and Mary had come up from the kitchen and were talking in whispers with Mrs. Pulley and Mr. Stevens in the hall; I couldn't hear what they said, but Louis asked me in a timid voice, "Is Susan going to die?"

"Hush. Of course not."

Still, I felt something shift inside me. It was unlikely that a healthy young woman like Susan would be in very grave danger from such an illness, but if she was out of the way, even just for a week or two, it would be a welcome respite.

Mrs. Eversham was pacing up and down the breakfast room. She turned to look solemnly at Louis and warned us both to avoid the servants' quarters.

"Have you ever had the illness, Mrs. Lennox?"

I shook my head.

"Nor have I, nor has Louis. Mrs. Pulley and Lacey have had it as children and should be relatively safe. Stevens and Carter can keep their distance. I have told Lacey to send Mary away—she has never been strong—but she has no family and I hardly know where she'll go." She swallowed. "If you wish to leave for a time, we shall all understand."

I had nowhere to go any more than Mary did. I thought of Cornelia's letter, the "home" she had offered me, and balked at the idea. "I shall stay," I said, "if you will have me."

She nodded and the relief was clear in her face. "Thank you."

After a quick breakfast—even Louis seemed to have lost his appetite—I tried to carry on our lessons with some pretense at normality. Louis still seemed upset. Every now and then he'd sniff and rub his eyes, and his concentration seemed to wane.

And then, halfway through arithmetic, he fell asleep at his desk. When I leaned over him, I felt his forehead again, hot, sticky—and where earlier I had assumed it was a product of his sudden tearfulness, now I felt panic creep over me.

I ran to the bell and rang it hard.

I tried to rouse him. I shook his shoulders gently, as he coughed and spluttered himself awake. I splashed water on his face from the jug on my desk and tried to get him to speak to me, but he only moaned and put his head back on his arms, splayed before him on the table.

"Come, child," I said, tugging at his arm. "Louis, it's all right. Tell me what hurts."

I heard a noise and turned to see Mrs. Pulley in the doorway. The flicker of displeasure on her face for having been summoned was gone in a moment, and her eyes widened.

"Step back, Mrs. Lennox."

She spoke loudly, authoritatively, but I didn't move.

"Mrs. Lennox, you are in danger. Step back. The boy is ill."

"But—"

"Mrs. Lennox," she said, more softly now, "you will do him no good if you are ill yourself. Step back and leave him to me."

I stood back from Louis, my heart thumping, my head in a whirl. He was such a thin, little child. Measles had killed or maimed stronger children than him. It had torn through families my father had treated when I was a girl, had been death to the friends of my younger years.

My stomach churned, but I stood back, helpless, useless, as Mrs. Pulley lifted Louis in her arms and carried him from the room.

VOLUME THREE

CHAPTER I

"Now," said Dr. Rogers, "I need you to all listen to me very carefully."

The household had been summoned to the entrance hall—all of us except Lacey, who was upstairs, watching Louis and Susan. Mrs. Eversham looked pale and overwrought, and I could see her hands shaking with agitation. Mrs. Pulley was as inscrutable as always. Stevens looked a little anxious, Mary as though she had seen another ghost. I was standing near the back of the hall, angled toward the doctor so I could listen carefully. Paul was just behind me, and I tried not to look round at him, tried to quell that urge to turn to him, put my hand in his, pull him close. I knew that if I looked at him, I would see it on his face—that concern, that worry, that love of Louis we shared. I could not bear the thought of Louis unwell. It hit me now, the full force of how much I had come to care for him.

"It is imperative that you do not allow the contagion to spread any further than it has," the doctor went on. "Measles can be dangerous, but recovery is probable if it is managed correctly. You should all feel hopeful. But if every person in this house sickens, the chance of adequate treatment and therefore recovery are far slimmer. Every one of you, as far as at all possible, must avoid all contact with the two patients upstairs. Miss Lacey and Mrs. Pulley, who I understand have had the disease before, will be to a certain extent protected against future attacks, but must still be careful. Stuff your nose with tobacco, rue, or tansy when entering the sickrooms, to keep the miasma off.

For the rest of you, you must keep away entirely. For the next fortnight, certainly for the next week, you must not visit the patients. I will come here when I can and will let you know when it is safe."

As he spoke, his eyes lingered on Mrs. Eversham. She was standing in front of me, so I could not see her face, but I saw her twist the cuffs of her sleeves hard between her fingers, as though she were in physical pain.

"Do you understand what I am saying, Mrs. Eversham? You cannot see your son."

There was a moment's silence and then she nodded. She said, "I understand," and her voice was hoarse.

The doctor continued. "We must confine the illness to as small a section of the house as possible. Susan has already been moved to a room opposite Master Eversham's, and I must warn all of you, emphatically, to avoid that end of the corridor upstairs. With your permission, Mrs. Eversham, I would suggest we implement a kind of barrier—chairs, tables, whatever you can spare, to block off the far end of the corridor." He gave a slight, almost involuntary smile. "Such a barricade can hardly fend off any miasma, but it will remind you all to go no further."

"Mrs. Eversham's bedroom is beyond Louis's," said Mrs. Pulley.

The doctor turned to Mrs. Eversham. "You will have to move, ma'am. You have a room spare?"

"Yes." She said nothing more, as though she could not trust herself to speak.

"Very good. Move any things you require as soon as possible, but after that, do not return to your room. I would also advise that one room on that corridor becomes a washroom. If there is a spare basin, bring it, and as much soap as you have in the house. Mrs. Pulley, you and Miss Lacey, whenever you move from one half of the corridor to the next, must wash your hands and change your clothes, and no one must wash your clothes except yourselves. Do you understand?"

In front of me, Mrs. Pulley nodded once.

"I will be here as often as I can, but the best thing possible would be for you to hire a nurse to care for the patients, and to confine that nurse to the far end of the west wing."

I saw Stevens glance round at Mrs. Pulley here, and she seemed to look at Mrs. Eversham in turn. Mrs. Eversham's hands had started to shake.

"Try anyone known as a midwife first—I can give you some names—but any competent village girl should suffice. All we need is somebody who has had the illness before and who can take instruction from me." He looked over the group, taking in each of our faces. "Do you all understand what you must do?"

I nodded. I saw the others around me nod, though Mrs. Eversham's movement was barely perceptible.

Dr. Rogers pulled out his watch, frowned. "I had better check again on the patients, and there are others in the neighborhood I must see today. I will return tomorrow morning to see how they fare."

And then he was gone, up the stairs with a sure step.

The group in the hall dispersed. Mary left quickly, heading for the servants' stairs as though she could not get away from the rest of us fast enough. Paul glanced at me before turning to leave, and I steadily avoided his gaze.

I heard Stevens say, "What are we going to do about a nurse?"

He was standing close by Mrs. Pulley and Mrs. Eversham, at the foot of the stairs.

"I don't know," said Mrs. Eversham. Her voice was hoarse, thin. "I can't think."

"Is it really necessary to bring in an outsider? If we think of the risks . . ."

It was only then I realized they did not know I was still here, that they thought I had left with the others. I hesitated, unsure what to do, whether to move, to announce my presence. I did not want to be caught eavesdropping.

Mrs. Pulley spoke now. "I am sure if I were to nurse them myself, Lacey might manage the household."

Stevens was shaking his head. "There will be too much to do already, with Susan unwell, and if Mary is sent away . . ."

"Surely we can manage," said Mrs. Eversham. She seemed on the verge of tears. "To think of a stranger here, one of those Hartbridge gossips, and when Louis is ill and might not be . . ." She shifted her weight from one foot to the other, and as she did, she caught sight of me, still standing in the hall. She started, and the others turned. Stevens was pale, and Mrs. Pulley looked at me warily.

"We are trying to work out whether or not to hire a nurse," Mrs. Eversham said at last.

I frowned. Mrs. Eversham was private, of course, and she did not think highly of the village—I knew all of that—and yet it seemed unthinkable that she should let such a prejudice, such a whim, stand in the way of her son's recovery.

"But surely there is no question if that is the doctor's recommendation," I said.

They all looked at me. They must have heard the surprise in my voice. I saw Mrs. Eversham breathe in. "Yes," she said, and her voice cracked. "Mrs. Lennox is quite right. We will do just as the doctor says."

—⟩✦⟨—

Within the hour, Mrs. Pulley had left for the village to try to find a nurse. I sent with her a note to pass to Mrs. Welling, explaining the trouble up at Hartwood Hall, and asking for her assistance if she knew anyone who might help.

In Mrs. Pulley's absence, Stevens took charge, and he and Paul began to carry chairs upstairs to bar the west-wing corridor. I was left with Mrs. Eversham.

She seemed scarcely capable of standing, let alone thinking clearly. I all but forced her into the chair in her study, made her drink a cup of tea. I tried to reassure her—and myself—that many children survived measles, that both Mrs. Pulley and Lacey had come through it, that as the doctor had said, we had every reason to hope. There was no immediate cause for alarm.

"Can I do anything?" I asked. "Might I move your things for you to one of the spare rooms upstairs? What do you need?"

She seemed to catch my kind meaning—that if I did it for her, she would not have to pass by the sickrooms, be so close to Louis and unable to reach him. Mechanically she listed belongings: a few dresses and undergarments, her hand mirror and comb, the book on her bedside table. She trailed off after a few items. "I am sure that will do, Mrs. Lennox." She looked up at me, smiled weakly. "Thank you."

Upstairs, the corridor already smelled of the sickroom. I could taste the vinegar in the air; the harsh scent of it almost masked the smell of bile. Stevens and Paul had lined chairs up against each other, leaving only a small gap to act as a path for the doctor and whatever nurse we might manage to find. Through the open door of the nearest room, I saw an old, chipped washstand, a few hard bars of soap lined up along the top.

There was a pouch of tobacco left on one of the chairs, and I stuffed up my nose with it—it was uncomfortable, the smell intoxicatingly unpleasant. I must get this task over with as soon as I could.

I passed down the corridor quickly. The other doors were closed, but I knew where Louis slept, knew which room Susan had been placed in. I felt queasy as I passed those barred doors, and then I heard a cough, distinct and hoarse. I had a sudden image of him, his face worn, his eyes bleary. Louis in pain, Louis suffering. I thought of the scar on his back, of what he had said about his father, his sister. What a life this child must have led. So full of loss and pain.

I pushed that thought away. He would be well again soon—of course he would. And as for Susan—well, I did not know what I felt about her illness. If she was unwell in bed, out of sight, then I was safe. No more questions, no more threats. And now that she had been moved to a new room, I might even manage to find an opportunity to search her old chamber for my letter. I felt a kind of cruel longing for her to stay where she was, to give me a week or two of relief at least. But a twinge of guilt followed. If Louis's life had been short and hard, Susan's must have surely been so, too. I knew little of her experiences before Hartwood Hall, but I did not think she could have acted as she had done had she not disliked her life, had she not been reaching for something else, something more.

I tried to focus on the task in hand as I opened the door to Mrs. Eversham's room and stepped quickly inside. I had never been inside her bedchamber before, but I barely took in the neat bookshelves, the red walls, the fine carpet. I gathered clothes from her wardrobe, items from her dressing table, picked up the volume of *Dombey and Son* from beside her bed. Then I carried my bundle down the corridor, refusing to look at those shut doors. I heard Lacey's voice from behind one and made myself keep walking.

After I had rid myself of the tobacco and scrubbed my hands, I headed to the spare bedchamber beside the schoolroom. I hung Mrs. Eversham's clothes in the empty wardrobe and left her things in the dresser.

→ ⋅ ←

For the rest of the afternoon, Mrs. Eversham and I stayed together in her study. We tried to read, to sew, to talk through our worries for Louis as though it might comfort us. Mrs. Eversham even tried to write. She told me she was supposed to deliver a short story to a London magazine next week, and sat with her pen poised, staring at blank pages for half an hour, before laying her papers down in frustration.

I kept thinking of Isabella. There was no doubt that Mrs. Eversham was an anxious mother, and how much worse must it be to see a child weaken and sicken when one child had already been lost? Isabella, too, had been taken ill, so it was not hard to imagine what Mrs. Eversham must be feeling.

Every now and then, Mrs. Eversham would rise, pace the hall, check the clocks, and wonder why Mrs. Pulley had not yet returned, or call up from the foot of the stairs to Lacey, to ask if she had any news. Lacey would shout down that the patients were just as they were, that Susan was complaining, that Louis was tired, all in a tone that made it clear she did not relish her current tasks.

I was as restless as Mrs. Eversham. I tried to leave the room once, but she called me back, asked me to stay. She was my mistress, I little more than an elevated servant—and yet we stayed at each other's side, because we both loved the child lying in bed upstairs.

CHAPTER II

At six o'clock, Mrs. Pulley finally returned. Her face was as grave as always, but there was a new tinge of sadness in her eyes as she reported to us in the study.

"Well, Ruth?"

I had never heard Mrs. Eversham call Mrs. Pulley by her Christian name before, and I must confess it surprised me. She was not the sort of woman one thought of as having a Christian name.

Mrs. Pulley only shook her head.

"No help?" Mrs. Eversham's voice was strained. "None at all?"

"Mrs. Welling and I did our best," said Mrs. Pulley gravely. She glanced toward me. "Your friend was most helpful, Mrs. Lennox. She has offered their house as a safe place for Mary to stay for the time being—and for you, too, ma'am, should you wish it."

I was pleased to hear that Mrs. Welling had been generous. Still, I shook my head. "I will remain."

She nodded once, then turned to Mrs. Eversham. "We went to every house Mrs. Welling could think of where there might be women in need of work—first to the midwives Dr. Rogers had given us names of, then those who we knew had nursed sick children of their own, next to any we thought the most desperate, but—" She broke off, shook her head.

"They are all afraid of contagion, I suppose," I said slowly.

"I do not think it is that. Several of the women I spoke to have had the measles themselves, and I dare say had it been someone in the village . . ." She glanced at Mrs. Eversham. "Nobody wishes to come here," she said plainly. I had never seen her flustered before, but I heard the catch in her voice. "Mrs. Welling offered to come herself and nurse the child, but she has never had the illness and I could not in good conscience let her risk it."

Mrs. Eversham raised her hands to her face in exasperation. When she looked up, I saw tears in her eyes. "And so these people will let a child and a young woman die because they suspect me, because they distrust this house?" She spoke loudly, and I heard the anger in her voice. "Because they believe in ghosts and spirits and curses? Or because they think I am a woman of low character, that I have never had a husband? Dear God, are these the people we live among!"

There was an appalled silence. Mrs. Pulley stared at the floor, and I did not know where to look. Despite myself, my eyes strayed to Mrs. Eversham's hand, her plain wedding ring. Was it possible that it was a sham, that she had never been married? Was that the secret Susan had hoped to find in her mistress's letters? I shook the thought away. Whatever Mrs. Eversham was not telling me, this was no time to dwell on it.

Before any of us had a chance to speak, there came a knock on the study door. Mrs. Eversham called wearily, "Come in."

The door was pulled back and Mary appeared in the entrance. "Someone's come about being a nurse," she said. "She's here in the hall."

We all stared. Mrs. Pulley moved at once, stepped into the doorway. I saw her shoulders start, and I was just about to follow her out of the room when she closed the study door quickly behind her. I heard the sound of rapid voices moving further away, though I could not make out the words.

I looked across at Mrs. Eversham. She had sunk back into her chair and raised her hands to her forehead. "At last," she muttered.

The voices in the hall were growing louder and I caught the words "but surely it is not—" from Mrs. Pulley, suddenly distinct. I recognized her voice, and yet the tone was one I had never heard from her before—not angry exactly, not demanding. No, her voice was traced with fear.

I moved quickly to the door and wrenched it open. The voices fell quiet, and both women turned to look at me. Mrs. Pulley's lips parted in a silent O, her brow furrowed. She wore an expression I could not read: dismay, annoyance, confusion. Her right hand was clenched into a fist.

Beside her stood a stranger, a woman I had never seen before. She was pale, with fair hair and blue eyes. She was simply but neatly attired, in a light-gray stuff dress with white trimmings. From her face I might have thought her nearer forty than thirty, but her slight frame, short stature, and girlish figure made it hard to tell. She, like Mrs. Pulley, looked startled—but there was a determination in her face that puzzled me. Mrs. Pulley had dropped her eyes, but this woman met my gaze steadily.

And then Mrs. Eversham was at my side. She was wide-eyed and staring, her face flushed.

The stranger spoke at once. "If you please, ma'am," she began, with a slight curtsy, "I heard there was a child taken ill up here and have come to offer my services as a nurse."

I breathed out. Thank God. *Thank God.*

I glanced at Mrs. Pulley and saw none of the relief in her face that I felt. I could not understand why I had heard fear in her voice before. I wondered if it was possible that she might know this woman, that she had heard something ill of her.

"Did Mrs. Welling send you?" I asked. "Are you from the village?"

"Not Hartbridge—Medley."

I nodded. I remembered Mrs. Welling telling me she did charity work in Medley.

"My name is Miss Davis," the stranger went on. She hesitated, glancing between me and the mistress. "Are you Mrs. Eversham?" she asked me.

I looked toward the real Mrs. Eversham, who was still standing at my side. She looked weary, and the silence stretched long before she gathered herself together. "I am Mrs. Eversham," she said at last. "You have . . . had the measles yourself before?"

"A long time ago, yes."

She did not speak like a local girl. Her voice was soft, polite, educated.

I waited for Mrs. Eversham to reply, but she said nothing. I saw tears in her eyes and she blinked them back. "I . . ." she began, but she said nothing more. She seemed simply too exhausted to act.

I turned to Miss Davis. "My name is Mrs. Lennox," I explained, "and I am the boy's governess. Have you cared for the sick before?"

"Many times. If the doctor will advise me, I am sure I can manage." She hesitated. "You have not found another nurse yet, I think?"

Mrs. Eversham spoke now. "No."

"I trust you will find me satisfactory. I am competent and quick and discreet." A pause, and then, "I should like to help, if I can."

Something seemed to switch in Mrs. Eversham's face, and she turned to Miss Davis with a softened expression in her eyes. "To be sure," she said, at last.

I only noticed how tight Miss Davis's shoulders had been when she relaxed them.

"Louis is upstairs," Mrs. Eversham went on. "For the love of God, take care of him." Her voice caught, and this time I did not stop myself from reaching out. I touched her arm, once, just enough to make her turn and attempt a smile.

Miss Davis followed Mrs. Pulley upstairs, and I caught the sound of their voices, too soft for me to make sense of, as they ascended the steps.

"She seemed reliable," I said gently.

"True," replied Mrs. Eversham, and her voice shook. "Margaret—"

"Yes?"

She shook her head, moved away from me, tried to smile.

"Nothing. Oh, I am afraid, of course . . . You think you have protected them from everything and then—" She shuddered. "But Louis is strong. He is strong enough."

She turned back into her study and closed the door hard behind her.

I thought of the Louis I knew, slight and skinny, short for his age and often pale. He was not so very strong as she seemed to think.

CHAPTER III

THE FOLLOWING MORNING, MRS. EVERSHAM AND I SAT DOWN TO A solemn breakfast together. It seemed she had passed a sleepless night. Her face was ashen, her eyes red, and her hands shook as she reached for the bread.

"How are they?" I asked.

"Louis is asleep. Miss Davis said he looks quiet enough, though his fever is high and he had a nosebleed during the night. He does not have the rash yet, but Susan's is spreading. Miss Davis says that she cannot see—she cannot open her eyes." Mrs. Eversham broke off. "Susan is stronger than Louis, of course. I am sure she will be well again soon."

"I am very glad a nurse was found."

She nodded wearily, and a picture of Louis in his bed upstairs flashed through my mind. I could see it: his pale face, his fevered brow, his weak frame.

I tried not to think of Susan. Susan with her sharp tongue and her streak of cunning. Susan, who stole and threatened, whom I had feared and half wished harm.

If one of them were to die, surely it must be her. Louis was so young, so innocent, so universally loved. Louis's life was golden.

Susan had spoiled mine.

I shut my eyes. It was dreadful, to weigh one life against another. I tried to kill the thought.

Mr. Stevens brought in the letters with a quick bow.

"Has Mary gone?" Mrs. Eversham asked him.

He nodded. "Left half an hour ago. Carter's taken her down to the village in the cart."

As Stevens put the letters down on the table, he asked gravely, "How are Louis and Susan?"

Mrs. Eversham gave the butler the same answer as she had given me, and he turned with a nod and—to my amazement—a quick touch on his mistress's arm. Then he left the room.

What a strange house this was. But of course I had done the same yesterday, when I saw her in distress—and I was not much more than a servant myself.

I sat across from Mrs. Eversham, tracing the pattern on the china, trying not to think, not to dwell on everything that was happening. Perhaps I should have gone away like Mary, for I was no use here, a governess without a charge. Since I had arrived at Hartwood Hall, my hours had been filled, and I had managed to keep the ghosts of my marriage at bay—and now, nothing. Emptiness. Uselessness.

"Mrs. Eversham," I said, "is there anything I can do?"

She looked at me, her expression pained. "I have some correspondence to attend to this morning, and I must try to write, but . . . well, perhaps this afternoon you might come and sit with me. I think I shall need the company." She gave a weak smile. "I am glad you are here," she said. "I am very glad you are here."

—⟶⟨⟵—

I did not know what to do with myself until the afternoon. I half thought of offering my assistance with household matters, but the servants seemed too busy to talk. I thought of Susan's old bedroom downstairs, empty now, and wondered again if my letter and watch might still be there. Surely they could not have been in Susan's pockets when she fell ill or the doctor would have found them by now. The corridor downstairs was too busy today, Lacey and Mrs. Pulley always passing by, but I must watch, wait for a chance to try to retrieve my letter.

I sat in the schoolroom, ordering the books, tidying the shelves, cleaning the blackboard, planning out lessons for when Louis was better—but it was too sad, too melancholy, to be in the empty schoolroom without him. I could not stand it. I went to change my shoes for my boots and headed down the stairs.

It was a fine autumn day, a cool breeze in the air, red-brown leaves strewn about the grass, the woods a sea of auburn and gold. I pulled my shawl around me and began to walk, trying to focus only on moving my feet. I passed through the formal garden, through the rose garden, and stopped. I could not see the window to Louis's room from this side of the house—his faced out onto the courtyard—but I could see Susan's sickroom. The curtains were half drawn, the window open to let the air in, and in the space between the fluttering curtains I could see movement, the shadowy silhouette of Miss Davis carrying something past the window. I swallowed. If Miss Davis was with Susan, that meant she was not with Louis. My poor child, ill and afraid, was lying on his own.

I would not let myself watch the window. He would be well again soon. I must trust to the doctor's skill, to the nurse's care. I must try not to worry. I kept walking, rounded the back of the house and found myself at Louis's garden. I sat down heavily on his swing and focused on the sway of the lavender, the colors of the oak tree's leaves, green slipping to gold. I tried to forget the world.

I was still there an hour later when Paul returned from taking Mary to the village. I supposed he noticed me from the stables when he came to put the horse away, but I did not see him approach. The first I knew of him was a murmured "Margaret?"

I turned. He had spoken softly, carefully. Almost reverently. He said my name like I had seen him tend the rosebushes.

I was suddenly very aware of my visible agitation. I wanted Paul to leave, to walk back the way he had come and let me be—and I wanted him, dreadfully, to stay.

"Are you all right? Is there any—any bad news?"

"Nothing worse than to be expected," I said. I repeated what Mrs.

Eversham had told me at breakfast. I hesitated, then moved to make space for Paul on the swing. He sat down beside me, and the rope and wood eased and moved, sending us a little backward, a little forward, a brief pendulum before it slowed and stilled. I thought of Louis sitting on this swing, pushing the ground with his legs to make it go faster.

"You left Mary with the Wellings?"

Paul nodded. The swing was not quite big enough for both of us, and I could feel the press of his leg against mine through the layers of my skirt. He was warm from riding, and I smelled mud and horses on him, earthy and familiar. I leaned my shoulder against his, almost without meaning to, felt the comfort of his presence still my beating heart.

I glanced up at the house. If someone saw us, what would they think? Somehow I could not, in this moment, muster the energy to care.

I shut my eyes. Paul was sat on the right of me, and I could hear him clearly, the soft sound of his breathing, the rustle of his clothes as he shifted.

"I know you must be very worried about Louis," he said at last.

I nodded. I did not trust myself to speak.

"As I am." His voice cracked a little, and I knew he meant it, knew he loved that child, too.

I looked round at him, studied his face. His eyes were red, his hair ruffled by the ride. He looked anxious and beautiful.

"You have known Louis a long time, Paul."

He nodded once and his eyes filled with tears. "I have watched him grow up," he said.

I reached for his hand. I laced my fingers through his, because he needed comfort as much as I did, because all my fears of losing my place seemed to shrink beneath the weight of my fear for Louis, beneath the need for something, anything, to support me, to hold me up. I needed Paul. He held my hand tight, and his warmth seemed to spread through me. We sat there for a long time, saying nothing, our hands bound together, as Louis's swing creaked in the breeze.

—→⋆←—

I spent the afternoon as promised with Mrs. Eversham. For a long time, we did not talk. We both sat in the library with books in our hands, each turning the pages as little as the other. It did not feel right to read without Louis.

I do not know how long we had been there before Mrs. Eversham asked abruptly, "Was your husband long ill before his death?"

The question startled me. My first thought was of my letter, of Susan's threats. Had she said something to Mrs. Eversham, before she fell ill? I made myself speak as evenly as I could. "Several months."

"That is a long time to watch a person suffer. It is a hard way to lose someone."

"Yes," I said carefully. I wondered if she could hear in my voice that I was not sorry, not truly, to have lost him, if she could tell that I had wished for it, had longed for it, that I had found it a weary trial to live for another and not for myself.

"It must be difficult for you," she said, "to be in a house of sickness again."

I breathed a little more freely. Of course: her anxiousness made her thoughts turn to sickness, to death, and so she had asked about my husband. That was all, surely. Susan could not have told her anything, or she would have said more.

I told myself again that I was safe, for now, that Susan was lying unwell upstairs, in no position to harm me.

I looked at Mrs. Eversham, her tired eyes, her solemn expression. I longed to ask her about her daughter, about Isabella, but I knew I was not supposed to know, that I could not mention her without explaining that I listened to village gossip, or that I spent more time than I ought with the gardener. Then I thought of what Mrs. Eversham had said yesterday, that the people in Hartbridge thought she had never had a husband.

"Was your—was Mr. Eversham long ill?"

She shook her head. "No. It was all quite—sudden."

I watched her expression carefully, but I could not read it. "I suppose it has been hard for Louis," I said, "to have no memories of his father."

Mrs. Eversham stiffened. "He has never needed a father."

Her tone was sharp, almost angry, and I heard within it a note of bitterness, the sting of dislike. She looked down at her book once again, as though determined to break the conversation, to warn me off asking more.

It must be true, then, the story Louis had told me of the scar on his back. Mr. Eversham had not been a good man. Mrs. Eversham valued her freedom, her release, just as I did mine.

CHAPTER IV

THE NEXT DAY STRETCHED EMPTY BEFORE ME. MRS. EVERSHAM SAT at the barricade of chairs, watching and waiting for Miss Davis to come out of Louis's or Susan's room with news. Dr. Rogers had already been and gone early this morning; Louis's rash had come on in the night, and Susan's cough was worse. I joined Mrs. Eversham for half an hour, but after a while I could stand it no longer: the smell of vinegar, Mrs. Eversham's high-strung nerves, Miss Davis flitting from room to room.

I sat alone for an hour in the morning room, trying and failing to focus on my book, straining my good ear to listen to the house. Everything seemed so quiet. No closing and opening doors, no mumbled conversations. The autumn sun was streaming through the windows, and I missed Louis dreadfully. I wished I could climb the stairs and stand at his bedside, put my hand on his forehead, read him stories in his sleep.

I put my book back in the library and headed for the kitchen. Lacey would talk to me, surely. Lacey, ever full of gossip, perhaps lonely now that Mary was gone—she might want the company.

She bustled about me, muttering under her breath, lighting fires and loudly stacking pans. She scowled and cursed and chopped and peeled, and I turned as she moved to better listen to her tirade, knowing I should not have come.

"As though I don't have enough work to do, without special concoctions for invalids, endless soup and broths, barley water and balm tea and goodness knows what. Dr. Rogers says they must have licorice and where, I ask you, am I supposed to find licorice in a place like this? And of course I must bring it upstairs myself, for the nurse cannot go beyond that corridor. And not to mention there's another mouth to feed now she's come—two, indeed, if the doctor stays for refreshments every time he's here. And all this work with Mary gone, and me scrubbing my own dishes. I ought to have said I'd never had measles and taken myself off as Mary has. It's my belief she'll never come back, for she's always hated this house, always complaining about noises in the night and voices that aren't there." She finally drew breath and gave a long sigh. "At least the food's stopped disappearing from the larder."

I frowned. "Oh?" I remembered her mentioning this, weeks ago. Was it possible it had been Susan all along? I wondered if she might have done it simply to scare Mary, if it had given her the same kind of pleasure she had got from stealing my letter, from taking the ring I'd found in the lake.

"I've sometimes thought it was Louis, and turned a blind eye—for he's the master and a growing lad—but I wondered about Mary or Susan, too, whether they were eating it all up themselves or had some follower, village lads sneaking up here of an evening, you know. And now Susan and Louis are lying sick and Mary's off in the village, it stops. I wonder . . ."

All the time she'd been speaking, she carried on working, hands moving rapidly, kneading bread for tomorrow's breakfast.

"Should you like some help?" I asked. "When I was married, we had only one servant and I did some of the cooking myself."

She stared. Then she screwed up her mouth, and I could see she was torn; she wanted my help but felt it was improper to ask for it. At last she said, "No, ma'am, no—I'm busy and I know I have a tongue on me sometimes, but I'm above asking a lady to do my work for me. I know my place, Mrs. Lennox, and you know yours."

I shrugged my shoulders. "Are you certain?"

"Oh yes, I'm certain." But she smiled anyway, and when she turned back to the stove, I slipped away. I had disturbed her long enough.

In the corridor, I ran into Mrs. Pulley. She frowned at finding me in the servants' quarters but stopped only to tell me that she was going down to the village to buy the supplies Lacey had been unable to fetch earlier in the week.

I turned the corner toward the back stairs, and stopped when I saw the door of Mr. Stevens's office ajar. He was at his desk, writing fast in an accounts book, and he looked up when he saw me in the doorway.

"Good morning, Mrs. Lennox. Any news from upstairs?"

"There is little change." I hesitated, then asked, "Are you busy?" with a wave at the papers and books lining his desk. "I don't mean to disturb you."

He shook his head. "Oh, it's all right. These will be a strange few weeks, I think, with Susan ill and Mary away. I haven't scraped out fireplaces and swept hallways for years, but I did enough of that this morning." He gave a slight smile. "Mrs. Pulley and I are splitting the household work between us, but there are still accounts to be done and bills to be paid."

"Will you let me help?" I asked.

He hesitated. I saw him glance down at the ledger with a flicker of anxiety, then up at me.

"Lacey has already refused my help," I said, "but I cannot sit idle. Give me something to do—anything, please. I can light fires well enough myself, and I am not any more above sweeping a room than you are. I can add up accounts and keep records and write to tradesmen. Please, I cannot do nothing."

Stevens looked at me. He bit his lip, hesitated. "It is not your responsibility," he said at last.

"No," I said, "but you are two servants down and I have nothing else to do. I am quite capable. I will do anything asked of me. Please."

He smiled. It was a pained smile, but still a smile. "Very well," he said, but when I opened my mouth to thank him, he held up a hand.

"I must ask Mrs. Eversham first, of course, but I am sure that both Mrs. Pulley and I could do with the help."

—→⋅←—

When Mrs. Eversham gave me permission, even Mrs. Pulley seemed pleased. Once she was back from the village, I spent the afternoon helping her with the laundry. It was not so very long ago that I had helped my own maid with this work, rolling up my sleeves whenever Richard was out of the house, plunging my hands into hot water, scrubbing aprons on the washboard, turning and turning the mangle, pinning up sheets and clothes to dry.

Once, Richard had come home early and found me with my apron on, scrubbing the tiles, and was appalled. *This is beneath you, Mrs. Lennox.* He never approved of my helping with the household duties, but I had grown used to doing what I could whenever he was out of the house: I knew well enough that he would have found fault with me for not managing our servant better had he come home to dusty floors or dinner not on the table.

Mrs. Pulley and I spoke little as we worked. I tried to engage her in conversation, asking a few light questions about her life before Hartwood Hall, but I did not get very far. I learned, in increasingly brief replies, that she was from Surrey, that her husband had been a gamekeeper and had died many years ago—and then Mrs. Pulley remarked, "I am grateful for your help, Mrs. Lennox," in such a pointed way that I gave up my efforts.

All the while, I was aware of the other work going on around me, the sounds and smells and movements of a household caring for the sick. A tin bath was taken up to Louis's and Susan's rooms, and pails of lukewarm water carried up and down the stairs. In the kitchen, Lacey pounded together sugar candy with spermaceti that the doctor had brought to ease their coughs, and boiled up salty broths, adding spirits of vitriol and lemon juice as the doctor had instructed.

When Mrs. Pulley was summoned upstairs by Mrs. Eversham, I carried on scrubbing the worst of the laundry by myself. When I had finished, I emptied the dirty water, rinsed out the pail in the scullery, and emerged into the corridor.

I hesitated as I passed Susan's old bedroom. This might, perhaps, be the opportunity I needed. Lacey was now out in the vegetable garden; Stevens and Mrs. Pulley were upstairs. I had not tried the door to Susan's room for some time.

I reached out, wondering if it was possible it had been left open when Susan fell ill.

I tried the handle—but nothing gave. It was still locked.

I breathed in, breathed out. I reminded myself that while she lay ill in bed she was no threat to me. I was safe from Susan, for now.

————>·<————

When I met Mrs. Eversham at dinner, she asked if I would stay with her afterward. It was clear that she was as anxious as she had been yesterday, though there was no change in Louis's condition. She had spent the day moving between her study and the upstairs corridor, trying—and failing, she told me—to write, her mind constantly on Louis. She ate little, and it was only when I told her she must eat to keep her strength up that she even seemed to notice the dishes before us.

Later, in the library, she opened her book, stared at it, and did not move. Her elegant face was paler than usual, her eyes shadowed, and she had bitten her lower lip until the skin was raw.

"Mrs. Eversham," I said, as gently as I could, "you must distract yourself. You cannot spend every moment in anxiety. You will wear yourself out."

She shook her head. "How can I do anything? How can I concentrate on anything when Louis is unwell? I can't sleep. I can't think. I can't write. I can't bear to eat."

I crossed the room toward her and pried the book from her hands.

"Have you a pack of cards, Mrs. Eversham?"

"What?"

"We are going to play whist," I told her.

"I cannot play cards, Mrs. Lennox, when Louis may be dying."

"Louis is not dying," I said, as firmly as I could. "We should have every hope of his recovery. Mrs. Eversham, I know it is hard, but you cannot be of use to Louis at the moment. When he is better, when he is out of danger, that is when you will be able to help him—but if you are ill yourself, you will be of no assistance. Please, listen to me."

A knock on the door. Mrs. Eversham started violently and I turned to open it.

Mrs. Pulley stood in the doorway. "Good evening, ma'am," she said, glancing at Mrs. Eversham. "Miss Davis says both patients are asleep, so she has time to report to you, if you would like to come upstairs."

Mrs. Eversham nodded quickly. She stood up, then glanced back at me. "Mrs. Lennox, I am sure you would like to know how Louis is?"

So I followed her out of the library. Mrs. Pulley left us at the foot of the stairs, and I went up with Mrs. Eversham, then down the west corridor toward the barricade of chairs.

Miss Davis stood a few feet back from it. She glanced once at me but made no comment on the fact that Mrs. Eversham had not come alone. Her face was as pale as Mrs. Eversham's, her smile tight and anxious, but when she spoke her voice was steady.

"They are both sleeping, and I thought you would wish to know how they are. Dr. Rogers has promised to be here again tomorrow morning and will be able to tell you more, but . . ." I saw her swallow. "In truth, both are . . . suffering. Susan is in great pain and Louis is very weak. Bathing seems to give some relief to Louis's rash, and steam is helping Susan's cough, but . . . well, there is no denying that they are both very ill." She hesitated. "Dr. Rogers will bleed them, when he comes tomorrow. It will help lessen the fever."

Mrs. Eversham winced. "And that is all you have to tell me?" she asked, her voice trembling.

"There is nothing more."

"Can I do anything?"

"No. I will see to everything. You can trust me."

There was a pause, and then Mrs. Eversham gave a weary nod. I heard a cough from one of the bedrooms—Susan's cough, lower and rougher than Louis's. With another glance at Mrs. Eversham, Miss Davis moved to leave.

"Wait a moment, Miss Davis," I said. "Will you help me to persuade Mrs. Eversham that she needs to eat and rest, that she will make herself ill if she refuses to try to distract herself?"

It was impertinent—I knew it was. And yet Mrs. Eversham looked so worn, so unsteady, that something must be done.

"I have told her so already," the nurse said. She glanced at Mrs. Eversham. "Listen to Mrs. Lennox; she gives you good advice. The doctor may be able to give you something tomorrow to make you sleep."

Mrs. Eversham was already shaking her head. "It would be wrong to—"

"It is not wrong to keep yourself well."

"You are not overtired yourself?" I asked, looking to Miss Davis. "I know it is hard work."

She gave a slight smile. "Oh, I am used to irregular hours," she said, with a glance at Mrs. Eversham. "I am quite well. Rest, please. Louis will be all right."

Another cough came from down the corridor, and Miss Davis turned to walk away. I caught the smell of vinegar and licorice as the door to Susan's room opened and shut, but I could see nothing within.

Mrs. Eversham and I stood alone in the corridor. I turned to her, put my hand on her arm. When she looked up, her eyes were bleary with tears.

"Whist, then?" she said. "Why not? Anything that can make this dreadful time pass cannot be so very bad."

CHAPTER V

WE MADE OUR WAY TO CHURCH IN NEAR SILENCE. I WATCHED PAUL as we drove, the creases in his jacket, the flick of his hair beneath his hat. It felt wrong to go to church without Louis at my side, but I did not wish to stay away. I needed the comfort of it, the normality of it, to ease the surge of anxiety spreading through me. Dr. Rogers had been at the house early again this morning, and when I asked him if it was inadvisable for me to go into the village, he said I should have no fear to, that if I was well myself and was keeping my distance from the patients it was safe to go out.

The sun danced through the branches, illuminating spots in the darkness as we rode on and on. I didn't look into the trees today, didn't search for glimpses of the sort of spirits Mary would see, didn't listen for the rustle of movement. I kept my eyes on Paul, listened only to the charged silence between us.

I did not know what to say to him. We had agreed it must be over, but I could not quite tear myself from him—certainly we had not sat together as strangers that day in Louis's garden. And all I could think of was that I had seen this man undressed, that I knew the precise shape of his arms beneath his shirt, that I had touched every inch of him, kissed his neck and mouth with hungry kisses, that he had clasped me to him fast.

I did not want to ride in silence with him to church. I wanted to kiss him, to hold him close, to peel his clothes from his skin.

As we emerged from the woods, Paul asked quietly, "How is Louis?"

I felt a stab of guilt that I had not been thinking of Louis, too. "Struggling, Miss Davis says."

"And Susan?"

"The same." Images came unbidden in my mind—her smirk in the music room, my watch in her hand, her locked door. I shook the thought away. "Paul?"

"Yes?"

"Do you think Louis will be all right?"

I knew he did not know, that he could not predict the future any more than I could, but somehow I needed to hear it said.

"Yes," he said softly. "Yes, I think he will."

———✦———

We arrived early, and the church was still quiet. Mrs. Welling was sitting in the box, waiting while her husband leafed through the Bible at the front. There were a few people already in their seats, and I saw Paul's family at the back of the church. Somewhat to my surprise, I also spotted Mary, sitting with Jenny, the Wellings' maid, in a front pew. They were whispering softly together. Although she had been gone only a couple of days, I could see a change in Mary. She looked less shrunk than she did at Hartwood Hall, less nervous.

She started when she saw me, as though I might carry illness on my clothes, on my skin.

I looked round at Paul, and he gave me a single nod, then turned to join his family. No one looking could have known there was anything between us.

I stopped to speak to Mary on my way to the box and asked her how she fared.

She shrugged and glanced at Jenny. "I like it here. It's different in the village." She pursed her lips, leaned toward me, and said, very quietly, "I shan't come back."

I stared at her. "I beg your pardon?"

"I said I shan't come back. Jenny says she'll help me advertise. I don't want to go back to Hartwood. Jenny says"—she glanced at her new friend—"Jenny says everyone in the village knows it's haunted, that the girl Lacey told me died away from home—well, Jenny says that everyone here knows she *walks*."

"Walks?" I repeated slowly.

"Yes, *walks*." She bit her lip. "I always knew there was something wrong with that house. All those noises in the night. All those times I thought I'd seen something . . . Lacey says I'm just nervous but I swear it's a bad place, Mrs. Lennox. I'm not going back."

All the time she had been talking, cold was stealing over me. And yet I knew—didn't I?—that it was all in my head, that Paul was right when he said it was just a house, just people, that Mrs. Eversham was nothing more sinister than a reserved woman with a sad past. I had not heard unexplained noises in the night these last few days, since Louis had been ill, since I had been distracted by other things.

I thought of Louis, suffering in bed, and my anger rose against anyone who dared disparage the family at Hartwood Hall.

"Mary, you are being ridiculous." Even as I said it, I felt a twinge of guilt. I knew I was playing a part, forcing out the words I ought to say. I was letting Mary down, just as I had a few weeks ago when her room had been wrecked and I said I'd seen Susan in the courtyard.

"She's not," said Jenny matter-of-factly. "All the folks here know what kind of house Hartwood is. We all know that it's a dead place, that the shadows don't fall right there, that the woods at night are the darkest in the county. We know that the deer all left one day, years ago, because they were afraid. And Mary's not the only one who's seen it—the ghost that bides there. Why d'you think no one from around here works up there? Why d'you think you've got sickness and we haven't? 'Cause God knows that the Evil One's up at Hartwood Hall."

I ignored her, turned back to Mary. "You must see that all these fears are irrational. Hartwood Hall is a good place. You have a good position there. To give it up—"

"I won't go back," said Mary. "You shouldn't either. You ought to run as fast as you can."

"But this is preposterous," I said, and I was aware even as the words left my mouth that I had used the voice I adopted to upbraid misbehaving children. Jenny claiming Louis's illness was some sort of punishment had rankled me. "Mary, I won't stay to listen to your nonsense. Think carefully before you do anything rash—that's all. Good day."

I moved away before she could say anything else, and made my way up to the box. I sat down slowly at Mrs. Welling's side.

She was glad to see me, full of eager inquiries about the situation up at Hartwood. I told her what I knew, and saw her expression grow grave as she took it all in.

"How is Mary getting along?" I asked, with a sideways glance down at the pews.

Mrs. Welling gave a slight smile. "Oh, well enough, I think. She has been helping Jenny with the housework."

"Thank you again for taking her in."

"Are you safe, Mrs. Lennox? I know you have never had the illness."

I smiled. "I am safe enough. We are very careful, and the sufferers are kept quite separate, or else I should not have ventured to church today. And the nurse, Miss Davis, is very good—it was you who sent her, I think?"

Mrs. Welling frowned. "No, I am afraid I don't know any Miss Davis."

I looked at her in surprise. I tried to remember what Miss Davis had actually said the night she came—we had all been so worried for Louis that it was almost a blur. I thought of the note of fear in Mrs. Pulley's voice in the hall, Mrs. Eversham's confusion, and something did not quite add up.

"Oh, I had thought . . . Miss Davis is from Medley, and knowing about your work there, I assumed . . . well, I suppose I must have been mistaken."

"I have never heard of any Miss Davis in Medley." Mrs. Welling gave a slight smile. "I am glad to hear you found someone, but I am afraid it was nothing to do with me."

CHAPTER VI

PAUL WAITED FOR ME AT THE BACK OF THE CHURCH WHEN THE service ended. He said nothing as I approached, but he smiled, broad and dimpled. My heart beat fast, and my conversation with Mrs. Welling, my questions about Miss Davis, my worries for Louis, my stolen letter—everything seemed to slip away.

I had never met anyone like Paul. All the men I had known were stiff and formal. Paul was calm but never cold, his actions careful but never studied. He was always easy with me, as though whatever this was between us was the most natural thing in the world. He did not want me because I seemed a suitable person, an appropriate candidate to fill some hole in his life. He wanted me because he *wanted* me. It was too much, and it was enough.

I followed him to where the horse and cart were waiting. The weather had turned during the service, and the sky was a dark gray now, threatening rain. Paul held out his hand to help me up, and when our fingers touched he held on tight, just for a second, before he released his grip.

He climbed up to the front, lifted the reins—and then the cart began to move, wheels trundling forward, down the village roads, past shops and thatched cottages, past clusters of people, away and out into the fields, where the streets turned to hedges, the bricks and roofs to grass and red-leaved trees.

"Mary told me that she does not intend to come back," I said, when we had left the village behind us.

Paul did not turn. He kept his eyes on the road in front of us, but I saw his shoulders shift, saw him nod. "I heard that."

"There will be so few of us."

"There have never been many."

"I suppose she is afraid. Of—the house. Hartwood Hall is, in a way, a strange place."

"Hartwood Hall is a wonderful place," Paul replied, and his voice sounded so earnest, so sincere, that I smiled.

We were entering the woods now, the clouded sky ahead blocked out by branches, the grass beneath the cart fading to dirt. Paul's figure seemed shadowy, lost in the dark. I breathed in, breathed out.

The darkness around me was too vast, pressing down on me from every side. It was only early afternoon, and yet the clouds beyond the treetops were black now. I squinted, trying to concentrate on what I could see—the dim outlines of branches, Paul's silhouetted form before me. I tried to focus on the sound of the wheels, turning and turning over, crunching twigs and leaves beneath them.

"Margaret?" Paul's voice was low, gravelly, and gentle. He must have remembered what I had told him about the dark.

I opened my mouth to speak.

And that was when I saw it. In among the dim trees, a ripple of movement. Something, out there, walking through the woods.

A deer.

No, a figure.

Isabella.

"Can you see that?" I whispered.

Before Paul could reply, the horse reared up. Whinnying and snorting, it bucked and brought its feet down with a crash, then was up again in a moment. The cart was jerked from side to side, pulled by the horse's frantic movements.

The horse had seen it, then. That was my first thought.

And then I thought of nothing but holding on as the cart lurched. Paul was on his feet, calling gently to the horse to quiet it, pulling sharply on the reins. I could see him dimly in front of me, one arm outstretched.

The horse stopped abruptly, kicked the ground hard, and the cart lurched again. I was thrown forward, grasping onto the seat to break my fall—and when I looked up, Paul was gone.

I think I cried out. I could see so little, the outline of the cart dim and obscure, the horse's frame a mere shadow. The horse was whinnying more softly now, a low whimpering sound, and it seemed to have stopped moving.

Paul.

He must have been thrown off his feet.

He had been standing up and—

"Paul?"

I heard a groan but no words. I scrambled down from the cart, felt my boots sink into the mud and stared around me, searching in the darkness. Nothing on this side. Nothing but black earth and endless dark trees. When I looked into the undergrowth, there was no sign of the figure that must have upset the horse.

I paced around the cart, my hand against the wood to guide my way. I went around the back, not daring to go too close to the still-whinnying horse. And there, lying on his back in the mud, was Paul.

He shifted as I approached, and my relief at seeing him move was almost overpowering. He propped himself up on his elbow, wincing.

"Are you all right?" I whispered.

"I—I think so."

"Nothing broken?"

"No, just bruised, I think. Damn, that hurt." He gave a low whistle. "You weren't thrown, too, were you?"

"No." I knelt beside him on the ground. "What was it? I thought I saw a—a figure, in the trees."

"It must have been an animal," he said.

I hesitated. "You are sure you're not hurt, Paul?"

"No harm done." In the dark, I saw him grin. "Why, were you worried?"

I could not help but smile back. "Only a little."

I reached out my hand—and whether it was because he'd heard the anxiety in my voice or because we were together in the darkness of the woods, I didn't know, but instead of letting me help him up, he pulled me down toward him and kissed me.

I told myself to pull back, to say this was a mistake, that we couldn't risk it, that we shouldn't—but though the words formed in my mind, I couldn't quite bear to say them. I could not resist him, the warmth of his smile, the gentle tenderness of his hands, the pull of everything he was. The last few days, the misery of Louis's illness, the mixed guilt and relief of Susan's pain—it all faded at Paul's touch and a kind of joy rushed through me. This must be what it felt like to be in love, that intangible sensation I had searched for with Richard again and again and never found.

So I kissed Paul back, put my arms around his waist and hugged him to me. I held him in the dark and kissed his lips, his face, his neck, ran my fingers down his shirt. I closed my eyes, forgot the darkness, forgot Louis's illness, forgot the figure in the trees, and thought only of the feel of his body beneath mine.

And then, moments later, I heard something.

"What was that?"

What or where it came from, I could not make out. But I had definitely heard something. I started up, broke from him. Behind us the horse seemed content now. It stood still, nosing at the grass.

"It was nothing, Margaret."

"But I heard—"

He sat up, cupped my face in his warm hands. "Just the horse."

"And did you not hear anything, just now?"

"No."

"But—" I broke off. What, after all, did I think I had seen, had heard? Surely there could be no one here.

Paul's arms were snaking around my waist again, and this time I did not even think of stopping him. I felt my fingers clasping around his, felt my lips brush against his cheek. I could drown the dead out of my mind. I could forget the darkness close around us. It was not so very difficult.

I pulled Paul closer to me and kissed him hard.

———>–‹–—

It was another hour before we were back at the house. The horse still seemed quiet, but we walked just in case it was not, letting it drag the empty cart behind. My black dress was muddy, the skirts crumpled, and as we walked up to the house, I felt nervous. Someone would know, I thought. Someone would see us and work it out.

But we saw no one as we approached the house. The grounds were quiet, deserted, and the courtyard empty.

Paul turned toward me. "Margaret?"

"Yes?"

"I know that this is . . . complicated . . . but—" He broke off, blinked. He was struggling to find the words for just what he wanted to say. I was standing close enough to see each breath, each hesitation. "The other week, when you said—I just . . . I don't want this to be over."

"Me neither," I whispered.

"No, but . . . I mean—" He stopped again, and I saw that his hands were shaking, his breath ragged. "Margaret, I know our positions here at Hartwood . . . I know it is risky and foolish, but—"

"I am not sure I care anymore," I said. I spoke the words quietly. I barely heard my own voice.

Paul's face broke out into a grin. "Yes," he said. "That's just it."

———>–‹–—

I saw no one as I opened the front doors, as I climbed the stairs, as I made my way to my room. The house was quiet, the barricade of chairs in the corridor deserted. I hurried to my bedroom and changed for dinner, removing my dress, scraping off the mud, before pulling on another gown. One good thing about always wearing black was that no one could tell if you had changed.

I twisted the wedding ring around and around on my finger.

What would Richard say, if he could see me today?

I heard the words in my head, his voice precise and cold: *I always knew you were a whore.*

CHAPTER VII

I HAD JUST LEFT MY BEDROOM EARLY THE NEXT MORNING WHEN, glancing up the corridor, I saw Mrs. Eversham sitting by the barricade. She looked exhausted, and I wondered if she had sat there all night.

Then Louis's bedroom door opened. From where I stood, I was angled well enough to see in, and for a second I caught a glimpse of him, bathed in candlelight, his small form on the bed, his skin pale and red in patches. His body abruptly creased with the effort of a cough—and then Miss Davis stepped out, wearing her usual light gray dress, and closed the door behind her.

Mrs. Eversham rose and Miss Davis came to meet her. I stood back, watching them. They spoke in low voices, and I could not hear what they said, but I saw Miss Davis's earnest face, saw Mrs. Eversham nod, then turn away. She walked slowly toward the bedroom that was for the time her own.

Miss Davis was moving toward Susan's room when I stopped her with a word and stepped closer to the barricade myself.

"I am glad you have persuaded Mrs. Eversham to rest."

"She needs it."

"She does." I glanced down the corridor. "How is Louis?"

An almost imperceptible shake of the head. "His fever has been high, but we bled him yesterday, and he is cooling. Dr. Rogers is still hopeful."

I swallowed. The thought of Louis's broken skin, his fevered brow, brought a pang to my heart.

I looked at Miss Davis carefully. She worked hard, forever in and out of Louis's and Susan's rooms. As Dr. Rogers had instructed, she never left the part of the upstairs corridor in which she worked. She even slept at their sides, in the large armchair in Louis's bedroom or the smaller one in Susan's. When I saw her flitting between the rooms, her cheeks ruddy with exertion, her eyes tired, it was very hard to think anything other than highly of her. But Mrs. Welling's words in church would not leave me. If Mrs. Welling had not sent her, who had? How had she even known that a nurse was needed?

I spoke as lightly as I could. "I meant to ask—how did you hear about this position?"

A frown crossed Miss Davis's face. Something unreadable flickered in her expression. And then, "Oh, a woman in my village knew of it from a friend in Hartbridge." She glanced over her shoulder, at some sound I did not catch. "I had better see to Susan. Good day, Mrs. Lennox."

"Good day."

The door of Susan's room swung shut behind her and as I turned to go, I put the thought out of my mind. Miss Davis was so practical, so measured, that it seemed impossible to doubt her.

———— ⋅>⋅<⋅ ————

That night in the library, Mrs. Eversham asked me to distract her. After an hour of us both trying to read—and neither of us managing very well—she shut her book, sat forward. "Tell me something, Mrs. Lennox," she said abruptly. "Tell me a story or something about your life or—I don't know. Please. I can't think, I can't talk—I am so useless." She shook her head, shut her eyes, leaned back in the armchair. "Tell me about your life, Mrs. Lennox."

I stared at her. What was I to say?

I could tell her about my childhood, about my parents, how my father was always out on his rounds, how my mother helped at the village school. I could tell her about the day I was too curious, looked too far over the side of a well and slipped. I could tell her about how long I lay there, the bandages I made from my dress, just as I had seen my father make them from calico, the ropes they lowered to help me out. Or how I lay in bed for weeks afterward, refusing to leave my room, experimenting with the hearing I had left, putting my good ear to the pillow and straining and straining to hear anything, crying when I could not. I could tell her about the sounds of church, the rush of noise and how it thrilled me. I could tell her about my education, how my parents scrimped and saved for it, how I went out as a governess as soon as Father died.

I could tell her about my charges, the boys and girls I had taught. Clever children, kind children, spoiled children. I could tell her about the Russels, how the girls pinched and shoved me, how the parents did not give me leave to see my mother when she was dying.

Or I could tell her about my marriage, how I had once met a man in a church and mistaken him for an escape, how I had sought to buy freedom with the promise of a family and only bought myself struggle. I could tell her how I had failed to love him, how he had watched me fail, how his feelings for me had withered. I could tell her how we had longed for children, how Richard had told me it was my fault when they did not come.

I could tell her about the night he died, how he had raised his failing voice to reprimand me one last time—how something in my spirit had snapped. I could tell her about his cold, hollow form the next morning, about that vial on the dresser.

And what would Mrs. Eversham have done, if I had told her about Paul? That I had fallen for her gardener, that I knew every scar and mark on his skin, that I was, by the world's standards, fallen and broken and ruined.

In the end, I told her nothings. I told her about the meadow in the village where I had grown up, how I had liked to sit by the river and watch the water. I told her that my father had been a surgeon, that he had cured children like Louis, brought them back from the brink. I told her about the artist whose daughter I had taught, about his drawings, how the house smelled forever of paint and charcoal. I told her about my journey here, about how much I had come to love her son.

I told her little things, moments and details that did not add up to a whole, and she sat there, with closed eyes, murmuring her surprise or amusement, until eventually she drifted off to sleep.

I covered her with my shawl and left her in peace.

CHAPTER VIII

THE NEXT EVENING, MRS. EVERSHAM DID NOT NEED ME. SHE HAD slept so ill the night before that Miss Davis persuaded her to retire to bed early, and I was left to my own devices. After dinner, I asked Mrs. Pulley and Stevens if I could do anything for them, but they never allowed me to work into the evenings.

"It is one thing to help," said Stevens, with a smile, "but you are a governess, Mrs. Lennox, not a housemaid." Mrs. Pulley only pursed her lips and shooed me away, but I supposed she meant the same.

I even tried Lacey, asking if I could be of assistance, if I could help bake bread, scrub pans, do *anything*. But she didn't dare accept my help when Mrs. Pulley and Stevens had refused.

They did not understand that I did not want evenings to myself. Time to myself was dangerous. I did not want to read, to sit and wait, to feel as powerless as I was.

So instead I went to Paul. When I showed up unexpectedly at his door after dinner, he grinned. "Well then," he said. "Come in."

I fell asleep afterward, and when I woke, nearly an hour later, I found that Paul had fetched a pillow from the hayloft and placed it beneath my head.

I looked around the room, took it all in. There was Paul, dressed again, smiling at me as though we were a couple married a few weeks, holding out my chemise and corset. It felt strange, foolish, to be playing at domesticity, when we both knew what a fragile, fleeting thing this was.

It was worth it, I thought, looking across at his familiar face, his ruffled hair, the curve of his jaw. It was worth the risk, for this, for him.

He tied my corset for me, fastened my petticoats, helped me put on my black dress. He fastened the buttons he had undone so quickly an hour before, and then raised his hand, hesitantly, to my hair.

"Do you have a glass?"

He nodded and brought me a marked shaving mirror. I sat down at the table, propping up the glass, and took out pin upon pin, until my hair was loose. I was just about to fasten it up again, to fix it, when Paul put his hand in my long hair, and stroked it, his fingers moving from the top to the end.

"You're beautiful," he whispered, and I felt my cheeks flush.

"Not like you," I said.

Paul laughed, with such sudden shy surprise that I wondered if he truly did not know he was handsome, if a life up at Hartwood Hall, away from the world, meant no one had ever told him.

I plaited my hair slowly, then twisted it up and pinned it in place behind my head. I looked at myself in the mirror, with my neat hair and my black gown.

"Respectable?" I asked Paul.

He tucked one stray hair behind my ear and smiled.

"I had better get back to the house."

He nodded. And then, "Margaret, I know you are worried about Louis," he said, "but he will be all right. He's a good man, Dr. Rogers."

"He seems it."

A pause. And then Paul said, "He tended my mother before she died."

"Oh." I looked at him, met his solemn eyes. We had not talked much about our lives beyond Hartwood. We spoke only of the present, not of the future or the past. "Was she long ill?"

"She was ill for most of my life."

Paul was silent. I reached for his hand, laced my fingers through his. He reached out his other hand, played with the cuff of my sleeve, and I supposed because death and illness were on his mind he was thinking of who I wore that dress for.

"Margaret, all this must remind you, of . . ." He trailed off. "Forgive me. I know you rarely speak of your husband."

Paul spoke very gently, but still the words seemed to ricochet around the small room. It took me a long time to reply. I did not want to talk to him about Richard. I did not know how to do so without changing his opinion of me.

"There is not much to tell. We were . . . not happy."

"You told me you didn't love him."

I said nothing.

Paul drew me closer to him. He did not ask me the unspoken question that lingered between us. I kissed him gently. "It was never like this," I said, and I heard the soft exhale of Paul's breath.

"But you married him?"

"Yes." A dozen words and stories lingered on my lips. I wondered what he would say if I told him everything, up until the last. But instead I pulled him closer, drew him to me, worked kisses up his neck. "Let's not talk about this," I said. "What about you? Tell me about the women who came before me."

"What women?" Paul smiled, his lips close to my ear. "There has been no one but you."

———>·<———

His words replayed in my mind as I walked back up to the house, tramping through the dusk. I did not know whether to believe Paul that there had been no one else. And if it was true, what did that make me? He was five years younger than me. He was below me in station, in the house, in the world. I was endangering a place I had held for a few months, and however safe Paul might feel his position was, he was still, as far as I could see, endangering a place he had held for years.

I had never before felt hungry for someone in the way I did for him. I had never been so brazen, so careless of all those rules the world and God had laid upon us. Everything about him seemed to intoxicate me—the thrill of his touch, the feel of his skin, the look on his face when his eyes met mine. I loved the scent of him, the way he ran his hands through his hair, the gentle tones of his voice. I loved the solemn sincerity of his affection for Louis, the care with which he worked, the freedom I felt when I was with him. I loved that he thought me better than I was.

He made me feel like I was someone else, like the person I wanted to be.

Somehow, when I was with Paul, I could forget all the rest of it. The noises in the night, Isabella's face in the locket, the rash on Louis's skin, Susan's fingers closing on the gold watch, Richard's cold expression, the guilt that lingered forever at the corners of my mind—everything fell away, and all that was left was his warmth wrapped around me, his skin on my skin.

I wanted nothing more than what we had—snatched moments, fleeting happiness, hidden passion, love and lies. But he must know that. He was not like Richard, all convention and rules and propriety.

I felt a rush of guilt, but there was something else mingled with it, too—a kind of triumph, as though I liked proving to myself, to Richard, that I deserved some kind of happiness, some kind of love.

I let myself back into the house carefully. The entrance hall was quiet, the stairs deserted. Mrs. Eversham was still asleep, I supposed, and Mrs. Pulley, Stevens, and Lacey were at work in other parts of the house. I bolted the doors behind me and walked steadily up the stairs.

As I turned along the corridor to reach my bedroom, I heard loud, hurrying footsteps on the stairs behind me, and I thought for a second that somebody had seen me, that somebody would know—and then I saw Miss Davis, standing at the barricade of chairs, an anxious frown on her face.

"What is it?" I asked, moving nearer. A moment later, Mrs. Pulley had gained on me.

"You rang the bell? Is everyone all right?"

"I—" Miss Davis broke off, looking between us both. "There has been a turn for the worse. We need to send for the doctor at once."

CHAPTER IX

I TRIED TO SLEEP, AT FIRST, ONCE DR. ROGERS HAD ARRIVED AND both he and Miss Davis had told me there was nothing I could do. I dozed fitfully for an hour, maybe more, and then roused myself. The flare of candlelight from the corridor, the conversations too urgent to be whispered, the footfalls past my bedroom door—it was all too much.

When I went out into the corridor, I found I was not the only one awake. Mrs. Pulley was standing at the barricade, tobacco stuffed up her nose to ward off contagion. She was carrying a pail of water, evidently on the doctor's instructions. Mrs. Eversham was sitting on the floor in her nightgown, leaning back against another chair, an untouched cup of tea beside her. Her hair was loose, her face was strained, and Mrs. Pulley was talking to her in a low voice.

I heard the words "He is delirious," and I felt my heart plummet. Louis, with his bright laugh, his familiar smile—Louis suffering, Louis insensible. I could not bear it.

Mrs. Pulley said, "He thought he was talking to . . . to Isabella."

"Oh God," said Mrs. Eversham. "Oh God, my poor boy."

I moved forward and they both looked up, noticing me for the first time. Mrs. Pulley gave me a stiff nod, then turned and moved back down the corridor.

A moment later she was pushing the door open to Susan's room, and two things happened at once: Susan's voice became suddenly audible, low and rasping, muttering indistinct syllables between coughs—and I saw her face. I thought she was bruised until I realized what it was, purple and blackish spots nestled among the red measles. It had been only a week since she fell ill, but she looked thinner than ever.

A moment later the door was shut once more.

"Any news?" I asked Mrs. Eversham gently, sitting down at her side.

"Susan is very bad," she said. "The fever and delirium have taken hold, and Dr. Rogers says he fears inflammation of the lungs. He has given her opiates to calm her. Miss Davis says she is seeing things— ghosts in the walls and faces that can't be there. She has been talking for nearly two hours—they cannot quiet her. Most of it makes little sense, but . . ."

A kind of horror stole over me. What if, in her fevered state, she said something—something about me? Susan, always so in control of herself, of her words—what if, slipping in and out of dreams, of fevered madness, she let out all the things I had worked so hard to make her hide?

I tried to quell my panic. I must trust that anything Susan said in her delirium would not be taken seriously by the rest of the household. And yet I thought of my watch and my letter, tucked away somewhere in Susan's room. The knowledge of my past shut behind that locked door made my heart hammer.

"And how is Louis?"

Mrs. Eversham shook her head. "His delirium is not so violent as Susan's, but Dr. Rogers says he is having waking dreams. They asked Mrs. Pulley to come up, too, to help." Her voice cracked. "I *hate* being useless. I hate everything feeling so . . . so futile." She turned to me, almost abruptly, as though she had been speaking only to herself before. "What is the point of anything, Margaret, but being here? I try to read, and it feels heartless. I try to write, and it feels preposterous at such a time. I try to sleep, and all I see is a blank, ruined future." Her eyes glistened in the candlelight. "You think you can save somebody, that you can protect them, that you can shield them from all the pain and misery and mess that is this world, and somehow—somehow the rot seeps in."

I laid my hand on her arm. "Louis will be well again. There is every reason to hope."

"Not just Louis, I . . ." She trailed off. Her voice was tight but she was looking at me differently, carefully, as though she had realized what she was about to say, as though she were weighing up her words.

And I thought, for one aching minute, that she was going to tell me about Isabella. Whatever bond had formed between us this past week, however Louis's illness had pulled the two of us together, it had been enough. Finally, somebody would tell me the full truth about Louis's sister.

And then the door of Louis's room opened, and Miss Davis stepped out. The spell was broken.

"How is he?" was Mrs. Eversham's first question. "Tell me—please."

"He is quieter than before. The poppy syrup has helped a little. I must see to Susan, too—it is having less effect on her. I am afraid it will be a difficult night." She was looking at Mrs. Eversham now, at her pale cheeks, her agitated manner. She said softly, "Are you all right? Should you not rest?"

"How can I rest when others do not?"

"Did you sleep last night?"

There was a moment's pause before Mrs. Eversham said, "Barely."

"Then go to bed," said Miss Davis. "Sleep. Please."

She only shook her head.

Hours passed like this. Mrs. Eversham and I kept watch. We sat in an anxious silence, broken by the sound of hoarse coughs from Louis's room, by stifled cries from Susan's, by indistinct conversations between Miss Davis and Dr. Rogers. I sat sideways on my chair, my good ear toward the corridor, straining to hear whatever Susan might be saying, but I caught no distinct words, only the vague hum of muttering through her door.

Every now and then, Miss Davis or Dr. Rogers or Mrs. Pulley

would cross the corridor, going between Louis's room and Susan's. We asked them, each time, for news, but there was little to tell. That Susan was quieter, or fiercer, that the opiates were taking effect or wearing off, that Louis was asleep or restless, that this would be a long night.

At about three o'clock in the morning, when Mrs. Eversham was almost falling asleep on the floor, I finally persuaded her to go to bed. I had to help her up, support her along the corridor and open the door. She sat down wearily on the bed, raised her hands to her face as though in despair.

I was at the door, leaving her to sleep, when she spoke.

"You would not think, would you, Margaret, that I had once thought myself a strong person?" Her voice was weak. "I have conquered things you cannot imagine—taken risks that would shock you to your core. I have always stood firm, been unshakable, but this—*look at me*," she said, "broken by a child's illness, ruined because my boy is sick and I cannot see him and I cannot bear it. And it feels—it feels like a punishment. But I cannot lose him, Margaret. I cannot lose him, too."

And then she began to weep, gasping, rasping sobs escaping from her, tears falling down her cheeks. I put my candle down on the dresser and went back to her, put my arms around her to steady her. She did not flinch away from me; she barely seemed to know who it was that held her. It did not matter that I was her son's governess, her paid subordinate. It did not matter that she did not know me, not really. Tears sprang to my own eyes and I blinked them back. I kept my arms around her as she cried, until, exhausted, she fell asleep.

Then I laid her down gently on the bed, took up my candle, and closed the door quietly behind me.

As I reached the barricade, I heard the sound of coughing from one of the rooms and looked up to see Susan's door opening and Miss Davis looking out.

"Mrs. Lennox?" She moved forward a few steps, letting the door ease shut behind her. "Can you do something for me?"

"Of course—anything."

She sent me down to the kitchen with instructions to fetch barley water and linseed for Louis. I moved down the stairs as fast as I could, candle flickering, descending into the dark belly of the cellars. A few minutes later, I was back, turning down the west-wing corridor.

The smell of vinegar and poppy tea hit me afresh. Medicine always seemed to smell of my father, of my childhood; it seemed half comfort, half fearful. I placed the tray on one of the barricade chairs, and hearing me, Miss Davis appeared once more. She had barely managed to thank me before she turned at the sound of some commotion from Susan's room, and the next moment I heard Dr. Rogers cry, "Miss Davis—Miss Davis!"

Miss Davis left the tray on the chairs and all but ran back into Susan's room, leaving the door wide open behind her in her hurry. Susan's voice was suddenly louder. It was hoarse and breathless, almost unrecognizable. She was muttering at first, and I could not catch the words. I could see through the open door from where I stood, and in the candlelight I saw Susan struggling up from the bed. They were trying to restrain her, but Susan—restless, fierce—threw them off. Her voice rose and suddenly I heard one distinct sentence: "I know what you are."

It was hissed sharply—and then her eyes seemed to flick in my direction.

I held my breath. If she meant what I thought, if she said something more—what on earth would I do? I tried to control my thoughts. Her eyes were wild, her movements erratic. Her hair was matted across her forehead with sweat, and in the candlelight her face was ashen and glistening. If she spilled my secrets now, no one would believe her. Surely, no one would believe her.

Dr. Rogers's voice came clear and hurried. "Miss Davis, open that window. The fever is at its height. We need to cool her, *now*."

The window was wrenched open, and the door slammed shut in the sudden breeze.

I rushed back to my own room, leaned over the basin, retched. I had a sudden vision of Richard like that, diminished and feeble, broken and scornful. And if someone that indomitable could be brought so low, what hope was there for the rest of us? I poured myself a glass of water, drank until the liquid ran down my neck.

Then I lay down heavily on my bed, breathing hard.

I intended to rise again in a moment, to go back out into the corridor, to make sure Louis was all right, to see if Susan was less agitated, to assure myself that she had said nothing that might harm me. But I was bone tired, and I found I could barely move. I lay there in the dark and before I knew it, I was slipping into sleep.

I dreamed of Isabella and Louis, sitting together on the swing in Louis's garden, pushing their feet against the grass to make them go faster, higher, with no fear that they might fall.

CHAPTER X

I WOKE TO THE SOUND OF FIERCE KNOCKING ON MY DOOR. I RAISED my head, rubbed my eyes. Beyond the curtains, all seemed black. I was still exhausted, and I could not at first work out what was happening. Last night came back to me in flashes. Several more seconds passed before I had the wherewithal to get out of bed and hurry to the door.

Miss Davis was standing a few feet back. Her face was white, her eyes wide. It was the only time since her arrival that I had seen her beyond the barricade of chairs.

My heart beat fast. "What is it—is it Louis?"

"No, no—he is a little better, but—I need you to go and rouse Mr. Carter. You must ask him to ride to Hartbridge at once for Dr. Rogers. When he left not long ago, we thought—well, it doesn't matter. Will you go? Mrs. Pulley is with Louis and the rest of the house is asleep."

I stepped back into my room only to grab my dressing gown and pull it around my shoulders. "What has happened?" I asked, my heart pounding.

"Susan is barely breathing." She glanced over her shoulder. "I must go back."

And then Miss Davis was gone, back past the barricade of chairs, back into Susan's room. I was left standing alone in the corridor, my heart in my mouth, suddenly horribly awake.

Susan.

Susan, who threatened any happy future I might have at Hart-wood Hall.

I had been relieved, had I not, the first moment I heard she was ill, relieved to be spared her constant looks, the fear that crept over me when I was in her presence. I had been relieved.

And last night, the way she had looked at me from her sickbed, the draining fear that had spread through me . . . I wanted rid of it. Of her.

I hesitated for a moment. I could linger, or I could run. The thought crossed my mind that Susan's life was half in my hands.

Susan's life.

She was only twenty. She had barely lived at all.

I ran down the corridor, as fast as I could. I cursed Mrs. Eversham for her mad anxiety as I did so. There were too many bolts, and every moment was a moment lost.

I could not have another death on my hands, another ghost to haunt me.

I battered hard on Paul's door when I reached it. A few seconds passed before I heard the bolt pulled back and Paul appeared in the doorway. His first instinct was a sleepy smile, but when he saw my face, the smile slipped.

"Louis?"

"Susan. Miss Davis says she's much worse. Can you ride to Hart-bridge for Dr. Rogers? He only left a short while ago, but—"

Paul had already stepped back into his rooms, leaving the door wide open, and he was pulling on trousers over his nightshirt, grabbing his jacket from the hooks by the door, pushing his feet into his boots.

As he passed me in the doorway, he grabbed my hand and pressed it to his lips. And then he was gone, into the stables, saddling up one of the horses. I stood still, my back against the wall, watching the sun creep up above the hills, my heart pounding.

Half a minute later, I saw Paul riding out of the stables, down the track toward the woods, moving swiftly. He shouted back to me to close the doors behind him, and I did so, pulling the wooden bar across, locking the other horse inside.

When I turned back to the grounds, Paul was out of sight.

———⟶✦⟵———

I did not know what to do when I was back at the house.

Upstairs, Susan was dying. And if she died, what in the world was to stop Louis dying, too? I could almost see it: Louis's face white and still and cold, Mrs. Eversham losing a child for the second time, me losing whatever this boy had become to me. Too much. Too much. My husband had died and I had not shed a tear. But if I lost this boy, I would break.

If Louis died, would he haunt me, as Richard did? Would Susan? Would I see their faces in the dark when I shut my eyes? Would they follow me from place to place, the maid I had feared and the little boy whom I had come to love?

I had tried to distract myself, to forget how afraid I was. I had lost myself in household chores, in helping Mrs. Eversham, in Paul. I had kept the reality of Louis's illness at bay for so long that it now seemed to hit me with all its full force.

It was cruel to think so much of Louis when Susan was in danger. I knew that, and I could not help it. If I could have traded her life for his, I would have.

I stood up. I paced the hall, until the regular sound of my boots on the floorboards brought me comfort. I stopped only at the sound of loud knocking, and I raced to the front doors to wrench them back.

Dr. Rogers headed for the stairs with no more greeting than a nod, and though he was not a young man, he moved fast. The fear in his face made my head ache.

When I finally looked up, I saw Mrs. Eversham at the top of the stairs. She must have heard the commotion and come straight from bed, for she was in her nightdress, her hair loose.

"What is it?" she asked, and I heard the sharp panic in her voice. "The doctor just passed me. Mrs. Lennox, is it Louis—is he—?"

I shook my head and hurried up the stairs to reach her. "Susan," I said.

Another voice, somewhere, said, "What is it?" and when Mrs. Eversham looked down, I followed her gaze. Mrs. Pulley and Stevens were standing at the foot of the stairs.

"It's Susan," murmured Mrs. Eversham. "The doctor has come. She—"

Abruptly, she turned around. I followed her gaze, and saw the door to Susan's sickroom open. Miss Davis and the doctor both stepped out. They stood in silence in the corridor, their faces ashen. Mrs. Eversham and I started toward them—but we did not get far. Miss Davis was softly shaking her head, and the doctor gave a long, deep sigh.

At once I was back in the parsonage, my red shawl wrapped around me, sitting in the armchair in Richard's room as the doctor gazed down at the frame of the man who had been my husband. Then and now I felt relief and guilt surge through me, so muddled together that I did not know where one ended and the other began.

"It is over," Miss Davis said. She spoke the words so quietly I did not hear them but read them on her lips. "Susan is dead."

CHAPTER XI

WE STOOD BY SUSAN'S COFFIN—MRS. PULLEY AND STEVENS, LACEY, Paul, and me. It was a quiet funeral, the churchyard more or less empty. Miss Davis could not leave Louis, for though his fever was passing, he was still very weak. Nor would Mrs. Eversham leave the house. Mr. Welling was here, to read the service, and Mrs. Welling had come, to stand at his side. Mary had refused to accompany them.

As the sexton lowered the coffin into the ground, I spotted a man lingering at the edge of the churchyard, watching. He was youngish, dressed in workman's clothes, with his cap pulled down so that I could not see his eyes. I wondered who he was—perhaps Susan's young man, the person she had been to see that time she crept away from the house? And for all the dislike and fear I had felt for her, the bare fact of her humanity dawned horribly on me.

The young man slipped off into the rain before I could ask the others if they recognized him. I was not sure anyone had noticed him but me.

It had rained incessantly all day. It turned to a downpour as Mr. Welling read the same words that had been spoken at my husband's funeral, three months before. We threw wet flowers down into the grave and turned, slowly, to leave.

"Had she no family?" Mrs. Welling asked me gently, as she walked with us toward Paul's cart.

"None," I said. Mrs. Pulley had told me that Susan's parents had died young, and she'd been put into service straightaway. Over the last seven years, she had worked in five different households, moving from place to place. I wondered what her life had been like before she came here, what had made her feel so powerless that she had sought to grab influence wherever she could, to wear other people's secrets like armor around her skin.

She was a young woman grasping at scraps of power because she had none, and I knew how that felt.

We seemed such a sparse, forlorn group. Two thoughts pushed themselves into my brain: one, how sad that was, that there were none but us to mourn her—I, who had been afraid of her; Mrs. Pulley, who had often upbraided her; Stevens and Lacey, who had been too removed from her by age and position to truly know her; and Paul, who had barely known her at all. My second thought was that this would be what my funeral was like, no one to mourn me but the household I worked in.

"It is a sad day," said Mrs. Welling.

"It is."

"How is Louis?"

I looked up. "A little better today. His fever has died down now, and he seems to be past the most dangerous time. We are all hopeful."

Mrs. Welling nodded. "You will write to me, won't you, if—if anything changes?"

"Of course," I said. And then, "Thank you."

"For what?"

"For coming. It is more of a kindness than you know."

⟶＞＜⟵

We were all silent in the cart returning to Hartwood Hall. Paul sat up front, guiding the horse, while the rest of us squashed together in the back. Mrs. Pulley's silence was customary, but Stevens was solemn and quiet all the way home, and even Lacey seemed unable to think of anything to say. Paul drove us back along the country roads and all the while the rain fell fast. We barely noticed.

I kept my eyes on Paul, watched his every movement, as though the sight of his steady, familiar figure might ground me, might drown out the tumult of my thoughts.

We were nearing the woods now. The trees had turned, the branches smothered in reds and golds, the ground a carpet of fallen leaves. When the darkness took us, the trees sheltered us from the rain, and the soft feel of drops was replaced by blindness and silence. A shuffle to the right, a dim glow in the darkness before me—I heard Lacey stifle a mutter, and my hands began to shake.

This was foolishness. This was madness. I was safe in a cart with four other people on a rainy afternoon, and soon we would be home. Susan was dead and Louis seemed a little better and here I was, my hands shaking, my heart thumping, and for no other reason than because I feared the dark.

If Isabella and Richard had left ghostly footprints in the woods before, now there was one more ghost to join them.

Eventually we emerged into the dim gray afternoon. I felt my heart rate ease.

We alighted at the edge of the courtyard. Paul held out his hand to help each of us down, and though he held my hand a little longer before he let it go, no one seemed to notice.

Suddenly Lacey spoke. Her voice sounded odd after an hour of silence. She said to Mrs. Pulley, almost mournfully, "I suppose we shall have to get another housemaid now."

Mrs. Pulley nodded, and that was all. She reached into her skirt pocket for the keys and walked toward the front doors. She was the first to vanish into the house. Next was Stevens, and then Lacey, and finally Paul and I were left alone in the courtyard, standing in the rain, our clothes sodden.

At last he said, "I had better take the horse back." He glanced at me, his lips set, his eyes shining, as though he were trying to tell me a thousand things he could not say. Then, "Tea?"

I nodded. As he led the horse to the stables, I walked forward and shut the front doors. Then I followed him, slowly, around the back of the house.

My hair was wet beneath my bonnet, my clothes soaked, my body tired. I waited in the rain as Paul tied up the horse, waited as he pulled the bar back across the stable doors, as he unlocked his rooms. Then he opened the door wide, took my hand, and pulled me in.

His hand slipped from mine and he went to light the stove. I watched the spark flicker, felt the warmth creeping toward me. Paul took off his wet jacket and strung it up before the fire. Then he turned to me, raised his hands to my face, untied my bonnet strings, took it off, and laid it, gently, on the table.

"You're shivering," he said.

"So are you."

He put his arms around my waist, drew me closer. His whole body was wet and warm, and as I wound my arms around his neck, pressed my face into his shoulder, I felt safe, just for a moment, as though the world could not harm us here. Time would stop and leave only us. I hugged him closer to me, not with passion, not with longing, but because he was a refuge, a shelter from the storm.

"You are quiet today," he said into my hair. "All through the service. Were you thinking of—him, your husband? I know it must be—"

I shook my head to silence him. The words seemed too much. Tears pricked at my eyes, and I did not know whether they were tears of sorrow or relief.

"Margaret," Paul said, "do you believe in heaven?"

I pulled back almost without meaning to. "Of course. Do you—do you not?"

He gave a weak smile. "Probably. Sometimes. I don't know."

"But you are so regular at church, I—"

He shrugged. "It's when I see my family. I don't much like going back to the farm. They always call it home and it is not my home."

I looked at him, his solemn frown, the wisps of hair curling at his temples. His hands were on my shoulders, as though he could not quite let me go.

"After my mother died," he said slowly, "sometimes I didn't . . .

want to believe, I suppose. I didn't want a God who took my mother. I didn't want to think she was somewhere else, in paradise, without us."

"So what do you believe in?"

He looked at me. "Gardens," he said, and then he laughed at himself, and somehow I found a smile on my lips.

"I suppose heaven would be a garden for you."

"And for you?"

"I hardly know. Somewhere loud and full. Books and flowers and blackboards, I suppose."

He smiled, and then his smile slipped. "I wonder what Susan's heaven is like."

I said nothing. I thought of her stare in the music room, her shadow in the corridors, her insistent, threatening voice, how she had made me lie for her, tried to make me steal. And for a moment the words were on the tip of my tongue. I could tell him. I could tell him everything.

"Paul," I said, meeting his gaze, "what did you . . . make of Susan?"

He frowned. "I barely knew her. She always seemed like a pleasant enough girl to me."

I couldn't do it. I stared at him and the words failed me. I could not take the image he held of me in his mind, his heart, and smash it. I loved it too much, the way he looked at me, the way he loved me.

"Why do you ask?" he said, and because I did not want to answer, I kissed him instead, hard, wrapping my arms around him. My confession died on my lips as he sank into me, hands on my back, in my hair. I could not be close enough to him. It was not enough to kiss him, not enough to feel his bare skin against mine. I was blinking back tears that I did not understand as I pulled Paul closer to me, my skin on his skin, his body wet with rain and sweat. As I kissed him, I dared not shut my eyes or look round, for fear I would see Susan's pale dead face, watching us, judging us, from beyond the grave.

CHAPTER XII

I LOOKED CAREFULLY AROUND ME BEFORE I BEGAN MY WALK BACK
from the stables to the house, but I met no one, not even once I was
through the front doors, not even when I took my usual place for dinner. I sat alone at the empty table, my heart thumping. Today had
stretched an age, and it seemed impossible that it had been mere hours
since we buried Susan.

A quarter of an hour after the usual time for dinner, it occurred to
me that no food was coming today. Perhaps Lacey had gone to bed
early after the funeral. Or perhaps—my mind balked—perhaps the
house was distracted, perhaps Louis was not so much improved as we
had all thought this morning.

I stood up, crossed the room, hurried toward the stairs. At the top,
on the landing, I nearly knocked into Lacey.

"Ah, Mrs. Lennox, there you are. I have just now taken up a plate
of supper to Mrs. Eversham—she's worn out and eating in her room.
I meant to bring something for you as well—it'll just be bread and
cheese today, but after the day we have all had I dare say—"

"Of course, Lacey, that's all right."

"I'll put something in the dining room for you."

"Do you know how Louis is?"

"Better, by all accounts," said Lacey, and I felt my heart lift. "Not
much of a cough this afternoon, Mrs. Eversham says. Poor little
mite—and he's such a little thing you'd think a breeze would carry
him off, but here he is, and a tall grown girl like Susan's gone and . . ."
She trailed off, shook her head.

"Are you all right, Lacey?" I asked, as gently as I could.

"Oh, you know me, Mrs. Lennox, I always make the best of things. To be sure, this last fortnight has been a chore, and Susan—well, it was a shock." She yawned, covered her mouth. "Mrs. Pulley has given me the night off, so once I've brought something up for you, I'll go to bed. What a day."

She bustled away down the stairs, and I was about to follow her, to go back to the dining room, when I heard voices. I could not at first tell where they were coming from, but when I turned the corner, I saw Miss Davis and Mrs. Pulley standing together, one on each side of the barricade. I went toward them, meaning to ask after Louis, and as I did their words became clearer, and I saw that Miss Davis had something in each hand, that she was holding them out to Mrs. Pulley.

One of them was a stopped-up bottle; the other was a key.

"We ought to have done this sooner," Mrs. Pulley was saying.

"Dr. Rogers says it will be all right—it has been twelve days since she was moved from her room in the cellars, and the contagion will have died out by now, but just as a precaution, he thought it wise. It's quite simple—open the bottle, carry it about the room to fumigate it, then leave it overnight to fill the air."

"I had better do it tonight. Then we can start going through her things in the morning." Mrs. Pulley took the bottle and looked down at the key in Miss Davis's palm.

"It seems a little sad, does it not," the nurse said, "that she kept it in her pocket all the while she was ill, thinking she would go back there? She wouldn't let me take it off her."

I stared at the key as Mrs. Pulley put it into her pocket. Susan's key. The key to Susan's bedroom in the cellar, the room that had sat abandoned and locked since she fell ill. The room where, surely, she had kept my watch, my letter.

I felt a sudden rush of headiness.

Mrs. Pulley turned to leave. I was close upon them now, and she bid me good evening as she passed by. Miss Davis did the same as I drew near.

"How is Louis?" I asked.

A faint smile lit her lips. "Oh, better, I think. He is still weak, but he has hardly coughed at all today, and the rash is almost gone. Dr. Rogers will be here again tomorrow morning, and then we should know for certain. I am so relieved." Her voice cracked a little, and I heard the earnestness in it, the cautious joy. She had become so fond of Louis so soon, just as I had.

"Of course," I said. "As am I."

—→⋅←—

I ate a solitary dinner of bread, hard cheese, and apples. I could barely keep my hands still as I ate. All the time I was thinking about my letter, my watch. Mrs. Pulley had said she would fumigate Susan's room tonight—she must have already been in, and if I was lucky, she would have left the door unlocked overnight. I would have an opportunity, for the first time, to look for what Susan had taken from me—the only opportunity, in fact, if Mrs. Pulley was to clean out the room tomorrow. I could not risk waiting longer.

I must steal my letter back. I must at least try.

The hours passed fitfully as I waited for the household to go to sleep. I changed into my nightgown. I tried to read, to distract myself. I leafed through the pages of *Jane Eyre* for a full chapter without reading a single word. I did not want to read about death, about missed chances, lost family. In the end I sat at my desk, watching the clock on the mantelpiece, trying not to think about Susan. It did not feel quite real that she was dead, that she could not harm me anymore.

At two o'clock in the morning, when everything seemed quiet, I picked up a black shawl from the dresser and pulled it round my shoulders. Then I took my candle in my hand, stepped out into the hall, and closed the door behind me.

The corridor was empty, the chairs deserted. No sign of Mrs. Eversham tonight.

Yet I could not still my beating heart as I stepped, carefully, down the corridor toward the stairs. I tried to look only in front of me, watched my candle sputter and tried not to think what I would do if it went out—or worse, what I would do if somebody saw me. Until I reached the servants' quarters, I was safe enough—I need only say I had been struggling to sleep and had gone downstairs for a book—but after that, any meeting would be suspicious.

I would have to be completely silent.

I made my way down the steps that led to the kitchen and the servants' rooms.

Now that I was here, I knew my light was foolish, that someone might see the candle from below their bedroom door. Yet without it, how could I search for my letter?

I finally reached Susan's room and put my hand on the doorknob.

It turned easily, and the door eased open a crack. I breathed out, but my relief at finding the room open did not last long. I shuddered. I did not want to go into a dead woman's room.

I did not believe in ghosts. I knew I did not believe in ghosts.

And yet.

I made myself step inside. The first floorboard creaked, and I stopped, held my breath, waited.

Nothing.

I pulled the door shut behind me and looked around. It was a dull, sparsely decorated room—a sturdy bed, a wardrobe and chest, and a washstand and pitcher in the corner. The floorboards were bare, and the furniture cast long shadows on the white walls. The whole room smelled of acid; I could almost taste the salt, the anise, in the air. I saw the open bottle standing on the floor in one corner, and held my shawl over my mouth and nose to block out the smell. The high window was open a crack and the whole room was icy cold.

Received any more letters lately, Mrs. Lennox?

Shadowy forms flickered on the wall as I placed my candle on the washstand. As I opened the wardrobe, the soft rasp of the door seemed to cover the noise of panting breath behind me.

My own, of course. It could only be my own.

I searched the wardrobe methodically. Work dresses and stays and chemises. A sewing kit, washcloth, and boots thrown hurriedly down. That was all. I felt around at the bottom, but it reached the floor: no space for hidden drawers—and what was I thinking anyway, that a servant would have a thing like that?

I closed the wardrobe, breathing hard.

Nothing wrong with a dead man's watch. Not like he's going to haunt me.

I put the candle on the floor and gingerly opened the chest. I searched through blankets and undergarments, nightgowns and caps. No sign of the watch. No sign of my letter. I lifted every item out slowly and carefully, until the chest stood empty and the floor was spread with a patchwork of Susan's life: aprons and handkerchiefs, piles of patched clothes and darned stockings. At the bottom of the chest, I found a battered little Bible and opened it quickly, half expecting to find my letter pressed within. But instead I found the crumbling petals of a dried flower and the title page marked with three handwritten names: *Edward Potter, Sarah Potter, Susan Potter.*

I closed the cover. It was dreadful, to do this to the things of a woman who was dead. I placed it all back, one item at a time. I sat on the floor without moving, hearing nothing but my own choking breath.

Then, something new.

I turned sharply.

No such thing as ghosts anyway.

It was only a mouse, dashing out from under the bed toward the skirting boards.

Ah, under the bed. I had not thought of that.

I closed the chest, took my candle in hand, and lay down on my stomach on the floorboards. I used one arm to push myself forward, to tuck myself into the tight space beneath her bed. My heart was pounding, my breath short and fast—but I saw it, sure enough. A wooden box, pushed right into the corner, where it would be hardest to reach. I put the candle down and pulled the box toward me, shuffling back on the floor.

When I was finally able to sit up, my nightdress was thick with dust. I sat cross-legged on the floor, candle at my side, and pried open the lid.

It was stuffed full, and in the dim light spreading from the candle, it took me a few moments to make out what I was seeing. A box, packed with an odd assortment of things: papers, letters, a patch of cloth, a child's toy, the tarnished wedding ring I had found in the lake, a jeweled bracelet, a loose button, a ribbon, a book with its spine in tatters, a—ah, Richard's gold watch.

I lifted it toward me and pressed it into my palm. The metal was cold against my skin, and when I opened it, I saw it had stopped. It must not have been wound for some time.

I put it down beside the candle and began to search for my letter. There were dozens of papers here. I sifted through them, barely able to make them out in the darkness, catching only scattered words—the name *Mrs. Eversham* once, the names *Lucy* and *Charles*, the words *Come at once* underlined in one letter, and *I have no news* in red ink at the top of another. I found a faded page addressed to *John, my love*—Stevens: that was his Christian name. This must be some love letter, I thought, and half wondered if I had been right, if Susan held something over him, too. But I made myself pass it over, because behind it at last I saw the words *My dear Margaret* at the top of a page and allowed myself to breathe out.

I looked down at the box again and found my eyes drawn to a newspaper advertisement that my letter had hidden. The edges of the paper were neat, and it looked new. I lifted it, squinted at it in the darkness.

> **Should any person have information regarding the following individuals, please write to MR. BROWNE at this newspaper. They will be compensated for their time.**

Then a sound, distinct. A footstep.

I looked up, my breath coming fast, and saw a light, dim, from beneath the door. I put the lid back on the box and blew out my candle. I folded the papers into my pocket, closed my fist on the watch, and pulled myself under the bed.

I lay there, in the darkness, the mattress mere inches above me, holding my breath.

I was going to be caught. Stevens or Lacey or Mrs. Pulley was about to step into the room and all would be lost. I would be dismissed at once, as a thief or a madwoman.

I would never see Paul again.

I would never see Louis again.

I bit my lip to stop the cry that rose up at the thought, pressed my fingernails into my palm to distract myself. I watched, from beneath the bed, as the door opened, as bare feet stepped into the room.

"Is anybody there?"

It was unmistakably Lacey's voice, though less steady than usual. The amber circle of light from her candle was shaking, just as her hand must be. I held my breath, lying still as the dead, my heart in my mouth.

I had my good ear to the room, and I was glad of it, for I could hear her footsteps as she moved about. My heart was hammering so hard I was half sure she would hear it.

The light was receding. She was moving away. She muttered something under her breath that I could not hear—and then, more distinctly, "Mary was right."

I heard the creak of the door, and the light was gone.

I lay there for what felt like an age in the dark, turning the watch over and over in my hand, breathing in and out. Then, when enough time had passed that I was sure Lacey would be asleep once more, I got out from under the bed as quietly as I could. I held the watch in one hand, the candlestick in the other. I felt the crinkle of paper in my pocket as I moved, softly, toward the door.

I had no way of relighting the candle, and even if I had, I might not have dared. So I stepped out of Susan's room into the darkness, feeling my way along the corridor. I stopped at the foot of the servants' stairs, but there was only silence. No eerie footsteps, no voices of the dead.

I tried to think of something else, tried to concentrate on what I had found beneath Susan's bed. Mrs. Eversham's name, Stevens's. I thought of Mary's ransacked room, all those weeks ago, and wondered what, if anything, Susan had found among her things. Who else had she threatened? And why?

Up the stairs I went, my breath coming fast. I had stolen from a dead woman who had first stolen from me, and now her face was in the moonlit shadows of the main hall, her voice in the sound of my footsteps as I ascended. Her open palm seemed to stretch before me as I reached for my bedroom door.

And here I was. Safe again.

I felt for the matches on my bedside table and lit my candle. As light enveloped me, I felt my breathing slow. It would be all right.

After all, as Susan had said, there was no such thing as ghosts.

I bolted my door and lit the fire. Then I knelt down in front of the flames and held out the letter. In the flicker of the firelight, I caught sight of Cornelia's handwriting, her neat mentions of *accusations*, of *poisons*. The words sent a wave of nausea through me. I wanted to destroy them, to blot them out forever.

I did not want to face my guilt. I did not want to think of what I had done.

I let the letter fall. I sat on the floor for a long while, watching the pages curl and glisten, watching the writing burn.

VOLUME FOUR

CHAPTER I

WHEN I WOKE THE NEXT MORNING, MY BODY ACHED. I ROSE SLOWLY, pulled myself out of bed, and stumbled toward the washstand.

My nightgown still lay on the floor. I would have to beat it myself before it went into the laundry, in case anybody asked about all that dust. I caught sight of a scrap of paper folded beneath it, and remembered that in the hurry of last night it was not just my own letter I had taken from Susan's box. I was about to lean down to pick it up when I caught sight of the clock on the mantelpiece—I was already late for breakfast. I shoved the nightgown and the paper hastily into the corner of my room and hurried to the door. It would have to wait until tonight.

On my way downstairs, I spotted Dr. Rogers in the entrance hall, but he did not see me as he closed the oak doors behind him. It was an early hour for him to be here, and a twinge of dread stirred inside me. I hurried to the breakfast room, where I found Mrs. Eversham at the table, one hand raised to her cheek, tears pouring from her eyes.

I stood horror-struck in the doorway, staring at her. I heard a sob erupt from her lips, and a lump formed in my throat.

Louis.

My poor, poor child.

And then she turned to me, and I saw that she was smiling, that though tears were streaming down her face, what I taken for a sob had been a laugh.

"Oh, Margaret, good morning," she said, wiping her eyes. "You will forgive me, I am sure. I know Susan is only a few days dead, and it is wicked to be so happy, but—well, I am so relieved. Dr. Rogers has just told me that Louis is finally out of danger. He is well enough to be seen."

I blinked. The relief was immense, and for a moment I thought I might not be able to keep myself from laughing, from crying, as his mother did. But I controlled myself. "I am very glad," I said.

She must have heard how true that was from my voice, for she gave me a warm smile.

"I think it will be another week or so before he is ready to learn again." She let out a long sigh. "Oh, I have missed him so much."

"As have I."

"I know." Mrs. Eversham shook her head. "It has been a strange first few months for you, Margaret, but I am glad you have stayed. I will go up and see Louis as soon as I am recovered. I don't want him to . . . to see me upset." Her voice cracked a little. "I have not seen him for nearly a fortnight." When she raised her teacup to her lips, I saw that her hand was shaking. "You would like to see him, too, I am sure. Come up this afternoon."

I spent the morning helping Stevens and Mrs. Pulley, sweeping, cleaning silver. There was a cheerful mood in the house, despite Susan's funeral yesterday. Everyone had heard that Louis was truly better. Lacey was singing to herself in the kitchen as I walked by, and even Mrs. Pulley could not quite keep a small smile off her face. Stevens was beaming, his shoulders less tense than they had been for days. I thought of the letter addressed to him that I had spotted beneath Susan's bed, and wondered who it was from, what Stevens's life beyond this house had been.

Before luncheon, I found time to sneak away into the gardens. Working away from the house as he did, Paul might not yet have heard. I found him at last in the shrubbery. He turned, startled, at my approach, and when he saw the expression on my face, he almost dropped his shears.

"What is it? Margaret, what—?"

"It's Louis," I said. "He's going to be all right."

Paul moved toward me, then halted, pulled back. He had been about to throw his arms around me in joy, and had stopped himself just in time. He glanced, hesitantly, up toward the house, the open curtains of the west wing, the many windows glimmering in the sun.

He bit his lip to stop his grin. We looked at each other, standing a respectable distance apart, the picture of polite fellow servants. Then Paul laughed.

"Thank you for telling me."

"But of course."

"And he's truly going to be all right?"

"Truly," I said, and my voice cracked. "Truly he is."

—⸻⸻—

At two o'clock, Mrs. Eversham sought me out in the library. There was redness in her cheeks today, brightness in her eyes; her faded beauty seemed to have come back and she looked years younger.

"How is he?" I asked.

"He is weak," she said, "but he is conscious." She almost dropped into one of the armchairs. "I had better take you upstairs," she said. "Louis was asking after you."

I tried to ignore the rush in my heart when she said that. "Let me go by myself," I said gently. "Rest. You need it."

She nodded. "Yes. Perhaps you're right."

Upstairs, Stevens and Mrs. Pulley were dismantling the barricade across the corridor. I helped them shift the last few chairs before heading to Louis's room.

I knocked softly, and could not help but glance round at the door opposite, the room where Susan had died.

"How is he, Miss Davis?" I asked, when she opened the door.

She smiled. She, too, seemed brighter today. Her face was less drawn, her expression less harried. She looked almost as relieved as Mrs. Eversham did, her eyes shining, her cheeks flushed.

"You can ask him yourself," she said. Then she opened the door wider, showed me in, and stepped out of the room to leave us alone.

Louis was lying in bed in his nightshirt, his sheets pushed down to his chest as though he was still too warm. The rash was gone, but he looked pale and thin. Yet he smiled cheerfully when he saw me, and reached out his hand.

I hurried toward him, sat down gently on the end of his bed, and took his hand. It felt very small in mine.

"Mrs. Lennox," he said, and his voice sounded sleepy, distant.

"How are you, child?"

"Mama says I have been very ill."

"And so you have. But you are better now."

"I suppose I am," he said. "The doctor says so." Then, in a quieter voice, "Mother told me that Susan has gone up to heaven."

I nodded my head solemnly. I thought of what Paul had said, what Susan's heaven would be like. "I am afraid it is true."

Louis glanced toward the window, and I followed his gaze to the courtyard, the closed curtains of the east wing. "I wonder why God wanted Susan and not me," he said. His grip on my hand was weak. "I thought I was going to die, like the girl in *Jane Eyre*. I thought . . . I thought I'd see God."

"Hush, Louis. You're well now."

"When I was ill," he said, "I saw Isabella. She was sitting in the corner of the room, reading one of her books, and she told me I must be very good always."

I felt my skin prickle. "You were dreaming, Louis," I said. "It is lonely, being ill."

"But I wasn't lonely," said Louis softly.

"Miss Davis and Dr. Rogers were good to you, I hope."

"Everyone is good to me," said Louis. "Isabella says if you're good to other people they will be good to you. Except the bad ones. Except the monsters."

"You're tired, I think, Louis," I said. I squeezed his hand, drew a lock of his hair away from his face. Then I stopped. There was something strange about his hair. For a moment I thought the illness had made a streak of it turn white. And then rationality set in and I realized what it was: the roots of Louis's hair, before the pitch black began, were fair, blond, just like the hair of the girl in the locket I'd found in the east wing.

His hair was dyed. There was no doubt about it. Louis's dark mop, his black hair, so perfectly like his mother's, was a lie.

I frowned. Why on earth should Louis color his hair? Had Mrs. Eversham done it so that the boy looked less like his lost sister? I could make no sense of it at all.

"Will we have lessons again soon, Mrs. Lennox?" Louis was asking now, rousing himself a little.

"As soon as you are well."

He smiled. "Could you read to me?" he asked gently.

"Of course. What should you like me to read?"

"*Jane Eyre*, please."

"Very well."

Louis asked me to start from the beginning again, and I was nearing the end of the second chapter when his eyes began to close. I shut the book softly, and as I did, he stirred.

"I don't know why she is afraid of her uncle's ghost," I heard Louis say, under his breath. "I shouldn't be afraid to be haunted."

And then he was asleep, and I sat for a long time at his side, watching the rise and fall of his chest, thanking God that he was alive.

>———⤬———<

I spent the evening in the schoolroom, pulling together papers and books, planning lessons for Louis's return. The work felt almost blissful. I wrote lists of dozens of books we would read together, new topics we ought to discuss. He would still be weak for some time, and lessons must resume slowly, but we would build them up, a few hours a day at first, until Louis was fully recovered.

He would be fully recovered.

The thought made my heart fill with joy.

It was late before I went back to my bedroom, and as I stepped through the doorway, candle in hand, I was greeted by the sight of my dusty nightgown pushed into the corner. Yesterday abruptly loomed large in my mind, and the cheerfulness that had enveloped me all day seemed to slip away. What would they all think, Louis, Mrs. Eversham, Paul, if they knew that last night I had robbed a dead woman's room?

I shook my head and lifted the nightgown. I brushed it down, wiping the dust in smears from the fabric to the floor. Then I took it to the washstand and poured water from the ewer over it. I draped it over the top to dry, and turned back to pick up the scrap of paper from the floor.

Slowly I unfolded the newspaper advertisement I had glimpsed last night, saw the words flicker in the candlelight. There was no date on it, but it looked recent, the paper still white, the ink not yet faded.

> Should any person have information regarding the following individuals, please write to MR. BROWNE at this newspaper. They will be compensated for their time.
> SEEKING—one MRS. AND MASTER GREY, the former thirty-five years old, the latter ten years of age. Mrs. Grey is small and delicately built, with fair hair, blue eyes, and pale skin. Master Grey is a young boy of similar appearance to his mother, small and slight in form, with blue eyes and fair hair.

I thought of the blond roots of Louis's hair this morning, of all the things about this house that had never quite made sense—the lack of servants, Mrs. Eversham's evasiveness, Louis's hatred of secrets.

I read the advertisement again. The ages were right. Louis's hair was dyed. Mrs. Eversham's might well be, too. Her eyes were a greenish blue. True, I would not have described a woman so much taller than myself as small, but she was thin, slight, delicate.

What if, after all, the Evershams were not who they said they were?

CHAPTER II

"Good morning, Mrs. Lennox. I am afraid you have just missed Miss Davis."

I blinked. "Missed her?"

Mrs. Eversham nodded. "Yes. Dr. Rogers came early on his rounds this morning, and as Louis is doing well, he said a nurse is no longer required. She left half an hour ago."

I sat down at the breakfast table, oddly sad that I'd not had the chance to say goodbye. She seemed like a good woman, Miss Davis— hardworking, kind. She had, perhaps, saved Louis's life. And she was like me. She both was and was not a lady, and she had come to this house to care for Louis. Now she was banished, and I remained.

"She was a very good nurse," I said.

"Yes." Mrs. Eversham smiled. "We could not have done without her."

———⊱⊰———

The next few days passed quickly. I spent hours sitting in Louis's room, talking with him, reading to him, playing chess with him, discussing what we would study when he was well. His mother sometimes joined us, or sent me away with a word or a look, so that they might be alone.

With Louis growing stronger every day, Mrs. Pulley and Stevens began to refuse my help around the house, even when I had nothing else to do.

"You shall be back to your own work soon enough," Stevens said with a smile.

So I would sit in the schoolroom and plan out lessons for Louis, waiting to be summoned back to his side.

I kept thinking of what I had found in Susan's room, of the blond line in Louis's hair. What did it mean, if the Evershams were not who they said they were? I thought of what Mrs. Eversham had said, when we could not find a nurse—that people in the village did not like her because they thought she had never had a husband. That might be true. It would be one reason to live under an assumed name, though it hardly explained the dyed hair. Or it might be, instead, that she had been married, that her husband had died like mine, in circumstances that made her want to run, to forget.

———⟫⟪———

I asked Paul the next time we were together. I said it cautiously. "Paul, did you ever hear of Mrs. Eversham going by another name?"

He stiffened at my side. "No."

"Mrs. Grey, perhaps?"

He shook his head. We were lying together in the hayloft, and he reached for me gently, turned my face toward him. "What on earth makes you ask that?"

"Oh, it doesn't matter. I expect I am mistaken." I chose my words carefully; I could not tell him, of course, about Susan, about the box beneath her bed. "I found a newspaper article, advertising for a Mrs. and Master Grey, and it sounded very much like them, only—well, it said they were fair-haired, but Louis . . . Paul, his hair is dyed. I noticed it, a few days ago, fair roots beneath the black. And I wondered—"

Paul shifted. He turned onto his back. "They're good people, Mrs. Eversham and Louis."

"I know that. You know I know that."

"Then don't . . . pry."

I stared at him. I was not *prying*. I did not know how to explain myself, without telling him about Susan, about where I had found the article; but if Mrs. Eversham and Louis were not who they said they were, if Susan had known that, then they had been—perhaps still were—in danger of being discovered. What that might mean for them, I could not say, but it made me uneasy. I could not bear the thought of anything bad happening to Louis. I could not bear the thought that he, like me, might feel the press of the past.

What had Susan said to me, a week or two before she fell ill? *What if I told you that this family, this house, is going to come crashing down?*

Paul was looking away from me, frowning.

"Paul," I said slowly, "do you know something I don't?"

He stared at me. He looked pained. "I know there is nothing for you to be afraid of." He paused, and then the frown was gone and his soft, broad smile was back. "Margaret, stop this. Stop trying to uncover secrets. Let them be. They're good people; that's all that should matter to you."

CHAPTER III

MRS. EVERSHAM AND I WERE AT BREAKFAST WHEN STEVENS CAME in with a tray of letters. He handed the majority to Mrs. Eversham, and then one to me. I stared, surprised, then opened it hurriedly.

It was from Mrs. Welling. She told me that she was sorry to say Mary was refusing to go back to Hartwood Hall, that she had found a family in the next county in need of a kitchen maid. She enclosed a letter from Mary.

I unfolded the letter, and a passing glance was enough to show me the words *ghosts* and *noises* and *unexplained* before I realized it was addressed to Mrs. Eversham. I handed it to her.

Mrs. Eversham's brow furrowed, and she read fast. When she finished, she was still frowning. "I'm afraid Mary will not be coming back. She has found another position. A shame, of course, but I dare say Lacey will manage. We will find someone new in time. Of course we must advertise for Susan's position, too." She sighed. "The household is shrinking fast."

I looked across at her, her careworn face, her green-blue eyes. I thought of the newspaper advertisement folded in my dresser drawer. Mrs. and Master Grey. Had Susan done anything with it before hiding it in the box beneath her bed? Had she answered it before she grew ill? Had she written to the person who was looking for them? Or perhaps she had demanded money from Mrs. Eversham, too.

I would never be able to ask. I sipped my tea and tried to smile.

———⟶⟵———

That evening, I did not go to Paul. I went to the library instead, opened a copy of *Agnes Grey*, and made myself read. I told myself that it was because we ought to be more careful now, that every day Louis grew better Mrs. Eversham was more aware, more likely to find us out. In truth I was frustrated with him, and did not want him to know it.

I could not tell whether he was being entirely open with me. Sometimes I half thought he knew something about the Evershams that I did not, and the next moment would upbraid myself for not believing in his sincerity. And besides, if I did not trust him, what then? I could not bear the thought of being without him, without the familiar warmth of him, his precise movements, the thrill his soft voice gave me, the way his touch made my heart beat fast—everything that made him *him*, everything that made him perfect. I knew I could only keep away for so long.

Richard had accused me, once, of having a love affair. His words still rang clearly in my head: *You will not make a mockery of me, Mrs. Lennox. You will tell me who this man is that you have been to see.*

I told him he was mistaken. I promised him that it was madness, that I would never betray him, that I was not that sort of woman.

But I wondered now if what I had said was true. It had not taken much for me to fall.

I stared down at *Agnes Grey*. I had been reading the same page over and over again and I had taken nothing in. I had tried to drown my thoughts in words, and I had failed. The clock read eleven and I had done nothing for hours.

Richard was not here. He was dead and gone and I was free. Free to be the person he had despised.

I put the book down and stepped out of the library. Across from me, the door of Mrs. Eversham's study was open a crack, candlelight flooding out. I stepped forward to bid her good night.

Then I stopped, pulled up sharp. Mrs. Eversham was sitting at her desk, a wooden box open before her.

I knew it at once.

The box from beneath Susan's bed.

Mrs. Eversham was searching through it, methodically taking out one item after another—putting a letter in one pile, throwing another on the fire, folding a newspaper clipping neatly into a second stack. She took up the old wedding ring and the jeweled bracelet, put the first into her desk drawer, and slipped the other around her wrist.

Had it been hers, then? Had Susan stolen it, forced it from her, as she had forced Richard's watch from me?

Did Mrs. Eversham know about the advertisement? Was she searching for that, too?

She looked up and, seeing me through the slim opening of the doorway, she quickly shut the box.

"Mrs. Lennox?"

"I only came to say good night," I said, opening the door a little more, pretending I had seen nothing unusual.

"Thank you." She smiled, but her manner was distracted. "Louis seemed so much better today," she said. "I wondered if he might be well enough to start lessons on Monday—just a few hours, perhaps."

"Certainly."

She nodded, smiled. And then she looked down at the box and the papers spread over her desk, as though to remind us both that she was busy, and I knew I was dismissed.

CHAPTER IV

"It is dreadful about Susan," said Mrs. Welling, "but I am so, so relieved that Louis is well."

I was sitting at her side in the box. Louis was still too weak to go as far as church, so I had come without him once more.

"I suppose you will be starting lessons soon again?"

I nodded.

"Do you miss teaching, when you are not doing it?"

"Very much," I said, almost without thinking. I had not quite realized how true it was—but I missed it dreadfully. Not just recently when Louis had been ill, but in the years with Richard, too.

I had tried, in the first year of my marriage, to set up a Sunday school. But Richard told me that it would not do, that for a gentleman's wife to teach farmers' children on a Sunday was unwomanly, unrespectable.

I say you shall not do it, Mrs. Lennox, and you shan't. That is all.

He had always called me Mrs. Lennox, not Margaret, when he wished to make a point—when he wished to remind me that I was, above all, his wife.

That I was more his than I was my own.

Just as Mr. Welling stepped out to the front, his wife leaned toward me and, with her usual smile, said quickly, "It has been an age since we saw you at our house. Won't you come and dine soon?"

"Of course, I'd love to. I doubt Louis will be well enough to join me."

"Then come alone. We would both be glad to have you. Next Sunday?"

"Certainly."

She smiled at me and turned back to watch her husband. I watched her, the look of pure love in her eyes, as though everything beyond him faded away as he began to speak.

I glanced out into the congregation, searching for Paul, waiting for him to look up at me.

And instead I caught the eye of a different man. The young man I had seen lingering in the churchyard at Susan's funeral.

———→—<—→———

"Did you see that man at church?" I asked Paul that night. We were lying up in the hayloft, my head on his chest, his arm around my shoulder.

"What man?"

"I don't know if you saw, but there was a man, at Susan's funeral, watching—I had almost forgotten him, but I am sure I saw him again at church today."

Paul frowned. He ran his finger across my shoulder. "I don't remember seeing anyone."

I wondered if he really had been Susan's young man, if she had lain like this in that man's arms, if she had felt for him what I felt for Paul.

I heard a low sound and sat up sharply.

"It's just the clock," murmured Paul.

"What time?"

He counted. "Eleven."

"Eleven?" I scrambled to my feet. "It cannot be so late, surely."

Paul rose slowly beside me. "I suppose it is."

"Damn." I was already reaching for my clothes, pulling on my undergarments, trying to tie my stays.

"Margaret, what's the matter?"

"Mrs. Pulley will have bolted the doors by now." I pulled on my dress, fastened my buttons. "I am never this late. We are always so careful. How on earth am I supposed to get back in?"

"Ring the bell. Say you've been out late walking."

"Until eleven at night? They will either think I'm mad or guess some part of the truth."

"Then stay with me. Stay all night."

I looked round at him. I thought about it, what it might be like to wake at his side, morning sun streaming over us. An intimacy we had never shared. Then reality set back in and I shook my head. "And have someone notice I am not in my room in the morning? Are you quite mad, Paul?"

He looked a little chastened. Then he stood up, reached for his undergarments. "There is another way," he said.

——>·<—·——

We tramped across the grass together. My skirts would be thick with mud. My hair was in a state of disarray and I hoped to God that everyone was asleep. I followed Paul around the side of the house with a thundering heart. We would have to be more careful in the future. I should have known to be more careful tonight.

We reached the door at the side of the east wing where I had tumbled into Paul six weeks before. I hesitated as he searched for the keys in his pocket. I could not help the shiver working its way through me. I did not want to walk through the east wing alone at night. "I can't understand it," I said, because talking, even in a whisper, was the only way to stop my teeth from chattering. "Why does Mrs. Eversham have ten bolts on the front doors and yet this door can be opened by a key?"

"Well, there's another two locks before you get to the main section of the house," said Paul.

I frowned. "But that day I went into the east wing . . ."

Paul shrugged. "An accident, I suppose. Mrs. Pulley must have left the door to the east wing unlocked after cleaning in there. The door will almost certainly be locked tonight."

I blinked, my panic rising. "Then how will I get in?"

"I have the keys."

"You're coming with me?"

"Of course," he said, and in my relief I felt a sudden wave of love for him. He knew I would be afraid, and he would come with me to make sure I was not. He knew me, at least a little—for all that he did not know my past, he saw some part of me for who I was.

I reached for his hand and pressed it tight in mine.

"Margaret."

"Yes?"

"It's quite hard to unlock doors with only one hand."

I laughed. I couldn't help it. Paul grinned at me in the dark and I withdrew my hand, watching as he pushed the key into the lock. It was locked from the other side and he had to maneuver his key to push the other out of place. I heard it fall to the floor with a click.

"Why *do* you have the keys, Paul?"

"I've had the keys to Hartwood Hall longer than anybody else here." He shrugged. "I think I told you that my brother and I found a set in the stables once. I kept them, just in case."

A few moments later he put his hand back in mine and eased the door open.

The east wing was just as dark as the gardens. At first, I could see nothing. I was aware only of Paul's pressure on my hand, the muddy ground changing to floorboards beneath my feet, and some low sound—just the creak of the door behind us, of course; I must not be so foolish as to imagine it more.

We stepped forward together, through another door, then down a long corridor. I half remembered the layout of the east wing, but I had run through it last time, clattering through its corridors, passing through its rooms at speed. I could not imagine now how I had been so afraid with daylight streaming through the gaps in the curtains—I would give everything for sunlight now, for anything other than relentless darkness. My hands were clammy with sweat, and though I knew the only footsteps I heard were Paul's and mine, I could not help shuddering.

All that darkness—black walls, black ceiling, black sky—and suddenly I was thirteen years old again, trapped down the bottom of the well, my head bound up and bleeding still, the sky getting darker and darker above me, until I could neither see nor hear, until the only thing I could feel, sense, taste, smell was pain, pain, pain, and my chest was heaving, my sobs coming crushed and strangled, not loud enough, for nothing would ever be loud enough again, and—

I would not cry. I was a grown woman now, walking through a house in the dark. That was all.

As my eyes began to adjust, I saw shadows in the corridor, shapes I told myself were furniture, and dared not reach out in case I was wrong. Paul's hand was still in mine, and though I would know his hand anywhere by now, though it was as familiar to me as my own, though I could trace the scars and cuts on his palm, still I said softly, "Paul?"

"I'm here."

"I hate it."

"I know. I should have brought a candle."

"But then someone might have caught us."

He gave a quiet laugh, then pulled me toward him and kissed me.

And that was when I saw it. Somewhere beyond us in the dark.

A light, flickering.

"Paul," I whispered, and he must have heard the urgency in my voice because he stiffened.

"What?"

"Turn around."

I felt him turn, out of my arms, and as he did I reached for his hand, laced my fingers through his, held on tight. He could see what I could now, and I tried to read his face in the dark. He was nothing but a shadow.

There was light seeping out from beneath one of the doors, where it was not flush to the floorboards. Bright yellow candlelight.

"Someone's there," I whispered. "*Who?* No one comes here."

"Mrs. Pulley might have come here to clean. Mrs. Eversham might have decided to wander into this part of the house. Either of them might have left a candle burning. Come, Margaret."

He moved a step forward, and another. I felt our arms stretch, but still I could not move.

"Margaret?"

He was wrong. I knew he was wrong. Not because nobody ever came here but because the pool of light spilling onto the floor was irregular. It was flickering, moving in and out. A shadow was moving across it.

Someone in that room was walking up and down.

My first foolish thought was that ghosts did not light candles.

"Margaret, come on," Paul said, and his voice was so quiet it was a strain to hear, even with my good ear next to him. "You said yourself we don't want to get caught. If there is someone in that room, it must be Mrs. Eversham or one of the servants. We should move."

I wanted to move. I wanted to run, to run out of the house and into the fresh air. And I wanted, more than anything, to know who or what was behind that door.

I turned the handle fast before I could change my mind, and wrenched it open.

It was just an empty room, sheets thrown over shadows of furniture, light flickering at the edges of the walls, a lone candle burning on the table.

No one here.

Just a candle.

But candles did not light themselves. Candles did not burn for hours. Even if someone had left it here—

A hand on my shoulder. I started round.

It was only Paul, trying to pull me onward.

"Just like I said," he murmured. "It's only a candle."

I was still looking around the room when he blew it out and we were plunged into darkness. I caught my breath—but I had seen it, hadn't I? Just before the light was extinguished, I had seen, on the other side of the room, in among furniture and shadows, another door.

Paul was pulling me out into the corridor, soft step upon soft step. I did not want to follow him. I wanted to check the other door. I wanted to tell him that it was nonsense to say it was nothing, that candles are not left burning in empty rooms, that it was madness to say that no one had been there, that—

He let go of my hand. I heard the low clatter of metal on metal, and when I squinted I could see that Paul was moving. I stretched out my hand and felt the wooden door before us. We had got to the end. In a moment's time I would be back in the main part of the house. In a minute or two more I would be safe in my own room.

"Who was it?" I whispered, as Paul turned another key in another lock.

"What?"

"In the room—there was someone there. I saw another door, Paul. They must have left just as we entered and forgotten their candle. You know that must be true."

"If there was someone, it must have been Mrs. Eversham."

He was lying. He must, surely, be lying.

My mind was whirring, my head sore. I thought of the footsteps I had heard in the east wing before, the sound of singing. I thought of the advertisement, the name Grey. These were people on the run, people hiding. Hiding something. I thought of the silhouette by the lake, the figure in white.

Paul touched my hand with his. "Listen, it's all right," he said gently.

I turned on him. "Paul, you are unlocking an interior door with multiple keys and the front doors have ten bolts and there are candles lit where there should not be candles and noises where there should be silence. Nothing about this house is right."

"Mrs. Eversham is a nervous woman. The house is old and the servants are overworked. That is all." But I heard something in his voice I had never heard before: fear, perhaps, panic. "There is nothing here to be afraid of, Margaret. Trust me."

I stared at him. He asked me to trust him, and I almost, almost did. If he could have spared me my fears, surely he would have told me all he knew.

And yet.

He pushed the door noiselessly open. In the hall, the staircase and carpet were dimly lit by moonlight, and everything was familiar—the grandfather clock, the chest, the console table, the marble floor.

"Here we are," said Paul. He squeezed my hand, then let go.

I could see his face now in the moonlight, the way the shadow fell across his smile. He looked so ordinary, so unperturbed by what had just happened.

"Paul—"

"I had better go back," he whispered. "Good night, Margaret."

I blinked. His first words were spoken quickly, almost anxiously, and yet he said my name so gently, so tenderly, that it seemed almost impossible to doubt him. I found myself saying "Good night."

I watched him close the door, listened for the sound of the keys turning in the locks. Then I crept up the stairs to bed.

—————⟶⟵—————

That night I dreamed of Isabella, a thin slip of a girl walking the lonely corridors of the east wing, her skin pale, her feet bare. She was wearing a long white dress, her fair hair done up in ribbons, her face smiling in the dark.

I did not know, even when I woke, if the girl I had dreamed of had been dead or alive.

CHAPTER V

My LESSONS WITH LOUIS BEGAN AGAIN THE NEXT DAY. I TRIED TO push all thought of the night before out of my head, to focus entirely on Louis. Whatever secrets this house held, I would have to dwell on them later. If Paul knew something—and I could not deny to myself that he *might* know something—I would have to make him tell me. I had asked in the darkness of the east wing and discovered nothing, but if I bided my time, if I found the right moment—surely, he would tell me.

Now that Susan was gone and Miss Davis had left, it was I who woke Louis in the morning, who helped him dress and brought him down to breakfast, who put him to bed at night. I liked the extra hours we spent together—after so long separated from him, it was something to feel I could be of use, of comfort, that I was once more part of his world. I was the one helping him choose his clothes for the day, teaching him how to comb his hair, and reading him stories before bed.

That day when I arrived in Louis's room, he was already awake, an eager grin on his face. At breakfast he spoke to his mother of nothing but lessons, and all the way up to the schoolroom he seemed to be wearing himself out with delight. He was happy to be back—not merely, I thought, because he liked learning, but because lessons meant he was well once more.

His energy was still not quite what it was, so we agreed to finish our studies at lunchtime for a few days. But first—arithmetic, slow and steady. I sat at my desk, turning over the chalk in my hand, watching Louis write, and something shifted inside me. I was so glad he was well, so grateful, so relieved. I felt more strongly than I could have expected.

I thought of all the mysteries about Hartwood Hall—noises in the night, things I had seen of which I could not make sense, the names the Evershams had gone by in the past, the blond in Louis's hair, too many locks and too many secrets—and if all these things meant that Louis was in danger, I must do what I could to protect him. That must come above everything else.

---><---

That night, he told me shyly that Susan used to fetch him a warm cup of chocolate to drink before bed, and so I did the same. When I went down to the kitchen to make it, I found Lacey in another of her moods, muttering about there being too much work.

"I've seen no sign of them looking for anyone else, no one to fill Susan's place, let alone Mary's. I can't do everything on my own. And, would you credit it, Mrs. Lennox, food's started going from the larder again. I was so sure it was Susan. Perhaps it was always the young master after all." She sighed heavily. "Sometimes I think leaving's the only wise thing Mary's ever done . . ."

I could not imagine Louis stealing down to the cellars each night in search of food—especially not now, when he was so weak and tired at the end of every day. I wondered if it was possible that this story of the missing food was merely a tale of Lacey's, something she had thought up to have a reason to complain—but there was no reason for her to invent a break in the pilfering. And when I remembered the candle flickering in the east wing, I knew—I almost knew—that this was not nothing.

I shook the thought away, forced myself to brighten. "Can I help, Lacey?"

She drew herself up. "Oh no, Mrs. Lennox, not when you've got Louis to care for now. You're very good, warming up his chocolate yourself and such like, but I couldn't ask more. I have my pride, ma'am."

I took the chocolate upstairs for Louis, along with a cup of my own, and I sat down on the end of his bed.

"How are you feeling?" I asked him.

Louis looked up at me, smiled sleepily. "Not quite ordinary," he said, "but better. Almost well." Another pause. "I won't get ill again, will I?"

I hesitated. "I cannot promise that, Louis. But you are well now, and that is what matters."

"I don't like being ill," he said quietly. "I was afraid. I thought—I thought I might die, and when Mother told me Susan had died, I thought perhaps it had all been a mistake that I was alive, and that I should have been in the ground like Susan." His voice caught, and I steadied him by taking his hand in mine.

"It's all right, Louis. You are much better now."

"Have you ever been ill, Mrs. Lennox? Have you ever been close to death?"

"Once," I said softly. "When I was a girl—just a little older than you are now—I fell down the well a mile from my parents' house. I cut the side of my head, badly, and I sat in the dark for hours before anybody came."

"But you were all right?"

"Yes. But that was what took the hearing in my left ear."

Louis was looking at me, curious. "Do you miss it?"

I hesitated. "Sometimes," I said. "It means I can't always tell what sound comes from which direction, and anything to that side of me is harder to make out. But I am used to it now. I can tell if I need to move to hear better, and those I know well stand to the right of me, because they know I will be able to hear them."

"Like I do?"

I smiled across at him, propped up in bed, chocolate in hand. This little boy I had come to prize. "Yes, Louis," I said. "Like you do."

—>—<—

I was leaving Paul's rooms the following night when I saw something, a flicker of movement in the dark. It was nearing ten o'clock and the gardens were quiet. But there it was, something in the dimness. A figure, moving, somewhere across the grounds.

I did not stir at once. I watched it, a silhouette in the moonlight. The figure was walking, making a slow circuit of the lake, carefully passing the summer house. This was not some trick of the light. I was certain.

I hurried back to the stables, wrenched open Paul's door. For a moment a smile spread across his face, a flicker of amusement, of pleasure. Then it fell at my expression.

"There's someone out there," I whispered.

Paul frowned. "Margaret, there's not—"

"Paul, I swear." I felt a familiar twinge of annoyance, the same feeling I had felt in the east wing the other night. "Come and look."

He hesitated. I saw something like frustration on his face, and then he moved past me, into the doorway, and looked out into the night. I followed his gaze and saw that the figure was closer now, around the back of the summer house. I watched Paul's face change. "See?"

"It looks like a man," he said, and his voice was slow, confused.

A new thought struck me, a different kind of fear. I thought of the newspaper article tucked away in my room. If Susan really had answered it, if she had brought someone here—

"What do we do?" I heard my voice shake.

Paul reached out to pull the door closed, to shut us in. "We wait," he murmured. "It will just be some youth from the village, come up on a wager. It's happened once or twice before. He'll go."

I put out my hand, held the door open. "We can't do that. What does he want? Why is he here? For all we know he is about to rob the house. Paul—" I broke off. The clouds had drifted on ahead of us, and the figure was suddenly bathed in moonlight. I saw his face clearly. I recognized him. "It's Susan's young man," I said. "The man I saw at the funeral."

I walked quickly out across the grounds, and though Paul hissed something after me, I did not look back. The thought of the advertisement, of Susan's cold voice, the effortlessness with which she had made threats—it forced me to move. I strode toward him and when he turned, startled, on my approach, I saw his eyes widen.

For a moment he looked like he might run.

Then he stopped, looked me up and down, pursed his lips. I saw his shoulders slump.

He was clear in the moonlight. The cap that had been pulled down at Susan's funeral was higher now, and I could see his whole face, his dark eyes, his pinched nose. He was older than I had thought at first, perhaps thirty, dressed in the clothes of a traveling workman.

"What the devil are you doing here?"

He did not answer. He was looking past me, and I turned to see Paul come up at my side. I swallowed. If we had to turn him in, bring him up to the house, tell Mrs. Eversham, summon the constable— well, what would we say? Mrs. Eversham thought that I was in the schoolroom, planning lessons. We would have to claim that I had been walking late at night and had knocked on Paul's door to ask for help when I saw an intruder, but it was hardly credible. I glanced at Paul. He was in only his shirt and trousers, his hair still ruffled from my hands.

The man smirked. "No need to ask what the devil *you* are doing," he said. His voice was softer, more educated, than I had expected. It did not match his clothes.

"You were at Susan's funeral, weren't you?" I kept my voice as steady as I could. "Who are you? Were you . . . courting?"

He laughed. "That bitch? Dear Lord, no. I met her once, to be sure, but only that. Not much good she proved, in the end. Promises upon promises and then she goes and catches something foul and that's it."

"Who are you?" I asked again. "What do you want?"

The man shrugged. "I don't care to give my name to strangers. I was looking for someone, that's all. But it's the wrong woman, wrong house. I saw her today, in the garden, with the boy, and she's not who I'm looking for. One last look around tonight and I'm done. Waste of my time, and of someone else's money."

I stared at him. He had seen Louis. He had *watched* Louis. Something shifted in my stomach. And what did he mean—a waste of someone else's money? "Who sent you?" I asked.

The man grimaced. "Oh, I don't care to tell you that either."

"Then you will have to tell it to a constable," said Paul. It was the first time he had spoken but his voice sounded firm.

"Will I?" said the man. "And what will you do when I tell your fine mistress here what the two of you have been up to?" He looked between us. "Let's see . . . the housekeeper, I suppose, or the governess? And the groomsman, perhaps the gardener. One wedding ring and black dress, one bare finger. Doesn't look very respectable, does it?"

I felt sick. "This is ridiculous," I said, though I felt the heat rise to my face. "You are talking nonsense."

The man shrugged. "But will you risk it?"

I looked at Paul, and he looked at me. Paul, always so steady, so calm, looked suddenly anxious.

"Thought not," said the man. "Besides, I told you—it's all a mistake. Wrong woman, wrong house. You shan't see me again."

He took a step back, away from us.

I ought to have reached out, grabbed him, held him fast, asked him more.

We ought to have taken him up to the house, roused Mrs. Eversham, sent someone over to the nearest town for a constable, however long it took.

But neither Paul nor I moved. We stood there, not looking at each other, and watched the man disappear into the darkness of the woods.

CHAPTER VI

ALL THE NEXT DAY I COULD NOT CONCENTRATE. I TRIED TO FOCUS
on Louis, on the lessons, tried to help him with sums, to write clearly
on the blackboard and concentrate on his reading. But I could not get
that man from the grounds out of my head.

I was angry with myself for not stopping him, for not pressing
him—and I was angry at Paul, too, for being as much a coward as I
had been. What had that man meant by *the wrong woman, the wrong
house*?

Was it possible, perhaps, that Susan had made a mistake? That Susan, looking for secrets, had found one where there was none? That this
man had been sent to look for Mrs. Grey and not found her? That Mrs.
Eversham was indeed Mrs. Eversham, that Mrs. Grey was another
woman altogether, that the Evershams had nothing more to hide than
eccentricities and the tragic loss of a daughter?

But then again, what if Susan had not made a mistake after all?

I could not make sense of it. Paul and I had barely had time last
night to discuss what had happened; I'd had to creep back into the
house before it was locked up. Paul had said we must not tell anyone,
and that was all. I was almost sure I agreed. But then, I did not know
what he knew—and he did not know what *I* did. I wanted to tell him
everything, all I knew of Susan, what she had been like—and I could
not do it. I could not break the spell that held him to me.

That afternoon, when I took Louis on his walk in the grounds, I
could not help looking for Paul. We strolled through the courtyard,

Louis beaming at me as he kicked up fallen leaves from beneath the apple tree. I took him to his own garden, where he climbed up on the swing and asked me to push him. I did so, watching his face light up as he moved backward and forward.

"I've missed my garden," said Louis. "I've missed it all."

It was not long before Paul approached. I saw him from the corner of my eye, coming up from the stables where he'd been feeding the horses, and my heart quickened at the sight of him. He came toward us.

"Good afternoon, Louis. Mrs. Lennox." Paul was smiling. "How are you, lad?"

"All better," said Louis, with a broad grin, kicking his legs as the swing rose higher. "Better and better and strong as a horse."

"Strong as me, eh?"

"Stronger," said Louis, beaming. "Aren't I, Mrs. Lennox?"

I laughed.

"And cleverer, too, no doubt," said Paul. "Back to learning, are you?"

"Today we read six chapters of *Jane Eyre* and did thirty-five sums, and I remembered all the kings and queens of England and said my Shakespeare well, didn't I, Mrs. Lennox? And now my brain's as strong as my body and I shall be all right."

Paul smiled. "You'll be a fine lad yet."

"I'm a fine lad now," said Louis. As if to prove it, he jumped down from the swing and began to run, bounding up through the grass.

The moment Louis was out of earshot, I turned to Paul.

"That man, yesterday. Paul, I think something isn't right. What if—?"

"Don't dwell on it. It was a mistake. He said so."

"But what if it wasn't? Who on earth was he?"

Paul shook his head. He spoke quietly, quickly. "Someone looking for someone. Not anyone here."

"But he knew Susan. He said—"

"Susan might have made a mistake, too."

I stared at him. "Paul," I said slowly, "I really think—"

"Mrs. Lennox!" Louis was calling. "Mrs. Lennox, look how far I've run!"

I looked round, smiling as brightly as I could, to see where Louis had stopped, panting for breath. I glanced back at Paul, once, but his expression was unreadable. I walked up the hill after Louis.

———✕———

That night, I could not sleep. I had not gone to Paul. I was angry with him, because he had not listened, had not taken me seriously, because he was not as worried as I thought we ought to be—and I was angry at myself, for being angry, for he might well be right that this man, whoever he was, had gone and would not be seen again. Still, it all unsettled me. Susan was cruel, but Susan was clever. Surely she would not have kept that advertisement, have written a response to it, unless she had been sure?

The previous night kept pushing into my mind, and just as I was drifting off, I heard, somewhere out in the darkness, the sound of a harp being played. I started up, listening, but the sound had ceased.

Mrs. Eversham must have been playing downstairs and had stopped. That was all.

I lay back, but my mind would not rest. I listened to the soft creaks and moans of the house, my eyes open and staring into the dark. I thought of Paul, his gentle dismissal of my fears, his certainty that the man in the grounds had only been here by mistake.

It was impossible that Paul had never noticed anything strange about Hartwood Hall. He had seen the candle in the east wing with me. He had spoken to the man lingering in the grounds.

And still he told me it was nothing.

I sat up in bed, passed a hand over my forehead. I trusted Paul. I knew him. I knew every mark on his skin, knew the sound of his laugh, the way he made tea, how his eyes lit up and his cheeks dimpled when he smiled. I knew the exact movements his fingers made to clip a flower from its stem. I could tell from his voice whether he was tired or solemn or happy. I *knew* him.

But I thought of all the secrets I kept, all the things I had never told him, the words we had never said.

What, then, might he be keeping from me?

I lay back down, my mind in tumult.

I passed a weary night, tossing and turning, slipping in and out of indistinct dreams. Susan's ghostly hand on my arm. Isabella's footsteps pacing the corridors. The man from the grounds, silhouetted in the moonlight. The towering frame of Hartwood Hall twisting and turning into rounded walls, until the courtyard was the well and I was lost, trapped, somewhere forgotten and out of sight.

And then Richard was there, haggard and skeletal, staring at me from across the well. He strode forward, his arm outstretched, and when his hand touched my cheek, it was as cold as the dead.

He held my face in his hands, an icy caress.

Why are you here? I asked.

He pressed his lips together, half a sneer, half a smile. *I am your husband. I am always where you are. I own you, Mrs. Lennox.*

CHAPTER VII

I woke panting, my face slick with sweat. I sat up, pulling back the bed curtains, breathing hard. I reached for a match on the bedside table and lit the candle quickly. The room was bathed in light.

I took it all in slowly, the familiar room, the chest at the end of the bed, the wardrobe, the fireplace, the bookshelf, the dressing table. When I drew the curtains, it was still dark, but Richard's watch told me it was past five o'clock.

I stood in silence by the window, watching the darkness, twisting my wedding ring around and around on my finger. I wished that I could hurl it into the lake, let it tarnish like the one I had found there, let it sink deep into the mud.

He was gone. He was dead and he was gone and he could not come back now.

I did not want to go back to sleep. I did not want to stay here, with Richard's ghost lingering in the corners of the room, with uneasy guilt caught in the back of my mind. Instead I washed and dressed hurriedly, then made my way downstairs.

I walked slowly, my mind still fuzzy with lack of sleep. I was nearly at the bottom of the stairs when I saw the footprints.

They were not large footprints. Small feet, a child's or a slight woman's. A line running indistinctly from the back stairs toward the east wing.

Muddy footprints, like someone had been outside and then run into the house.

I stood and stared. I almost thought I might be dreaming, that my tired mind had conjured them into being.

Then I stepped forward, bent down, touched the tip of my finger to the footprint.

Mud, fresh mud, came away on my hand.

I heard something, and started up. For a moment I could not make out what I had heard, until the sound came again. Voices. Raised voices. I was surprised to hear anyone up so early. I pivoted where I stood until my good ear found the sound. It was coming from Mrs. Eversham's study, and though I could not quite make out the words, I heard Mrs. Eversham's voice, sharp and taut, and then Lacey's.

The door was wrenched open and Lacey's voice came clear. "I won't stand for this, Mrs. Eversham. I know what I saw."

She was in the doorway of the study, her back to me, her shoulders set. Beyond her I could see Mrs. Eversham, her face pained, one hand outstretched.

"Lacey, really—"

"It's enough, ma'am. That's all."

"You'll give us a week, Lacey."

"I shan't do anything of the sort. I shall be gone by the end of the day."

I stared in amazement, but Lacey was already turning, pushing past me, her face a mask of anger—almost, I thought, of something like disgust. I stood in the hall, bewildered, until Mrs. Eversham's gaze met my own.

"I am sorry you had to witness that, Margaret."

"Whatever is the matter?"

"Lacey has given warning." Mrs. Eversham sighed. "Well, not much warning, as it happens."

She looked anxious, almost afraid. She stepped back, and I moved forward, into her study. She closed the door behind me before sitting down, and signaled for me to do the same.

"Are you quite well, Mrs. Eversham?"

She closed her eyes, leaning back in her chair. "What are we to do?" she murmured. "That leaves only Mrs. Pulley and Stevens and Carter."

I said, hesitantly, "I suppose it is because there is too much work, without Mary and Susan?"

She opened her eyes, blinked at me. "I—yes, of course. Goodness knows how we will cope without her. Mrs. Pulley will have to cook, and as for the rest of the work—"

"I can cook," I said, leaning forward in my chair. "If I can be of any help, I will be."

Her brow creased. "I wish I could cook, could work, could do anything! Dear God, is there nothing more useless than a *lady*?" She shook her head. "You could teach me, Margaret. Would you? You and Mrs. Pulley together—I am sure I could learn."

"Of course," I said. "But you can find more servants, Mrs. Eversham. Others will come."

She raised a hand to her forehead. "It is so hard to rely on people. It is so hard to know who is trustworthy and who—" She broke off, shook her head. "We have had an unlucky few months. That is all. I am being foolish." She smiled abruptly and rose quickly to her feet. "You are up early, Margaret," she said, and her voice seemed different, falsely cheerful. "It looks to be a pleasant day. Warm for October."

"To be sure."

She nodded, but her smile was slipping. She moved round me, put her hand on the doorknob. "I had better speak to Mrs. Pulley," she said, in a lower voice.

"Of course."

When we stepped out of her study together, the footprints in the hall were gone.

———>•<———

By the time we'd finished the day's lessons, Lacey had left. Mrs. Pulley and I made dinner together. We brought bowls of stew upstairs and found Louis and Mrs. Eversham waiting for us. Mrs. Pulley was just about to leave the room when Mrs. Eversham called her back.

"Ruth, wait—stay. At least, go and find Stevens. We may as well all eat up here when there are so few of us. Does Carter usually eat with you?"

"Sometimes, ma'am."

"Then fetch him, too. We will all dine together tonight."

I blinked. I never saw Paul inside the house; I was not used to it. I rarely saw him in anyone's presence but Louis's. All of a sudden, ours seemed such a vast secret to hide.

Stevens and Mrs. Pulley came to the table, and Paul followed. No embarrassment seemed to trouble him; he sat at Louis's side and chatted to him easily, while I kept my eyes downcast and avoided Paul's gaze.

In no other house would the mistress have invited the servants to eat at the table with them. In hardly any other house would *I* have eaten with her.

Yet here we were, the six of us, the diminished household of Hartwood Hall, sitting together as the sun set beyond the windows.

————✶————

I went to Paul that night. I was hesitant but I could not resist the thought of him; it had been so hard to sit with him at the dinner table and say nothing—and besides, I was sure now that he was keeping something from me, and I wanted to see him, armed with that knowledge, to find out what it changed.

He was smiling when he opened his door to me, but his smile flickered a little when he saw my face. I supposed he noticed something amiss in my expression, but he opened the door wider, as always, to let me in. "Tea?"

"Please."

He turned to light the fire beneath the kettle, and I looked around this room I had come to know so well, at this man I had thought I knew.

"Paul," I said, slowly, carefully, "do you not think we should tell Mrs. Eversham—about the man in the grounds?"

He did not turn. He poured boiling water into the teapot on the sideboard.

"Paul, how can it not be troubling you?"

"Because he said it was a mistake."

"And if it wasn't?" I kept my voice hard. "What if—what if someone is looking for Mrs. Eversham, what if someone is looking for her whom she does not want to find her? What if she and Louis are in danger?"

Paul was frowning, his brow furrowed. "Hartwood Hall is safe," he said, and he sounded so certain that I almost believed him. Then I thought of what he had told me, how he had come here so often when he was a boy, how he had hidden in the grounds after his mother had died. It had always been a safe refuge for him, but that did not mean it was safe.

"Paul—"

"Mrs. Eversham has been safe here for years. Why would anything change now?"

He was standing in front of me, close enough that I could almost feel him, that I could smell him, that scent of grass and tea.

I could ask him. I could ask him what he knew, what he was keeping from me. I could ask him who the Evershams were, really, and why they lived here, like this, in isolation, hiding from the world. I could ask him—and either he would tell me, or he would lie.

And if he lied, it would all be over. This fragile thing between us would snap. I knew that. Without trust—without a pretense at trust—what would we do?

And if he told the truth—what then? What would I do with all the secrets that I had kept from him?

It would be so easy to ask. Just a few words.

What do you know about Hartwood Hall that I do not?

But he leaned forward and kissed me, and the words died on my lips. I would ask him another day, I told myself. Tomorrow perhaps, or next week.

And then his lips were on my neck and my hands were in his hair and I made myself stop thinking.

CHAPTER VIII

HARTBRIDGE WAS BUSY THAT SUNDAY. IT WAS ALL HALLOWS' EVE, the night of ghosts and spirits, and as Paul and I passed through the village, I saw a few jack-o'-lanterns placed outside front doors and one child helping her mother bring a great barrel of water and apples for bobbing into the yard. I remembered such traditions from my own childhood, and how the village girls had told me that on All Hallows' Eve any one of us might see the face of her future husband, if she ate the right apple facing a mirror, burned the right nuts, peered into a basin of water in the right way. But no magic had ever shown me my fate.

At church, Mrs. Welling waited for me in the box, with her usual smile.

"How is Louis?" she asked.

"Much better, but he is still easily worn out, poor child. He is at home with his mother today."

The organ began and the congregation rose to their feet. I glanced back at the crowd filling the church—farmers and mill workers in their worn Sunday best. I tried to catch Paul's eye, but he was looking down at the ground. There was something new in his expression that I could not read. I searched the faces for the stranger from the grounds, just in case—but he was not there. He must have done as he had promised and left.

But I met someone else's eyes. A man I had never seen before was watching me. He was at the back of the church, sitting beside a fair-haired young woman, who was staring down at her Bible. He must have been about forty-five, with graying brown hair and iron eyebrows. His jaw was hard and set, and while the rest of the church sang, his red mouth did not move. There was something else, too, something about him that was different.

He blinked. I broke his gaze and turned back to the front.

It was then I realized what it was that had unsettled me about this man. Unlike everyone else in the congregation, he wore the clothes of a gentleman.

—>—<—

When I stepped out of the church an hour later, I found Paul at my side within a moment, his face pale, his manner agitated.

"Margaret—" He stopped, colored. His brother was only paces behind, seemingly waiting for him. "Mrs. Lennox, I have to—my father is unwell, and—"

"I am sorry to hear it," I said. "Of course you must go and see him. Has Dr. Rogers been sent for?"

He nodded, and I saw from his face that he was truly worried. I wanted to reach out, comfort him, take his pain away.

"Is it very serious?" I asked softly.

Another nod. "I have no idea how long I might need to stay." Then, in a quieter voice, with a glance back at his brother, "I wish you could come with me."

The earnestness with which he spoke surprised me.

I took a step back, almost without meaning to. "You know I cannot. I am dining with the Wellings. Besides, it—"

"I know," he said softly. "I know. If he is as bad as my brother says, I am not sure—I hardly know how I can take you back in the cart later, but—"

"I will walk," I said.

"Are you sure? It is a long way. You will not leave late, will you? You will go back to Hartwood before it gets dark?"

"I will be careful, of course. Now go—your family are waiting. I hope you find your father better than you anticipate."

He shook his head solemnly. "I will see you tomorrow," he said, and because I knew it was half a question, I nodded.

I watched him walk toward his family, watched as his brother glanced over at me.

When they were gone, I turned back to the church. The air was cold, the wind picking up, golden leaves darting between the gravestones. The congregation had mostly cleared, but Mr. and Mrs. Welling were waiting near the doors. On the other side of the graveyard stood the man I had noticed in church, his back to us all, looking out over the village.

The Wellings and I ate roast beef and potatoes for dinner. Jenny served us, casting odd glances in my direction every now and then, before she retired to the kitchen. Beyond the vicarage, we could hear noises in the street. I could not make out what they were, but Mr. Welling told me the village was making preparations for All Hallows' Eve.

"It pains me to see it, especially on a Sunday, but the people here have always been superstitious. They come to church every week, but I rather think they fear ghosts more than God."

We talked of the village, of Hartwood Hall, and I told them both how Louis fared, how my lessons progressed.

"And you have been there nearly three months now, have you not?" asked Mrs. Welling.

"Two and a half," I said. "It feels like longer."

"I hope you will stay."

"I hope so, too."

She smiled brightly, and I thought again how very lonely the people were here, how solitude seemed to spread through the air like miasma.

"I have been so worried, after all Mary told us about Hartwood

Hall, all her fears and—well, I don't know what—that you, too, would feel you were not able to stay."

"Mary is not much more than a child," I said. "She was scared of shadows. That's all." Even as I said the words, I thought of the east wing, the candle burning in the dark, all the things Paul was not telling me. There were more than shadows at Hartwood Hall. I knew that. But I could not bear the thought of Mrs. Welling thinking badly of the place, of the family.

"Mrs. Eversham has not found a replacement yet, I suppose?" Mrs. Welling asked.

"Not yet."

"Nor for Susan?"

I shook my head. "There have been one or two answers to her advertisements, but they have led to nothing. And now our cook has left as well, saying there was too much work."

"Oh, how difficult," said Mrs. Welling.

"I keep thinking of that poor young housemaid—such a tragedy," said Mr. Welling, and he shook his head softly. "We will let you know if we hear of anybody looking for a place."

After dinner, Mr. Welling went to his study to read his Bible—a pretext, I supposed, for leaving his wife alone with me. Mrs. Welling and I drank tea together in the drawing room. I liked Mrs. Welling. I liked to sit at her side and talk about village matters, about church goings-on and neighborly feuds. I felt as though, with her, I were someone else, the person she had perhaps assumed me to be—a truly grieving widow who had lost a husband as good as hers. It was as though I were looking through a window into a life I might have had, in another world. If I had met a different man, married a different man, I might have had a marriage, a life, like hers, like my parents'— quiet, respectable, full in its way. I might have been another person altogether.

"You seem happier, you know, than when we first met," said Mrs. Welling.

"Do I?"

"Yes." She smiled. "Time truly is a great healer."

I swallowed. I wondered what she would say if she knew the truth about me, this respectable clergyman's wife, this woman who was everything I was not and could not be—loving, kind, honest, proper, meek.

She might have turned me out of her house.

"I am so glad you came here," she said.

So I kept up my mask, my pretense. I turned to her and smiled.

CHAPTER IX

IT WAS NEARING DUSK BY THE TIME I LEFT, THE SUN NO LONGER visible behind the clouds, the sky a dim gray-blue. I ought to have left earlier, as Paul had told me to, but I had been enjoying myself. And there was something else, too, something in me that wanted to do the opposite of what he had said. Paul was nothing like Richard—I knew that—and yet the moment he had told me not to walk back too late I had thought of my husband. All those rules. All the times I had broken them.

Mr. and Mrs. Welling expressed some concern about me walking back alone, especially on All Hallows' Eve, when the village streets might be busy, but I waved them off. It was not much after four, for all that the sky was dimming, and I could walk an hour without harm. I was nervous of going through the woods in the dark, but I pushed such thoughts away. It would not take long, and there was no other choice. I would be back at Hartwood Hall very soon.

I had barely left the vicarage garden before I heard the All Hallows' celebrations. The sound of a fiddle, a pipe, a harmonica, an accordion, and then shouts and cries, jeers and laughs. I smiled despite myself. I loved noise, noise so loud I could hear it without mistake. I turned down toward the main street and paused, watching. Scores of people lined the cobblestones, apple bobbing and dancing, masks perched upon nearly every face. There was a bonfire in the village square, flames crackling in the growing dark. Candles and jack-o'-lanterns were now lit on each doorstep, and everything before me was shining and bright.

These people would not laugh so heartily at ghosts were they at Hartwood Hall, I thought—and then I chided myself for being foolish. There was no such thing as ghosts, after all. The dead were dead.

I wondered, for a fleeting moment, what would happen if I joined them, if I strode into the midst of all this joyous magic. Would they string me up above the bonfire and burn me like the witch they thought Mrs. Eversham was, or would they ask me kindly to join in apple bobbing and give me a soul cake for my journey home?

Better not to find out. I walked quietly around the edge of the festivities, cut down a back street and down a lane—and then out into the open country, orderly orchards and fields upon fields.

I knew the way well. I followed the wide road that led up to the woods, keeping my eyes on the rising moon above me.

I had gone perhaps half a mile when I heard a shout.

My heart thumped.

I looked back to see the silhouette of a man hurrying after me.

Was it the man from the grounds, come back? Or one of the village folk, who'd seen me watching, and had come for me, because I was from Hartwood and Hartwood was feared?

I walked quickly on, steeling myself to break out into a run.

"You there—wait!"

It was the voice of a gentleman.

I turned again—and there, close upon me now, was the man I had seen watching me in church.

"Please wait. I beg a word with you. I can see that you are a lady. Please."

The urgency in his voice gave me pause; he sounded like a man near desperation.

"It is growing dark," I said. "I must get home."

"I will take but a moment of your time."

I had stopped walking. I stood in the dusk, facing this stranger, his graying hair, his lined face. He looked weary, worn out.

My silence seemed to satisfy him, and I saw a look of hope pass across his face.

"Listen, I believe you may be able to help me. I am looking for someone—for two people, in fact. I am most eager to find them. Do you know of a woman called Mrs. Grey? Lucy Grey?"

A chill crept over my skin.

What had the man in the grounds said? *I was looking for someone. But it's the wrong woman, wrong house.*

What if it was not the wrong house, after all?

I said, "I know no one of that name."

I kept my distance from him. I was all too aware of this lonely situation, the path stretching empty before and after us, the woods looming in the distance. The village was too far back to run to, Hartwood Hall too far ahead.

"Are you sure?"

"Quite sure."

"Nor anybody called Thomas Grey? He is a boy of ten."

I swallowed. "I know no Thomas Grey."

His face fell. He winced, bit his lip, and when he raised his hands to his forehead, I saw them shake. "Do you know a woman called Susan Potter? Do you know where she works?"

Susan, whom the man in the grounds had met. This, then, must be the person who had sent him.

I breathed in. "No. I know no one of that name. Excuse me. I must go home."

"Wait, wait—please, listen to me. Are you sure you have not heard of Susan Potter? She wrote to me—she told me she was a servant to Mrs. Grey, that she could tell me where she was, but—well, she wanted money. I sent a man to meet her, someone to act on my behalf. He met her, agreed to the terms she laid out, and she was to meet him again—but she did not keep her appointment. I have been waiting and waiting—and then two days ago I received a letter from him telling me that this Susan Potter had died, that he believed she was mistaken anyway, that he found out where she worked and Mrs. Grey was not there. But I had thought—I had thought, finally, that I had found them. So I came to see for myself—" He broke off. The sweat on his brow was clear in the moonlight. "Please, if you know anything, if you are a lady of any honor, you must tell me."

I said, "I know nothing." All the time my mind was racing.

"I have been looking for them for years," he said. "This is the closest I have ever come. Listen, my name is Charles Grey. Lucy Grey is my wife, Thomas is my son. Please—"

I blinked.

I thought of the scar on Louis's back.

Father threw something at me.

Father was a devil.

I had thought that Eversham might be a false name. I had thought they might be hiding from something, some scandal involving Isabella. I knew that Louis's dyed hair must be more than a whim.

But it had never once occurred to me that her husband might still be living.

My face must have betrayed me. It was enough for Mr. Grey to dart forward and grab my wrist hard.

"Let me go!"

"You know something," he said, more urgent than ever. "What do you know?"

"Nothing," I said, trying to keep my voice steady. "I have never heard these names before."

He grabbed me by the shoulders. He was a big man, bigger than Richard, bigger than Paul. His hands were large, his frame broad, his grip fierce. "Did that man of mine lie? Speak, woman!"

"I know nothing!" I repeated, louder now. I was trying not to shake, trying to think, think. There was always a way out, always a solution. He had me by the shoulders, an iron grip, and yet, surely, if I thought, if I stilled my mind, I could do *something*.

"She is my *wife*. I have a right to her. She ought to be with me. He is my *son*. No woman should steal a man's son."

I wanted to say *He is her son, too.* I bit my tongue.

"I have been looking for her for years. I could tell you things about Lucy Grey that would make your blood run cold. Do you understand what I am saying?"

"I told you—I don't know the people you speak of."

"You are lying to me!" His grip increased, his fingers digging into my shoulders. I could feel his nails, the press of each rough fingertip through my dress and cloak. He was standing so close that I could feel his breath, see the fury and fear in his eyes.

Desperate men are dangerous. But they are also weak.

I raised my boot and stamped down hard, running the leather toe fast down his shin, slamming the whole sole of my foot down on his.

He cried out, cursed, and his grip slipped. I took my chance. I swung my fist at his face and as he stumbled backward, I ran, my boots pounding on the muddy ground, my whole body shaking.

Not fast enough. I felt myself suddenly lurch backward and realized he had trodden on my skirts. I tried to turn—and could not. Tried to flail, tried to reach out—and could not. I tried to pull myself free, and finally the fabric tore and I stumbled forward, hands out to break my fall, struggling to regain my balance.

I don't know what happened next. I don't know whether the movement was enough to knock me over, whether I tripped, or whether he pushed me. But somehow I lost my footing, and before I knew what had happened, I fell sideways, crashing hard into the ground.

A rush of pain shot through me. Everything screamed. My heart was thudding, my head dull, and for a moment faintness seemed to overcome me.

Then he was standing over me, his face pale in the darkness, his eyes livid. And suddenly the pain didn't matter anymore, and the faintness was nothing, and the only thing in all the world that mattered was that this man did not get to Louis.

Louis. Thomas.

Mrs. Eversham. Mrs. Grey.

So that was it, after all—the grand secret of Hartwood Hall. They were not who they said they were. They were hiding; they were afraid. Mrs. Eversham had married the wrong man and run.

Slowly, gingerly, I moved my hand from my stomach to the pocket of my skirts.

My fingers closed on what I had been searching for. My penknife.

I reached out, lunging forward. I caught him in the leg. Only a cut—but it was enough. Enough that he swore and clasped at his ankle. Enough that he stumbled backward, blinking, dazed. Enough that he was unsteady on his feet.

Enough time for me to scramble up.

Enough time for me to run.

I had never run so hard in my life. I had never been so afraid. I ran, barely looking where I was going. I ran, despite the pain in my legs, despite the thumping ache in the base of my belly. I ran, despite my shaking hands, my chattering teeth, my torn skirt. I ran and ran, and though the night was cold I was bathed in sweat. I ran until my breath caught and my heart ached and my head swirled.

It was only when I reached the woods that I dared to turn. I stopped, panting, and looked back along the dim path.

No one.

Nothing.

CHAPTER X

IN THE DIMMING LIGHT I COULD NOT SEE FAR, BUT I COULD SEE NO silhouette approaching, no shadow on the road. I tried to listen for a second, but all I could hear was the thudding and ringing in my head, and my own hard breathing.

I carried on.

It was pitch black among the trees. I could barely see my own hands when I held them out in front of me. I tried to quell the shudder that ran through me. After all, the trees might be my friend tonight. It would be harder for him to follow me through the dark woods.

The path was straight enough. I knew that. If I kept on walking, I would come out on the other side, close to Hartwood Hall, to home.

But I could feel the blood pumping in my ears. My eyes would not get used to the dark and my legs ached—and there it was again, that stabbing pain in my belly, that dreadful ache. The woods seemed to be spinning around me. Had I hit my head, when I fell, when he pushed me? I could not remember. All I knew was that I hurt everywhere, that my mind was all shadows, that my whole body was shaking.

I stepped on, walking more slowly now, my feet feeling in front of me for roots and dips in the ground, sinking into dirt and piles of fallen leaves, on and on through the darkness.

Another stab of pain in my stomach.

Then something else, too. As I moved, I began to be aware of something new, an unpleasant sensation, a kind of stickiness between my legs.

I thought first that my courses had come, but it was too much, too wet, for the first day. And in the faint fogginess of my mind, another thought began to float to the surface, as my feet stepped on and on. When was the last time I'd had my courses? Mine were never consistent; I could never tell the phase of the moon by my own body's clock. And I had been so busy at Hartwood, so anxious about Louis's illness, so lost in Paul, that I had not thought. But now that my blurred mind reached back, the last time I had bled had been weeks ago, months—shortly after my arrival at Hartwood Hall.

Surely not.

It was impossible.

But then—

I let out a kind of cry. I did not mean to. I clasped my hand over my mouth. If somebody heard, if Mr. Grey had followed—

Nothing happened. Nobody came; nobody cried back. I walked on in darkness and silence, until the pain in my stomach was too much.

No, not in my stomach.

Suddenly, I saw light. A glimmer of it, in the distance. A way out into the moonlit grounds. I hurried forward, my hands clutched over my belly, stumbling, my head heavy, and as I burst out onto the open grass, the moon seemed to sway and the whole world spun.

I had reached the edge of the lake when my legs gave way. I let myself fall sideways, felt the mud take me, warm against my cheek. My good ear hit the ground and the world fell silent.

The last thing I saw was the swinging of the summer-house door and a figure running toward me in the moonlight. A girl in white.

Isabella, I thought. The dead, coming to claim me.

Well, it was only a matter of time.

Only, no. It was no girl at all. A fair-haired woman in a white dress was running toward me, her mouth open, crying out something I could not hear. And as she drew nearer, her face came into view, and I stared, not comprehending, pressing my hands into my belly, as Miss Davis ran to my side.

My first mad thought was that it was a good time for a nurse.

And then the moon seemed to grow and the sky spun, and at last the world went gray.

VOLUME FIVE

CHAPTER I

THE NEXT FEW HOURS WERE A BLUR TO ME. THE FEEL OF SOFT sheets beneath my back. Warm hands undressing me, wet rags washing me down. A soft nightdress pulled over my head. A flannel on my forehead.

I was in my own room. I knew that, though the room was out of focus, swimming before my sight. I was in my own bed, and there were figures filling my vision. A woman. Another woman. One taller with black hair, one short and slight and fair. They moved around me, speaking to each other, to me, trying to give me water, muttering words I could not hear.

Mrs. Eversham. Miss Davis.

Miss Davis.

What was she doing here?

I tried to move, but I was too weak. I tried to open my eyes fully, to speak, and found it impossible. I tried to remember, and could not bear to. There was an ache, a deep ache inside me, and when I shifted and tried to turn, the ache seemed all-consuming.

So I let my eyes slip closed again, let sleep take me.

I dreamed that the pain was something else, that I was in childbed, that the base of me was being torn out. There was a midwife at my side, her hand clenched in mine, and across the room stood a man.

Richard, I thought, at first—but then he had Paul's face, and when I looked up at the midwife she was Miss Davis.

And that was when the child started to cry. Loud and fierce. Over and over again.

———>—<———

The next time I woke, the curtains were still drawn and a candle burned on the dresser, casting shadows about the room. I blinked my eyes open, just a little, and through tears and confusion I caught hold of the scene before me.

Wake. Breathe. Remember.

Be rational, Margaret.

I would lose my place.

That was my first thought. They would know, of course, about Paul.

And then I thought of the child, the child slipping out of me, pouring out of me, bleeding out of me, and it did not matter anymore.

For three years Richard and I had tried, and this was the furthest I had ever got. Blood between my legs and an ache of emptiness in my belly.

I had lost my child.

I would lose my place.

I would lose Louis.

Louis.

Thomas.

Mr. Grey.

I tried to sit up. I heard a sound, something like a cry, and I supposed it came from me.

"Hush, Margaret. It's all right. Lie still."

From under dipped eyelids, I saw Mrs. Eversham back away. She thought me still unconscious, and I was not awake enough to prove her wrong.

Instead, I watched. Watched as she reclaimed a chair beside the only other person in the room, watched as she reached out and laid her hand on Miss Davis's arm.

When Mrs. Eversham touched her, they looked at each other, held each other's gaze for a moment.

They smiled.

And there was something about their expressions that seemed familiar to me, that I had seen before.

It was the expression Mrs. Welling wore on her face when she looked at her husband, the expression on his when he looked at her.

It was a look of love.

Despite my cloudy mind, the pain in the base of my stomach, despite the way the room loomed in and out of focus, despite the sweat beading on my forehead and the ache between my legs—I saw it all.

I knew who it was—the person who burned candles in empty rooms, who took food from the larder, left warm tea in the summer house. The person whose footsteps I had run from in the corridors, whose figure I had caught a glimpse of on the stairs. The person I had spotted by the lake.

I understood why Mrs. Eversham had acted strangely when Miss Davis offered to nurse Louis, why Mrs. Pulley had been anxious.

I knew who lived in the east wing.

Not Mrs. Eversham's daughter, as I had once or twice thought, but Mrs. Eversham's lover. Miss Davis. My mistress's mistress.

CHAPTER II

WHEN I NEXT WOKE, THE ROOM WAS EMPTY. IT WAS STILL DARK AND when I pressed the repeater on Richard's watch, I found it was not yet midnight. Still, a few hours of sleep had done me good. The pain deep in my belly was deadened now, though my bruised skin was still tender. And there was another pain, too, that I could not shift.

I had lost a child. I had lost a child I had not known I had.

I sat up in bed, breathing hard. They had put me in one of my white nightgowns, and it was stained with blood.

I put my hands to my flat stomach and blinked back tears.

What would I have done, had the child lived and grown within me? We might have lived together somewhere out of sight, where no one knew my past. I would have told the world that the child was my late husband's, and though I would not have been able to be a governess, I might have taken in sewing, and lived quietly, and when the child was old enough, I might have started a little school. It would have been all right. I was used to keeping secrets. We would have found a way, this child and I, this child who might have been like Louis, who would have been clever and free and mine.

My almost child.

I had lost so many almost children. All the way through my marriage, every time I bled again and the chance was lost, I mourned a child that might have been.

But this was the closest I had come. This child I had not been able to keep hold of.

I did not think of Paul in all of this. I could picture him in my mind, but suddenly his image did not move me. It did not feel as though it were his child I had lost, only mine. I did not long for his arms around me. I did not long for the comfort of his smiles. I felt only waves of sadness, crashing and crashing into me, until I could bear it no more, and I curled up in my bed, arms wrapped around my legs, and sobbed.

I do not know how long I lay like that before the door eased open and I saw Paul framed within it. His face was deathly pale, his eyes red and wet, and I felt a strange stab of anger, as though I wanted all the grief to be mine alone.

"What are you doing here?"

He closed the door behind him and moved quickly toward me, catching me in his arms. I shrank back.

"You shouldn't have come," I said, keeping my voice low. "What if someone saw you?"

"They're all asleep. I had to see you, Margaret."

I tried to disentangle myself from him. His arms had always been a comfort, his presence had always calmed me—but not now. I did not want to touch him. I wanted to sit alone in my grief.

"Margaret, is it true? Mrs. Eversham told me that you had lost a child, but—"

"It is true," I murmured.

Paul nodded. And then he began to sob, thick drops slipping fast down his cheeks. He fell back from me, clasped a hand over his mouth to stop himself from crying out. I watched in a kind of dreamlike dismay. I thought about reaching out my hand, touching him, comforting him, but I did nothing. I watched some part of him break, and all I did was sit there.

Yesterday, if I had seen him in this state, I would have pulled him to me, held him close. But then, yesterday, I had loved him. I had thought I loved him. I had almost known it. And now—I was not so sure. Everything seemed hazy, blurred, less certain. The last few months, the snatched moments in his rooms, the feel of his hands on

my skin—it all suddenly seemed like a strange dream. And I had
woken to blood, to loss, to this.

"What happened?" he whispered at last.

I told him, stumbling through my words. Even to me it felt foggy.
I was still exhausted, drained, and I ached where the fall had bruised
me. I remembered the path home, Mr. Grey, too many sensations all
at once, the feel of my body hitting the ground. I remembered the
woods, the darkness, the pain in my stomach.

"I think—I think this Mr. Grey may be Mrs. Eversham's husband."

Paul stopped crying. "What?"

"I think she may be in danger."

"But . . ." He frowned. "Her husband? Alive? I—I had no idea."
And then the effort of surprise seemed too much, and his hands began
to shake. "Oh, Margaret, you ought not to have walked back alone,"
he said. "If I had come for you with the cart, none of this would have
happened. You would have been all right. You and . . ." He shut his
eyes tight.

Yesterday afternoon came rushing back to me. "How is your
father?"

He shook his head. "Dying," he muttered, and his voice shook.
"Oh God. I should have stayed with you. And now the child, and . . ."

"Paul," I said. I reached out for his hand now, half to comfort him,
half to silence him, and the moment I touched him, he turned and
clasped me in his arms.

He held me tight. Not like he usually held me, not passionately,
hungrily, tenderly. Now he held on to me like a drowning man.

"Paul," I whispered again. "Paul, maybe it's for the best." Even as I
spoke the words, I heard the quiver in my voice.

I felt rather than saw him shake his head.

"What would we have done, Paul?"

"It would have been all right," he said, and I had to strain to hear
him. "We would have married sooner, that's all."

"Married," I repeated, and for a moment I was too stunned to say
anything else. My grip slipped from him; my hands fell from his back.

"Of course, you'd have still been in mourning and people might have talked, but—well, what would that matter?" Paul's voice was still low. "You have no family, and mine have given up objecting to anything I might do. And of course I love Hartwood—I wouldn't want to leave, but . . . well, if we couldn't have made it work here, we would have gone to another village, found a house together, raised the child, like any other young married couple. I would have found another place, been a gardener at a house where I did not need to live on the grounds, or else one that would let you live with me, too. You wouldn't have had to work anymore—I would have looked after us all. And in five years' time, no one would have known or cared that you had been married before, that you had still been in mourning when we married, that our child had been born not that long after the wedding."

I pulled back. These words were not words of a moment. This dream was not one brought into being by the events of the last few hours. This was a full future, a life, thought out for us, for me. All this time, I had thought he understood. We had never spoken of the future, of marriage. We had never planned anything beyond the following day. I loved him—of course I loved him; what other name did I have for this but love?—but I always knew it was impossible, that we would have to part one day, that even if I had wished to marry again, the difference in our stations, our circumstances, would throw up all sorts of obstacles. I had thought that a man who spoke of love with looks, not words, a man content to wait for me night after night, a man who never spoke of the future—I had thought he wanted what I wanted: a secret love, a life uninterrupted. A life unchained.

I stared at him, this man I had known just a few months, this man I had wrapped myself around night after night, thinking only of the moment, thinking only of his warmth and his kindness and his smile, of the constant need to escape myself. This man I did not quite know, who had been building a future in his head all this time.

It did not sound like so very bad a life. Children. A man I liked.

"Paul," I whispered. "There is no child. Not anymore."

"I know," he said. He pulled back from me, took my hands in his hands. His eyes were wet. "But there might be. One day. Not yet. I know—I know it is soon, for you. I know that. I know your husband has not been dead long, but—one day, Margaret."

What would happen, I thought, if I were to marry him? What would my life be like? Paul was kind. With him, I could erase my past. We could live quietly, have children perhaps. After all, if one child had begun within me, another might one day come. Perhaps it had never been my fault, as Richard had once had me believe, but merely some incompatibility between us. I could have with Paul the kind of ordinary life I had once sought with Richard.

And yet.

You wouldn't have had to work anymore, he'd said.

But I wanted to work. I wanted to teach. I wanted a life of my own. And I did not want to be married. Not again. Never again.

I opened my mouth but I could not bear to speak the words, to tell him that I did not want to be his wife, to be anybody's wife. A mother, yes. I wanted to be a mother—my whole body ached with that want. But I did not want to be a wife.

So I said instead, "Paul, when I fainted by the lake, it was Miss Davis who found me. Louis's nurse."

He was motionless, staring down at our joined hands.

I looked at him carefully. I thought of all the times he had told me not to pry into the Evershams' secrets, all those moments he had tried to make me trust him, to not question Hartwood Hall. I said, slowly, "I think she lives in the house, Paul. I think she's the person in the east wing."

Paul moved. A slight, almost imperceptible jolt. Then he looked up, his face clear in the darkness, his brow furrowed. There was not a glimmer of surprise in his face. He said, "Yes."

And even though I had told myself he must know something, still it stung. Still resentment welled up inside me and I tore my hands from his. "You knew?" I said, and I could not keep the anger from my voice. "All this time, you knew there was someone living in the east wing and you told me it was nothing. You wanted me to think—what? That I was going mad, that I was hearing things, seeing things?"

"No," he said, startled by my outburst, his face full of concern. "Margaret, no. I—I always told you, there was nothing to be afraid of."

"Who else knows?" I asked. "The whole house? Am I the only one kept in ignorance?"

"I—well, Mrs. Pulley and Stevens know, I think, but Lacey and Mary did not, and I do not think Susan did. I am not supposed to know—no one knows I do."

"I suppose I am right," I said, "that she is—well, Mrs. Eversham's mistress?"

"Yes." Paul reached for my hands again and I pulled mine away. "Margaret, listen to me. It was not my secret to tell. You understand that, don't you? As far as Mrs. Eversham is aware, I know nothing. The old head gardener, he—he saw them, once, together, in the summer house. I came upon him just afterward and he told me everything. I don't think he meant to tell me—I don't believe he ever told anybody else—but in the first moment of shock he told me it all, told me that he was leaving at once, and why, told me I ought to leave, too. But I didn't want that. It didn't trouble me, and I—well, I liked Mrs. Eversham. I liked the children. I'd always loved Hartwood Hall. Why would I leave, over a thing like that? Over love? So I kept silent. I let them think I didn't know."

"What else do you know?" I asked sharply. "The man, Mr. Grey—you didn't know about him?"

Paul shook his head. "No. I know nothing else, I swear."

I tried to push him from me, tried to rise from the bed. "I need to warn Mrs. Eversham. I need to tell her what happened."

"Margaret, you have to rest, you—"

I shook my head, shook him off. I turned away from him. I did not want to look at him, this man who wanted to marry me, who had lied to me, who had eyes like our child would have had. And there were other things at stake now.

"You had better go, Paul."

"Margaret, please."

I said nothing. I kept faced away from him, back straight, body sore. I felt sick. There was an ache inside me, a piercing, numbing pain that seemed to spread from my feet to my heart.

I heard the door click shut as Paul left the room. I sat still on the bed for a moment, my head reeling, trying to make sense of it all, to catch my crumbling life in my hands.

We would have married sooner.

But I did not, could not, want that. Not after last time. Not ever, ever again.

CHAPTER III

I HAD THOUGHT I COULD MAKE MYSELF INTO A GOOD WIFE. I HAD thought I would grow to love Richard, that when we had children we would become a real family.

I do not know if he ever loved me. He certainly tried, perhaps harder than me. I think he loved some idea of me that wasn't me. He liked the notion of having a wife, and there I was. The right age, the right station—respectable, willing. I suited his ideas just enough, and so he had married me.

But he wanted more from me than I could give. He wanted a companion and a lover and a friend, but he wanted a wife, too—a wife to read him the newspaper and sit sewing indoors, not a wife who roamed the countryside on her own and wanted to *do* something. He wanted a wife who would take his word as law and follow his lead, not a wife who thought for herself, who had worked every day of her adult life and longed for employment, for occupation. He soon found me out. After a few months, he realized that I did not love him, and he tried to woo me. His own wife. He was kind and courteous, bought me serious books he thought would interest me, picked me flowers, took me on long walks.

And then, when it made no difference, he stopped being kind. It was then I think he realized that I was not the woman, the wife, he had thought. I was not meek. I was not passive. I was not loving. I was not his shadow to be led.

He did not beat me. He rarely raised his voice. Instead he tried to educate me, to control me, to change me. I must read the books he read, must forget novels and stick to sermons. I must give up the piano-forte. I must never go out alone. I must stay in the house we shared, must focus on my duties at home, my duties to him. I must hold my tongue.

If we'd had children, it might have been different. I might have grown fond of him through them, and he might have grown fond of me.

But no child ever came.

Richard blamed me. Me and my cold heart.

I suppose it was around then I began to hate him.

And not long after that, I began to hate myself.

When I would not change for him, he tried to make me. He burned my books. He took and hid my letters. He told our servant not to listen to me, told my few acquaintances I was not at home when they tried to see me. He told me that it was my fault he had married me, that I had drawn him on, bewitched him.

The spell was well and truly broken.

I was trapped. I was tied for life to a man I did not love, did not know, did not understand—a man who could not and would not understand me. Whatever he thought I was, it was a lie. He expected me to live my life entirely for him—and I could not do it.

Even if I had loved him, I could not have done it.

I began to long for an escape. I began to dream of what I would do if he died, if I left him, what I would have done had we never met, had we never married.

And then he fell ill.

It was not my fault, of course. I could not have helped the illness, could not have prevented it. I am almost sure that is true.

Yet I had wished him gone a thousand times. If I had cared for him, watched over him, would I have seen it sooner? If I had loved him, could I have nursed him better?

Every day I was grateful for his illness, for his absence in every room of the house but one. And every day I damned myself for thinking such thoughts. Every night I prayed to God to make me love him, to make me wish for his recovery.

The doctors never knew, really, what the disease was. Some slow, dreadful illness, something wrong inside his stomach. It sapped all of his strength, brought this once-powerful man, this man I had feared, to nothing. I almost pitied him, and yet I could not help the constant thought: if he died, I would be free.

I would be *free*.

In his sickness, he hated me more than ever. Perhaps I did not hide well enough my relief at his illness, or perhaps he merely resented my strength when he was weak. But he would rage against me, upbraid me, accuse me of neglect. Unknown to me, in the last week of his life, half delirious, angry at the world, he wrote to his mother and said that I was the cause of his illness, and he sent for his solicitor to change his will.

On his last night in this world, he told me that it was my fault, that he blamed me, that he would not be dying if he had never met me. He accused me of poisoning him so that I might marry another man. He called me a whore and a harlot and a harpy and he *swore*—my respectable, formal husband, racked with pain and brought so low. He said words I had never heard on his tongue before. I left the room, shut the door behind me.

I did not sit up with him, as I had done so often through his illness. I locked myself in my room and tried to sleep.

Later that night, he called out to me. I heard him through the wall that separated my room from his. I heard him shout out in pain, heard him call my name distinctly, ask for me, for something, water, help.

And I pressed my good ear to the pillow and shut him out.

And in the morning, he was dead.

It was only when I saw the vial of medicine on the dresser that I realized I had forgotten to give it to him, that in the hurry and stress of his outburst, I had missed the previous night's dose. It was an accident, a mistake, and yet—

And yet I poured the vial away, just in case. I put the empty vial back in its place. Then I looked down at my husband's pale and cold body, took the watch from beside his bed, and went downstairs to summon the doctor.

I had lived with the shadow of it over me ever since.

CHAPTER IV

I STUMBLED FROM THE BED AND THOUGH MY BODY ACHED, I DRAGGED myself to the washstand. I must warn Mrs. Eversham. It could not wait until the morning—the danger was too real.

I stripped off my bloodstained nightgown and cleaned the blood from my skin. I wound rags between my legs as I did for my courses, and tried to dress myself. I was badly bruised on my left side where I had fallen, and my skin stung as the petticoats touched me. Fastening my stays was painful. My mind was blurred and my body aching and exhausted, but there was no time to rest.

I reached for the first dress I found in my chest—not a black gown but a navy-blue one. I pulled it gingerly over my head, wincing as the fabric nestled against my skin.

I lit a candle and stepped out into the dark corridor. The house was still and silent—no creaks or footsteps tonight. My candle threw up vast shadows on the walls as I hurried toward Mrs. Eversham's room. I knocked hard.

It was a few moments before Mrs. Eversham appeared. She was in her nightgown, a lilac shawl around her shoulders and a candle in her hand. She looked as though she had been fast asleep, and she stared at me for a moment in astonishment.

"Mrs. Eversham." I heard the urgency in my voice. "There is something I have to tell you—something important. I know I owe you an explanation, an apology, but please, for now—you must listen to me."

A shadow of confusion passed over her face. "You must rest, Margaret. There is time to discuss everything later."

"Mrs. Eversham, please—*Mrs. Grey*."

She stopped. Her face paled, and when she looked up at me her eyes were wide with surprise and confusion.

"Listen to me," I said. "There is no time to lose. I should have said so at once but I was in no fit state to . . . Listen, Charles Grey is in the village. He told me himself who he was. He was the one who accosted me. He is the reason I fell. He was asking me about Lucy Grey, his wife, about a ten-year-old boy named Thomas. You realize what I am saying, Mrs. Eversham? Your husband has found you. He has come."

She stared at me. "I—"

"I think there is still time," I said. "I—well, I think I injured him, a little, in the tussle. Enough to slow him down. And he wasn't sure—he knew you were near but not the name of the house, I think. But it will only be a matter of time before he is able to find out what he needs from the people down in Hartbridge. You have to leave as soon as you can."

"I don't understand," she murmured. "How could Grey have—? We are so careful."

"I think . . . I think Susan brought him here."

"Susan?" she repeated. She sounded stunned, dazed. She seemed to be weighing up how much to say. "She had more than enough money from us to keep quiet. I suppose it was not enough. I thought . . ."

I was right, then, about Susan—that she had taken Mrs. Eversham's money, too, traded in her secrets.

"Listen, Mrs. Eversham, do you see what I am saying? You have to leave. Your husband is coming."

She shook her head. She spoke so quietly I did not hear her next words; I read them from her lips. "He is not my husband."

"But in his eyes you are still his wife. And Louis is his son. Mrs. Eversham—"

"No," she said, her voice shaking. "You don't understand me. Louis is his son, but I am not his wife. Margaret, I am not Mrs. Grey."

I stared at her. For a moment I could not make sense of her words, and then understanding hit me.

Of course.

Why live shut up in the east wing unless you were hiding, unless you were running for your life?

I thought of the advertisement. *Small and delicately built, with fair hair, blue eyes, and pale skin.* Which did not describe Mrs. Eversham so much as . . .

"Miss Davis," I said. "You are not Mrs. Grey. She is."

Mrs. Eversham stared at me in amazement. Her face showed nothing but confusion and then, slowly, she began to nod.

CHAPTER V

Mrs. Eversham hurried downstairs to rouse Stevens and Mrs. Pulley. One of them was to keep watch over Louis in the coming hours, the other to begin packing what was needed for a long journey. Mrs. Eversham intended to flee Hartwood Hall as soon as day broke.

There was little time to lose, but we knew it would be too difficult to travel in the dark and had calculated that we should be safe from Mr. Grey until morning. He did not know the name of the house, nor exactly where it was—that much had been clear when we met—and he would be hardly likely to find his way through the woods and to Hartwood Hall in the dark, especially with an injured leg.

We met at the east-wing door and I followed slowly, almost nervously, as we stepped inside. The corridor was quiet, lit only by the sputtering light of our candles. I thought of the last time I had been in the east wing, with Paul. I had to remind myself that there was nothing to be afraid of.

I knew this house's secrets now.

I followed Mrs. Eversham around the corner, down the long upstairs corridor. Mrs. Eversham knocked three times on the mirror image of the door to her own room in the west wing. A few moments later, it swung open.

And there stood Miss Davis—Lucy Grey—in a white nightdress, her fair hair messy around her shoulders, her eyes wide with surprise. Beyond her I could see the room—not shut up and smothered in sheets like the rest of the east wing, but a finely decorated, comfortable bedroom and sitting room combined.

"It's all right," said Mrs. Eversham. "She knows who you are." She reached for Lucy Grey's hand, stopped, pulled back, glanced between me and her. "Listen, Lucy, I'm sorry to wake you but it cannot wait until morning. It has happened, as we always feared it might. He has found us."

Lucy stared at her. She took a few steps backward, found her way to a chair. She sat down heavily and I saw a flicker of a tear in her eye. It was gone in a moment, controlled, smothered. She looked up at me.

Mrs. Eversham had closed the door behind us and moved to take a seat at Lucy's side. I followed, took the chair across from them. I did not realize how weak I still felt until I sat down.

"Listen," I began, "I met Mr. Grey this evening. He followed me home. He is the reason I fell, why—" I broke off, blinked back sudden tears, shook the thought away. "He told me that Susan had written to him about you, that he had sent someone here looking for his wife but they dismissed it as the wrong house, the wrong woman—I suppose because he saw Mrs. Eversham, not you. But Mr. Grey was not convinced, and so he came himself. He is in the village now."

Lucy was nodding slowly, her face pained. "Did he—did he mention Isabella? He might have called her Anne. Did you see her?"

I stared at her.

Isabella.

Isabella?

Isabella, the girl Paul told me was dead. Isabella, whose image I had seen in the locket, whose ghost I had dreamed of walking through Hartwood Hall.

What if, after all, she had not died? What if Mr. Grey had come for her, when she was away from home, as he was coming for Louis now?

"My God," I murmured. "You mean she is alive? I had heard about her, but I was told—" I remembered, suddenly, that there had been a young woman sitting beside Mr. Grey at church. I had thought nothing of it at the time, had not even realized they were together. But it was possible. "I saw him earlier in the day," I whispered, "at church. There was a young woman beside him, fifteen or sixteen, with fair hair."

Lucy started. "She's here."

"I don't know that. It might not have been her."

"She is here," she said. "I know it. Perhaps he thinks he can use her to make me return to him. For five years he has kept her—for five years we have been searching for her, and God knows what her life has been." Her hands trembled with anger. "My husband, he . . ." She trailed off, looking down at her bare ring finger. "No, he is not my husband. He has no right to such a title. Mr. Grey, then—he is a bad man, Mrs. Lennox, rotten to the core."

I thought of the wedding ring I had found in the lake. *LG*. She must have thrown it there, because she could not bear to look at it.

"Mrs. Grey," I said gently, "Lucy, you do not have to tell me."

"You know enough." She glanced at Mrs. Eversham, who nodded, and I saw a thousand unspoken words flit between them. "There is no harm in you knowing it all. I know Charlotte trusts you, and I trust her completely." She glanced once at the clock on the mantelpiece. It was nearly one o'clock in the morning. "There is time. We cannot leave until it is light."

I was close enough to see her swallow.

"I was seventeen when I married him," she told me. "I did not know him at all. My parents were dead, and the uncle I lived with liked Mr. Grey, because he was rich, because he served good wine at dinner. That was all.

"I soon found out my mistake. He raised his voice to servants—raised his hand, too. He drank too much. He gambled away his fortune faster than he could make it back. He took lovers. He made me swear not to leave the house without him or some companion of his choosing."

I stared at her. I thought of Richard, all the times he had told me what to do.

"I lost the first child I was with because of his violence," she said. "After that he was more careful. He shouted at me, but he did not strike. Not until my daughter was born. He was angry that we had not had a boy. I wanted to call her Isabella, after my mother, but he said she must be Anne, after his. Charlotte and I gave her the name Isabella after we left.

"Some years later, Louis was born—Thomas, as he was called then—and Charles was glad, at first. He was always demanding to see his boy. He had him carried into dinner once, laid out on the table like a feast before all his drunken friends. And once, when Charles was angry because he had lost money on a horse, Thomas would not stop crying. He was just a year old. I tried to take him from the room and Charles said I must not, that he must learn to obey his father. And when the baby did not stop screaming, he threw a wineglass at him."

I exhaled sharply. The scar on Louis's back.

"It cut him badly. I had to lie to the doctor, saying he had fallen on it, that it was all some dreadful accident.

"But that night changed everything. He had hurt me enough, but he had never laid a finger on the children before. I began to think my life unbearable, to wonder if I could leave him, if it might be better to—to kill my husband to save the children from him. I tried to save scraps of money, planning some escape I might never dare to make.

"And then one day, I met a woman called Charlotte Williams."

She glanced over at Mrs. Eversham.

"That is my real name," said the woman I had worked for these last few months. She glanced at the ring on her finger, raised her hand to the light. "Of course you must realize by now I was never Mrs. Eversham. I bought this at a pawnshop in London." She paused. "I met Lucy through my brother—he was a friend of Mr. Grey's, and there was some other acquaintance of his staying at Grey's he hoped to make me marry. He wanted to get rid of me, I suppose. So he brought me to the house. During the day, he forced me into society, and at night, I was hidden away with Lucy while the men drank."

"And I had never met anyone like her," Lucy said. She was smiling now. "It did not take me long to realize that nothing would ever be the same.

"I found I could tell her everything, and I knew she would understand. And somehow, in that dreadful house, while the men hunted and drank themselves to death, we fell in love."

They both glanced at me, perhaps to see if I flinched.

I did not.

"We planned it out together," said Charlotte. "How we would leave, where we would run. We would fly into the night, taking the children with us, hide ourselves away in some distant spot, shake off the lives we had led before."

"I had something saved out of the little Charles gave me," Lucy went on, "and Charlotte had money of her own from the reviews and stories she'd had published. She thought she might be able to support us by her pen once the rest of the money ran out. So we made our plan. I would save my children. I would save myself.

"It was hard, at first, when we ran away. We moved from place to place for a year, fearing detection, constantly afraid. We all went by new names. We lived in squalid lodgings and hotels. I don't know whether my husband came after us. I think he was half glad to be rid of me. I suppose he lived wildly for six months before he thought to remember that he wanted a son, that he wanted a wife, that he missed having someone to hit. I don't know. Nearly a year after we had run away, two things happened. The first was that Charlotte's aunt passed away and left her some money, and we found ourselves rather better off than before. And then I saw an advertisement in London asking for information about us, and we realized we needed a new plan.

"So we came here," Lucy went on. "The most isolated spot we could find. A house mostly shut up, a village that didn't interfere. Hartwood Hall was being sold off cheaply by its owner, who had fallen into debt, and we decided we would live a life of our own. We knew that Charles would be looking for me but not for Charlotte—we had concealed the extent of our friendship from him. So we dyed the children's hair and I hid. Charlotte became the children's mother, said she was a widow. I kept myself safe in the east wing. We hid from the past.

"We wrote to people we knew could be trusted as servants. Ruth Pulley had been my nurserymaid when I was a little girl. I had not seen her since she left my parents' house to be married, but I knew that her husband had died some years before. She was not happy in London and came as soon as she heard from me. Charlotte knew John Stevens—her brother had dismissed him from his service a few years earlier, after he found out that . . . Well, Stevens is . . . like us, you see."

I thought of the love letter addressed to him in Susan's box. That, then, had been the secret of his that she held.

"It was just the six of us at first," Lucy was saying. "That meant I could live a little more openly within the house, but it wasn't long before people in the village began to ask why we had so few servants, why the gardens were still so overgrown now the house was occupied. We knew that above all we must not draw attention to ourselves, that we could not risk talk about us spreading and giving rise to suspicion, so Charlotte hired more servants, and kept me a secret from them.

"We spent most of our savings purchasing the house, so we have lived off the income from Charlotte's writing. The east wing has been my home—and Charlotte's, and Louis's, too. He comes here often, as did Isabella. It has been hard to train Louis to keep the secret, but he understands, especially now he is older, how important it is, how he needs to help keep me safe.

"We thought we might do without a governess while the children were younger—we taught them ourselves, as far as we were able. But as Louis grew, we began to feel it was unfair. He so wanted to learn, and there was only so much we could do ourselves. He understood why he could not go away to school—and I do not think he ever wanted to be parted from us—but he began to ask and beg for a governess, and . . . well, here you are."

I asked, slowly, "What happened to Isabella?"

Lucy glanced at Mrs. Eversham—Charlotte. I saw her look to the clock as it chimed one, and then she swallowed hard.

"It all happened so fast," said Charlotte. "She was ill, you see—she had suffered from trouble with her lungs since she was a young girl, and there was a doctor in London, a specialist, who had treated her before. We did not want to risk Lucy being seen, so I took Isabella to London myself. With her dyed hair, and now that she was a few years older, we thought we might be safe from recognition. But we should never have risked it. The doctor, after all, was not to be trusted. He sent an express letter to Charles Grey, and he—" She broke off. Tears were slipping down her cheeks.

Lucy put her hand over Charlotte's. "It was not your fault. I have never blamed you."

"He took her," I said.

Charlotte nodded. "He sent someone to the inn. Isabella was asleep in our room, and I had gone down to the landlady to order our breakfast. I was only gone for a few minutes. We heard a commotion and ran upstairs to find the door broken in—and Isabella was gone." Her eyes were wet. "We told Louis that she had to go away for a time, that he mustn't worry—but he was so young, and he has always struggled to understand it. We had to tell the servants she had died, to explain her absence, but we have been searching for her ever since. We have found Grey once or twice, but she never seemed to be with him. I think she has been kept away at boarding schools or goodness knows where. We have tried to find her, while still running from him. When I leave Hartwood Hall, that is where I go."

Things fell into place. Her trips away, her overwrought anxiety about Louis—I understood it all better now.

"But if she is here with him now, then . . ." Lucy's voice cracked. She shook her head, as though she could not bear to speak.

The house was dark and still around us, and the candlelight flickered. On the mantelpiece, the clock ticked toward a quarter past one. Lucy and Charlotte held each other's hands fast.

"What happens now?" I whispered.

"Now?" said Lucy. "Now I try to get my daughter back, as soon as it is light. Then we leave. Forever."

Charlotte's eyes fell on me. I don't know what she saw in my pale face, my flat stomach, but after the rush of worry, her memory of what had happened now seemed to come back to her. "Oh, Margaret," she murmured. "We have been talking of all these things and I had almost forgotten . . ."

"It is all right," I said softly. "I am well enough now."

"But, Margaret, you have lost a child."

"Yes." I heard my voice catch.

The two women looked at each other, then back at me. Then Lucy said softly, "You and—Paul?"

Of course. Lucy had been the figure I saw through the window of Paul's rooms all those weeks ago—not Susan but her. She had seen us. And when she left a candle burning in the east wing, when she hurried from one room to the next to avoid being seen—she must have heard us then, too.

"You knew," I said.

A faint smile. "Yes, we knew. When you are a house's mystery, you learn the rest of its secrets pretty fast."

"I suppose you fell in love," Charlotte said softly.

"I don't know." I bit my lip, closed my eyes. "I thought so, but perhaps, after all . . ." I swallowed. "It was very foolish—we have both been very foolish. And I know that it was unacceptable, that I have been in a position of trust in this house . . ." I shook my head. "Of course I did not think I would get with child. I thought—I thought it was impossible, that I could not . . . Well, it does not matter now." My voice caught in my throat. "The child is gone, like all my other children who have never been."

"Oh, Margaret."

I heard the kindness in Charlotte's voice, and I let tears build in my eyes.

Then Lucy said, "I gather your marriage was an unhappy one, Mrs. Lennox. Was he a cruel man, your husband, like mine?"

I whispered, "Yes."

I had never truly admitted it before. I had told myself again and again that I was a bad wife, that if Richard was unkind I deserved it. I had known since the moment I found him dead that I was glad he was gone: I was a bad wife, a bad widow.

But he was bad, too. Rotten, like Mr. Grey.

No, he did not strike me. But there are other ways to break a person, other ways to ruin someone from the inside out.

"It is my fault he died," I said. The words were out before I knew what I was doing, before I thought them through.

Charlotte's voice was gentle. "I am sure it is not."

"But it is. I mean it. It was my fault and I—I am not sorry." I looked up to face them now, for the first time, and saw their expressions: curious, anxious. But I did not see judgment.

I looked at them, Mrs. Eversham—Charlotte—this woman I had lived with for three months, whom I had both known and not known. Lucy, whose son I had come to love so dearly, who'd had a marriage not so very different from mine.

I told them everything.

And when I was finished, when my words finally dried up, I sat with them in silence and stared down at the floor.

"You did not kill him, Margaret." Charlotte's voice was soft, gentle. She had listened to every word with attention and did not once speak until I had stopped. "It was an accident."

I shook my head. "I didn't do it consciously. I didn't mean to, but—"

"He was dying," said Lucy.

I swallowed. "He changed his will, just before he died. He left everything to his mother."

Charlotte sighed. "Oh, Margaret."

"His mother told me that she believed I had killed him. And I barely had the courage to look her in the face and tell her she was wrong."

"You did not kill him," said Lucy.

"Not purposefully. But my mistake . . . And besides, I wanted him dead and that frightens me." I took in a shaky breath. "And then I came here, where no one knew what I had been, where no one knew what my marriage was or what my mother-in-law had said. And I found you, Mrs. Eversham—Charlotte—and Louis, and I liked being one of you. And Susan—you said you gave her money, to keep the secrets she had found out; well, she found one of my letters and threatened me, too. And so when Paul admired me, I—I think I got lost in it all. It was different, to want someone. I had not thought it possible."

Charlotte said, in a whisper, "And now, to lose a child."

"Yes." I stared down at my dark blue dress. No black, not now.

Charlotte looked up. "You have been happy at Hartwood Hall, I think?"

I nodded. My eyes were dry but I felt so weary. My body ached, and the base of my stomach was sore.

"I will give you a good character," said Charlotte. "No one ever need know about all this."

I looked round at her, my heart heavy. So, this was it. This place I had been nearly happy in, this place where I had been alive. All gone.

"Or—"

I blinked. "Or?"

Charlotte looked at Lucy, and Lucy looked back at her. Another silent conversation seemed to pass between them. Then Charlotte said, "You might come with us. Lucy, Louis, and I—we have to do everything we can to reclaim Isabella. And if we can, we will run from this place and we will never look back. We will keep on moving, place after place, praying Charles Grey never finds us. We must never become so complacent again. We thought we could give Louis the sort of upbringing we'd both had, but I think it is time to try a new kind of life." Her lips quivered. "I can trust you, Margaret. I do not think I can trust everyone. Mrs. Pulley and Stevens will come with us, I think. Louis will still need a governess. Isabella, too, if we are able to . . . Of course, I know it is all beyond irregular, and it might be dangerous—Grey is a dangerous man—and of course Lucy and I are . . . together." She reached for Lucy's hand, held it steadily in hers. "Well, if you object, if you say no, I will not be surprised. I will not be offended. I know that to come with us would be to give up normality, society, conventionality, everything—I know that. You may leave Hartwood today, if you like, and never think of us again."

She breathed in deeply, her face set, and I saw in her expression that she wished me to say yes and thought I would say no. I had been here less than three months, and she trusted me. With her secrets. With the children who had become her own.

"Are you sure?" I looked between them, my question as much for Lucy as for Charlotte.

"Yes," said Lucy. "We are sure."

"What do you say?" asked Charlotte. "Will you come with us?"

I looked at them both. I thought of Lucy, who had run toward me so fast as I fell to the ground. I thought of Mrs. Eversham—Charlotte—her gentle voice, all those times she had scolded and forgiven me. I thought of Louis, his eager face and the scar on his back. I thought of Isabella, alive, the girl I had once thought might be walking the corridors of Hartwood Hall.

I said, "Yes."

CHAPTER VI

THE NIGHT PASSED IN A RUSH OF PACKING AND PLANS. WE CLOSETED ourselves in the study to plot out our journey, Charlotte, Lucy, and I, sometimes joined by either Stevens or Mrs. Pulley.

We were to leave just before daybreak. Mrs. Pulley, Stevens, and Lucy would take Louis straight to the nearest railway station and set out for London. Charlotte and I would go to the inn. I would ask for Mr. Grey, tell him that I had reconsidered, that I had information for him. I would arrange another time to meet him, would distract him while Charlotte found their room and took Isabella back. They would run, and I would follow. Charlotte, Isabella, and I would meet the others in London and travel onward together.

We were to go abroad. That, we had decided, was safest. They had money enough saved up from Charlotte's recent literary successes, and there was still capital remaining from the money her aunt had left her. We would head to Dover and take a steamer to France, then travel across land as far as we could. Mrs. Pulley suggested Vienna. Charlotte wanted to go to Rome. Lucy thought Spain. Somewhere warm, she said.

At some point, Stevens brought Louis to the room.

He stood there, sleepy-eyed and tired, looking between the three of us. Me, still pale and bruised, in my blue frock. Lucy, standing by me, in her white day dress. Charlotte, on the other side of the room, a teacup in her hands.

She held out her hand to him and he came toward her, glancing back at Lucy and me as he did.

"Does Mrs. Lennox know now?" Louis asked softly.

I had not had time in the last few hours to fully take in Louis's part in this. How had Louis, little Louis with his wide eyes and bright face—how had this child kept such a secret from me?

I hate secrets, he'd said to me once.

He had painted another figure into our picture of Hartwood Hall. Not his sister, as I had thought. His mother. His mother, who had lived and hidden in the east wing.

My dear child.

"Yes, my love," said Charlotte. "She knows everything. And soon there will be no more secrets. We are going to go on a journey."

"A journey, Mother?"

"Yes." She hesitated. "I am sorry for it, for I know you like Hartwood Hall. But we are going to move somewhere else, somewhere beautiful and sunny and away from here."

It was a few moments before he replied. Then he asked, "Why?"

I saw Charlotte glance at Lucy and realized that the boy did not know everything after all. I knew he was afraid of the memory of his father; they must have told him, to spare him, that he truly was dead. That must have been why they were unable to tell him the full truth about Isabella.

He turned to Lucy. "Why, Mama?"

She smiled at him, a wide smile that did not reach her eyes. "Because we must," she said.

—————>×<—————

"What should I tell Carter?" Stevens asked at about four in the morning. Mrs. Pulley had taken Louis upstairs to help pack his things.

Mrs. Eversham—Charlotte—hesitated. She glanced at me and I felt warmth rush to my cheeks.

"He's a good man, a good gardener," Stevens went on. "He is very fond of Hartwood. It is a hard way for him to lose his work—his home."

Charlotte winced. "Pay him a quarter's wages. And—" She sighed. "I will have to speak to him myself. I suppose we had better wake him, or we will be gone before he rises. Will you bring him here?"

"Of course."

A moment later, Stevens was gone.

I glanced at Lucy. I said quietly, "Charlotte, he knows."

"What?"

"Paul knows about Lucy. He's known for years, since the other gardener left."

Lucy stared at me, taken aback.

I saw a faint blush of color on Charlotte's cheeks and knew she understood.

"He didn't tell me—not until I had worked it out for myself. He has kept your secret well."

Charlotte nodded. "Then I am grateful to him." She hesitated. "Margaret, if you wish me to ask him to come with us, perhaps . . ."

I thought of Paul, this kind, good man. I had loved him, almost known him. I thought of what he had said in my room, hours before, that life he had mapped out for us, for me.

In another world, there might have been a future for me and Paul. If I had met him before Richard, if I had been the person I used to be, the person I had tried, with Paul, to make myself into—perhaps we might have made something beautiful.

But the life he wanted was not the life I wanted. We could never be what the other needed. I knew that now.

"No." I spoke quietly and I heard my voice quiver. "No," I repeated, a little more firmly. "I don't think so."

Charlotte understood. One quick nod and the subject was dismissed.

"I had better speak to him alone," she said. "You must both have packing to do."

I was up in my chamber, hurriedly packing my things, when I heard a soft knock on the door. I pulled it open and there stood Paul, candle in hand. His face was flushed, his mouth an anxious frown.

Though it was cowardly of me, I had half longed to leave Hartwood, to leave the country, without seeing him. I was tired and weary, my body weak, my mind struggling. I did not know how to explain myself. I felt stronger in my purpose, without him there. I did not know how to say goodbye.

"Paul," I said, as I stepped out into the corridor. My voice sounded strange. I stood back from him, a few feet apart, and the cavernous distance between us seemed too great to conquer.

"Mrs. Eversham has just told me that she is leaving Hartwood Hall forever, that I am dismissed, that they will leave me with a character and a quarter's wages and nothing else, that Hartwood Hall is going to be shut up—that you are going with them." His voice was shaking and I could see he was struggling to hold back tears. "Everything, my whole life, just—gone. Is it all true? Are you going for good?"

"What else can they do?" I kept my voice to a whisper. "Mr. Grey is coming. They are all in danger."

"And Hartwood Hall is really . . . it's really over?"

"Yes," I said, and I saw the pain in his eyes. He loved this place. His life had been this house. And this blow, on top of his father's illness, on top of the child we had lost . . . I wanted to reach out, to put my arms around him, and I did not dare let myself. If I did, it would all come, the rush of feeling, the pain of parting. If I broke my resolve, if I asked him to come with us, this would only happen again, in a few months, a year, when we realized we wanted different lives.

"Why go with them?"

I looked up at him. His eyes were blue and shining. I had always loved his eyes.

"Margaret, I know you love Louis, I know that, but—surely, you would not give up your own life for him, for Mrs. Eversham?"

"I am not giving up my own life," I said. "I like my work. I like Mrs. Eversham. I trust her. I trust Lucy."

He opened his mouth, then shut it again. "You would leave me?" he murmured.

Pain was seeping through me, and I had nothing left to give him. I looked up at him, his beautiful, familiar face, lips I had kissed a hundred times, eyes I knew all too well.

"Stay," he said gently. "You have had a life here. You can have a life again." He swallowed. "Stay, Margaret. Marry me."

I stared at him. I could not speak.

"Margaret, tell me where you wish to live and I will follow. There are gardens all over the world. I can build beauty anywhere. We can start again. Live a quiet life. You won't have to teach anymore. We could be happy together. You know we could."

I stood in the dark, empty corridor with this man whose bed I had shared. I knew every mark on the back of his hand. I knew the distance between each of his ribs, the subtle indents and scars on his shoulders, the precise shade of his eyes. But I did not know him, not really.

And he did not know me either.

I thought of all the moments we had spent together: his lips pressed to my lips, my skin—his soothing voice—his arms tight around me. I thought of him telling me why he loved Hartwood Hall, how he'd stretched his arms wide and told me he'd never found any place so beautiful.

I had loved him, in a way. I had felt for him more than I had felt for Richard, perhaps for any man, all my life.

But I did not want the future he had planned for me. I did not want a future chosen by anyone but myself.

This love between us was precious, but it was not enough.

"I can't, Paul," I said softly.

"Why not?" His voice was suddenly brittle. "Because you are a lady and I am not a gentleman?"

"No. Of course not."

"Because you are a little older than me? If it does not trouble me, then—"

"It is not that, Paul."

"Is it because I lied to you, about Lucy?"

"No. That hurt me, but it does not change anything."

"Then why—why leave me, why not . . . marry me?"

I felt my lip tremble. "Because I was married once," I said, "and I never want to be married again."

He stared at me. "But I love you," he said. "And you love me. At least, I thought—" He broke off.

"I know," I said, and I heard my voice tremble. "I know, Paul. I did—I do—love you, but—but I am not sure that it is enough. I do not think we want the same kind of life. I will miss you, I will, but—" I breathed in. "I do not want to be someone's wife, Paul. I do not want anyone to own me."

"I don't want to own you, I want—"

"But you would," I said, as softly as I could. "You would. I'm sorry, Paul, but I can't."

He stared at me. I watched his face crumple, and sorrow and confusion seemed to sweep through him.

We stood there for some time in silence. I could not meet his eyes.

"Margaret, do you know what you are giving up? I don't mean me, I mean—life, normal life. You will be running from a man you cannot predict. You will be living outside society. Margaret, you know that?"

I swallowed. "I know that. But I am not sure I want a normal life."

He nodded slowly. "Then I wish you all the happiness in the world."

"And I you, Paul. Truly."

He didn't look at me. "I am leaving right now."

"It's still dark."

"I don't care. I can find my way well enough at night. I am packing my things and going to see my family—" His voice caught. "I can't be here. I can't see you all leave."

"I'm so sorry, Paul."

He shook his head. His eyes and cheeks were wet and he was looking at me with desperation, and there was nothing I could do, nothing I could bear to do.

"I'm sorry," I said again. I reached out to touch his arm, but he flinched away. "Goodbye, Paul."

He turned. "Goodbye, Margaret."

He said my name like he always did, soft and lilting, bursting with tenderness. Tears sprang into my eyes.

And then he was gone, walking fast down the corridor, his hand raised to hide his face.

I covered my mouth to stifle a sob.

Half an hour later, he was gone.

CHAPTER VII

IT WAS JUST AFTER SIX O'CLOCK IN THE MORNING WHEN WE GATHERED in the courtyard, and the sky was still dark. Stevens brought the cart and horses round, pulling them over the cobblestones, kicking fallen leaves out of their way. Charlotte and I would take one horse, to travel to the inn; the cart would take Stevens, Mrs. Pulley, Lucy, and Louis. As I helped Louis up, placing him among the boxes and trunks, he reached for my hand and held it hard.

"Are you afraid, child?" I asked gently.

He nodded.

"Don't be," I said. "It's all right. Everything is going to be all right now."

The morning air was chill and I wound my cloak tight around me. Louis was buttoned up in his little greatcoat, but still I saw him shiver as I stepped back to lock the doors. The moon was dim now, and I could see a sliver of light above the wings of the house. Stevens and Mrs. Pulley were loading up more bags and trunks around him, and Charlotte had just saddled her horse when, turning, I saw something.

A light in the distance.

I was used to glimmers in the dark, to figures in the distance. And yet—Lucy was here. Everything was explained.

I narrowed my eyes and saw it again. Somewhere beyond the courtyard, near the woods, I could see a burning torch. Then the glimmer of light showed me the silhouette of a figure on horseback.

"Someone is here," I said, as loudly as I dared.

Everyone looked at me save Louis, and then their eyes turned slowly to follow my line of sight.

Lucy began to shake. I saw her in the darkness, her trembling hands, her quaking shoulders. She steadied them in a moment.

We had miscalculated. We ought to have left hours ago, risked the dark, sent Louis and Lucy on while Charlotte and I waited to try to get to Isabella.

Mrs. Pulley pulled the last of the bags onto the cart and stepped up herself. "We have to go now," she said, "while we still can."

She was right. We were in the courtyard, surrounded by three walls of the house. A minute more, and we would be cornered.

But he was galloping, the horse moving fast, too fast. I heard Louis whisper, "I'm afraid."

He was close by, a foot above me in the cart, pressed in against the bags and coats. "It's all right," I said.

"Who is the man? Is it the devil, come to take us away? Is it Father? Bella always said—"

But Mrs. Pulley tugged the reins and the cart trundled away from me, just as Lucy found her seat. Charlotte was on her horse, but before I had time to pull myself up behind her, I heard Grey's shout.

He was fast upon us now, barely yards away. I saw his face in the darkness, livid and maddened and hopeful all at once.

It was only then that I saw he was not alone.

Behind him on the horse was a girl.

I saw her wide eyes fall on the cart and her lips whisper the word "Mama."

I saw the shock in Louis's face, as though he could not quite believe his eyes, as though he dared not hope she was really here.

Mr. Grey's horse stood at the edge of the courtyard now, blocking our way out. "Lucy!" he was crying, and within the cart she drew back, closer to Stevens, to Louis. She had seemed so steady until now, so determined and fierce in the study, so tough and formidable throughout Louis's illness, though all the time she was nursing her own sick child. And now she seemed to shrink, to grow smaller before my eyes.

"You think you can hide from me? You think you can rob me of my son? I have tracked you down, at last. Enough, Mrs. Grey. Enough."

A sudden strength seemed to seize her and she stood up in the cart.

"That is not my name," she said. "It will never be my name again."

"You are my *wife*." He spat the word. "You will come back with me. Do you hear?"

"Never," replied Lucy, and now her voice was steady. She turned her gaze to the girl cowering behind him on the horse. "Isabella, Anne—are you well, are you—?"

"Don't speak to her!" Grey's voice was fierce. "You lost all claim to our children when you ran from my house, when you threw in your lot with sinners and reprobates. You can speak to Anne when and only when you come back. Now listen to me, Lucy. You are my wife. I own you. You will bring the boy and you will come back, and if I do not punish you for all you have done, so help me God . . . You are mad. I know that now. It can have only been madness, to make you run away with that ungodly strumpet"—he waved a hand toward Charlotte— "and break all natural bonds. Yes, I know all about that now. You thought you'd deceived me but I found out at last. Now come back. Prove you are not mad."

"No," said Lucy. "Nothing on earth would make me do it."

"What, nothing?" Grey shifted his position. He reached into his coat pocket, and as he fumbled, he dropped his torch. It fell to the ground and with a roar the fallen leaves beneath the apple tree went up in flames. The horses reared and trampled and grew wild, while Mr. Grey drew a pistol from his coat.

I flinched, and Stevens gave a cry. Behind Grey, Isabella was sob-bing, but she was moving, too, tugging at something at her waist— and it was then I saw, in the light of the moon and the spreading flames, that he had tied her to him with rope, that she was bound.

The apple tree was burning now, and the dead leaves around us were aflame.

I expected Grey to point the pistol at Lucy, but he did not—he turned it toward Charlotte. "Come, Lucy," he said. "What if I tell you I'll kill your whore?"

There was fear in Lucy's eyes again now. She opened her mouth to reply, but before she could there came a burst of flame. The cart pitched and everyone within started up. The wheels were burning. The fire from the leaves had caught the cart—and more, too: the flames from the apple tree had spread to the ivy trailing up the east wing. I heard a window smash in the heat.

Mrs. Pulley was the first to climb out, lifting Louis down after her. Stevens scrambled out next and had to all but pull Lucy with him. She seemed hardly aware of what was happening. The horses moved wildly, pitching the burning cart into the side of the house before Stevens managed to lead them away. Lucy seemed to see nothing but Charlotte and the gun her husband pointed at her head.

"Pull the trigger if you dare," said Charlotte. To my amazement, her voice was steady. Charlotte, Mrs. Eversham, whom I had seen so often flustered and anxious, so often afraid. Now she stood her ground, anger burning in her eyes.

Lucy started. "Charlotte—"

"Do you think, Mr. Grey," Charlotte went on, her tone low and fierce, "that I would not give my life for Lucy? I would die for her freedom, if I thought it could save her from you. And if you do not understand that, then you know nothing of love. Put your gun down, sir—I am not afraid of you."

Grey looked between Charlotte and Lucy. His eyes were wide with surprise. He could not understand it, I thought—such love was unfathomable to him.

And then Isabella jumped. She had been working at the knot all the while her father was distracted, and now she threw herself down from the horse, ropes slipping off her, and stumbled to the ground. She ran, as fast as she could, toward her mother.

But Grey was off the horse in a moment. He grabbed her by the wrist and wrenched her back. She let out a gasp of pain.

"Stop it!" screamed Lucy.

"What do you say—will you exchange your daughter for my son? Give me Thomas and you can have her. I'll leave you alone."

Lucy stared at him, then at her daughter. She glanced back at Louis, who was standing with Mrs. Pulley on the cobblestones, tears of fear in his eyes.

She said slowly, steadily, "You cannot have him. I will never give up either of them."

And then something in Mr. Grey snapped. He pushed Isabella from him, sending her stumbling to the ground. The pistol still clasped in his hand, he ran forward, barreling into the group by the burning cart and grabbing Louis hard by the arm. He wrenched him away from the others, his grip tight, and raised the pistol to his son's temple.

Louis was trembling. I saw every quiver of his breath, every shudder in his arms. He looked from Lucy to Charlotte in panic, in dread. I stared, my heart pounding, sick with fear. Surely Grey would not do it. Surely he would not kill his own child.

And then I thought of the scar on Louis's back, the way Grey had held Isabella, the rope bound around her arms.

Lucy jolted forward.

"Move and I'll shoot."

She stopped. She was shaking all over. Charlotte cried out, moved to dismount, and Grey gave her a warning glance.

"All of you," he said. "I mean it—I'll do it. Better for him to be dead than disgraced by such a mother."

"You are the disgrace, not me." Lucy's voice shook, with fury as well as fear. "Louis," she said, as gently as she could, "it will be all right. Don't move. We'll save you. No one will hurt you. No one will ever hurt you."

"His name is Thomas," said Grey, "and you have already hurt him. If I pull the trigger now, it is you who have pulled it. You understand that, don't you, Lucy? You are killing him. You are killing him."

I turned automatically to hear better and was only aware of what I had done when it was too late. I expected Grey to round upon me at once—but he did not. It was then I realized—he could not see me. It was still dark, despite the flames working their way up the ivy, across the east wing. I was in the shadows of the house, half behind Charlotte's horse, too far to the left of him. He had everybody else in view—but he could not see me.

I saw my opportunity. It was the only way.

I own you, he had told Lucy.

And so I rushed forward. I, who had known Louis only a few months but who loved him like my own. I loved him, though love came hard to me. I loved him, though he had two mothers already. I had loved him from the first, when he put his hand in mine.

I was still weak from the fall but I pushed all my strength into this. For Charlotte, for Lucy. For Louis, and for myself.

Charles Grey was not Richard, no, but they were two of a kind, like coins minted from the same mold.

I rushed forward, launched myself at Grey, and wrenched the pistol from his hand.

I do not know what happened next, not really. I know that Louis ran to Lucy, that someone cried out. I know that Grey tried to wrestle the gun back from my hands, that we scuffled and fought and fell. I know that he struck me, and that I did not care, for all that mattered in the world was that Louis was safe.

And then my fingers found the trigger and I heard a gunshot, loud and clear, ringing through the night, and I fell back in the darkness.

CHAPTER VIII

I SAT ON THE COBBLESTONES, WHILE THE OTHERS STOOD IN STUNNED silence, looking at the place where Charles Grey lay on his back, a dark stain spreading like ink around his motionless body.

I had killed a man. I was, finally, what Richard's mother had thought me. A murderer. I looked at the blood seeping out of him, this thing, this no-longer man.

No longer a danger. No longer a threat.

I was safe. Louis was safe. Isabella was safe. Charlotte and Lucy were safe.

I heard Lucy whisper, "My God," and it sounded like a prayer.

Charlotte murmured, "Is he really dead?"

I nodded numbly. "I think so. I—" I broke off.

Three things happened at once.

Louis let out a soft cry.

Lucy ran to Isabella.

We were all suddenly, dreadfully, aware of the heat.

I had forgotten the fire; it had been lost in the panic of Mr. Grey's pistol, in the terror of the moment—but now I heard it, felt it, smelled it, saw it—the crackle of wood, the warmth of flames, the choking scent of smoke and burning, the blazing, blinding light of fire.

We were at the edge of the courtyard, and Hartwood Hall was burning around us.

It had spread from the leaves and the apple tree to the house, caught the ivy, caught the window frames.

And now, all three sides of the house around us were burning.

"Water," said Mrs. Pulley. "We need water. At once."

But Charlotte was shaking her head. "It's too late," she murmured. "It's too late."

"We have to move," said Lucy. "Now. Before it spreads more."

So we ran. I took Louis's hand in mine and pulled him quickly down the hill, away from the fire, away from the house. Lucy walked with Isabella leaning on her arm, and Louis kept turning to stare at his sister, as though he could not tell what was real and what was not. Charlotte kicked her horse into motion, and Stevens mounted the other horse and followed quickly after us. Mrs. Pulley caught up with Charles Grey's horse, now grazing a little way down the hill, and took it by the reins. Without the cart, we would need it.

The cart was still burning, so we left it behind. All our belongings, everything we had—save the clothes we wore and the money in our pockets—everything would be gone.

We were out of the courtyard and halfway down the hill when Mrs. Pulley stopped us.

"What about him?" She was looking back at the figure who still lay in the courtyard, and nausea stole over me. "We ought to . . . move him," she said. "He won't burn there."

The words sounded terrible, inhuman, even though the sense of them dawned on me. I could not speak.

"She's right," said Stevens.

Charlotte was nodding. "If he burns, it will take a long time for anyone to find him," she said slowly. "And if they do, how will they know who it is? No one knows he was here. No one need ever know."

I hesitated. "There was that man—the man he paid to watch the house. He might make the connection. And if Grey does not settle his bill at the inn . . ."

An uneasy silence spread between us, filled with the crackling of fire.

"There is nothing we can do about that," said Charlotte at last.

"And if anybody does come after us—well, it is not as though we have never run before."

There was another pause, and then Lucy let go of Isabella's hand and stepped forward. We watched her as she walked up to the bright flame-lit courtyard, put her hands on her husband's corpse, and tried to drag him toward the pyre. She struggled with his weight, and looked up to the rest of us for help. Charlotte stepped forward.

—>—<—

I do not know how long we watched the house burn. We watched the flames dance as dawn broke behind it. It was too late to save Hartwood Hall—we all knew that. The heat, the smoke, the blaze—it was too intense to stand near, and so we pulled the horses further down the hill, closer and closer to the woods.

The flames were high now, lapping at the roof, smothering the gargoyles. It would be a ruin, a gaping hole where a house, a home, had been. The only structures not taken by flames were the summer house and the stables, set far enough back from the house. I glanced across at the stables, Paul's home, where we had spent so many nights together, and tears came to my eyes. It had been so much. So much, and not enough. I wondered if he would ever come back here, to the wreck this house would be. Paul, who had loved this place more than any of us. Paul, who had a spare set of every key.

Louis was crying intermittently, more quietly now. He was still staring at Isabella, as though she might disappear if he took his eyes off her for a moment. He said not a word, but he kept his hand in mine, and I saw that he was grateful, not afraid, that he did not draw back from me.

And then, finally, I heard Isabella speak for the first time.

She said, her voice low and unsteady, "Mama? Mother? Is he really dead?"

She had been watching the house around him burn for nearly an hour, and still she asked. I wondered what her life must have been like, with such a man.

"Yes," said Charlotte. "He is."

Isabella looked over at her mother. "Then we are free," she said, and her voice shook.

I saw Lucy nod. "Yes, my love, we are."

Isabella was clutching her mother's arm, her eyes scanning the rest of us. I saw her take in the faces of Stevens and Mrs. Pulley, saw her smile. Her eyes fell on Louis. She held out her hand to him with trembling fingers, and his hand slipped from mine as he moved toward her, put his arms around her waist. He burrowed himself into her, his arms tight around her, his cries muffled in her dress.

He whispered, "Bella, Bella," like a prayer.

Lucy put her arms around them both, and Charlotte did the same.

This, I thought, was love. This was family. This was what I had been forever seeking and had never found. I watched them for a moment: there was Louis, the boy I knew so well; Charlotte, whose secrets I had found out; Lucy, whose marriage had been a little like mine; Isabella, the girl I had dreamed of at Hartwood Hall. I watched them, their tight embrace, their wet eyes, and I felt my own prick with tears.

And then Louis turned, reached out his hand, searching for mine. When he found it, he grasped it within his own.

And I knew then that these were my people, too, just as they were one another's. I knew that Mrs. Pulley and Stevens respected me, that Louis loved me, that Charlotte and Lucy trusted me, that Isabella would learn to. I knew that I would follow them wherever they went next, that it would be my choice. A life of my own making.

I held tightly to my boy's hand, this boy I loved for all the children I had never had. I held tightly to his hand, as the sun rose beyond the burning house.

A few minutes later, we climbed onto the horses and turned our backs on the flames.

ACKNOWLEDGMENTS

There are so many people without whom this book would not be what it is.

First, I want to thank my wonderful editors: Jessica Leeke, Maya Ziv, and Emma Plater. Thank you for all your notes, and for your belief in and love for this novel. It has improved beyond measure in your hands.

Thank you also to my cover designers, Chris Lin and Dominique Jones in the US and Lee Motley in the UK, for producing such stunning designs.

Thank you to the rest of the team at Penguin Random House, on both sides of the Atlantic. At Dutton, thanks go to: Lexy Cassola, Alice Dalrymple, Susan Schwartz, Ryan Richardson, Nancy Resnick, Christine Ball, John Parsley, Amanda Walker, Stephanie Cooper, Caroline Payne, Hannah Poole, and everyone on the PRH sales team. And at Penguin Michael Joseph, thanks go to: Ciara Berry, Steph Biddle, Nick Lowndes, Alice Mottram, Deirdre O'Connell, Kate Elliott, Katie Corcoran, Natasha Lanigan, and Hannah Padgham.

Thank you to my sensitivity readers, including Reina Gattuso, for your insightful feedback. Clare Bowron, thank you for your cutting and trimming and working with me on pacing. Thank you, too, to my eagle-eyed copy editors, Emma Horton and Amy Schneider, for helping me with (among other things) my failure to understand how fires start and how sunsets work. And thank you to my marvelous proofreaders, Jill Cole, Liz Cowen, Andrea Monagle, and Leah Marsh.

A huge thank-you to my agent, Karolina Sutton, for loving and understanding this book right from the start; I am so lucky to have you fighting in my corner. Thanks also to Claire Nozieres and Rachel Goldblatt, and the rest of the team at Curtis Brown.

Thank you to Louise Buckley for being an early champion of my writing and for your editorial work on this novel.

My work as an editor has been a major influence on my writing—so thank you to all my colleagues over the years at Octopus, Bonnier Books UK, and HarperCollins, for helping me understand the world of publishing from the inside, and for all your support for my writing.

Thank you to the BookTube community. I'm enormously grateful to everyone who is a subscriber to my channel, "Books and Things," and I am so thankful for the community's support for *The Secrets of Hartwood Hall* in the run-up to publication. Special thanks to Marissa and Jenny, for years of friendship and buddy reads.

Thank you to the MA program at Bath Spa University, to the tutors who worked with me and to the other writers on the 2014–2015 course. Thank you for teaching me to be a better writer and editor, and for slowly helping me uncover exactly what I want to write.

Thank you, too, to the people behind Writers' HQ and their Plotstormers online course, which helped me substantially with the early planning stages of *The Secrets of Hartwood Hall*.

Thanks also to the 2023Debuts Twitter group, for being a sounding board and a source of comfort for the past eighteen months. It's been a privilege to begin this journey with you all.

Thank you to my fantastic writing group, who for the last seven (!) years have shared and shaped my work. Thank you for being amazing critics, champions, and friends. Special thanks go to George, for running the group so adeptly and for all his support; and to Hannah and Andrew, for being among the earliest readers of the first draft (with double thanks to Hannah for her undying love for Paul Carter).

Thank you to all my friends, with a few special mentions: to Steph, Sophie, Jenny, and Sarah, for sending me baked goods when I got my book deal; to Lexy, for all the writing chats; to Molly and Céline, for all their excitement—with extra thanks to Céline for listening to the outlines of my unwritten novels when we were teenagers. Huge thanks to Jess—for never refusing to play games in imaginary worlds when we were little, for being one of the novel's very first readers, and for all those lockdown writing sprints, during which many scenes within this novel came into being.

Thank you to my family, immediate and extended, near and far. Thanks to both of my parents for believing in me for such a long time, and for not thinking it too strange all those years ago when your teenage daughter started waking up at six a.m. every day and hogging the family computer to write. Plus, thanks to my dad for introducing me to the theater, and to my mum for giving me *Jane Eyre* to read when I was thirteen—I doubt this novel would exist if you hadn't. Thank you also to my brother, Jim, for spending hours taking author photographs with me, for being my very first editor when we were children, and for creating imaginary worlds with me long ago, which somehow began it all. My first Brontë-related memory is of going around Haworth as a family, long before I knew who the Brontës were; we were so excited about all the maps they had drawn of other worlds when they were children, because that was what we did, too.

Last but not least, thank you to my husband, Nick: for understanding and loving my writing right from the start, for liking my books as books (and not just because I wrote them), for all your support and belief when I've failed to believe in myself. Thank you, too, for pouring hours and hours into reading and thinking about and talking about my work. Thanks for bearing with me when you give me very sensible editorial thoughts and I furiously tell you you're wrong (before quietly implementing your suggestions five hours later). Finally, thank you for reminding me, after I'd written the first draft, that it was just not right to end a novel in conversation with *Jane Eyre* without burning down the hall. *The Secrets of Hartwood Hall* wouldn't be the same without you, and neither would I.